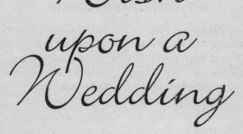

Wish upon a Wedding

A CRICKET CREEK NOVEL

LuAnn McLane

A SIGNET ECLIPSE BOOK

SIGNET ECLIPSE
Published by New American Library,
an imprint of Penguin Random House LLC
375 Hudson Street, New York, New York 10014

This book is an original publication of New American Library.

First Printing, May 2016

For more information about Penguin Random House, visit penguin.com.

ISBN 978-1-101-98980-7

Printed in the United States of America
10 9 8 7 6 5 4 3 2 1

This book is dedicated to brides-to-be.
May all of your wedding wishes come true!

Acknowledgments

I would like to take this opportunity to thank hair stylists for their creativity and hard work behind the chair.
Getting pampered at a hair salon is a treat a woman
treasures, especially on her wedding day. Thanks to
Cara McLane for answering all of my many questions
about the hair industry. Someday I will finally learn
how to French-braid your hair.

Thanks so much to the entire editorial staff at New
American Library. The gorgeous cover captures the
heart of Cricket Creek, bringing the story to life.
Thanks so much to the copy editors for the attention
to detail and grammar and to sales and marketing for
getting the book on the shelf. I couldn't ask for a better
team! I want to give a special thanks to my wonderful
editor, Danielle Perez. From brainstorming new ideas
to tackling revisions, you continue to make me a better
writer.

As always I want to give a heartfelt thanks to my
agent, Jenny Bent. Your knowledge of the industry and
confidence in my writing made my childhood dream of
becoming an author a reality.

Thanks so very much to my loyal readers. From reading my stories to posting reviews, your continued support means the world to me. My goal is to bring you
love, laughter, and of course a happy ending!

1

White Lace and Promises

"**S**OPHIA GORDON, NOW JUST WHAT IN THE WORLD ARE you doin' reading *Good Housekeeping*? For pity's sake, that's for my older clients, not for a young cutie pie like you."

Sophia looked over at Carrie Ann through her foil-covered bangs. "Well, there's a recipe for—" she began, but Carrie Ann tugged the magazine from her fingers so quickly that the salon chair swiveled sideways.

"This is what you should be reading, sweet pea." Carrie Ann placed the latest issue of *Cosmopolitan* in Sophia's hands.

Sophia gazed down at the scantily clad model on the cover and looked at the hair and makeup with a critical eye. "That eye shadow is way too shimmery."

"Oh, forget about that and turn to page thirty."

"Page thirty?" Sophia flipped through the magazine until she was staring at a hot male model lying in bed wearing nothing but boxer briefs and a wicked smile.

"Twenty-five surefire ways to drive your man wild?" When Sophia shook her head and laughed, the foils made a light tinny sound next to her ear. "Well, unfortunately, I don't have a man to drive wild."

"I've seen you hanging out with handsome-as-sin Avery Dean a time or two. I'm pretty sure you could drive him wild all twenty-five ways and think of a few more to add to the list."

"We're just friends," Sophia insisted, but her pulse beat a little bit faster at the mere suggestion. She glanced at the article with renewed interest. Number two involved a feather trailing over certain body parts. "Oh my," Sophia said when the image of Avery popped into her head. She squeezed her eyes shut but the image remained.

"Share, please."

"These ideas are just silly."

"Really? I think this falls into the category of don't knock it until you've tried it." Carrie Ann looked at Sophia in the mirror. "My motto is to always be prepared." She arched an eyebrow. "Know what I'm sayin'?"

Sophia chuckled at the owner of A Cut Above. In her mid-fifties, Carrie Ann Spencer had the hair and curves of a vintage pinup girl and a sassy Southern attitude to match the look. She'd been styling Sophia's hair since last summer when Sophia arrived in Cricket Creek, Kentucky, to help out at her pregnant sister-in-law's Walking on Sunshine Bistro after Mattie had been put on bed rest. "You crack me up."

Carrie Ann fisted her hands on her hips and tilted her head. Her big auburn hair was so full of product that it barely moved. "I'm serious, girl. Hey, how about me and you head over to Sully's Tavern after your hair is all done up with those highlights? I'll be your wingwoman."

"Have you forgotten that I'm heading back to New York City soon?"

"No, but if you ask me, you don't seem in any big hurry." Carrie Ann took a seat in the chair beside her and swiveled it around. "But now that your mama, sister, and brother all live in Cricket Creek, I was hopin' that you might consider moving to this sweet little town too. I've grown fond of your smiling face here and when I have breakfast at the bistro." She leaned in closer. "Don't tell Mattie I said so, but I think you've mastered her melt-in-your-mouth biscuits," she said in a low voice. "I just add some strawberry jam and it's like there's a party in my mouth."

"Oh, thank you, Carrie Ann. And you know I'm fond of you too." Sophia shifted in her chair and inhaled deeply. Of course she'd thought about staying in Cricket Creek, especially recently. The peace and quiet of a small town drew her in more than she'd expected and she would sorely miss living in the same town as Garret, Grace, and her mother once she moved back to the city. "But Lily is nearly six months old and Mattie is back full-time at Walking on Sunshine. And while I love cooking and had enjoyed filling in as a chef, I'm a hair stylist and makeup artist. I've worked hard to develop my clientele, and it's time for me to head back to New York before I lose them. I really need to get ready for the June wedding season. I've already extended my stay way longer than I intended and my bosses are running out of patience with me. They will only hold my position open for so long before I'm permanently replaced at the salon."

Carrie Ann pressed her deep red lips together and gave her a level look. "And just why did you extend your visit?" she asked, but continued without waiting for an answer. "Um, maybe because you want to stay in Cricket Creek?" She raised her eyebrows. "Hmm? And you could have a chair here." She waved her arm in a wide arc. "I could certainly use someone with your reputation and skills. Girl, after you helped out with updos for the Snow Ball dance, requests for you started pouring in."

"You've mentioned that a time or two."

"Or ten." Carrie Ann gave her a slight grin.

While Sophia loved the little salon situated in the heart of Main Street and honestly didn't miss the drama of the bridezillas she had to deal with, her expertise was in updos and makeup for elaborate events and weddings. But how could she tell Carrie Ann that working at A Cut Above wouldn't be enough of a challenge without sounding uppity and rude?

"Hey . . ." Carrie Ann raised her palms upward and inclined her head. "I know what you're thinkin'. You're used to the hustle and bustle of that fancy salon in New York City and this wouldn't be enough for someone with your skills."

"Carrie Ann . . ."

"Hear me out, sweet pea."

"Okay." Sophia gripped the magazine and and waited.

Carrie Ann nibbled on the inside of her cheek for a few seconds as if gathering her thoughts. "We've been slow today but A Cut Above still holds its own against the chains popping up outside of town. I have lots of loyal local clients and I could use a couple more stylists." She put her hands on her knees and leaned forward. "But I've been tinkerin' with the idea of opening a salon up in Wedding Row. You know in that pretty strip of wedding shops overlookin' the river?"

Sophia nodded her foiled head and felt a warm flash of interest. "I've been up there with Grace. If I remember right, there's a florist, jewelry store, and lovely bridal boutique, among other things."

"You're right. From This Moment is owned by Addison Monroe, daughter of Melinda Monroe, the famous financial guru."

"I know." Sophia nodded slowly. "Um . . . Addison was engaged to my half brother Garret before she married Reid Greenfield. It was a messy story in the tabloids until my mom's ex-husband came to Cricket Creek to straighten out the crazy lies. Rick Ruleman was a rock legend with a reputation to match, but he would never have had an affair with Garret's fiancée." Sophia shook her head in disgust.

Carrie Ann slapped her hand to her forehead and winced. "Well, hell's bells, how in the world could I have forgotten about that little detail?"

"Addison and Garret are on great terms now." Sophia lifted one shoulder. "My mom and Rick have mended their fences too. I never thought I'd see the day when he'd settle down in a small town." Sophia chuckled. "Life is so weird."

"Tell me about it. Did you ever think that your fashion model mama would marry a bass fisherman and run a fishin' camp for underprivileged kids?"

"Not in a million years. But she loves it."

"How about your Grace swooping in and helping Mason Mayfield save his craft brewery?" Carrie Ann picked up the mixing bowls and walked over to the sink.

"Now that I would have believed. Unlike me, Grace loves a challenge."

"That's a whole lotta movin' and shakin' going on. I'd say your family is pretty doggone awesome."

"Why, thank you. I totally agree," she said with a firm nod.

"And they're all here. This is why you need to consider staying in Cricket Creek." Carrie Ann walked over and checked one of the foils. "Not done processing yet." She folded it back into place.

"Carrie Ann, why are you so adamant about me staying?" she asked, but had an inkling of where this conversation could be heading.

"What would you say to opening up a wedding-themed salon as partners? I'm thinking I'd like to call it White Lace and Promises," she said in a dreamy tone.

Sophia's heart thudded with excitement but about a dozen questions popped into her head all at once. While her mom and sister were all about taking financial risks, Sophia was much more conservative. "Would there be enough weddings to keep the business brisk?"

"Good question. I spoke with Reid Greenfield's sister Sara who said that she's getting big barn weddings booked from Nashville, Tennessee, and Lexington, Kentucky. Sara's wedding reception venue with the gorgeous river setting is growing by leaps and bounds. She's also booking more intimate receptions at Wine and Diner right here on Main Street. We might be a small town but we're close to some big cities. And don't forget that there's a convention center down by the baseball stadium now. I'm sure there will be some black-tie events, which could mean even more business. Sophia, sugar, with your expertise and reputation I truly think the clientele would grow quickly." Her voice picked up speed and her hands did the talking as she became more and more excited. "The businesses up on Wedding Row support and feed off one another. There's a shop available for lease right next to Flower Power and it's located just two doors down from the bridal boutique! And it's already set up to be a salon. Can you believe it?" She paused to take a breath. "So what do you think? Not that you have to give me an answer right now. But thoughts . . . Give me some feedback."

"I think the idea has potential, for sure."

"So you're interested?"

"I'm . . . intrigued."

Carrie Ann smacked her knee. "Sweet! I've been thinkin' about this ever since Wedding Row opened up but I didn't have anybody like you who could take the reins for me. And I have to keep on top of things here at A Cut Above. My mother opened this shop and I want to keep the doors open in her honor." She raised her arms skyward. "This is so perfect! We definitely need to head to Sully's or down to the taproom at the brewery and celebrate."

"Carrie Ann . . . I said I'm intrigued." Sophia carefully added a note of caution to her tone. "I'm not making any promises, though."

"Okay then . . ." Carrie Ann flipped her palm over and put her index finger to her opposite pinkie. "Let's start a list of reasons why you should do this. You'd be your own boss. I would basically let you run the whole thing. You'd live in the same town as your family. The cost of living is nothing compared to New York City. You already told me that you love your condo overlooking the river." She leaned forward and put her hand next to her mouth and whispered, "And you already know that most of the hot Cricket Creek Cougars baseball players live there. Thought I'd toss in that tidbit."

"I hadn't noticed," Sophia said.

"Oh . . . well, maybe that's because someone else in this town has caught your eye. And that someone just might be Avery Dean."

"Pffft . . . no way." She pointed to her eyes. "Not caught. We're just friends."

"Right. And I'm a natural redhead."

Laughing, Sophia pointed to her own hair. "And I'm *about to become* a natural blonde."

Carrie Ann sat back in her chair. "You're gonna look that way because of my expertise. Actually, those highlights will be just the perfect little boost to your gorgeous caramel color. A very Jennifer Aniston look. You kinda remind me of her . . . So pretty but not in a flashy way."

"Coming from one of the flashiest women I know."

"At my age I have to pile on makeup and bling to camouflage my flaws."

"Oh, stop! You're gorgeous."

"Ah, bless your heart, Sophia. But, sweetheart, you're a natural beauty."

"The girl next door, right?" While Sophia didn't have the stunning long-legged beauty of her mother and sister, Grace, she was content with her looks, for the most part, anyway. Although it was irritating that Grace could eat whatever she damn well pleased and not gain an ounce. Having a slow metabolism really sucked. While she also didn't share the big personalities of her mother and sister, Sophia was happy to stay in the background. She'd much rather do hair and makeup than be in front of the camera. But being the quiet one also gave her the ability to get away with some pretty epic practical jokes. Garret and Grace were always blamed for things first, so there was a definite upside to flying under the radar. But she thought about Carrie Ann's offer and wondered if it was about time that she busted out of her comfort zone. But decisions didn't come easy to her. Here she was a hair stylist and it had taken her two weeks to decide to add a few highlights.

"Why so quiet? Did I say something wrong?"

"Oh no." Sophia shook her head. "Not at all. I'm just trying to process what you've thrown in my lap."

"You mean the twenty-five ways to drive your man wild?" Carrie Ann asked with a chuckle.

"No, I'm just a little blown away that you'd want to go into business together," Sophia replied, but glanced down at the article. Visions of Avery slid back into her brain.

Carrie Ann stood up and checked the foils again. "About another ten minutes." She patted Sophia's shoulder. "No rush on your answer. It's good enough for me right now that you're considering my offer," she said and hurried off to answer the ringing phone.

Because Sophia had come in rather late everyone else was gone for the day. She glanced at her reflection in the mirror and winced, thinking that she looked like an alien Medusa with the silver foils sticking out everywhere. The blond highlights were a bit of a whim but she was glad she'd finally made the decision to go for it. Of course, hair stylists should always be up for something different, but change, even something as simple as highlights, took Sophia longer than most people and it was so frustrating sometimes.

With a sigh, she started scanning through the article just for fun. The suggestions were mostly silly, in her opinion. The painting of each other with chocolate syrup and then licking it off seemed a little messy. She stopped short at the thought. Dear God, was she becoming a . . . *fuddy-duddy*? Yes, because she was pretty sure nobody her age even thought of expressions like *fuddy-duddy*.

Determined, she kept her eyes closed and tried to imagine the chocolate syrup scenario. Perhaps if you used thick chocolate fudge and warmed it up? Oh, now that might just be very nice. . . .

"Are you sleeping?" asked a whiskey-smooth male voice that slid over her just like the chocolate fudge she'd been daydreaming about. She smiled thinking that this body-painting thing might be the ticket after all. "Um, maybe I shouldn't interrupt," the voice continued cutting through her chocolate-coated fantasy.

Oh shit.

Sophia opened her eyes and looked at the sexy country boy who had been invading her thoughts and dreams over the past few months. "Avery!" Foils sprung from her head and *oh dear God* the magazine in her lap was open to the twenty-five ways to drive your man wild. She gripped the armrest, wishing there was an eject button. "Hi." Her smile probably looked like a wince.

"Hey, Sophia. Haven't seen you in a while." He put his toolbox down and shrugged out of his jacket.

"I've been busy babysitting Lily a lot."

"Oh well, I miss seeing you at breakfast," he said,

which created a vision of him sitting across a kitchen table in the morning all sleep-tousled and sexy.

She swallowed hard. "I miss you . . . I mean seeing you at the bistro, too." She glanced down at the nearly naked model. Her fingers itched to turn the page.

"Watcha readin'?" Panic set in when he angled his head at the glossy pages in her lap.

"I . . . um . . ." She felt heat creep into her cheeks. "I was just, you know, thumbing through a random magazine, while my hair is processing." She looked over at Carrie Ann who was chatting away on the phone. "What, um, brings you here?"

Avery jammed his thumb over his shoulder causing Sophia to notice the bulge of his biceps that stretched the sleeve of his red T-shirt. "I'm here to fix the washing machine that's been giving Carrie Ann fits. I would've been here sooner but I was slammed with repairs all day. But it sure is a bonus to run into you."

"It's good to see you too, Avery."

"I'm sure glad you think so." He gave Sophia a grin that caused his cheek to dimple. His chestnut brown hair had grown out a bit since she'd last seen him, the dark tendrils curling around his ears and forehead. As though reading her thoughts, he shoved his fingers through his hair.

"I know. I need a haircut. Just been too busy to get it done."

"I like it longer," Sophia heard herself say, and lifted one shoulder in a shrug.

"Well then, maybe I should keep it that way." He shot her a grin.

"As a stylist I'm always thinking about hair," she responded quickly.

"Oh, I'd forgotten that was your career. If you ever decide to stay a cook you'll never be broke either." He flashed another grin that made her melt like the ice cube in "How to Drive Your Man Wild," number five. "I really do miss you at the bistro, Sophia."

"Oh, I was getting pretty good, but Mattie is still the best cook around."

"I was referring to your company," Avery said in a sincere but slightly flirty tone. "Your sweet smile was a great way to start my day."

"Why, thank you. I must look a fright right now, though." She pointed to her head and caught her bottom lip between her teeth. "Sorry."

"Aw, you still manage to look pretty," Avery said just as Carrie Ann hurried over.

"Hey there, Avery. You gonna take a look at my washing machine from hell?"

"Sure thing." Avery nodded. "Sorry I'm late. Been a busy day."

"Oh, that's okay. Still cold out there?" Carrie Ann peeked beneath one of the foils.

"Yeah, but I hear the snow is gonna miss us," Avery said.

"Humph, well, last time the weatherman said it was going to miss us, we got six inches. You're just about ready to get rinsed," she said to Sophia, but looked back at Avery. "We're thinkin' about heading up to Sully's Tavern later. Stop on in and I'll buy ya a beer."

"Well, now, that's an offer I can't refuse," Avery said, and angled his head toward the back of the shop. "I'd better get working." He picked up his toolbox, causing another delicious ripple of muscle. "See y'all tonight," he said, but his gaze lingered on Sophia.

"Let's get you back to the bowl, sugar."

"Carrie Ann!" Sophia said in an urgent whisper. "Just what do you think you're doing?"

"Gettin' an early start on bein' your wingwoman," she whispered back. "Avery Dean's got the hots for you, Sophia. And judging by the blush in your cheeks I think you're sweet on him too. That whole we're-just-friends thing you keep saying is a bunch of hogwash. Why are you not taking advantage of the situation?"

"Because when we first met at the bistro he was just getting over a broken engagement. I don't want to be his rebound girl, and I didn't intend to stay here so I didn't want to hurt him all over again either."

"Well, now, I'd say enough time has passed since his breakup. And I'm hoping you'll take me up on my offer and move here."

Sophia stood up and had to grin. "I think you're playing matchmaker to give me another reason to stay."

Carrie Ann placed a hand over her ample chest. "Would I do something like that? Little ole me?"

"In a heartbeat."

Carrie Ann laughed. "Ah, child, you already know me too well. That's why we're gonna make great business partners. You just wait and see."

Sophia shook her head as she followed Carrie Ann back to the shampoo bowls to get rinsed. Through the open door to the laundry room she could see Avery bent over the washing machine. She couldn't help but admire his very fine denim-clad butt.

Carrie Ann turned and caught her staring. "What?" Sophia sputtered with a lift of her chin, desperately trying to appear innocent, which of course only made her appear guilty.

"Friends . . . ha." Carrie Ann laughed. "Thought so . . ." She clapped her hands softly. "I do love it when a plan comes together."

Sophia rolled her eyes, but when Carrie Ann turned around, Sophia angled her head to get another glimpse of Avery. Of course he picked that very moment to straighten up and look in her direction. She did one of those lightning-quick look-away moves but she caught the blur of his smile in the corner of her vision. A warm tingle of awareness washed over her as she leaned her neck against the cool porcelain bowl. She and Avery had been tap dancing around their attraction and for very good reasons. She firmly reminded herself that nothing should change if he showed up at Sully's.

No matter what matchmaking scheme Carrie Ann was cooking up, Sophia knew she needed to make her decisions with a clear head that wasn't clouded by the desire to know what it felt like to kiss Avery Dean.

2

Under My Spell

AVERY SLID HIS TOOLBOX INTO HIS TRUCK, AND hopped up into the driver's seat, anxious to grab a cold beer at Sully's. The thought of hanging out with Sophia sent a jolt through his system.

"Cool your jets," he grumbled, shaking his head. He'd been telling himself for the past few months not to act on his attraction to Sophia Gordon. Of course, getting involved with someone who was heading back to New York would be a poor decision on his part. But ever since Sophia's sister and mom had decided to stay, a little part of him hoped that maybe she might end up moving to Cricket Creek as well. Then again, Sophia staying in town remained a great big *maybe* and he didn't want to set himself up for getting hurt again. Once in a lifetime was enough, thank you very much.

But what Avery hadn't seen coming was the punch to the gut reaction when he'd spotted Sophia sitting in the chair at Carrie Ann's salon. He had to grin. Even with those silver foils sticking up everywhere, she still managed to look absolutely pretty. When he'd caught a glimpse of what she was reading, he just had to tease her. When Sophia blushed, he thought it was the cutest damn thing in the world.

Avery sat there for a minute trying to decide whether to head over to Sully's or to stop home first to take a quick shower and change out of his work clothes. Fixing the washing machine had taken longer than it should have but he'd been distracted by Sophia's voice while he attempted to do the repairs. And when he'd heard her soft, sexy laughter he'd dropped his hammer onto his foot. Thank God for his steel-toed boots.

Seeing Sophia made him realize just how much he'd missed the easy banter they'd shared nearly every morning at the bistro, when she'd been working there. The sweetness of her smile had soothed the searing pain he'd felt right after his fiancée Ashley had cheated on him several months into their engagement.

Ashley worked in marketing for the Cricket Creek Cougars baseball organization. Oddly enough, her tearful confession that her one-night stand with a baseball player was a horrible mistake had hurt much worse than if the guy had actually meant something to her. If she'd somehow fallen in love, at least the guy would have meant something to her instead of just being a roll in the hay.

Avery scrubbed a hand down his face. "Oh man, you're past that shit. Don't even go there," he mumbled.

Deciding he'd like to take the shower first, Avery reached up to start the engine. But the ping of his cell phone had him reaching into his pocket instead. After fishing his phone out, he looked down at the text message from his sister asking him to come to dinner. He leaned back against the headrest and groaned. Avery sent a message back to Zoe saying he didn't want to have dinner tomorrow night with her fiancé Max and her maid of honor, who just happened to be Ashley Montgomery.

Zoe messaged back: *Why not? We need to go over some wedding details.*

"Oh, please . . ." Avery inhaled a quick breath of chill air, held it and blew it out. Ever since Zoe asked Ashley to be her maid of honor and Max had asked Avery to be the best man there had been a not-so-subtle push for Avery and Ashley to get back together. "No damned possible way."

While Avery knew that Ashley regretted cheating, he simply couldn't move past her betrayal. He thought he knew her so well but how could he ever trust her again? Not only had they been engaged, but Ashley had been his sister's best friend since junior high school. So Ashley's behavior went way past just hurting him. She'd betrayed them all.

After her confession, Ashley had begged Avery not to tell Zoe, and he'd promised he would keep her dirty deed a secret. But because Avery had kept his word, there continued to be a lot of speculation as to why they'd broken up so suddenly. Unfortunately, the most popular rumor was that Avery had gotten cold feet, so most people—including his sister and Max—assumed that he was to blame. Apparently, his lame *we grew apart* answer wasn't good enough to satisfy small-town gossip.

When Avery's phone pinged again he gripped the cold steering wheel for a few seconds. While he would never break his word, this was getting pretty damned old.

After a long sigh Avery gave in and read the message: *Oh, come on, we'll go to the taproom at Broomstick Brewery. Karaoke night!!!* Three exclamation points meant that Zoe meant business.

Avery shook his head and felt an unwanted pang of sadness. Only a little over one year older than Zoe, he and his sister had always been close siblings. Avery loved to tease her, but they rarely fought and always had each other's backs. Other than this secret, Avery usually confided in Zoe, so it really felt odd not to be able to talk about such a big disappointment in his life.

But if Ashley came clean and told the truth, Zoe would be devastated and Avery knew the knowledge would put a damper on her wedding plans. Not only would Zoe most likely break off their friendship but his sister would have to find a maid of honor to take her best friend's place. "Maid of *honor,* my sweet ass," Avery mumbled. He ground his teeth together. "Ah what a damned mess you've caused, Ashley Montgomery."

After a moment Avery scrubbed a hand down his face. While he knew that Zoe couldn't possibly understand his reluctance to go to dinner with them, her persistence was becoming increasingly frustrating.

And Avery sure as hell didn't have a clue how to remedy the sticky situation.

When his phone pinged again he winced. "Ah, dammit!" He hated this. He loved his sister and missed Max. The four of them had been best friends since middle school, virtually inseparable all throughout high school and their early twenties. They'd created some really amazing memories together, but now, it all felt somehow . . . tainted. Avery still didn't know what to do with the happy times still lingering in his brain. Plus, this whole avoidance thing put a big damper on his social life.

He sighed. Zoe meant well but Avery finally felt as if he was moving past a difficult period in his life. Having his sister trying to drag him out for a night on the town and having to revisit the pain Ashley caused him wasn't what he needed. To the world he might look like a hard-ass country boy, but Ashley had shattered his heart into a million pieces. Hanging out with her was at the bottom of the list of things he wanted to do.

Fresh, unwanted anger at Ashley reared its ugly head and he took a few seconds to tamp it back down. Of course, part of the problem was the fact that he couldn't vent to anyone. But not only had he given his word but letting her affair out of the bag was the kind of small-town gossip that would be talked about God knows how long. And Avery knew the news would cause Ashley's mom and dad pain as well. He'd spent countless hours in the Montgomery household and he didn't want to be the bearer of that kind of news to people he still loved. So he was in a word . . . screwed.

Blowing out a breath Avery typed: *Sorry, I have plans tomorrow.* Truth was he didn't have a damned thing going on and now he'd have to come up with something because Zoe was sure to ask what he was doing. Keeping this secret was getting more and more difficult.

Avery put his annoying phone on vibrate and started up his truck. An ice-cold beer never sounded so good. Motivated, he eased out onto Main Street hoping to catch green lights all the way to his house on Cherry Tree Lane.

Five minutes later, he pulled into his driveway and hurried into his two-story brick house that he'd been restoring over the past few years . . . The house that he and Ashley were going to live in. He'd painted over colors she'd chosen and removed all of her possessions. Going down memory lane was the last place he wanted to travel but his sister had no way of knowing why. Most of what Avery had learned about repair and re-modeling had come from his uncle, Easton, whom he'd followed around like a shadow when he was a little kid. He'd had his own toolbox by the age of five. When other kids were playing video games, Avery had been busy finding stuff to take apart or fix.

When the family-owned Fisher Hardware store couldn't keep up with the big warehouse chains, Uncle Easton closed up shop and decided to go into the re-pair business. When he'd asked Avery to come on board as a partner it was a no-brainer. Five years ago he and his uncle never dreamed Fisher and Dean would lead to training and hiring a six-truck fleet! And they were still too busy to handle all of the calls from Cricket Creek and the surrounding areas.

Avery took the front steps two at a time and unlocked the heavy front door he'd recently painted a
deep shade of green. He smiled at the lemon scent of
furniture polish that hung in the air. Because of the
long hours, he'd recently hired a maid service to keep
the house clean and his laundry washed. Having grown
up doing chores around the house with his sister, Avery felt a little bit guilty at what his father very vocally
considered an extravagance, but to Avery, the expense
was worth being able to come home from work to a
spotless house every night.

After a quick shower, Avery towel-dried his hair
thinking he needed a trim. Having always detested his
curls, he'd usually opted for a close-cropped style, but
remembered Sophia saying that she likes it longer.
Nibbling on the inside of his lip, he peered at his reflection in the oval mirror above the pedestal sink. After
a moment he shrugged. Hey, if Sophia liked it . . . but
then shook his head. Doing things just because a girl
liked it could lead into dangerous territory. While he
might be over Ashley, opening his fool heart to that
kind of pain again was going to take a long-ass time . . .
like maybe never.

He decided on a button-down Western-cut blue shirt
instead of the usual T-shirt he would have worn and
tugged on his best pair of Wranglers and cowboy boots.
After a splash of spicy aftershave, he looked at his favorite University of Kentucky baseball cap but decided
not to wear it. Grabbing his phone and his keys, he clat-
tered down the hardwood steps stopping to put on his
Carhartt jacket, and hurried out the door.

Avery turned on a country music channel and sang
"Friends in Low Places" along with Garth Brooks. Music
was his go-to stress reliever. Ah damn, he missed karaoke
nights! But he pushed the thought away, not wanting his
hard-won good mood to evaporate.

When he pulled into the packed parking lot of Sully's, Avery thought that the honky-tonk seemed crowded for a Wednesday night, but then again, he hadn't been out in ages so this might be typical. "Gotta get out more often," he muttered as he drove around.

Finally finding a vacant spot, Avery killed the engine, but after he hopped down from his truck, he stood there for a moment. He was going to see Sophia. He could try to deny it, but the thought made him undeniably happy. When caution reared its ugly head, he squashed it. *This isn't serious,* he told himself. *I can at least allow myself to enjoy her company. No harm in that, right?*

And he was actually kind of . . . *nervous.*

A slow grin spread across his face as he started walking toward the entrance. His breath blew smoke into the cold night air and gravel crunched beneath the heels of his boots. This was a good kind of nervous energy and he found himself whistling softly.

The old school neon lights blinked a friendly honky-tonk welcome. When he opened the door laughter and music slid toward him, drawing him in. The sharp scent of Buffalo wings, French fries, and tap beer made his mouth water.

Yeah, it had been way too long since he'd been to Sully's.

Turning, Avery unbuttoned his jacket and hung it on one of the hooks lining the back wall. But he reminded himself that this wasn't a date and that it was actually Carrie Ann who had invited him. Still, coming out to spend time with Sophia sent a jolt of excitement racing through his veins. Avery hadn't felt this carefree in a long time and he had to admit that it felt pretty damned awesome.

Avery scanned the bar hoping to spot Carrie Ann's big red hair over the crowd but came up empty. The thought hit him that perhaps they'd decided not to come, but before he could explore the room more, a cold longneck was pressed into his hand. Avery turned around and was greeted by the grinning face of his friend Danny Mayfield.

Danny gave Avery's shoulder a nudge. "Dude, I haven't seen you out in forever. What's up with that noise?"

"I dunno." Avery shrugged. "Been busy."

"That's a lame-ass excuse of FOGO."

"What the hell is FOGO?"

"Fear of going out."

"Oh." Guilty. "That's bullshit."

"Well then, Mason has been having some kick-ass bonfires at the Broomstick Brewery. He's doing a pig roast sometime soon. You should come."

Avery took a swig of his beer and nodded. "Thanks, sounds like a good time." Avery had helped bartend at the grand opening of the brewery back in October. Sophia had helped out too and they'd hung around and had fun at the after party.

Danny jammed his thumb over his shoulder. "Me and Colby are playing some pool. Wanna join us?"

"I would but I'm meeting somebody here," Avery replied and glanced around again.

"Oh, yeah, who?" Danny asked casually but gave him a close look. "Anybody I know?"

"Is there anybody you don't know in Cricket Creek?" Danny's family owned Mayfield Marina where his brother Mason built the popular craft brewery.

"Why do I feel as if you're evading the question?" Danny tipped his bottle back, and waited.

"I'm meeting Carrie Ann Spencer and Sophia Gordon for a beer."

"Oh?" Danny raised his eyebrows. "Sophia? She's one of the sweetest people on the planet. Funny as hell too. She and I bartended the other night at the taproom, and damn, she had me rolling on the floor. She's all quiet, but has these one-liners that come outta nowhere."

"Really?" Avery asked evenly but felt a flash of jealousy. "You do that often?" Damn but his tone had a bit of an edge to it.

"Whoa there." Danny held up his hands. "Don't get your panties in a wad. She's like a sister to me."

"My panties aren't in a wad."

"Oh." Danny laughed. "So you wear panties?"

"Yeah, thongs."

"I knew it!"

"Wanna see my whale tail?"

"Thanks, but I'll pass."

Avery gave his friend a chuckle, and then took a swig of his beer.

"No, seriously, I'm glad you're hanging out with her. She's a cute girl." Danny tilted his head. "I can kinda see you together."

"Danny, she's going back to New York. I'm not an idiot. We're just hanging out."

Danny shrugged. "Well, her sister, Grace, was going back to London and now she's married to my brother. Her mother lives here now and so does her brother Garret when he's not doin' that singing show in London. I kinda think she might consider staying given the right reasons, if you know what I'm sayin'."

"I don't know what you're sayin'."

"Right . . ." Danny took a swig of his beer and shrugged. "Geez, don't look at me like that. I'm just makin' a personal observation. Look, I've got to get back to the game. It's cool to see you, though, man."

"Same here."

"Don't forget about the pig roast. I'll text you the date and details."

"Thanks, Danny. We need to get out on the water and fish when the weather warms up."

"Sounds like a plan." He clanked his bottle to Avery's. "Now go find your girl."

"She's . . ." Avery was about to protest that Sophia wasn't his *girl* but Danny pivoted and started weaving his way through the crowd. *His girl.* Avery shook his head. Wow, he had it bad and it must be written all over his damned face. He told himself once again to cool his jets, but then he looked across the bar and spotted Sophia sitting at a high-top table with Carrie Ann. She sat sideways so he could see her profile and when she tipped her head back and laughed at something Carrie Ann said Avery had to smile.

Damn . . .

The rest of the bar faded into the background when Avery zoned in on Sophia, taking in how cute and sexy she looked in dark blue jeans and a pink sweater hugging her in all the right places. The overhead lighting picked up the extra blond in her caramel-colored hair. He noticed that her cut was a few inches shorter, grazing the top of her shoulders in a bouncy, flirty way. She'd crossed her legs and when a new song came on she tapped her foot in rhythm to the beat.

Avery suddenly wondered how it would feel to have her in his arms, dancing. . . . Avery usually wasn't much of a dancer, but he wanted to dance with Sophia something fierce.

As he walked toward her, Avery felt another jolt of nervous anticipation. He racked his brain for something clever to say but when he reached her table all he could think of was "Hi."

Sophia gave him a rather shy smile. "Hello, Avery. I'm glad that you came out tonight."

"I wouldn't miss it," he said and felt silly. This wasn't an event, just a Wednesday night out.

"Um, hello, what am I, chopped liver?" Carrie Ann asked, and then made a face at him.

"Not hardly." Avery leaned over and gave her a kiss on the cheek.

"Well, now, that's much better. I'll buy you that promised beer after all." Carrie Ann gave him a little head bop. "Just keep the compliments comin'."

Avery chuckled but shook his head. "No, this round is on me, ladies. What are y'all drinkin'?"

Carrie Ann held up her pilsner glass. "Somethin' called Spellbound from Broomstick Brewery. Very tasty."

Avery looked at Sophia. "Same for you?"

"I, um, had Love Potion." She pressed her lips together and blushed. "We did a flight of some new ales but this one is still my go-to favorite. Would you like a sip?"

"Yes, thanks." He'd probably tasted the brew before but there was something about taking a sip of her drink that appealed to him. When she handed him the glass and when their fingers brushed he felt another zap of awareness. He took a swallow and licked the hoppy taste from his bottom lip. "Oh, a winter ale. I like it . . . What is it again?"

"Love Potion."

"Number nine?"

"No, this is my first," Sophia said, and then laughed. "If I have nine, you'll have to carry me out of here."

Avery laughed with her, loving Sophia's sense of humor. In truth, carrying her out of there held some serious appeal.

Carrie Ann tapped her glass to his. "Here's to having it work."

"Carrie Ann!" Sophia said, but Carrie Ann just shrugged and laughed.

"Love potion number ni-e-i-e-ine," she sang.

Avery chuckled. Carrie Ann was one of his favorite people. "I'll be right back." He handed the glass back to Sophia whose cheeks were blushed a pretty shade of pink, probably caused by Carrie Ann's comment. She looked so damned cute that Avery had the urge to pull her into his arms and kiss her. His gaze lingered on her mouth and when her eyes widened just a fraction he caught himself and turned away. As he walked toward the bar he knew that he didn't need a love potion. He'd been sweet on Sophia ever since she'd served him breakfast at Walking on Sunshine Bistro last summer. They'd flirted but it was all in fun and he needed to keep it that way. He sure as hell didn't need to get his heart shredded to pieces again, but try as he might he couldn't quite shake the excitement of being attracted to her.

Just as Avery approached the bar he felt a sharp nudge from behind. He turned around and grinned. "Well, hey there, Uncle Easton."

"Hey, yourself," his uncle said with his usual wide grin. "Son, I've been trying to get you out to grab a cold one for ages. What brings you here tonight?"

"I fixed Carrie Ann's washing machine over at her salon. She invited me out for a beer."

An odd look passed over Uncle Easton's face. "Really? You're here with Carrie Ann?"

"Seriously, Uncle Easton?" He'd always suspected that his uncle had a thing for Carrie Ann and now he was sure. "Don't you think she's a little . . . uh, mature for me?"

"I dunno." His uncle shifted from one foot to the other, appeared a bit flustered, and then shrugged. "She could be one of those . . . what do you call 'em?" He looked into his glass of beer as if it held the answer.

"A cougar?"

He looked back up and pointed at Avery. "Yeah, one of those."

Avery resisted the urge to laugh, and then clamped his hand on his uncle's shoulder. "Carrie Ann is here with Sophia and she asked me to come along out of politeness." And he suspected a bit of matchmaking had played a part in the invitation but he wasn't going to get that conversation started. His uncle had been all over his ass lately to get back into the dating scene. Avery considered it funny advice coming from a man who proclaimed to be a confirmed bachelor.

"Oh, I gotcha."

"Yeah." Avery nodded. "I came over to the bar to buy a round. I could use a hand carrying the drinks back to the table. Why don't you join us?"

"Sure, why not?" he said casually but seemed more than a little pleased. It didn't go unnoticed that whenever Carrie Ann and his uncle were in the same room they seemed to gravitate toward each other so much so that there'd often been speculation about them.

"Cool," Avery said and signaled for the bartender. Although his uncle made it clear that he never wanted to get tied down, he was actively social in and around Cricket Creek. A natural athlete of some local note, he'd play anything from softball to cornhole and you were considered lucky to have him on your team. He could two-step with the best of them, had an exceptional singing voice and a great sense of humor. He was one of those George Clooney kind of guys who aged well, a gene that Avery hoped he'd inherited. Avery handed Carrie Ann's beer to his uncle. "Ready?"

"Son, I was born ready."

Avery laughed, knowing that would be his uncle's response. They were stopped several times while trying to make their way back to the table and while Avery liked seeing his buddies, he kept glancing over at Sophia. He noticed that he wasn't the only one looking her way and when some dude approached her it was all he could do not to march over there and step between them. To his relief, Sophia shook her head at whatever the guy asked.

"Maybe you oughta hustle on over there and stake your claim," Uncle Easton said and gave Avery's arm a nudge, nearly making him spill one of the beers.

"I don't have a claim to stake."

"That's the whole point."

"Sophia might be leaving Cricket Creek."

"And she might not."

"Uncle Easton . . ."

"Just keep that in mind. That's all I'm sayin'. Ask

her to dance or somethin' before someone else does. What's the harm in that?"

The harm was getting something started that he shouldn't. "It's not that simple," Avery argued.

"I beg to differ. You take the drinks over to them, ask Sophia to dance and then take her hand."

"You're assuming she'll say yes."

"There's only one way to find out."

"I don't know . . ."

"Well then, ask her to play darts or pool or somethin'."

Avery nibbled on the inside of his lip, thinking. "Why is this so damned difficult?"

"It's not."

"How did I know you were gonna say that?"

"Make up your mind before these beers get warm."

Avery inhaled a deep breath. Decision time. "Okay . . ."

3

All My Single Ladies

AFTER SPOTTING EASTON FISHER STANDING ALONG-side Avery chatting away, Carrie Ann reached up and fluffed her hair thinking she should have used a Bumpit for a little extra oomph.

"Well, now," Sophia said in a suggestive tone.

"'Well, now' what?" Carrie Ann asked, wondering if she still had lipstick on and if her perfume still smelled nice.

"I caught you staring at Easton." Sophia angled her head toward the bar. "He's pretty hot for an old guy."

"I know." When Easton and Avery stopped to talk to Danny Mayfield, Carrie Ann quickly dug in her purse for her tube of lipstick. She applied a quick swipe of red gloss over her lips. "Wait . . . he's not *old*." She rubbed her lips together and made a face at Sophia.

"I'm just teasing." Sophia leaned forward. "So, what's the deal with you two?"

"There's no deal." She'd carried a torch for the man ever since high school, and Lord have mercy, if he didn't get better-looking every time she laid eyes on him.

And she laid her eyes on him whenever she got the chance.

Sophia glanced over to where Easton and Avery stood. "Why not? He's single, right?"

"Far as I know." She gave Sophia a slight shrug. She ran her tongue over her teeth and wondered if she should pop a Tic Tac in her mouth and head to the ladies' to spray on a little more perfume. "How do you know him, anyway, sugar?"

"Well, he came into Walking on Sunshine for lunch on a regular basis. He seems super nice. Friendly. I also seem to recall how you would somehow always be there at the same time," she said with a mischievous grin.

Carrie Ann flushed. Easton went way beyond just being a looker. The man oozed Southern charm and had a smile that made her melt like a cube of sugar in hot tea. And he could fix damn near anything. What more could a girl possibility want? The fact that he'd remained a bachelor puzzled all of the single ladies in Cricket Creek. She risked another glance in Easton's direction. The man looked mighty fine in his blue jeans and Western-cut shirt. While Carrie Ann vowed to never tie the knot, if Easton, by some quirk of fate, ever proposed to her, she would at least have to give it some serious consideration. It would be worth it just for the honeymoon. Mercy . . . but that thought had her needing to fan her face.

"So . . ." Sophia gave Carrie Ann a questioning tilt of her head.

"So what?" Carrie Ann tried to appear confused and hoped her face wasn't flushing again.

"Oh, come on." Sophia wagged her finger back and forth from Easton to Carrie Ann. "Why don't you make a play for him?"

"Because I like to be footloose and fancy-free," Carrie Ann answered firmly. But Easton was truly the one man who could change her mind about marriage.

If he put a ring under her nose, she was pretty sure she'd cave and accept. Still, even though he made her heart go pitter-patter, she kept her feelings for him locked away inside a safe place. "I don't need somebody snappin' his fingers and tellin' me I need to get dinner on the table or bring him a beer."

"Carrie Ann, relationships aren't like that anymore. And Easton doesn't seem like the type of guy to issue orders to a woman. You're a successful business owner. You wouldn't have to lose your independence if you fell in love."

"I'm just too set in my ways," she argued, even though she knew what her real issue was. When her daddy died from a sudden heart attack at the age of thirty-eight, Carrie Ann's mother bought A Cut Above and worked long hours while Carrie Ann went from captain of the cheerleading squad to being the caretaker for her two younger sisters. And although Mary Spencer put on a happy face for her girls, Carrie Ann could see the sorrow in her mother's eyes. Carrie Ann vowed never to fall in love and risk suffering that kind of pain. She wouldn't even get a dog for that reason.

"Are you sure about that?" Sophia looked at her closely.

"Yeah, who wants to be tied down?" Carrie Ann replied, but when she risked another glance at Easton, she reckoned that being tied down by him could be satisfying in more ways than one.

Oh boy . . .

Carrie Ann picked up her beer coaster and started fanning her face.

"You okay?" Sophia gave her a curious look.

"Damned hot flash," Carrie Ann explained, but left out that the sudden heat was brought on by the vision of being handcuffed to Easton Fisher's bed, not hormones.

"My mom gets those," Sophia said with a sympathetic nod.

"Are you kiddin' me?" Carrie Ann turned her attention to Sophia. "It's hard for me to imagine your supermodel mama breaking a sweat."

Sophia laughed. "Well, she does. Hey, not only has Jimmy Topmiller made her into an excellent bass angler, but he's gotten her into hiking and camping. And she loves running the fishing camp for needy kids. So yeah, she sweats and gets muddy. She even curses once in a while."

"Yeah, but with that English accent of hers, I bet it still sounds polite."

Sophia laughed. "True. But trust me—she's a lot tougher that she looks."

Carrie Ann reached over and put her hand briefly over Sophia's. "You know I'm just teasing, don't you, sugar? The charity work your mama and Jimmy Topmiller are doing with their fishing camp for underprivileged kids is just fantastic. Those kids probably don't know that they're being taught to fish by one of the greatest pro bass anglers to ever live."

"No, but Jimmy never would tell them. He's a pretty humble guy, and according to Mom, he wasn't ever comfortable with having money. She had to convince him that being rich isn't a bad thing if you put the money to good use."

"Smart woman, your mama. And Jimmy is damned easy on the eyes."

"Another hot old guy."

Carrie Ann narrowed her eyes, but Sophia only laughed.

"Speaking of hot old guys, Easton is heading our way."

Carrie Ann lifted one shoulder and tried to ignore the extra thumping of her heart. "Well, he has a hot young guy with him."

"I told you that Avery and I are just friends."

"Right. I know that the sudden flush in your cheeks has nothing to do with a hot flash, girlie."

Sophia plucked at her pink sweater. "It's a little warm in here."

"Ha, you can't fool me, young lady."

"And you can't fool me, either," Sophia shot back. "I think you should go for it."

"Go for what, exactly?"

Sophia leaned over and whispered, "A kiss."

"Oh, come on." Carrie Ann waved a dismissive hand but her heart thumped at the thought. "No way." She gave Sophia a level look. "What? I can see the wheels turning."

"I will if you will," Sophia said, but then pressed her lips together as if with instant regret. She glanced down at her ale.

"Seriously?" Carrie Ann was a sucker for a challenge. "So, you'll go for a kiss from Avery?"

Sophia swallowed hard but then nodded. "Yes." She looked down at her beer again. "Maybe this really is a love potion. Are you in?"

"Do we need proof?" Luckily Easton and Avery were still deep in conversation buying her time to back out.

Sophia shook her head. "The honor system will do."

"No . . ." Carrie Ann shook her head so hard that her hair actually moved.

"Chicken?"

"Oh, you fight dirty." Carrie Ann tapped her fingernail against her glass.

"Hurry up and answer," she said urgently. "They're heading this way again."

"This is insane," Carrie Ann whispered fiercely. "Girl, you're crazier than a bedbug."

"But it's kinda fun." Sophia bit her bottom lip. "I mean, a harmless little kiss never hurt anybody, right?"

Carrie Ann opened her mouth to protest, but the sudden scent of Easton's aftershave made her brain short-circuit.

"You in?" Sophia mouthed.

Carrie Ann closed her eyes, but then nodded.

Sophia smiled, but suddenly looked a little bit skittish.

"Look who I found," Avery said with a grin. He handed Sophia the glass of ale. "Sophia, you know my uncle, Easton, right?"

"Of course." Sophia nodded. "From the bistro. Nice to see you, Easton."

"It's nice to see your pretty face too, Sophia." He turned his gaze to Carrie Ann. "Always a pleasure, Carrie Ann." He placed the ale in front of her.

"Why, thank you, Easton."

"Avery bought it. I'm just your humble servant."

"Well then, thanks, Avery. I still owe you one."

"Oh no, I've got the next round." Easton tapped his chest.

"Well, I won't argue then," Carrie Ann said.

Easton shrugged and tipped his bottle back. "Wouldn't do you any good."

"You might be surprised. She can be very persuasive," Sophia pointed out and Avery nodded.

Easton lowered his bottle. "That so?"

"When I set my mind to something," Carrie Ann shot back, but her pulse quickened when Easton bestowed his sexy as all get-out smile upon her. The warmth in her cheeks had nothing to do with a hot flash and she had to put her hand around the cold glass in an effort to cool down. She often wondered if she had the same effect on Easton or if the attraction was one-sided. Well, she supposed Sophia's silly kiss challenge would get to the bottom of that.

"Avery, would you like to play a game of pool?" Sophia suddenly asked, giving Carrie Ann a go-for-it arch of one eyebrow. "I've gotten a little bit better since the last time we played."

"Sure, Danny and some guys are already over there playing," Avery replied. "Let's go tell them we've got the winners."

"Okay, sounds like fun," Sophia said.

"Good luck," Easton said, apparently oblivious to Sophia's blatant scheme to leave them alone at the table. Normally, Carrie Ann would be perfectly content to be alone with Easton, but the whole kissing thing bounced around in her head like a pinball. Well, she didn't *have* to do it, she reminded herself.

"Somethin' on your mind?" Easton asked.

Yeah, kissing you. "Oh . . . no, why?"

"You're frowning."

"No, I'm fine as a frog's hair." Carrie Ann forced a smile and took a drink of her beer.

"Frog's don't have hair."

"Then I'm pretty doggone fine."

Easton chuckled. "I'd say you're right."

"Tasty," she said, and took another swig of her beer.

"Mason Mayfield is a talented brewmaster. Danny just told me that they are thinking of expanding Broomstick Brewery again to keep up with the demand. Their beers are popping up in restaurants all over the county and I've heard they've won some awards."

"Another Cricket Creek success story," Carrie Ann said. "This little town has come a long way ever since Noah Falcon came back home and built the baseball stadium."

Easton nodded. "I agree. Tourism sure has breathed life back into Cricket Creek. I guess the whole 'if we build it they will come' thing is really true. But I still wish I could have saved Fisher Hardware."

"Your repair business seems to be going like gangbusters, though."

"Yeah, more than Avery and I dreamed. Just goes to show you that when one door closes . . ." He tapped his bottle to her glass. "And your salon seems to be busy."

"It is." Carrie Ann nodded slowly, wondering if she should share her idea for White Lace and Promises with him.

"There you go frowning again."

"Sorry. I have some things on my mind."

"Anything I can help with?" As Easton looked at her with gorgeous blue eyes that were full of sincerity, it suddenly hit Carrie Ann that if she went through with the silly-ass kiss challenge that she risked ruining a perfectly good friendship. No, she wasn't going to go through with it.

"No, but thanks for askin', Easton."

"You can bend my ear whenever you want. You know that, right?"

She nodded and took another sip of her beer.

"Hey, would you like to dance?"

"D-dance?"

"Two-step."

"Oh, Easton, it's been ages since I've danced," she said, instantly feeling like a loser for admitting such a thing. But the last time she'd danced, she'd been at a wedding and it was to the song "It's Raining Men."

"Just follow my lead."

Carrie Ann opened her mouth to protest, but when he stood up and offered his hand, she was powerless to resist. "I gotta warn ya, I might break all of your toes."

"A risk I'm willing to take," Easton said as he led her to the dance floor. Others were already twirling around in the outside circle.

"Oh, you say that now . . ." she mumbled.

Easton was a smooth, effortless dancer—very easy to follow. His sure grip on her hip guided her around the circle and, before long, Carrie Ann relaxed and found herself smiling and laughing when his spins and twirls became a little bit more advanced.

"I knew you'd pick it up easily. After all, you were a cheerleader and on the dance team, if I recall correctly."

He remembered? "A million years ago."

"Well, girl, you've still got it."

And so did Easton . . . in spades. By the end of the

George Strait ballad, Carrie Ann felt flushed and breathless. But just as she thought they were going to exit the dance floor a slower song came on and Carrie Ann found herself swaying to the music in Easton Fisher's strong arms.

Easton threaded his fingers through her right hand and she rested her other hand on his shoulder. She could feel the warmth of his skin through the soft cotton of his shirt and the spice of his aftershave filled her head. After a moment, he pulled her slightly closer and she felt an ache, a longing so intense that her breath caught. She liked this feeling way more than she should. He sang "If I Know Me" in her ear and she was unsurprised to find that he had a great voice as well. Was there anything he couldn't do? Well, she sure as shootin' knew something she wanted him to do.

And then the song ended.

"Thank you for the dance," he said in her ear. The warmth of his breath caused her skin to tingle and damn if she didn't want to kiss him right there in the middle of the dance floor, no challenge needed.

Not trusting her voice Carrie Ann nodded. Her smile felt shy and when she looked into his eyes she saw a flash of something hot and aware. She accepted his hand as they weaved through the crowd and back to the round high-top table. Carrie Ann couldn't remember the last time she'd held a man's hand and it felt really nice.

"You were holding out on me," Easton said.

"What do you mean?"

"You're a terrific dancer."

She waved a dismissive hand nearly knocking over her glass. "Yes, you are. There's no use denying it, which leads me to my next question."

4

Slow Burn

AVERY LEANED HIS POOL STICK AGAINST THE WALL and gave Sophia a little nudge. "Check out my uncle and Carrie Ann over there looking cozy."

Sophia looked in the direction of the high-top table and turned to grin up at Avery. "I guess that slow dance got things heated up. How long do you think they've been in love?"

"In love? You really think so?" Avery asked because he wanted her opinion but he knew the answer. His self-proclaimed bachelor uncle needed a reality check.

"Absolutely," Sophia confirmed with a nod. "It reminds me of last year when my mom and Jimmy Topmiller kept fighting their attraction. It's pointless."

"So you're suggesting they should just give in and go for it?" Avery asked, thinking that Sophia's observation hit way too close to home.

"Yep. Why waste any more precious time?"

"You've got a good point."

"Thank you." When Sophia smiled up at him again his gaze landed on her mouth. Damn, he wanted to kiss her. As if reading his mind she licked her bottom lip and leaned in a little bit closer. Forgetting they were in public, Avery dipped his head . . .

"Uh, excuse me, lovebirds," Danny shouted from across the pool table. "Sophia, it's your turn."

"Oh!" Sophia blushed and stepped forward. "Sorry. We were talking."

"Right, talking," Danny said and gave Colby a nudge with his elbow. "Sure you were."

Avery shook his head at his friends pretending to take their teasing in stride but they were adding fuel to the fire that was already a slow burn. The problem was that Avery was torn between heating things up and cooling things down. But when Sophia nibbled on the inside of her lip and frowned at the balls on the table Avery thought about taking the opportunity to lean in close and help her. But before he could take advantage of the situation she bent over and angled her head, assessing the shot in the corner pocket. Because she was so short she had to stretch, giving Avery a mouthwatering view of her snug jeans hugging her curvy bottom. He swallowed hard and tried not to stare.

Sophia stood up, inhaled a deep breath and blew it out before she bent back to her task. She wasn't very good but concentrated so hard that Avery had to smile and by some miracle she made the rather difficult bank shot, sinking a purple ball into the pocket.

"Yes!" Sophia straightened up and did a cute little hands-and-pool-stick-in-the-air jig. When she turned and tried to give Avery a high five she grazed his hand but missed and hit him on the shoulder instead. She stumbled forward, giggling. "Oh sorry!"

"Whoa there." Avery caught her around her waist but she landed against his chest and the sensation of having her breasts pressed against him nearly made him groan.

"Um, I hate to interrupt again, but, Sophia, you need

to take another shot," Danny said. He rolled his eyes at Avery but grinned and gave him a thumbs-up

"Oh, right," Sophia said and turned around. It might have been Avery's imagination but she sounded a little bit breathless. She missed the shot horribly and stomped her foot. "Sorry," she said with a wince in Avery's direction. "That was ugly."

"Don't worry about it. You're getting a lot better," Avery assured her.

"You think so?"

No, not at all. "Yes, definitely. With some practice you'll become really good."

Sophia stepped closer and tilted her face up at him, within easy kissing distance. "Will you give me lessons, Avery? I'd like to be an asset rather than a liability."

"Sure." Out of the corner of his eye he spotted Colby making another tough shot. He rather handily cleaned up the table and then sank the eight ball, winning the game.

Colby picked up his beer bottle and tapped it to Danny's. "Now that's how it's done."

"No doubt," Danny agreed.

Normally Avery wouldn't like to lose but right now all he cared about was standing close to Sophia. Warning bells of caution pealed in the back of his brain but he ignored them and smiled at her instead of backing away.

"Want to redeem yourselves?" Danny asked.

Avery looked at Sophia in question but she shook her head. "Actually, I think I'd like a breath of fresh air. That strong ale has made me a little tipsy."

"No problem, I'll go grab our jackets. It's kinda cold outside but Pete should have the heaters going on the back deck." Avery turned back to Danny and Colby. "We'll take on you two goofballs next week."

"Ha, think you'll be ready for a rematch?" Danny asked and gave Colby a confident nudge.

Avery arched an eyebrow at Sophia. "What do you think?"

Sophia lifted her chin at Danny's challenge and nodded. "Game on." She turned and gave Avery a fist bump but when they walked away she leaned in and whispered, "I might have been a little overconfident so you might want to give me lessons."

Avery chuckled. "I can do that," he said, and realized it would be another way to spend time with her. "I heard Mason say they're adding a couple of pool tables to the taproom at the brewery. We can practice there."

"Sounds like a plan," she said with a smile, and then paused. "I need to use the ladies' room so if you wouldn't mind getting my jacket I'll meet you outside in a couple of minutes."

"Sure thing." Avery had the urge to lean in and give her a quick kiss on the cheek but refrained, quickly reminding himself that Sophia wasn't his girlfriend. But for some reason, it sure felt that way.

Avery walked over to their table and grabbed Sophia's jacket from her barstool. He smiled when he spotted his uncle and Carrie Ann back out on the dance floor. Looking at the empty glasses he had to wonder if there actually was some magic brewed into the Love Potion Ale. Or then again maybe his uncle finally realized that Carrie Ann was more than a friend to him.

Avery made his way outside to a deserted deck and that was just fine with him. A light breeze caused a nip in the evening air but a couple of tall heaters glowed with warmth and he gravitated toward one of them in case Sophia might feel the cold. Music and laughter from inside Sully's drifted Avery's way and he smiled a bit sadly, realizing with a little pang how much he'd missed nights out with friends. And he sure missed the company of a pretty woman. He sighed, thinking that letting go of the past wasn't all that difficult but shedding his fear of getting hurt again wasn't quite so easy.

Deep in thought, he rested his hands on the wooden railing and gazed at the river in the distance.

"Pretty view even when it's dark," Sophia said.

Avery turned and smiled as she approached. "The light of the full moon helps."

"And adds atmosphere." Sophia nodded, but then rubbed her hands over her arms.

"Oh, here." Avery reached for her denim jacket and held it out for her.

"Thanks." When she tucked her arms into the sleeves her hair got caught beneath the collar.

"Let me help." Avery enjoyed the feel of her silky strands slipping through his fingers. "Your hair is incredibly soft," he murmured, wishing he could kiss the delicate skin of her neck and then wrap his arms around her to keep her warm.

"Hair stylists use the best products."

"Well, it shows." Avery reluctantly took a step to the side and inhaled a deep breath, trying to clear his head, but all that did was bring the scent of her floral perfume his way. "Tonight's been a lot of fun. I don't get out as often as I should," he admitted, surprising himself.

"Why is that?" She tilted her head, waiting for his answer.

Avery finally shrugged. "A lot of reasons, I guess."

"Are any of them valid?"

Sophia's bold question surprised him.

"Not really, if you get right down to it."

"Then you owe it to yourself to get out and have some fun more often, don't you agree?"

"Yeah."

"So what's holding you back?"

"Good question." Avery looked at her and her sincere expression had him opening up. "Well, it doesn't help that my sister has it in her head that I should get back together with Ashley."

"Oh." Sophia frowned. "How do you feel about that?"

"It's the last thing I want to do. Zoe means well but she's driving me nuts."

"Hmmm . . ." Sophia nodded slowly. "Well, maybe if people see you out with me it will get back to Ashley and then maybe Zoe will back off."

"Hey, you know what? You could be right!" He grinned. "You just have to pretend to be totally into me and get a little gossip going."

"That would be the plan."

Avery nodded slowly. "You could be onto something."

"I have my moments."

"Think you could do that for me?"

"I do believe I could manage."

"Really?"

"Sure."

At the whoosh of the door opening Avery glanced over his shoulder and saw a few people heading out to the deck. He turned back to Sophia and felt a shot of anticipation. "Now might be the—"

"I've got this." Sophia reached up and grabbed Avery's jacket. She tugged him close and planted a hot kiss on his lips, lingering just long enough to have him longing for more. Still on tiptoe she tilted her head and smiled. "Well, that should get tongues wagging, don't you think?"

Avery wasn't sure about tongues wagging but the unexpected kiss sure got his heart thumping like a hardworking jackhammer. Temporarily speechless, Avery could only nod. "So, you would be willing to continue to do that for me?"

"Of course," Sophia said, but something flickered in her eyes that he couldn't quite figure out but before he could ask she tugged him close and kissed him again.

5

Wild Thing

"THANK YOU FOR DANCING WITH ME," EASTON SAID in Carrie Ann's ear.

"My pleasure. Shew, I've worked up a thirst."

"We can fix that." He took her hand and led her back to their table. After ordering a couple of ales, Easton cleared his throat. He couldn't believe that he was about to ask Carrie Ann out on a dinner and dancing date. It was true that he enjoyed her company and always gravitated toward her whenever he saw her out in a social situation. That, and he got his hair cut way more than he really needed to. But to toss anything remotely romantic into the mix could ruin a perfectly good friendship. "Tonight has been a lot of fun," he said, trying to work up the courage to take the next step. Carrie Ann nodded. "Yes, it sure has been."

"I'm glad we ran into each other." While Easton dated here and there, growing up with parents who argued on a daily basis had soured him on the idea of marriage. Unfortunately, as he got older, he found dating casually became more and more difficult. Women wanted at least the possibility of a future and Easton just wasn't the marrying kind. But he sure did enjoy Carrie Ann's company. And she seemed to be on the same page as him when it came to commitment.

So what the hell was he thinking asking Carrie Ann out on a damned date? "Well, I was thinkin' . . ." He cleared his throat again. Why the hell was this so hard? It was the slow dance that did him in. Damn . . .

"Yes? Are you gonna keep me in suspense, Easton?"

Maybe a date wasn't a good idea. But now she sat there looking at him expectantly and so he took the plunge off the high dive and hit with a big splash. "Would you like to go out to dinner? Wine and Diner added a dance floor and has a really good Frank Sinatra impersonator who performs on Saturday nights." There, it was out there now and he couldn't take it back.

Carrie Ann's eyes widened slightly. "Oh, well, I . . . sure. Yes, dinner sounds nice. Wine and Diner is one of my favorite restaurants. Kinda hipster comfort food, if you will."

Easton didn't quite know what hipster meant but he nodded. "Good!" Easton said brightly even though he wasn't sure if he'd just made a really bad decision. "I'll pick you up around seven-thirty, then?"

"Yes, seven-thirty works for me. I close the salon at six on Saturdays."

"Perfect." He nodded again, and then realized he must look like a damned bobblehead. "Hey, would you like something to munch on? Pretzels? Chips and salsa or something like that?" He wasn't really hungry but needed to get away and clear his head.

"Yes, sounds good."

"I'll be right back." Easton stood up. "Can I get you anything else?"

Carrie Ann glanced at her beer that was still half full. "No, I'm fine. Thanks."

As he walked up to the bar to get some snacks Easton glanced outside and spotted Sophia and Avery

out on the deck looking pretty cozy and he had to
smile. He never could get Avery to open up about what
happened between him and Ashley but he sure as
hell wasn't buying the popular notion that Avery had
simply gotten cold feet. It did his heart good to see
his nephew out having a good time with a sweet and
pretty girl. Avery was too damned young not to be having fun.

Although he worked hard, Easton spent most eve-
nings out doing something, whether it was playing softball, fishing, or at someplace social like here at Sully's.
He liked music, laughter, and mingling with people,
most of whom he'd known all of his life. Small towns
were like big families and he'd never really seriously
considered moving away even through the lean, tough
economic times. But lately, he'd been feeling a bit rest-
less, which made him wonder if he needed a vacation
or something new and exciting in his life to look forward to. Maybe a little sports car or a motorcycle . . .
or a boat?

Shit, was he having a midlife crisis?

Wait, he was fifty-five so he was, in reality, past midlife. Oh, now *that thought* was seriously sobering so
when he ordered salsa and chips he asked for another
beer.

"So, Easton, how've you been, buddy?" Pete Sully
asked in his big booming voice. He slid a bottle of Bud
Light down the long bar with amazing precision, and
then turned back to Easton.

"Pretty good. Busy."

Pete nodded and placed a basket of chips and salsa
in front of him. "Busy is a good thing."

"Yeah, been thinkin' I might need a vacation,
though. Any suggestions?"

Pete shrugged his wide shoulders. "I've been lookin'
into taking Maria on a cruise," he said but put his index finger to his lips. "But don't say anything. It's a
surprise for our wedding anniversary."

"How many years?" Easton asked. He'd been friends with Pete and Maria from when they were kids.

Pete slapped his dish towel over his shoulder. "Well, that depends if you count the first eighteen years we were married or add our second time around onto it." He chuckled.

"Good question. I'd go with adding the years together."

"Well, that means a bigger gift," Pete joked but shook his head. "But then again, I need to make up for the lost years," he added with a wistful grin. "The woman was crazy enough to say yes a second time. I'm thinking she deserves something special."

"I'd say you're right."

Pete slid a beer to a patron at the end of the bar and then chuckled. "You mean about her bein' crazy or deserving something special?"

"I'm not about to answer that loaded question." Easton picked up his beer and took a long swallow.

Pete nodded toward the table where Carrie Ann sat. "So this vacation you're talkin' about. You flyin' solo or are you thinking about some company?"

Easton shrugged. "Not sure yet," he said, knowing full well what Pete was getting at. There'd always been speculation about him and Carrie Ann being more than friends.

"Well, you'd best make up your mind before someone else beats you to the punch," Pete said and nodded toward the table again.

Easton watched Sam Hanson standing there chatting up Carrie Ann for about two seconds before feeling a flash of what could only be jealousy. He and Sam had been rivals on the basketball court back in high school. And while they were friendly, a little bit of that rivalry still remained. Sam leaned close and said something that made Carrie Ann laugh and he balled his hand into a fist. Okay, apparently a lot of that rivalry still remained. "I do believe you're right."

"Just a suggestion." Pete chuckled.

Easton paid Pete and picked up the beer and chips. Squaring his shoulders, Easton made his way over to the table so fast that he nearly lost the plastic tub of salsa twice.

"Hey there, Sammy," Easton said because he knew it would get under Sam's skin.

"Easton," Sam said tightly. A muscle worked in his jaw. "What's up?"

"Just wondered if Carrie Ann wanted to dance," Sam said and looked at her with a smile that Easton wanted to wipe off the man's face. "Well, sugar?"

Sugar . . . oh naw. He gripped his bottle tighter and gave Carrie Ann a glance.

"I . . . uh . . ." Carrie Ann reached for a chip and took a crunchy bite reminding Easton of that commercial where the guy sticks a candy bar in his mouth instead of answering.

When Sam gave Carrie Ann a please-dance-with-me smile Easton decided to answer for her. "Carrie Ann is with me."

Carrie choked a little bit on the chip and reached for her beer.

"Oh hey." Sam raised both hands, palms up. "Sorry. I didn't know you two were on a date." He looked at Carrie Ann for clarification.

"We're not . . . we uh . . . are, you know, hanging out," she finally answered and reached for another chip.

"Oh." Sam nodded although nobody seemed to be clear what that really meant. "Together?"

"Yes," Easton replied. "That's why we're sitting at the same table." He pointed at the two of them and then to the table so there was no mistake.

"Okay, then I'll let you two get back to 'hanging out.' Together. Have a good one," Sam said but gave Carrie Ann an if-you-change-your-mind wink and turned away from the table.

A wink? What a smarmy-ass thing to do. Kind of

made Easton want to march over there and punch Sammy right in the face. What the hell was up with that? He was usually the one to step in and break up a fight, not start one.

"Easton, what was that all about?" Carrie Ann asked lightly but tilted her head.

"I don't like that guy."

"Oh, Sam? He's full of hot air, as usual."

"What do you mean, as usual?" Did that jackass hit on Carrie Ann all the time?

"He's just a big ole harmless flirt." Waving a dismissive hand, she took a swallow of her beer.

Easton nodded but wasn't so sure about the harmless part.

"So . . . why did you tell him we were together?" Carrie Ann asked carefully.

Easton sat down and inhaled a deep breath. Usually calm and sure of himself, he suddenly felt really damned nervous. He sat there for a moment trying to gather his scattered wits. The thing was, his wits usually didn't scatter but stayed firmly in place. But something about Carrie Ann made it damn near impossible for him to think straight.

"Were you just lookin' after me?" Carrie Ann prompted. "Like Sam was bothering me or somethin'?" She picked up another chip but seemed to forget it was in her hand.

Easton blew out a sigh. "Nope, he was bothering me." He paused and tapped his chest. "Because he was flirting with you." He pointed at her but then lowered his finger and crossed his arms over his chest. "Can we pretend I just didn't do that pointing thing? I feel really silly."

"Some things you just can't unsee."

"Don't laugh."

Carrie Ann pressed her lips together but when she slid the chip through the salsa, a little chuckle erupted. "Sorry. But why do you care if Sam was flirting with me?" While her tone remained light she looked at him closely.

Easton uncrossed his arms and leaned closer. "Damn, Carrie Ann, isn't it obvious? I was *jealous*."

The chip slid from her fingers and landed on the little puddle of salsa on the round paper plate. "You . . . you *were*?"

Easton glanced away for a second, but then looked at Carrie Ann square in the eye. "Yeah."

"Well, you don't sound too happy about it." She picked up another chip that she still didn't eat.

Easton scooted his stool closer to hers not wanting anyone to hear what he was about to say to her. "Darlin', I value your friendship. I don't want things to . . ." He shrugged. "You know."

"Get weird?"

He nodded. "So, help me out here. Thoughts?" His thigh brushed against hers. It was something that must have happened a thousand times over the years, but this time the contact sent a slow, hot sizzle of desire through his blood. "Carrie Ann?" Did she just feel it too?

"I . . . I think perhaps we need to get out of here and talk about it."

"You want to finish your beer?" He sure as hell hoped not. He wanted to kiss her. Now.

"No."

"Me neither. I already paid the tab."

"Good." She dropped the chip and dusted off her hands.

"Do you need to tell Sophia?"

"I'll text her later. She seems content to be with Avery."

"You ready?"

She nodded.

"Let's go."

Easton wanted to hold Carrie Ann's hand but he thought that would be too obvious. Plus, he didn't want tongues to wag and so he stood back for her to go first, strolling casually when he wanted to pull her out the door and into his arms. The urgency of how much he wanted to kiss her blew Easton away.

But then again he supposed this intense need stemmed from years of suppressing his attraction to Carrie Ann. If he was honest, his feelings for her went all the way back to high school. But when her father died, she'd pretty much dropped out of his social life. Easton suddenly found himself wishing he'd realized how hard that must have been and made an effort to spend more time with her.

Well, he couldn't turn back the clock. But maybe it was about damned time that he opened his heart up to the possibility of a lasting relationship.

Easton helped Carrie Ann slip her arms into her coat before locating his jacket. He felt some curious eyes watching them but he didn't care. As a matter of fact, he should have held her hand and let people *like Sam Hanson* get the message.

"Oh, it's cold out here." Carrie Ann rubbed her hands together.

"Well, let's go someplace warm." He grabbed her hand and started walking.

"And where might that be?"

"In front of my fireplace. It's gas and lights up like magic. You game?"

Carrie Ann nodded. "My car is over there." She pointed to a sassy red Mustang.

"You know the way to my cabin up on Pine Ridge?"

Carrie Ann nodded. "Yeah, I think so but I'll follow you."

"Good, I'll just pull my truck around," Easton said. Part of him couldn't believe this was really happening, and the other part of him wondered how in the hell having Carrie Ann over to his place hadn't happened sooner.

The fifteen-minute drive along the winding road

hugging the river seemed to take forever and he kept looking in his rearview mirror to make sure that Carrie Ann's Mustang was still following him.

She was.

Easton smiled.

This was surreal, exciting, and scary as shit all wrapped into one wheel-gripping package.

Easton turned his blinker on to alert Carrie Ann that they'd reached the one-lane gravel road leading up to his cabin. The steep climb through the woods was tough in the snow, but the view up on the ridge overlooking the river was one hundred percent worth it. He'd paved a circular driveway that led into a three-car garage full of man toys.

Avery had spent many a day up here with his friends, playing with paint guns, four-wheeling, and shooting hoops. But lately the basketball hoop stood there silently wishing for players and he couldn't remember the last time he'd taken anyone out on the four-wheelers.

Easton hopped out of his truck and hurried over to open Carrie Ann's door. He offered his hand as she unfolded her long legs from her sexy sports car. "Welcome," he said as she looked around.

"Mercy, Easton, but I think you're living on the highest point in Cricket Creek, Kentucky."

"Could be."

"I bet it's a real pretty view in the daylight."

"It is. Kind of out of the way but I love it up here." It was on the tip of his tongue to say that he could arrange for that view in the morning, but he didn't want to push too quickly or have her think he'd brought her up here simply for a roll in the hay. Though, he wasn't sure how long he could hold off before going in for a kiss, but he was sure as hell going to try for a few minutes.

"That's one big garage."

"Full of all my adult toys . . . Wait, that didn't sound right."

Carrie Ann laughed. "I'm guessing you're referring to WaveRunners and four-wheelers."

"I am. And a bass boat . . . and a dirt bike."

"Is there actually a car in there?"

"Nope, but I've been thinking I might want a convertible." He pointed to her Mustang. "You ever put your top down?"

"Only for special people."

Easton laughed. "We're still talkin' about your ragtop, right?"

"Yeah."

Easton laughed again. "Well, I hope I'm one of the special people." He realized he was still holding her hand and led her over to the wraparound porch. "The view from the back deck is really spectacular no matter what time of day."

"I bet it is," she said as they ascended the steps. After opening the front door he flipped on the lights and then stepped back for her to enter. She gasped. "Mercy." She turned to look at Easton in surprise.

"I'm guessing you were expecting a sparse bachelor pad?"

"I suppose so . . ." She looked up at the floor-to-ceiling stone fireplace that dominated the great room. "Well, I'd heard that you have a nice place, but nice doesn't begin to describe your home, Easton. Your cabin is spectacular."

Easton felt a measure of pride. "It's taken me a few years to get it just the way I wanted." He grinned. "When I had to close the hardware store in town I decided that I wanted to move up here. I'm pretty handy with a hammer."

Carrie Ann gave a low whistle as she walked slowly around the room. "I'll say."

"Thanks." He walked over and helped her out of her coat. The light floral scent of her perfume filled his head and he took longer than needed to do the simple task. He wanted to brush her hair to the side, put his mouth on the graceful nape of her neck and taste her skin, but he walked over to the closet and hung her coat next to his instead. He wanted to kiss her more than he wanted to breathe but he told himself to take it slow. "Would you like the fifty-cent tour?"

She nodded. "Yes, please."

"How about a drink first? I have beer, wine, or bourbon. Maybe some rum. Sweet tea? Or water."

"I'll take a water."

"Really?" He was picturing cocktails by the fireplace and mood music. Bottled water ruined that image.

"No . . ." Her laughter seemed to light up the room. "This place is so pretty I think I need to walk around with a long-stemmed wineglass."

"Red or white?" He pointed to a wine rack to the left of a bar in the far corner of the room.

"You continue to surprise me. I usually drink Merlot because red wine is better for you. But I'm in the mood for Chardonnay, if you have it."

"I have a bottle chilling in the fridge."

"Do you drink wine?" she asked casually, but he had to wonder if she speculated that the wine was for female visitors.

"I enjoy a glass of Merlot now and then when I'm grilling steaks. My sister Carla likes Chardonnay, and so does Zoe, so I keep it on hand."

"It's nice that you're all close."

"Family is important. How's your mama doin'?"

"Mama loves the warm weather in Naples, Florida. She's got a whole slew of friends. I talk to her most every day. Her social life is way fuller than mine, let me tell you."

"Good, good. Haven't seen your sisters, Ava or Ella, in a while. How they doin'? Still in Lexington?"

"Both still happily married and really busy bein' soccer moms. I go up to watch the kids play but I don't get all of the rules. The offsides thing still has me baffled." She smiled but then a shadow passed over her features making Easton want to pull her in for a hug closely followed by a kiss. She must miss all of them dearly. "And I'm the crazy aunt that every niece and nephew needs. The one who brings a puppy for Christmas."

"You did that?"

"Naw." Carrie Ann laughed. "Just gerbils, but you would have thought I brought man-eating monsters into the house. I was banned from giving pets for presents."

Easton tossed his head back and laughed.

"Yeah, party poopers! Just little old gerbils, I mean come on. But I really miss them. I should go for a visit soon," she said. Easton sensed that there was more to it than she was letting on.

"We tend to hibernate in the winter. I'm sure you'll get to see them before too long. Or better yet, head south to see your mom. Put your toes in the sand." He understood. His parents finally split up for good right after Carla graduated from high school, but he still understood the value of family. He had close friends. He was financially secure. But something seemed missing lately.

"Oh, I bet Carla is having fun planning Zoe's wedding," she said a little bit too brightly.

"Yeah, she is," Easton answered, making a note to ask Carrie Ann to go with him. But he had to lead up to that one so he smiled. "Come on, wait until you see my kitchen." When he held out his hand she took it. He led her through an arched doorway and flipped on the recessed lighting to a state-of-the-art kitchen. He stepped away from her so he could get her full reaction. "Well? What do you think?"

Does this kitchen make you want to kiss me?

"Oh . . . wow." She stepped forward and ran her fingers over the shiny black granite center island. The warm cherry cabinets offset the sleek stainless steel appliances but his pride and joy was a six-burner gas stove that he'd recently installed. "Are you going to have the nerve to tell me that you're a good cook?"

Easton nodded slowly. "Let's just say I can do way more than scramble eggs and flip burgers."

"Where have you been all my life?" Carrie Ann asked with a grin.

"Maybe I'm the best-kept secret in Cricket Creek," he boasted, and then laughed.

"Well, maybe we should keep it that way." Carrie Ann stepped closer and gave him a playful tap on the chest.

Easton smiled, but then caught her hand before she could pull it away. "Ah, Carrie Ann?" He gave the back of her hand a light kiss. She looked at him expectantly but he just shook his head unable to put his feelings into words.

"I know," Carrie Ann said for him. "I feel it too."

"Yeah . . ." While the banter was light and flirty, Easton could feel something more bouncing around in the room. Admitting his attraction and asking her out on a date was one thing . . . well, two things, but bringing Carrie Ann to his home wasn't something he took lightly. But they both knew that this evening was about to alter their longtime friendship. He could see it in her eyes.

"Are you having second thoughts about bringing me up here?" When she frowned ever so slightly, he pulled her closer.

"Hell no," Easton said and meant it. Unable to wait any longer he dipped his head and kissed her.

When his lips captured hers, Easton felt a hot jolt of passion that felt like putting a match to kindling wood. He pulled her lush body flush against his and tipped her head back so he could kiss her deeply, fully. God, he loved how she tasted, sweet, sensual, and so damned sexy. When he lifted her up and placed her onto the island she wrapped her long legs around him and in that moment he knew that the days of them just being friends were one hundred percent over.

And it was about damned time.

Easton's heart thudded harder when she threaded her fingers through his hair. When he finally pulled his mouth from hers, he started a trail of kisses down her neck pausing to lick the rapid beat of her pulse. When he cupped her breast, he heard her breath catch and he got as hard as the damned granite counter.

"Easton Fisher, you are driving me wild."

"Mmmm, wild thing." He ran his thumb over her nipple.

"Now that song is playing in my head," she said with a low sexy laugh. "'You make my heart sing . . .'" she sang, but then gasped when he sucked her earlobe into his mouth and nibbled. "Mercy . . ." She arched her back offering him more and he gladly accepted. Easton wanted her . . . no he *needed* her in his arms, in his bed, and in his life. But he didn't want her to think he'd brought her up here just to get her in bed and so he pulled back and looked into her eyes.

"Carrie Ann, I didn't bring you up here to have my way with you," he said.

"Well, that's disappointing." She ran her fingertip over his bottom lip. "Because you make everything groovy . . ." she sang.

Easton chuckled but said, "It's important to me that you know that."

"No worries." Carrie Ann put her palms to his cheeks. "Pour me that glass of wine and let's see where the rest of the night takes us."

"I like that plan," he said, and then leaned in and kissed her. But when he started to pull away Carrie Ann held him captive with her legs. His heart thudded.

"Easton?"

"Yeah," he asked softly.

"Why don't we skip the glass of wine part," she suggested in his ear, sending a hot flash of desire due south. "We've been dancing around this heat for way too long."

"You're right, and I have to say that I like this plan even better," Easton admitted, and then helped her from the kitchen island. "As always, I was hoping to run into you tonight. I think it's high time we stop pretending we're just friends."

Carrie Ann smiled. "I'll just admit it. The slow dance and having you singing in my ear made me weak in the knees, Easton."

Easton cupped her chin and rubbed his thumb over her bottom lip. "Well, when Sam hit on you, I saw red. That kind of jealousy isn't something I'd feel about a mere friend. The thought of you in the arms of another man isn't something I could handle."

"No need to worry because it's your arms I want around me."

"That's what I want to hear. Come with me." Taking her hand he led her to his bedroom.

"Oh my," Carrie Ann said when they entered the large room made even more dramatic by slanted cathedral ceilings.

Easton dimmed the lights on the antler chandelier suspended from the ceiling. "You like it?"

"I am completely blown away." She nodded her head as she looked around. A rustic Aspen log canopy bed was the centerpiece of the room. To the left was a sliding glass door leading out onto the back deck overlooking the woods. But she could see that later. Right now he wanted her naked and in his bed.

"I'll show you the rest of the house in the morning," he said and pulled her into his arms. Clothes, shed with lightning speed, were tossed everywhere while they laughed and kissed, finally tumbling onto the bed. Easton slid his body up and over hers loving the silky feel of her skin. She was lush, curvy, and gorgeous with her red hair fanned out in contrast to the dark blue comforter.

"It's been a really long time for me," she admitted a bit shyly.

"I do believe it's like riding a bike."

"Well, that's good because I was really excellent at riding my bike. I could go for miles and miles. . . ."

"Ah, good to know." Easton chuckled deep in his throat. "I hope you like riding me even more." He explored her body with his hands and his tongue, loving her scent, her taste. When she wrapped those endless legs around him, he eased into her wet heat, thrusting deeply. She slid her hands up and down his back and then lightly raked his skin with her fingernails sending endless tingles down his spine. His heart hammered in his chest as he went faster.

Carrie Ann moved with him, clung to him, and when he dipped his head and captured a nipple in his mouth she became quite vocal with her moans and sighs of pleasure.

When she cupped his ass and pushed him even deeper, Easton felt his release coming. When she cried out, he let go, feeling the heady rush of an intense orgasm that left him shaking. He stayed buried to the hilt, loving the way she pulsed and throbbed and stayed wrapped around him like kudzu. He kissed her deeply, thoroughly wanting to stay buried inside her sweet body forever.

And in the morning he'd bring her breakfast in bed.

But for now they had the rest of the night, and Easton intended to savor each and every moment.

6

Highway to the Danger Zone

$\mathcal{E}$AGER TO GET OUT OF THE COLD, SOPHIA TUGGED open the door to River Row Pizza. The tantalizing scent of garlic, yeast, and marinara sauce nearly made her groan. Seriously, was there any cuisine in the world that smelled more enticing? But groaning would be embarrassing so she inhaled another delicious breath thinking that someone should create a River Row Pizza–scented candle. But then again the candle would make her crave pizza and pasta more that she already did, which was, well, a lot. And unlike her sister, Grace, Sophia failed to get the long legs and high metabolism gene from her mother.

Having White Lace and Promises located just around the corner was going to make the hand-tossed crust a tough temptation to resist. Not only did they serve amazing Italian dishes, but the owner, Reese Marino, made mouthwatering desserts including Italian wedding cake, which was hands down her all-time favorite. Mercy . . .

On tiptoe, Sophia glanced around for Avery but the packed dining room made it difficult to spot him. Although she'd been told that the restaurant had been there for only a few years, checkered cloth tablecloths and flickering candles gave the decor a cozy old-world atmosphere. If she didn't know better she could be somewhere in Italy instead of Cricket Creek and the food here rivaled any Italian dishes she'd ever eaten, including in New York City's Little Italy.

After a week of nonstop paperwork, Sophia and Carrie Ann Spencer were the proud co-owners of White Lace and Promises so Sophia was in the mood to finally kick back and celebrate. Carrie Ann had been right. She'd stayed in Cricket Creek longer than she'd intended because she really didn't want to leave, but didn't have a challenging career choice until now. While all of this business moved a bit faster than she would have liked and she still had some jitters, the nerves were also a good feeling. So when Avery called and invited her to dinner she eagerly accepted. She was about to send him a text, since it looked as if the wait at the hostess stand was several patrons deep, but after another quick look around, Sophia spotted Avery's dark curly head at a booth near the back of the cozy restaurant.

Sophia felt a familiar warm tug of desire that made her want to fan her face despite having just come in from the cold, breezy weather. She stood there for a moment while gathering her composure. Now that she knew she was staying in Cricket Creek, Sophia was beginning to wonder if she should let Avery know that if he wanted to, they could go beyond friendship instead of just having her pretend to be into him. Although her spontaneous kisses on the patio at Sully's had been fueled by a bit too much Love Potion Ale, she couldn't stop thinking about kissing him again.

But Sophia was still concerned that Avery wasn't one hundred percent over his ex-fiancée, so maybe she shouldn't go after another, much wanted kiss. On the other hand, maybe it was high time that Avery moved on for good—and another hot kiss might send him in that much needed direction. Well, a direction she needed, anyway.

Sophia's feet finally started moving and she made her way past the closely placed tables. Silverware clinked against dishes; patrons chatted and laughed while mood music softly played in the background. A beautiful wooden bar ran the length of the room to the left. Sophia noticed a few women with martini glasses and decided she could use one. Or two. This atmosphere actually reminded her of being in a pizza parlor in Brooklyn and then she remembered that owners Tony and Reese Marino had actually lived in Brooklyn before they came to Cricket Creek.

Because he was frowning at his cell phone, Avery failed to see her approach. "Hey there," Sophia said as she slid into the booth. When he looked up and saw her, Avery's frown turned into a quick smile but she had to wonder what was bothering him.

"Sophia!" He pushed the cell phone away and reached across the table to squeeze her hand. "Congratulations! Are you excited?"

"Yes!" Sophia nodded. "And of course Mom, Grace, and Garret are over the moon that I'm moving here for good. Grace is already starting to come up with a marketing plan. But it's all happened so fast that my head is still spinning." She made circling motions around her ears. "I'm usually much slower to make this kind of big decision."

"They're not the only ones happy that you're moving here for good." Avery gave her hand a tighter squeeze. "Let's order a bottle of champagne."

"Oh, you don't have to do that. . . ." Sophia protested but Avery shook his head causing his curly hair to dip over his forehead in such an adorable way. She had the urge to reach over and brush the curls back just to feel the silky texture between her fingers. The blue sweater brought out his eyes and was just snug enough to show off the wide set of his shoulders and defined arms. "Really."

"Too late. I already did. Besides, this is big news! We need to celebrate." His bright smile made Sophia long to lean across the table and get the kiss she'd been wanting but his phone pinged bringing another frown to his face. He glanced at it as if it was a snake ready to strike.

"Is everything okay?" Sophia tilted her head as she shrugged out of her coat.

"Yeah, it's just my sister's wedding plans again. To be honest, she's been driving me crazy."

"It's okay if you need to answer the text or give her a call." Sophia smiled. "I'm quite familiar with bridal jitters."

"Not this kind," Avery said, but before he could elaborate the server approached them with the bottle of champagne.

The young guy named Chad looked a bit nervous to pop the cork. "Thought I should warn you. I've only done this once at home and it didn't end well," he admitted as he untwisted the wire cage. "I have trouble enough with wine bottles."

"Should we duck for cover?" Avery asked.

"Maybe . . ." Chad looked at the bottle with trepidation.

"Hold it at a forty-five-degree angle and don't twist the cork at all," Sophia advised. "Twist the fat part of the bottle as you pull down."

"Well, now . . ." When Avery raised an eyebrow, she grinned.

"I've done lots of weddings and events where champagne was served. And I've seen my share of near disasters at parties."

"Only near disasters?"

"Well . . ." She winced, but when Chad's eyes widened she decided she'd better keep the cracked window incident to herself.

Chad bit his bottom lip and put a towel over the cork. "Here goes nothin'," he said, but the cork popped without mishap. "Hey, you were right." Looking pleased with himself he poured the bubbly into two flutes with a flourish. "I'll bring some fresh bread in a few minutes."

"Thank you," Avery said, and lifted his glass of champagne. "To White Lace and Promises."

Sophia tapped her flute to his. She took a sip and giggled when the bubbles tickled her nose. "Oh, very nice. Thanks so much, Avery. This is a sweet gesture."

"My pleasure." He smiled but his eyes appeared a bit serious. "I'm really glad you're moving here, Sophia."

"Me too." She took another sip of the champagne, and then played with the stem of her glass. "The decision was actually easier than I anticipated." She was about to say more when his phone dinged again.

"I'm sorry. I'll put it on silent, like I should have done to begin with." He picked up the phone, then groaned when he glanced at the message.

"Do you want to talk about it? I might have some wedding advice for your sister that could help calm her down."

Avery inhaled a deep breath. "I don't know if you can help." He paused when Chad brought a basket of dipping bread along with a dish of herbed olive oil. After they each took of slice of the fragrant loaf he continued. "My sister's maid of honor is Ashley Montgomery, my ex-fiancée. And I'm the best man."

"Oh . . ." Sophia felt a sinking sensation in the pit of her stomach. "Wow . . . So that must be awkward, I guess, right?"

"Yeah. It's weird. We were all best friends way before Ashley and I dated. Max, Zoe, Ashley, and I did just about everything together when we were growing up." He shredded the crust of his bread. "But since the breakup, of course, that all came to an abrupt end. Now that the wedding stuff is starting to get intense, my sister's been trying to get Ashley and me back together. It's driving me nuts." He took a big gulp of the champagne and nearly coughed.

"So it bothers you to be around her?" Sophia asked carefully. She dipped a warm piece of the bread into the oil and waited.

"Well, yeah, as you said it's awkward." He looked at the bread crumbs scattered on his plate as if wondering how they got there.

"I don't mean to pry—and you can tell me if it's none of my business—but why *did* you two break up?" Her heart pounded as she looked at him and waited. She'd wanted to know the reason for a long time.

Avery licked his bottom lip but remained silent.

"Hey, sorry—I shouldn't have asked," she said sheepishly.

"No, no, really, it's okay," he said. But he didn't look okay.

Sophia picked up her flute so quickly that champagne sloshed over the rim. She took a sip and said, "It's just, I know you said something about you two growing apart but that seems like something that happens during the marriage and not the engagement."

"Well . . ." Avery suddenly seemed so uncomfortable that Sophia wished she'd kept her mouth shut. "I can't go into . . . the reasons." He looked into his flute for a moment and then back at her. "But I don't want to get back together with her. I just don't know how to convince Zoe—and everyone else—of this. She means well but . . ."

"Do you know how Ashley feels about this?" Her heart thudded even harder. "Is she part of this plot as well?"

Avery lifted one shoulder in a shrug. "I haven't spoken to her about the breakup since it happened," he said but when he glanced away Sophia suspected that Ashley wanted him back and Avery knew it. He shook his head. "I just wish they would let this alone. And I sure wish I didn't have to be in this wedding."

"You mean be in the wedding with Ashley"

Avery nodded.

"So how is it when you've gotten together with them? Other than the obvious awkward undertones?" The fact that he got together with them bothered her more than it should.

"It's just weird. The night that Zoe and Max asked me to go out for dinner I figured that Max might ask me to be his best man. What they failed to tell me was that Ashley was going to be there, too."

"How did that go?"

"I mean, once I got over the shock of seeing her, after a few beers we sort of fell back into the good old times." He looked down at the table for a moment. "But there were also awkward silences while the elephant stomped around the room wavin' its big ole trunk all around."

"I can only imagine."

"I only went out for drinks with them one other time when Zoe insisted we needed to go over more wedding details. I instantly regretted it as soon as I got there, but Zoe just doesn't get it. I know that she misses all of us hanging out together and there is a hole in our lives now that wasn't there before, but I can't fill that void for them." He appeared so upset that Sophia felt guilty for bringing it up. "I just can't."

"I'm sorry. I shouldn't have pried, Avery."

"No really, it's okay." He paused, and then added, "I'm sorry for saying this so bluntly but this thing that Zoe is doing is just jacking around with my brain."

"I get that, Avery. But people do move on. I mean look at my brother Garret and Addison Greenfield. Not only were they engaged but their breakup was splashed all over the tabloids in a very public way and now they're on friendly terms. I know your situation is different but maybe you can just put the past behind you, where it belongs."

"That's what I'm trying to do. But it's not that easy in a small town."

She shrugged. "And maybe you could give Zoe more personal reasons for the breakup, something that might make her understand."

"It's not that simple." Avery scrubbed a hand down his face and appeared so crestfallen that Sophia wanted to do something more to help and then it hit her . . .

"Have you forgotten about our plan?"

"Plan?"

"For me to pretend to be totally into you?"

"Oh, Sophia, about that . . ."

"No, I'll do it." She glanced left and right and then reached across the table to cover his hand with hers. "To everyone watching, we'll appear to be on an official date."

"Yeah but I—"

"No worries, I'm happy to do it." Sophia squeezed his hand and smiled.

S OPHIA KNEW THAT PRETENDING TO BE SOMETHING that she kind of wished she *could be* was rather stupid but she wanted to help him out of this situation he found himself in.

Avery sat up straight. "Wait, Sophia . . . you don't need to do this."

"No." Sophia shook her head. "I want to. I mean why not?" Because I might fall hopelessly in love with you and get seriously hurt in the process? "It's the perfect plan." Except for the getting hurt part but she wouldn't dwell on that little detail right now.

Avery finally nodded. "Okay, if this is what you want to do."

"It is." Sophia smiled as she poured more champagne into the flutes, and then picked hers up. "Here's to perfection."

He tapped his glass to hers but his smile appeared a little bit forced.

"We only have to do this until after the wedding and then we can have a breakup."

"Okay."

Her smile faltered a little bit and an odd pang settled in her stomach. "Yeah, something big and public. I'll toss a drink in your face."

Avery finally laughed. "You're so damned funny. But seriously, this is gonna be a total game changer for me. I'm gonna owe you big-time."

"Aw, it's nothing. What are friends for, right?"

"Well, Sophia, this is going over and beyond the call of duty. You're the best." He tapped his glass to hers again.

"Yeah, the best." She smiled but felt a lump lodge in her throat. She was about to pick up her menu to hide her expression when Avery leaned across the table and gave her a light kiss on the mouth. The warm softness of his lips sent a tingle all the way to her toes. Oh boy, she was on the highway to the danger zone, and it was a zone she didn't want to be in.

"That will get tongues wagging again," he said but then frowned and took a sip of his drink, making her wonder what he was thinking. "You ready to order?"

Sophia nodded and lifted her menu. She looked at the selections without really seeing them and when Chad came over a moment later she had no idea what to order. She pretended to listen while he listed the daily specials but all she could think about was how this pretend-girlfriend thing was probably going to blow up in her face. When Chad looked at her expectantly she realized she was supposed to give him her selection. "The, um, today's special." She had no idea what it was but she doubted there was anything on the menu that she wouldn't like.

"One or two?" Chad tapped his pen to a tablet and waited.

"Uh, one," she replied, thinking it was an odd question.

"One meatball," Chad said. "Comes with a side salad."

"Oh, uh, the house is fine."

"Great choice. Tony Marino makes it fresh every day." He looked at Avery.

"I'll have the same thing but make my spaghetti with two meatballs. And ranch dressing for me."

"Gotcha. Need more bread?" Chad pointed to the nearly full basket.

"Maybe later," Avery replied and turned his attention back to Sophia. "Now where were we?"

"Talking about getting tongues wagging," Sophia said and dug deep for a grin. "Maybe we should eat our spaghetti like in *Lady and the Tramp*? That would certainly give them something to talk about."

Avery frowned for a second, and then laughed. "Oh, right, the Disney movie. When we were kids Zoe loved that one and I had to watch it over and over again." He put his hand next to the side of his mouth. "I pretended not to like it but I did."

"And I think Garret secretly enjoyed the tea parties Grace and I made him attend," she said with a grin.

"I wouldn't be surprised. So then, you're the pretty purebred cocker spaniel and I'm the street-smart mutt." He nodded slowly. "Makes perfect sense."

"Oh, but a very dashing mutt that the cocker spaniel falls madly in love with," Sophia said, and then wished for a trapdoor to swallow her up. Thankfully, Chad, bless his heart, arrived with the salads. Sophia gave an elusive cherry tomato her full attention even though she wasn't particularly fond of them and reminded herself that Avery asked her to pretend to be his girlfriend. *Pre-tend.* As in make-believe. Not real. She stabbed the cherry tomato hard but sent the little tomato torpedoing across the table. "Oh God!"

Avery laughed when he deftly caught it from careening into the dining room and onto someone else's plate. "If I'd been on the ball I could have caught that in my mouth. That would have been pretty sweet."

Ah yes, his mouth, and what a beautiful mouth it was.

She looked at the other tomato on her plate. "I could try to do it again but I think I'd fail," she said.

"You're so much fun to be with, Sophia. And a good friend for agreeing to do this . . . *thing* for me."

Sophia waved a dismissive hand. They were just friends. She needed to remember that important detail and quickly changed the subject. While they ate their salads Sophia entertained Avery with bridezilla stories from her salon days in New York City. She had him in stitches, and he seemed to enjoy her company so much that by the end of the main course Sophia had to wonder if their pretend relationship could become very real. Avery claimed to be over Ashley. Sophia was staying in Cricket Creek. While she knew she needed to tread softly, hope crept into her heart and did a little jig. Maybe this little ruse could have a happy ending for her after all.

7

Gone Fishin'

*A*VERY CAST HIS BAIT TOWARD THE LILY PADS AND looked over at Uncle Easton, who sat on the back-seat of the bass boat. The unseasonably mild weather had enticed them out onto the lake. Though the bass had been biting earlier, the morning activity had suddenly ceased. It was still great just to be outdoors, so Avery didn't mind if he caught anything or not.

"Be honest—do you think this pretend thing with Sophia is a good idea or am I playing with fire?"

"Little of both, I reckon." He reeled in his line, changed his bait, and then cast again.

"You gonna elaborate?" Avery asked, grimacing when he missed a nibble. His concentration wasn't what it should be.

"Well, as I see it, you're both single so I don't really understand where the whole pretend thing comes into play. It's obvious that you like the girl. I'm not sure I get it."

"Uncle Easton, I don't want to start something serious with Sophia."

"Somethin' wrong with your eyesight, son?"

"No . . . I just . . . I don't know," he said, but he did know.

"Lemme guess—you're scared shitless."

"Hell no!" Avery protested but as usual his uncle hit the nail on the damned head. "I'm just enjoying my freedom after . . . you know. Why would I want to put myself through that shit again?" Avery said and then clamped his mouth shut.

"No, I don't know because you refuse to talk about what happened between you and Ashley. I never did buy into the whole cold-feet gossip or the even more ridiculous 'you grew apart' baloney that you like to toss around."

Avery remained silent.

"You protecting her, son?"

"I really don't want to talk about it, Uncle Easton. My relationship with Ashley is completely over. That's all anybody needs to know."

"You still love her?"

Oddly, Avery immediately thought of Sophia and didn't quite know why. Or maybe he did know why and didn't want to face his growing attraction to her. He shook his head. "No, I don't love Ashley. I mean, a part of me will always care about her. We go way back to when we were kids. But I don't love her like *that* any longer and I wish to hell Zoe would get that through her thick skull."

"You sister loves you and means well. This has been really hard on Zoe. She misses how happy the way y'all used to be."

"I know." *That was the problem,* Avery thought, with a long sigh. That, and they unfairly blamed him and there wasn't a damned thing he could do about it. "Look, I'll admit that I miss hanging out with them, and the old times. But how the heck can I hang out with my ex-fiancée?"

"I get that."

"That's why I'm taking a page from your book and

staying single. The relationship with Ashley caused me nothin' but heartache. Why would I want to risk that again?" Avery looked back at his uncle and waited.

"Because maybe you don't want to grow into a lonely old man, like me. And just because it didn't work out with her doesn't mean it couldn't work out with someone else."

"B-but you always said—"

"Forget what I always said. I was a damned fool."

Avery reeled in his line and then cast toward a fallen log. "So, you're sayin' you wished you'd gotten married after all? I thought you said you didn't want to be shouting and arguing like Grandma and Gramps always did."

Easton reached up and adjusted the bill of his baseball cap. "It wasn't fun to be around constant bickering and fighting, always on edge. That's for damn sure."

"Mom never yells at Dad."

"Your mama married your daddy really young, Avery. I think partly to get out of the house."

"Do you think that's why Dad became a trucker? To get away from something he got into way too young?"

"No. I didn't mean it that way. I do believe your mama and daddy love each other. Your father simply made a good living but unfortunately it kept him on the road. And I think it pained Tommy to see me get to do the things with you that he wanted to do. I knew he was jealous of our relationship and used to treat me kind of shitty because of it. Avery, your dad used his grumpy moods as a shield against showing how he really felt having to be on the road all the time."

"Seriously?" Avery felt an odd pang in his chest. "How do you know this?"

"'Cause Tommy told me so. We almost came to blows one night after a few beers, and then we had a comin' to Jesus meeting."

Taken by surprise, Avery shook his head. "When was this?"

"Few years back."

"Damn." Avery lifted up his baseball cap and scratched his head. "I used to get so pissed at Dad for not being around. I guess it never occurred to me that he really wanted to be at my baseball games and school functions."

"Trust me—he sure as hell did."

"So why didn't he tell me and Zoe this stuff?" A bit of anger warred with sadness at the notion that he understood his father so very little. "I always wanted a closer relationship with him."

"It's never too late, Avery."

"But I just don't get why he couldn't have had this conversation with me."

"I dunno. Maybe he will someday. Pride can get in the way of a lot of things, Avery. Sometimes when something hurts, it's easier to lock it up inside rather than face it." He paused to cast his line and then looked over at Avery. "Or at least we think so, especially at the time."

Avery felt an ache settle in his chest. "Or pretend it doesn't matter, which is what I guess Dad often did." He sighed. "Honestly, I think that I really did know Dad wanted to be around rather than on the road. I guess bein' mad at him was easier than admitting how much I missed him. Stupid on both our parts, I'd say." Avery shook his head. "But Mom never complained even though she was basically a single mother most of the time. And rarely said a cross word to Dad even when he deserved it."

"I think she'd heard enough cross words and shouting to last her a lifetime. And Carla most likely understood Tommy's moods. Not that bein' a grumpy ass was right." He unscrewed the cap from a bottle of water and guzzled half of it. "But honestly, I think Tommy suffered from bouts of depression that none of us understood. I don't think he understood it either."

"Looking at it from another point of view makes more sense. Dad did often seem unhappy for no real reason. You'd think he'd be so glad to be home but it sometimes felt as if he couldn't wait to get back on the road."

"Yeah, as the saying goes, we can't walk in someone else's shoes so we're not to judge. I guess I should have said more about Tommy to you, but I didn't want to get in the middle of anything between you and your father."

"Maybe someday he'll want to talk to me about it," Avery said. His father was a quiet man so getting him to open up wouldn't be easy but it would be worth the effort.

"That would be a good thing. So tell me, did Sophia actually suggest doing this pretend-dating thing you were telling me about?"

"Yeah, it's only until after the wedding and then she suggested a big public fight."

His uncle gave him a measured look and then chuckled.

"What?"

"I've seen you two together. I think you're both foolin' yourselves."

"We've become good friends over the past few months. Maybe we don't want to screw that up. And she suggested this scheme, not me."

"Well, maybe you should suggest dating for real."

"I don't want to risk pushing her away, if dating for real isn't something she wants to do."

"And maybe it's well worth the risk."

"You should talk!" Avery waited for a comeback but his uncle suddenly went as silent as birds before a storm. "Well, now, did I just hit a nerve?"

"I don't know what you're talkin' about. Damn, I just missed a bite."

"Right, sure you don't," Avery said, and got a grunt in response. "Maybe you need to start practicing what you're preaching, Uncle Easton," Avery said and gave his uncle a look of challenge.

"Well, now, maybe I already have."

Avery nearly dropped his fishing pole overboard. "Come again? Are you seeing Carrie Ann for real?"

"Maybe."

"Well, it's about damned time," Avery said and meant it.

"Yeah," his uncle nodded. "Tell me about it. I mean, we're two old farts so I don't know where this will go but I think I'm ready to give it my best shot."

"You're a pretty good shot so I think odds are in your favor," Avery said with a grin. "Wow, this is some really cool news."

Easton chuckled, but then said, "Avery, even though you won't talk about it, I know that Ashley must have done somethin' to hurt you."

"I just want to move on."

Easton raised a palm in the air. "You don't have to admit to or say anything. I respect your privacy. But it's pretty easy for me to figure some of this out. You're protecting Ashley by keeping quiet about something. I know you too well."

Avery looked out over the water wishing once again that he could confide in his uncle. He knew that Ashley's secret would be safe, but he couldn't bring himself to divulge the truth, even if there was a part of him that wanted the whole damned world to know what she'd done to him.

"If you ever want to bend my ear over what happened you know I'll be here for you. And you know I'll keep my mouth shut."

"I know." Keeping this secret bottled up inside hadn't been easy or healthy, but when it came down to it, his word was his damned word and that was that. "Thank you, Uncle Easton," he said sincerely but decided to change the subject before he spilled his guts. "So you and Carrie Ann finally were spotted gettin' really cozy at Wine and Diner. Holding hands and dancing real close."

"People in this town need something better to talk about."

"You're dodging the question."

"We're not serious or anything."

"Do you want to be?" Avery asked.

"I've been sweet on her for some time but felt the need to fight my feelings." He grinned and pointed at his head. "Why do you think I keep my hair so danged short? I know what days she eats lunch at Wine and Diner and what time she has her coffee at Walking on Sunshine and I would just so happen to stop in at the same time. Son, guess I've been foolin' myself for a long time." He shrugged before casting again. "There's no fool like an old fool."

Avery laughed. "I pretty much had all of this figured out. I just wondered if you'd ever get up the gumption to go for it."

"Yeah . . ." Easton took a drink of his water, and then side cast his bait beneath a weathered dock. "But I do wanna tell you somethin'."

"Go on."

"Lookin' back, I see now that I let my childhood dictate a lot of my life. I decided early on that I wanted to stay single and not live an unhappy existence filled with constant turmoil. And I sure as hell didn't want to have children and put them through hell. I was pretty damned afraid of that happening."

"I understand, Uncle Easton. I told myself that if I ever had kids I'd be around for them. I mean, it's only natural to want to avoid or be the opposite of what causes us such pain."

"Yeah, but when it holds you back from happiness then you've got to do somethin' about it. I'm nearly fifty-six years old and it's about time I give fallin' in love a whirl." He shrugged. "If I crash and burn, so be it. What do I have to lose?"

"Well, the crashin' and burnin' part for starters," Avery pointed out but his uncle tossed his head back and chuckled. "So what are you tellin' me to do? I mean, you're assuming that Sophia would be open to the idea of somethin' real between us."

"Is that so far-fetched?"

"Are you forgetting that this pretend thing was her suggestion?" Avery suddenly thought about the *Lady and the Tramp* movie that they'd talked about. "I guess it's not completely out of the question."

"What, that Sophia could fall for someone hard-working, honest, and good-lookin' as you? I mean you do take after your uncle, after all."

Avery laughed. "Well, when you put it that way . . ."

"Seriously, Avery, you can look at this as pretending for the sake of getting Zoe off your back about Ashley. And hopefully it will work because your sister can be pretty damned determined."

"Tell me about it."

"But maybe you should consider giving this silly scheme a fighting chance."

"I know." Avery nodded but a cold shiver of anxiety slid down his spine.

"You don't have to say anything right off the bat but if something real starts to develop, then . . . you know what I'm sayin'."

Avery reeled in his line and looked for a frog to flip across vegetation near the shoreline. "Yeah, I know what you're sayin' but I've done the crashing-and-burning thing and it really sucks."

"Then go slow," he said. Then his eyes widened. "Hey, I got a bite!" He started reeling and then shouted, "Fish on! Get the net. We're gonna need it! Damn he's a fighter!"

Avery laughed and felt his blood pumping with excitement for his uncle. After a few minutes of laughing and cussing up a storm, Uncle Easton reeled in a huge smallmouth bass. Avery had the net ready and a moment later the fish was in the boat.

"He's a big one!" Easton shouted, and then gently removed the hook.

"Let me get a picture!" Avery reached in his jeans pocket for his phone.

"Yeah!" Holding the fish up high, he hammed it up for Avery's cell phone camera, and then tossed the prize back into the water. "Send that to me, will ya? That had to be about a seven-pounder. I need proof."

"I'll vouch for ya." Avery sent the picture to his uncle's phone but he also sent the picture to Sophia telling himself that it was just a friendly thing to do and it would bring a smile to her face. But he knew better— just like his uncle had seen right through the pretend dating It wasn't just a genius plan to squash the Ashley situation but also a way for him to keep his growing attraction for Sophia from showing. He'd wanted to tell her how he felt at the pizza parlor but she'd all but insisted on the fake-dating scenario, making him hold back. Pretending to pretend was a pretty crazy thing to do, but he just wasn't ready to let his true feelings show if it would end in him only getting hurt again.

Avery knew damned well that Uncle Easton was absolutely right about letting the past go and not letting pain get in the way of something good. He just hoped that someday he could muster up the courage to do it.

While he'd gotten past the pain of Ashley's betrayal, he didn't know if he'd ever trust someone enough to risk that kind of whiskey-drinking heartache again. Even though Sophia seemed so honest and so sweet, Avery just wasn't ready to completely let his guard down.

He liked her. He just wasn't going to let her know how much he wanted to date her for real.

At least not yet.

8
Let It Go

AS MUCH AS SHE'D LIKE TO SLEEP IN, CARRIE ANN always woke up to the first bird chirping outside her bedroom window. "It's Monday. The salon is closed," Carrie Ann mumbled. She rolled onto her side and refused to open her eyes. But her brain started ticking off all of the things she needed to do for White Lace and Promises and so falling back asleep wasn't remotely an option. Even though Sophia was going to run the creative end of the salon, Carrie Ann remained in charge of ordering products and keeping the books.

The early-to-rise habit dated way back to when she had to help her mama get Ava and Ellie ready for school. Ava insisted upon wearing outrageous outfits to kindergarten, causing quite a morning ruckus. Ellie, the little rascal, liked to sneak back into bed while Ava pitched her hissy fits leaving Carrie Ann almost no time for her own primping, usually resulting in a ponytail, jeans, and whatever top she could manage to round up. For a former cheerleader, this hasty morning ritual was far less time than she would have wanted.

But then again, primping became less of a priority when her social life waned.

Carrie Ann still lived on Oak Street in her family home where she grew up. Although the older house required a bit of maintenance, she never seriously considered moving, telling herself that the close proximity to the salon was the reason, but deep down she knew she didn't want to give up her ties to her childhood and to the father whom she still missed to this day.

Fingers of sunshine reached through the blinds into the bedroom, beckoning Carrie Ann to rise and make her coffee. But today, she resisted. Instead of immediately tossing back the covers and having her feet hit the cool hardwood floor, Carrie Ann stubbornly remained in bed, snuggled beneath the fluffy down comforter.

Sometimes, if Carrie Ann closed her eyes and remained very still, she could hear the echoes of the memories embedded in the walls. She did so now and smiled, remembering the giggles of her sisters coming from the bedroom across the hallway when they were supposed to be sleeping. Bedtime stories were a nightly ritual instilling a love of books in Carrie Ann and her sisters. When Carrie Ann was older she'd stay up past her bedtime and read with a flashlight, hiding beneath the covers until she dozed off.

Mary Spencer always cooked a big breakfast, even on school days, because their daddy enjoyed starting the morning with a hearty meal. Carrie Ann remembered the aroma of strong coffee and bacon tickling her nose. Pots and pans clanking always sounded cheerful and breakfast remained her favorite meal to this day. Her daddy, bless his heart, was a morning person, always singing and whistling, coming in every day to wake Carrie Ann up with a hug. He smelled of minty toothpaste and Irish Spring soap and even though she grumbled about getting out of bed there was nothing better than waking up to her father's smile.

Charley Spencer had laid carpet for a living and her

mama cut hair out of their home so she could be there when her girls got home from school. While they hadn't been wealthy, and they'd had their share of squabbles, love and laughter had filled the Spencer household.

And then, seemingly as fit as a fiddle, good-natured, hardworking Charley Spencer up and died of a sudden heart attack.

"Thirty-eight years old," Carrie Ann whispered and inhaled with a little hitch. She ran her fingertips over the edge of the soft sheet, letting the memories wash over her, something she rarely allowed herself to do because she'd always end up crying. But for whatever reason, this morning she wanted to remember.

They'd lived in a small town, a simple life free from the stress of wanting modern-day extravagances. When something broke, her father fixed it. Clothes were mended and passed down. Vacations meant camping by the lake or a trip to the Smoky Mountains now and again where they would walk the main strip in Gatlinburg, eating saltwater taffy and funnel cakes while taking in the sights.

"Oh Lordy . . ." Carrie Ann swallowed the hot moisture gathering in her throat. As a child she'd rarely cried and if she had it was usually from the pain of a skinned knee or tumble from her bicycle. But emotional tears almost never happened until the day her daddy died. And on the morning they'd laid him to rest she'd shed more tears than she'd thought was even possible to create without drying up and blowing away. And then she'd stopped crying, knowing she had to be strong for her heartbroken mother and little sisters.

If Carrie Ann had known how precious those early years were she would have savored the days and not taken one single moment for granted.

If she was honest, she supposed that one of the reasons she never married was that she didn't think she could capture the same kind of love her parents shared and would find her marriage somehow lacking. And of course, she never wanted to suffer the same kind of tragic loss that her mother went through.

But lately she started wondering if she'd let life pass her by. She'd never know what it was like to have a baby or hold the hand of her grandchild. While she'd fancied herself being in love a time or two, as soon as marriage was mentioned, she'd shut down and ultimately walk—no, *run*—away.

Carrie Ann fisted her hands in the sheets and felt another wave of emotion clog her throat. "Damned change-of-life hormones," she grumbled. For someone who had always managed to remain fairly stoic, nowadays Carrie Ann found herself blubbering at silly-ass commercials and if she watched a Hallmark movie, tears flowed like a damned waterfall.

Now as she brushed at a tear, she told herself that this was the very reason she rarely let herself travel down memory lane! Old photographs, hundreds of them, remained stored away in boxes because they were just too difficult to look at. "Get your sorry self up and start the day," she said, but her body refused to move and her brain continued to toss memories at her like a slide show on a projector screen.

Ava and Ellie were ages seven and five at the time of their father's death and so their childhood recollection of him remained a bit fuzzy. But for Carrie Ann, losing her daddy at the age of fifteen was a sharp searing pain that still came out of nowhere now and then.

Her mama had carried on. After all, what else could she do? Mary Spencer was a steel magnolia through and through. She kept her chin up, worked hard, and managed to keep laughter under the Spencer roof, but Carrie Ann could see that the light in her mama's eyes had dimmed and sometimes late at night she could hear her mother weeping.

The loud ringing of the phone jolted Carrie Ann from her musings. She reached over and grabbed the receiver from her nightstand pretty much knowing

who would be on the other end of the line at this time
of the day. She looked at the caller ID and nodded . . .
yep.

"Mama!" Carrie Ann answered the phone brightly,
somehow feeling guilty that she was still in bed after
eight o'clock. She cleared her throat so she wouldn't
sound groggy. Her mother was one of the few people
who called her on her home line this early and often
when Carrie Ann was thinking of her.

"Hey there, sugar pie, what's going on?" Mary Spencer asked innocently but the underlying tone in her soft
Southern drawl suggested otherwise.

Carrie Ann sat up and propped a pillow behind her
back. "You mean with White Lace and Promises?"
Carrie Ann asked just as innocently. "Sophia has been
working her tail off to get the salon ready to open in
time for spring weddings. Her sister, Grace, is a marketing whiz. We have a Web site, a Facebook page, and
gorgeous glossy pamphlets on display at all of the re-
lated shops in Wedding Row."

"Oh, I cannot wait to see it," Mary gushed.

"We're going to have an open house soon and have
some models brought in to do some updos on. Some of the
other shops are joining in with us for a day of festivities."

"You were always good at fancy updos. I didn't have
the patience for all that fluff."

"Oh, thank you, Mama, but Sophia does absolutely
stunning work. I'll send pictures, or better yet, you should
come up for a visit."

"I might just do that. Ava and Ellie are bringing the
grandkids down for spring break. Maybe I'll fly back
to Lexington with them and then rent a car and drive
down to Cricket Creek for a spell."

Carrie Ann wasn't too keen on her mother driving
but her mama would not even dream of giving up her
car keys. But even though years of standing on her feet
behind the chair had taken its toll on her physically,
Mary Spencer remained as sharp as a tack. Florida sun-

shine and the abundance of friends kept her going at a fast social pace and even though Carrie Ann missed her mama dearly, she loved hearing the happiness in her voice. And while her mother had never come close to remarrying, she was still a stunning, vivacious woman and had her share of what she referred to as "gentlemen callers."

"So . . . anything else going on?"

Carrie Ann rested her head against the pillow and grinned. "Hmmm, let me think. Well, I did Mabel Grammar's hair the other day. She brought me a dozen butter cookies from the bakery."

"Oh, those are my favorites. How is Mabel doing these days?"

"Just fine and dandy. She asked about you. Wanted to send you some cookies but we wondered if they would be cookie crumbs by the time they made it to Naples, Florida."

"Carrie Ann Spencer!" She cut to the chase. "Are you going to make me come right out and ask?"

"Okay, Mama, I've been . . . seeing Easton Fisher."

"Well, I know this very fact and I got this information via a group text message from my circle of friends in Cricket Creek. The two of you were spotted at Wine and Diner all lovey-dovey. Arrived together rather than your usual just-so-happened-to-be-at-the-same-place-at-the-same-time shenanigans you two like to pull. As if we all didn't see right through that nonsense."

"A group text message?"

"Hey, I know how to use my newfangled smartphone, thank you very much," she said, but then chuckled. "Well, I know some of the features. I do have a habit of sending texts to the wrong person, which can end up in some pretty sticky social situations, especially involving my gentlemen callers, but that's another story best saved for another time."

Carrie Ann rolled her eyes. "I won't ask."

"Let's get back to the subject at hand. Of course, I acted as if I was already privy to this vital information about you and Easton dating, but mercy me. Carrie Ann, why am I always the last one to know things?"

"Mama, I'd say you're usually the first to know and start spreading the news."

"Well, yes! I mean, being a hairdresser in the heart of town made me the queen bee at gossip central. You know as much. Not that I spread gossip, mind you."

"Seriously, Mama?"

A low chuckle reverberated through the phone. "Well, at least not *much* anyway. And I didn't ever repeat anything that I didn't know to be factual. As you know, being a good listener is part of a hairdresser's job."

"I'll give you that." She knew about affairs. lovers' spats, babies on the way, and any other news both big and small. Like her mother, Carrie Ann was much more of a listener than a talker, but being the first to know things was something she'd grown used to. And truth be known, she rather enjoyed it. "Well, yes, Mama, to answer your question, Easton and I are . . ." What were they really?

"He's your boyfriend."

"Boyfriend sounds so silly for someone my age."

"It's not silly at all." Her mother became silent for a few seconds and Carrie Ann could feel the emotion coming through the phone. "It's about time, sugar pie," she finally said with a slight tremble in her voice.

"Oh, Mama." Carrie Ann felt moisture gather in her throat. "I've been friends with Easton for so long that I didn't want to ruin it by doing something stupid."

"Falling in love is never stupid, even if it ends badly. You know all too well that I wouldn't have changed a thing in my life, even knowing what was going to happen. I treasure every moment I had with Charley even though he was taken from us way too soon."

"I know, Mama. I still miss Daddy every single day."

"Yeah, the old time-heals-all-wounds notion is a big bunch of bull feathers."

Carrie Ann was surprised by her mother's candor about a subject that they rarely discussed.

"But the sharp pain has dulled over the years. My big regret is that I didn't get a chance to say good-bye. It happened so suddenly without any warning. I mean, your daddy was a fit man and so young." She paused as if to regain her composure, and then chuckled softly. "And that morning I'd run out of his favorite lunch meat so I had to pack a peanut butter and grape jelly sandwich instead. Just to be funny I added a strawberry Fruit Roll-Up and a juice box like I did for you kids. Put a little note sayin' I was sorry and that I loved him. You know, I never put notes in his lunch. Funny how it happened that way."

Carrie Ann closed her eyes and inhaled a shaky breath.

"Used to bother me that a peanut butter and jelly sandwich was the last meal I gave your daddy but I just knew he found the whole thing amusing. He was so good-natured. Wasn't a mean bone in that man's body. He was just . . . good, you know?"

"Oh, I know. Shame I didn't get his laid-back disposition."

"You're a feisty one like me. But you know what? Your daddy could calm me down with a gentle kiss on the forehead. Or sometimes he'd just grab my hand and squeeze. He just seemed to have that power. Oh, but he wouldn't tolerate anyone disrespecting me—or anyone else for that matter. You didn't want to cross that line, let me tell ya."

"He stood up for what he believed in." Carrie Ann smiled because she knew all of this to be true. They didn't come any better than Charley Spencer. And it wasn't too difficult to understand that she'd never found anyone who could measure up to her father. Carrie Ann knew all too well why she had so many issues with commitment.

"Oh, Lordy." Mary sniffed and cleared her throat. "Anyway, Carrie Ann, what I'm trying to say is that you've got a lot of livin' left to do. You just don't know what's waiting around the corner. So embrace this relationship. From all I've ever known of Easton and the Fisher family, they're good solid folks."

"Yes, he's a good man. It's hard to believe he's remained single all these years too."

"Maybe Easton was waiting around for you to come to your senses."

"Mama . . ."

"Is he a good kisser?"

"Mama!"

"Well?"

"I am not going to kiss and tell!"

"Ah so you've kissed then! Ha, you fell right into that one."

"Mama!"

"Quit sayin' 'mama' like that."

"Well, then quit asking me those kinds of questions."

Mary chuckled again. "Aw, sugar. I sure wish I was there to give you a big ole hug. But next time tell your mother juicy news like this first, you hear me, child?"

"I promise," Carrie Ann said, and then smiled. "I sure do love you to pieces."

"Oh, now just hush before we both start blubbering and ruin our makeup. And it takes me a long time to look this good."

Carrie Ann pictured her mother fluffing her hair and smiled. "I'm still lollygagging around in bed. Can you believe it?"

"Well, you get yourself up and stop wasting daylight. And I want a full report after your next date with cutie pie Easton."

"You'll get one."

"Now that's more like it. Send me a selfie next time you're out with him."

"A selfie?" Carrie Ann had to laugh.

"Just remember to hold the phone up high and tip your head back so it looks as if you'd had a face lift. Or better yet get one of those selfie sticks."

"I'll keep that in mind. Thanks for the tip."

"Or even better yet, FaceTime me but do the same thing and hold the phone up or it puts a good ten pounds on you."

Carrie Ann had to chuckle. "I do believe you're savvier about this stuff than I am."

"I've got a lot of time on my hands, sweet pea."

"Are you kidding? Mama, you have a full social life."

"True, but I sure do miss my girls."

"I miss you something fierce too. Love you, Mama."

"Love you too, Carrie Ann. Well, time for my water aerobics. Gotta run! Or should I say 'gotta swim'? See you in the funny papers."

Carrie Ann smiled at the old-fashioned saying that her father used to say with a wave over his head when he headed off to work. She hadn't heard her mother say it in a while and perhaps chatting about the past was much more healing than Carrie Ann wanted to admit. Ava and Ellie had rebounded with the resilience of children, but for a long time Carrie Ann felt guilty about feeling happy. Well, it was high time that she put that silly notion to rest for good.

While shaking her head, Carrie Ann looked at the phone. Her mama was one piece of work. But it did her heart good to hear her mother's voice and to know that in spite of the tragedy she endured she'd managed to carve out a fulfilling life for herself.

Carrie Ann leaned over to put the phone back in the cradle, and then rested back against the pillows. If the news of her getting cozy with Easton at Wine and

Diner up on Main Street in Cricket Creek, Kentucky, had found its way down to Naples, Florida, then it was highly likely that she and Easton were the talk of the town.

And yes, Mama, the man was a good kisser and so much more than that. Carrie Ann closed her eyes and caught her bottom lip between her teeth. No, Easton was an amazing kisser. Thorough, deep, and yet somehow tender but with enough heat to make her simply melt. Just thinking about making love to him made her all hot and bothered. With a groan she reached up for the chain to her ceiling fan and yanked it up on high. She tilted her flushed face up to catch the breeze.

She wanted to make love once more to Easton Fisher. No, not just once more . . . but a lot . . . as in over and over.

"Oh, mercy, I should give myself a little overhaul." Carrie Ann looked down at her cherry red toenails peeking out from the edge of her pajama bottoms. Holy cow, it had been a long time since a man had seen her naked. Carrie Ann rested her palm against her forehead. Before had been spontaneous but now she had time to think about when it would happen again.

"Where do I begin?" Well, for starters she could use a manicure, pedicure, and facial. She needed to buff puff, exfoliate, tweeze, and moisturize from head to toe. Maybe drop a pound or two. Of course making love to Easton had been quite the workout. Maybe her weight-loss plan could be . . . sex-ercise. She chuckled at her own joke.

Carrie Ann looked at her light blue flannel pajamas and shook her head. "Lingerie. Candles." She looked her best in soft lighting. "Mood music . . . oh, mercy me, I need to make a list. No, several lists."

She'd invite Easton over for dinner, set the mood . . . and then have her way with him. Her heart thudded at the thought of having Easton in *her bed* this time and having his bare skin sliding against her body. She would take her time, exploring, teasing, kissing, licking every inch of him to her heart's content.

Reaching down, she cupped her breasts, lifting them higher. "Oh, girls, you aren't as perky as you once were." But even as a cheerleader she was never one of those as-skinny-as-a-stick kind of girls. She had curves and she liked to eat. But blow-drying and washing hair and being on her feet all day long kept her toned and in pretty darned good shape. While she primped and fussed with her appearance, she felt fairly comfortable in her skin. She just wasn't as confident about the whole naked part.

"I'm not one bit nervous," she told herself with a lift of her chin but her wildly beating heart told a much different story. Still, she smiled and hugged a pillow to her chest. "You can do this, Carrie Ann Spencer. Oh yes, you can."

9

Could It Be Forever?

EASTON STOOD ON THE FRONT PORCH OF CARRIE ANN'S house holding a bouquet of flowers in one hand and clutching a bottle of red wine in the other. He looked at the round doorbell but instead of pressing it, he stood there for a moment feeling a bit uncertain. He wanted their relationship to go to the next level, but he didn't want her to think he expected her to fall into bed with him every time they got together. Making love to a woman wasn't something he did casually. But thinking about her was becoming sweet torture and he wanted her naked and in his arms once more.

Her invitation to dinner at her home seemed like the perfect occasion to ramp up the romance but he didn't want to appear too obvious or too confident. He'd actually wanted to bring a box of chocolates along with the wine and flowers, but thought that might be going a bit too far. He told himself to just enjoy the night and to see where it led. But just thinking about Carrie Ann sent his libido into overdrive. In fact, making love to her was just about all he had thought about since he woke up that morning.

Easton took a breath of the cold evening air in an attempt to clear his head and calm his ardor.

Shouldn't have worn these damned tight jeans, he thought and nearly laughed. He hadn't been this revved up in . . . well, *maybe never.* Now that he knew what it felt like to make love to her all it took was thinking about it and he sure as hell was thinking about it right this minute.

Easton couldn't remember the last time he'd taken such pains with his grooming and appearance. His smoothly shaven face was as soft as a baby's behind. The new aftershave he wore was more expensive than he thought reasonable for a mere two ounces of anything, but the perky young clerk at Macy's assured him that the Acqua di Gio was certain to please.

Easton was the type of guy who spent more money on fishing gear than his wardrobe and a rare trip to the mall yesterday evening set him back nearly two hundred dollars. But if his new sweater and designer jeans impressed Carrie Ann it was worth every penny and then some. Even his boxer briefs and socks were brand-spanking-new. And because Carrie Ann was his hairdresser, he'd put a bit of pomade in his hair, slicking it back just a bit like she'd done in the salon. Most days he wore a baseball cap, but tonight, he wanted to look his best.

All in all he felt as if he'd cleaned up pretty well. Now if he could just muster up the gumption to push the damned doorbell, things would be just fine. Or so he hoped.

Easton looked at the flowers, wondering if he should have gone with the roses. "Oh for Pete's sake," he grumbled under his breath. Okay, just take it slow and easy, Easton told himself and then reached over and pressed his knuckle to the round button nearly dropping the bottle of wine in the process. Geez, could he get any more nervous? He felt like a teenager going to the prom. He squared his shoulders, put a smile on his face and waited.

A heart-thudding moment later, Carrie Ann opened the front door. "Hello, Easton. Come on in," she said breezily and stood back for him to enter.

When Easton stepped into the foyer he leaned over and gave Carrie Ann a light kiss on the cheek. "Something sure smells wonderful."

"Meat loaf," she said with a rather shy smile. "I wanted to make sure I fixed something that couldn't go wrong. I'm a decent cook, but I tend to get distracted and I always seem to forget to set the timer. Meat loaf is pretty much foolproof," she said as she took the bouquet of flowers from him. "These are lovely! Thank you!" She angled her head at him as if in question and Easton realized he was gawking at her.

"You . . ." he began but could only shake his head. She looked absolutely stunning in a dark green dress that clung in all the right places and showed just enough cleavage to make him want to put his mouth against the soft swell of her breasts. She wore a single strand of pearls and her hair was gathered up into some sort of sexy bun that had him imagining her taking bobby pins out one at a time until her the deep red mass of curls fell to her shoulders. And she was wearing high heels. Some strappy black things that were as sexy as all get-out.

"Easton? Everything okay? Am I overdressed?"

"No . . . I . . . you . . . damn, Carrie Ann. Well, obviously you've got me all tongue-tied and rendered me speechless. And that's pretty hard to do."

"In a good way, I hope?" She sniffed the flowers and looked at him.

"You take my breath away," he said as he shook his head slowly.

"Are you trying to get me to give you mouth-to-mouth?"

Easton laughed. "Are you making fun of my cheesy comment?"

"I don't find that cheesy at all. Thank you for the compliment." Her smile widened. "I tried on just about everything in my wardrobe trying to find something to make me look skinny." She shrugged, bringing his attention to how the fabric hugged her breasts. "I failed."

"You look perfect," he said firmly and truly meant it. He had a sudden image of her in nothing *but* the pearls and heels and had to disguise his moan with a slight clearing of his throat.

"Thank you again." She gave him a once-over and nodded. "Well, now, I have to say that you look mighty fine yourself, Easton Fisher. You can hang your jacket over there on the coat tree."

Easton put the bottle onto a decorative table and shrugged out of his coat. "I have a confession to make, too. Except for my boots and this leather jacket everything else I'm wearing is brand-spanking-new, including my aftershave."

Carrie Ann took a step closer and sniffed near his neck. "Oh, you smell divine," she said in a low tone that had him wanting to press her up against the wall and kiss her senseless. Instead he picked up the bottle of wine.

"I hope you like this Merlot. I was told this one is exceptional."

She looked at the label. "I do and only splurge on it for special occasions. Follow me into the kitchen and I'll put these pretty flowers in a vase. Did you get them from Flower Power?"

"Yes," Easton said as he walked beside her down the wide hallway. He loved the lemon smell of the polished wood. Older homes were comforting.

"Gabby does such a wonderful job with her floral arrangements. Sophia is going to work with her, weaving fresh flowers into some of the intricate updos. It's going to be so beautiful. I'm thrilled beyond measure that she is actually doing this with me."

"Sophia is such a sweet girl. I'm sure White Lace and Promises is going to be a huge success."

"I think it will be."

When Carrie Ann stood up on tiptoe to retrieve a vase from one of the cabinets, Easton tried not to stare at how the dress molded to her bottom. Okay, he didn't really try at all. He just stared. "Need any help?" He hoped she did so he could slide up next to her body and reach over her head.

"No, I'm like ten feet tall in these heels." She filled the vase with water and a little packet of mystery something before adding the flowers. After arranging them around a little bit she turned around and gave him sultry smile. "And I wore them just for you."

"I feel the need to thank you."

"You should. They are killing my feet."

"Well then, take them off!" *And anything else you like while you're at it.* "I'll help you. Give me your foot."

"No." Carrie Ann shook her head. "They make me feel sexy. This is the time of day when I'm usually in sweatpants and a baggy shirt."

"Let me tell you, you'd be just as sexy wearin' that too."

"You mean I did all of this for nothing?" She laughed, and then tilted her head. "Oh, but thank you, Easton. You're good for my ego."

"I'm not kiddin'. You are a beautiful woman, Carrie Ann. And those legs of yours seem to go on forever with or without heels." He put the bottle of wine on the counter and came up beside her. He looked into those gorgeous eyes that appeared more green than blue tonight. "And I want them wrapped around me," he said and put his forehead to hers. "Oh. Did I just say that out loud?"

She chuckled. "Yes, and I find it interesting because you must have been reading my mind."

"Really?" Easton stepped back and put his hands on her waist. "Well then, I'm glad we're on the same page." He pulled her against him. God, the feel of her lush body molded against his was almost his undoing. So much for taking it slow tonight.

Her eyes turned serious. "I think we've been on that page for far too long. Maybe it's time to start the next chapter." She pointed to the archway leading to the dining room. Tall candles flickered, casting a soft glow over an elegantly set table. For the first time, he noticed soft sultry music playing in the background. "Is there any question as to what I have on my mind?"

"Ah, so you were planning to seduce me?"

"Yes, indeed. That was the grand plan. Is it working?"

"No."

She made a face. "Do I need to try harder? The fireplace is lit in the living room. Would a glass of wine help my cause? A shot of fine bourbon? I do believe I have some Woodford Reserve."

"Nope." He tucked a stray curl behind her ear. "The fact is, darlin', you don't need to try at all. Carrie Ann, this was the longest damn day of my life. I couldn't wait to see you and have you in my arms."

"The feeling is mutual." She reached up and cupped his chin. "And I find the fact that you went shopping for new clothes to be just adorable."

"Adorable? That's probably the first time anyone has used that term to describe me." Easton turned his head so he could kiss the palm of her hand. He was falling in love with her. He knew it and truth be known, he had been crazy about her for quite some time— maybe all the way back to high school.

But a flicker of uncertainty in her eyes kept him from voicing his feelings. At least for now. And he knew where the hesitation came from. They'd been close friends long enough that they'd talked about her father's death and how much it scared her to fall in love. He'd also shared his fear of being trapped in a tumultuous marriage like his parents shared. It wasn't too difficult to understand that they both had issues that had caused them to remain single. Young love was different from falling in love at their age. At this stage of the game, they both had emotional baggage and daily routines that didn't include another person. They each had their own homes that they loved.

Was he too stuck in his ways to make room for another person in his life? How do you blend two lives together and make it work?

Instead of expressing his feelings, he decided to keep the mood light and playful. And as much as he wanted to sweep her up into his arms and carry her off to bed, he kissed her lightly and said, "Let's open the wine."

Carrie Ann nodded. "And sip it in front of the fireplace? Mine isn't as grand as yours, but it's cozy."

"I like that idea," he said even though he really liked the idea of taking her to bed a lot more. But he'd waited for this moment all week and he wanted to savor each touch, every kiss until he finally had her naked and between the sheets once more.

She handed him the corkscrew. "If you will do the honors, I'm going to turn everything down on low so we can enjoy our cocktail before we eat dinner."

"Dinner really does smell delicious, by the way."

"It's just meat loaf, mashed potatoes, gravy, and green beans. Oh, and cherry cobbler for dessert but I cheated and bought it at Wine and Diner on my way home from the salon. Nothing too fancy. Just good old-fashioned down-home cookin'."

"My favorite kind."

"After seeing your gourmet kitchen I got super nervous. I thought I knew you pretty well and I never would have pegged you for being a cook."

Easton laughed while uncorking the wine. "Maybe there's more to me than meets the eye."

"I have to admit I like what I've seen so far." Carrie

Ann accepted the glass that he handed to her. She tapped her rim to his. "Well, here's to finding out so much more."

Easton nodded and took a sip of the full-bodied wine. "Except for the occasional glass of Merlot, I'm not all that much of a wine drinker, but I think it's about time I expand my horizons," he said and took her hand and led her into the living room. "Maybe go on a day trip to a Kentucky winery?"

"I've always wanted to do that, Easton. I've heard there are quite a few lovely wineries in Kentucky. I'd love to take a drive through horse country and stop for a wine-tasting."

"Have you ever done the Bourbon Trail?"

"No." Carrie Ann shook her head. "But I'd love to do that too."

"And maybe stay at a bed and breakfast?"

"That would be divine. Since when did you become so romantic?"

"That's where the more-than-meets-the-eye part comes into play," he said, but the truth was that she brought out a romantic side of him that he didn't know he had.

"And cooking? When did you discover you enjoyed cooking?"

Easton took another sip of the wine. "Cooking is actually something I've gotten into in the past few years. I think watching the Food Network got me interested in doing more than tossing steaks on the grill. It relaxes me to putter around in the kitchen after a hard day's work."

"I do believe I'd like to see you in action. I'd be perfectly entertained sitting back and watching you cook up a storm."

"We can definitely make that happen."

They sat down on the sofa across from the crackling fire. Tony Bennett crooned in the background and for the next several minutes they chatted and sipped wine.

"I repaired Noah Falcon's dishwasher today and he said that the Cricket Creek Cougars signed a couple of good relief pitchers this past week."

"That's good news," Carrie Ann said as she toed off her shoes. "When Noah came back to Cricket Creek and built the baseball stadium it sure saved our town from financial ruin. I was always so proud of him playing in the majors, weren't you?"

"Sure was. We should go to some games this summer." He put his glass on the coffee table and reached down and lifted her feet onto his lap. "I think your feet deserve a massage. May I?"

She wiggled her toes. "By all means."

"You have very pretty feet," he said and started rubbing her cute toes.

"Oh my word, that feels just simply . . . oh . . . amazing." She leaned against a fluffy fringed pillow and sipped her wine. "My dogs tend to bark at the end of the day. This is pure bliss." She closed her eyes and sighed.

"You deserve it." It suddenly occurred to Easton that Carrie Ann didn't have anyone to pamper her, not even family since Ava and Ellie lived in Lexington and her mama retired to Florida. An odd ache settled in his chest and he looked over at her. Because her eyes remained closed he studied her face, loving the slight smile and soft moans when he massaged a little bit harder. The wine, the music, the warmth of the fire must be doing the trick. "I could get used to this," he said without meaning to.

Her eyes remained shut. "Isn't that my line?"

Easton chuckled but in that moment he realized with complete clarity that he really could get used to pampering Carrie Ann. He knew without a doubt that she'd never shout or argue with him the way his parents went at each other. She might be sassy, but she was also soft and sweet. He thought about the conversation with Pete Sully about the cruise he was taking with Maria and made a mental note to start researching vacations.

She said she used her free time to visit her mother and sisters but he had to wonder if she'd ever gone someplace exotic where she could just do absolutely nothing but just simply sightsee and relax. He imagined walking hand in hand on the beach or sitting in lounge chairs on the deck of a cruise ship. He'd take her to Disney World if that's where she wanted to go. Yeah, he needed to put that plan into action.

Easton looked at her sexy red toenails and felt a jolt of heat. He kind of wanted to kiss each toe but didn't know how she would react. Swallowing hard, he looked up. Her eyes remained closed and the flickering light from the fireplace danced over her features. Her chest rose and fell in a slow even rhythm making Easton smile.

"You're not gonna fall asleep on me, are you?" he asked softly.

"If I fall on you, rest assured that I won't be asleep."

Easton leaned his head against the cushion and chuckled. "Is that a promise?"

"Yes sir-ee."

"Mmmm, well now . . ." he responded and slid his hand up her smooth calf. She opened her eyes and met his gaze while his hand slid higher over her knee and up to her thigh. Easton's body reacted to the feel of her skin, warm, soft, pliant. He rubbed his thumb back and forth until her breath caught.

"Carrie Ann . . ." he murmured and when she nodded he moved his hand higher until he felt the silk of her panties. When he lightly grazed over her mound she gasped and nearly spilled her wine. Easton leaned over, took the glass from her, and put it on the coffee table. "Do you want me to stop?"

"Are you out of your mind?"

"Yeah, with wanting you," he said as he toyed with the edge of her panties. "I'd suggest right here on the sofa but we might end up injured. I think that our days of making out on the couch have passed us by."

"Then take me to bed."

Easton didn't need another invitation. He eased her legs over to the floor, stood up, and offered his hand. When he gently tugged her to her feet she stumbled against him.

"Sorry. I'm a bit unsteady." She smiled at him. "And it isn't from the wine."

"I can fix that," he said and scooped her up into his arms.

"Are plumb crazy? You're gonna throw your back out. Or pull something."

"No, I won't," Easton said. In truth, he was having instant regret, but he was determined. He started walking, gritting his teeth and trying not to grunt.

"Easton, seriously. I'm a big woman."

"I'm a strong man," he said, but his voice sounded strained and she started to laugh. "You are seriously ruining this very romantic moment."

"No, the romantic moment is going to be ruined when I have to dial nine-one-one," she replied with a laugh.

"I'm fine," he said but staggered and started laughing with her. He eased her to her feet. "Evidently I need to hit the gym."

"Evidently I do too," she said as he hugged her close.

"I think you are perfect just the way you are."

"And so are you," she said and stepped back and took his hand, leading him up the stairs and into her bedroom.

Easton took a second to absorb the fact that he was in Carrie Ann's bedroom, about to make love to her once more. She turned on a small lamp on a nightstand illuminating the room with a soft glow. Then, stepping back, she turned for him to unzip her dress. He kissed the delicate slope of her neck while he eased the zipper down, thinking there was something so intimate about this act. The dress slipped from her shoulders and pooled at her bare feet.

With a moan, Easton pressed his body against her back and cupped her breasts. He rubbed his thumbs over the silk of her bra.

"Oh my, that feels so very nice." Carrie Ann rested her head against Easton's shoulder, letting him touch her, caress her, sliding his hands lower over her torso until he reached her panties. He slid his finger beneath the waistband and felt the heat of her desire. Dipping his finger between her folds, he encountered the silky wet evidence that she wanted him as much as he wanted her.

"God, you are so very sexy." Easton longed to turn her around and see her standing before him in black lace and pearls but his hands refused to stop touching her, caressing her. Her breath caught and he knew she was close to climaxing. With a flick of his wrist, he unclasped her bra and cupped her breast. As soon as he flicked his thumb over her nipple she cried out with a throaty moan. He was sure she might have slithered to the floor if he hadn't hugged her against him.

"Dear God," she said, breathing a little hard. "I do believe you made my knees buckle, Easton Fisher."

"Good, but you ain't seen nothin' yet." He kissed her neck, and then turned her around to face him. She blinked at him and smiled, looking so damned gorgeous with her flushed cheeks that Easton smiled back at her. "Now sit down on the bed."

"Are you giving me orders?"

"Not at all, sugar. I will do whatever your little ole heart desires."

"I desire you. Naked."

Easton grinned. "Your wish is my command."

"Oh, I like this. I need to invite you to dinner more often." She let her unhooked bra slid down her arms and tossed it aside. Her breasts were lush and full with creamy white skin and dusky pink nipples. Youth might have passed them by but there was such beauty in her rounded curves and laugh lines. She looked at him, and while there was a hint of shyness in her eyes, he didn't see even a flicker of hesitation. She wanted this as much as he did and the thought made him feel . . . *happy*.

"I know I keep saying it but you're beautiful, Carrie Ann."

"You certainly make me feel that way."

Needing to be next to her in bed, Easton made quick work of shedding his boots and clothes, glad he'd purchased new boxer briefs in black. He didn't belong to a gym, but physical labor and sports kept him in pretty good shape and by the looks of Carrie Ann's smile, she liked what she saw. "I want to explore every inch of you," he said.

"Again, we are on the same page and, better yet, in the same bed. This day just keeps getting better." She scooted to the edge of the mattress and tugged his boxer briefs downward. When his erection sprang forward, she cupped his balls and ran the tip of her tongue from the base to the tip of his shaft. Easton shuddered and knew that if her hot, wet tongue teased him with another lick he would likely lose it. And when he lost it, he wanted to be buried deep inside her body.

"Ah, Carrie Ann," he said and she understood. When she scooted back he leaned over and tugged her panties down her legs and tossed them over his shoulder. Most of her hair had come loose from the pins and was spread out over the cream-colored comforter. Except for the sexy string of pearls, she was naked. Ready. And he'd never wanted a woman more than he wanted Carrie Ann Spencer.

Easton slid his body next to hers, loving the sensation of his skin on her skin. He pulled her into his arms and kissed her deeply, tasting the wine on her lips. She threaded her fingers through his hair and arched her body as if trying to get even closer and he understood how she felt . . . he couldn't get close enough.

Easton explored her body with his hands, his mouth, and when he grazed his teeth over her nipple she gasped.

"Please . . ."

"Please what?" He rubbed his thumb over her wet nipple.

"Please . . . don't *stop.*"

Easton laughed low in his throat. "There is zero chance of me stopping unless you want me to."

"Negative zero chance of that . . ."

"You feel good, taste good, and I can never get enough of you." He began a trail of kisses down her body and then parted her thighs.

"I want you inside me."

"Just one . . . *taste,*" he said and flicked his tongue over her core. She arched her back, gasping. "You . . . I'm going . . ." she said, but he came up and silenced her protest with a hot kiss and then entered her with one sure stroke. She wrapped her legs around him and moved in a slow seductive rhythm. Easton threaded his fingers with hers and made love to her the way he'd dreamed about all day long.

Oh, but the reality was so much better. He was learning the nooks and crannies of Carrie Ann's body, her pleasure points, and he made sure to pay close attention to each and every one of them. She liked to be kissed and nuzzled on the tender side of her neck, and his nipping her earlobe with his teeth made her breath catch. And her breasts . . . She loved to be caressed and teased; it drove her wild. The other night, after dinner, she sat between his legs and he'd brought her to climax by kissing the back of her neck and stroking her beautiful breasts.

Easton thrust deeper, faster. When she grabbed his shoulders and cried out, the sound of his name on her lips pushed him over the edge. But Easton's sweet release was so much more than physical. For the first time in his life, he felt desire to have a woman in his life and by his side. He pulled her close and held her. Brushing her hair to the side, he kissed her shoulder.

For a few moments neither of them spoke. Easton wanted so much to tell her that he loved her, but something told him to hold back. He knew when she didn't utter any wisecracks or playful banter that she was feeling the intensity of the moment, the shift of their relationship to something deeper, lasting.

He kissed her shoulder again, wondering if he should just take the leap of faith and say it . . . Let her know how much he cared for her. But would she say I love you back or run for the hills?

The words were on the tip of his tongue and he decided that he should just go for it. . . .

"Carrie Ann, I—"

"You worked up an appetite?" she asked as if somehow knowing what he was about to say.

"Yeah, I sure did." He tugged at her shoulder so that she rolled over to her back. Smiling down at her he kissed her lightly. "Let's go eat."

She smiled back but her eyes appeared stormy.

"Carrie Ann," he said and rubbed his fingertip over her bottom lip. "I want us to be . . . exclusive."

Her eyes widened slightly and she cupped his cheek. "Of course. Easton, you're the only man I want in my life."

"I mean, I knew that after—well, after *this*—that we would be but I wanted to say it. You've been my friend for a long time and now you're my girl."

She chuckled. "I like being called a girl. Makes me feel young."

"You're my girl," he repeated.

"I like the sound of that," she said, and although something flickered in her eyes, she seemed to relax.

Easton told himself to be content with this for now but he wouldn't wait long before telling her that he loved her. They weren't spring chickens and they'd lost years of what could have been nights like this. He only hoped that she would soon realize how good it could be from this day forward. He planned to do his best to chase away any remaining fear she had of commitment. He thought again about taking her away somewhere . . . Yes, then he'd tell her so there wouldn't be any chance of her running away.

"Why do you suddenly look as if you've got something up your sleeve?" she asked with a touch of her usual sass.

"Um, as you well know, I'm naked. No sleeves here."

"It's a figure of speech."

Easton shrugged. "I think there's something to be said for a little bit of mystery," he said with a hint of smugness that he knew would intrigue her to no end. When she opened her mouth to protest he silenced her with a finger to her lips. "Oh, sweet pea, you're just gonna have to wait."

"Come on, Easton." Carrie Ann narrowed her eyes and pouted but Easton wasn't about to tell her that he planned to sweep her away for a romantic vacation.

Easton rubbed his fingertip back and forth over her bottom lip. "My granny used to say that patience is a virtue."

"Something I am lacking in, by the way."

"And that makes this even more fun," he said, but when she tried to protest again he covered her mouth with a kiss. And a moment later, she forgot all about fussing at him and melted into his arms.

10

On and On

SOPHIA STOPPED SHELVING SHAMPOO AND CONDI-
tioner and watched her new washing machine in
the throes of a spin cycle. The massive machine spun
so fast that the towels were nearly dry by the time the
cycle ended. Sophia blinked at the stainless steel machines with wonder. Who would have thought that a
washer and dryer would bring her such joy? She smiled
and did the Snoopy happy dance. Her joy wasn't really
just about the washing machine, but the reality that she
was the half owner of her own bridal hair salon!

Carrie Ann had given Sophia full rein to run the creative end of the business while she tended to the books,
which was perfectly fine with Sophia. She needed a bud-
get and guidelines or she'd overspend, not in a frivolous
way but with too much enthusiasm. So instead, she'd
had fun this past week shopping at thrift shops and antiques stores, searching for bargains in and around
Cricket Creek. The result was a shabby-chic look, and
Sophia adored the elegant results.

Sophia brought one of the freshly dried oh-so-soft
towels to her nose. She inhaled the delicate scent of

lavender knowing all too well that brides-to-be needed the calming effects of aromatherapy. The piped-in playlist consisted mostly of laid-back jazz and old-school love songs setting a soothing mood. Brides needed to be handled with care, and over the past few years, she'd become an expert in the field of frayed nerves.

Earlier that morning, Sophia had coffee with Nicolina Diamante Monroe, owner of Designs by Diamante, a lovely jewelry shop two doors down from her salon. Nicolina showed her sketches for a complete line of White Lace and Promises hair jewelry that would be created exclusively for Sophia's clients.

Later in the week, Sophia had a meeting set up with Addison Greenfield, owner of From This Moment bridal salon, and Gabby Marino, the florist from Flower Power. Together, they could provide a total bridal party experience, all within walking distance of one another on Wedding Row. Grace was already working on pamphlets for the shops to share and a Facebook page chock-full of wedding planning tips. Her sister's unending ideas and suggestions were enough to make her head spin as fast as the new washing machine. Well, maybe not that fast.

But in fact, White Lace and Promises was coming together at a much faster pace than she and Carrie Ann had imagined. She'd already landed a few gigs for several weddings and they hadn't even had their grand opening celebration as of yet.

Grace assured Sophia that everything would fall into place but in truth a little bit of panic slipped its way past her excitement. Closing her eyes, Sophia inhaled another deep breath of lavender, rubbing the soft towel against her cheek.

Zoe Dean was scheduled to come in later in the week for a consultation. She thought of Avery and nibbled on the inside of her lip. She thought of Avery a lot . . . as in *all the time*. But while Sophia and Avery had been out and about in Cricket Creek for the past couple of weeks, Zoe apparently hadn't totally gotten the message that she and Avery were a thing . . . or at least pretending to be a thing. Zoe continued a push for Avery to hang out with her, Ashley, and Max. And even though Avery resisted, taking Sophia all around town, Zoe just wouldn't totally give up on the hope of reuniting Avery and Ashley.

The pretending part wasn't going so well for Sophia. In fact, her pretense was pretty much a complete fail. Try as she might, the hand-holding and public displays of affection felt all too real. In addition, Sophia thought about Avery throughout the day and looked forward to spending time with him. And while he ended all of their outings on Sophia's doorstep, thoughts of making love to him made for a fitful night's sleep.

Usually good-natured, Sophia found herself getting a little bit grumpy over little things that she would normally shrug off or even laugh about. So even though she remained extremely excited over the opening of White Lace and Promises, a little cloud hovered over her head, causing bouts of irritability that she couldn't seem to control. Unlike headstrong Grace, Sophia was a worrier and could slip into a blue funk now and again.

Like now, when she reached deep into the washing machine for a towel that was suctioned to the back of the tub. The towel remained stubbornly out of reach, making her spitting mad over something so small.

"Grrr . . ."

She leaned in farther, causing short-girl problems to raise its ugly head. "Damn it!" she grumbled and leaned in farther. "Aha, you little bugger," she said, using one of her mother's English terms that came out of her mouth every so often. "Come to mama!"

Her toes left the floor and she finally managed to pluck the towel away but when she lifted her head to ease out of the washing machine, the lid decided to flop down and smack her in the small of her back. "Well, damn it all to hell and back! I should have gotten the front-load model!"

Clutching the towel, she attempted to disengage herself only to realize that she was sort of . . . stuck. While she could rock back and forth, the lid remained shut and her toes failed to touch solid ground. Sophia let out a little squeal of pure frustration. "This is not happening!" She pushed with her hands and legs but had somehow managed to wedge herself even farther into the washing machine.

Normally Sophia would remain calm, maybe even laugh and then find a way out. But today she cursed a blue streak and her earlier good mood evaporated like rain on a summer sidewalk. To add insult to injury, her phone rang from where it rested on the table where she'd folded towels earlier.

Dear God, how long was she going to remain here before anyone came to her rescue? With renewed determination she wiggled and managed to move a bit sideways, thinking if she could get at least one arm free she could hoist herself up. Her phone rang again. "I can't answer; I'm stuck in a damned washing machine!" she shouted.

A couple of hours passed, okay more like a few minutes, but Sophia couldn't recall being this totally pissed off. As a hair stylist she'd learned to deal with crisis situations all the time. She had her share of color gone wrong, and she'd even snipped an ear a time or two. But for some reason this little incident had her totally annoyed. She struggled with renewed vigor but managed only to bang her head and bruise her ego.

And then she started to cry.

What began as a rather sad whimper quickly escalated into sobs that sounded really hollow and weird while submerged in a washing machine. For a wild second she wondered if this was the way she was going to die, but once she realized there was zero chance of her demise occurring, she calmed down *just a tiny bit*.

"Okay, just settle down." She inhaled what was supposed to be a calming breath, but for some reason, being stuck in this ridiculous situation forced her to take a look at her life or, more accurately, a look at her love life. Her fake love life that wasn't really so fake—well, at least on her end. Unrequited love really, truly sucked.

Seriously, her half brother Garret was happily married to sweet Mattie and their daughter, Lily, was the cutest baby in the whole wide world. Grace and Mason were totally in love and Sophia wouldn't be surprised if Mason popped the question sometime soon. And independent Grace had been adamant that she needed her freedom to wander all over the globe and could never be tied down. Ha! Funny how falling in love changed her sister's entire attitude about being tied down. While in Cricket Creek for the birth of Lily, her English-born fashion-icon mother met and fell head over high heels for Jimmy Topmiller, former world-class pro bass angler. Sophia didn't know that a person could become rich and famous for catching fish but apparently it was a real thing. Seriously, who would have thought that her city-born mother would end up with an outdoorsy type? That her mother would *become* an outdoorsy type? And that Rick Ruleman, Garret's famous rock star father, would give up his wild leather-clad ways and marry Maggie McMillian, a local real estate agent. Oh, and that Addison Monroe, Garret's former fiancée and owner of From This Moment bridal salon would marry Reid Greenfield whose sister, Sara, plans lavish barn weddings on their family farm!

This list in her head went on and on . . . and Sophia would like to make the Cricket Creek falling-in-love list too! Well, if you came right down to it she was already on the falling-in-love-with-a-local-boy list. She was just missing the all-important detail of having Avery's name on there with her.

"Well, this is just plain silly." Sophia inhaled a sharp breath of Tide-scented air. "Okay, sister," she grumbled, "you need to concentrate on the problem at hand, not the state of your love life. Seriously, who gets stuck in a washing machine?"

Surely, at some point someone would realize she'd gone missing. Wouldn't they? Her stomach gave a little growl reminding her that she'd had only a not-so-tasty, hard-as-a-brick granola bar for breakfast instead of the bacon and egg biscuit that she really wanted. And soon she'd have to pee. She had a bladder the size of a doggone walnut and it was quickly responding to the bottle of coconut water she'd guzzled earlier.

Sophia was contemplating if she should immerse herself farther and push up with both hands when she thought she heard her name being called. Cocking her head to the side she stopped and listened.

"Sophia?" She heard faintly.

Yes! Her savior had arrived. The UPS man? She hoped it wasn't someone she knew.

"You in here?" She heard more clearly.

Oh great . . . just her luck. Not the UPS man. Her savior was *Avery*. How embarrassing. Maybe she'd just keep quiet until he went away, but her bladder gave a cry of protest.

"Back here!" she shouted, hoping that her muffled voice reached him.

"Sophia?" Avery shouted again.

"Back here! In the laundry room!"

"So-phi-a?" When his voice sounded dimmer she wiggled, panicked, and hit her head again. Her phone rang, probably Avery.

"I. Am. In. The. Ouch! Laundry . . . Rooooooom!" She felt as if she was stuck on a desert island with a flare that failed to signal the rescue plane. She wanted to jump up and wave her hands. Panic gripped her. "Aaaaa-ver-eeeee!"

"Soooo-phia?" His steps sounded louder, closer.

"Here!" She panted. "Laundry room!" Who knew that being stuck could cause her to get out of breath?

"Oh my God!" His boots clumped in rapid fashion over the tile floor. "What the hell? Are you okay?"

"Define okay," she replied in a muffled, mortified, slightly watery tone.

"Here . . . let me . . ." he said a bit uncertainly. He lifted the lid upright off her back. "Stay still."

"Right . . . like I can move."

"So, you're stuck?"

"No, I decided I needed deep cleaning in the washing machine rather than a shower."

"What?" he sounded confused.

"Yes, I'm stuck!"

"Oh, well, I got this. I'm going to put my hands around you and hoist you straight up and out of there."

"Okay," reverberated in the washing machine. She felt his big hands on the waist of her jeans and realized with another hot flash of humiliation that her bum was in his face with a few inches of skin showing, most likely including the lace of her pink panties. At least it wasn't the whale tail of a thong. She didn't know how women wore those things wedged up their bum. His long fingers gripped her and as promised he lifted her up and out of her stainless steel prison. When her feet touched the blessed floor, she stood up quickly causing the blood to rush to her head. A wave of dizziness washed over her and she swayed.

"Sophia, God, are you okay?" The humor was gone from his voice.

"I . . ." She swallowed hard and inhaled a deep breath, trying to stop her world from spinning. "I think . . . so. I'm a bit light-headed. Just let me lean back against you for a minute." Or ten. All day might be nice, too.

"Sure, just take it easy." His arms remained around her. "Can I get you anything? Water?"

"My dignity would be lovely."

He gave her an uncertain chuckle. "Hey, I've gotten myself in worse pickles than this. You sure you don't want some water or something?"

"No, thank you." She shook her head, which was a big mistake when one was dizzy. She groaned thinking she might get sick to her stomach. Wouldn't *that* just top it off like a cherry on a sundae?

"Still dizzy?"

"High on Tide fumes, I think," she replied with a weak little chuckle.

"I have to ask. How did this even happen?"

Sophia raised the evil little towel still clutched in her hand. "I had a stray and had to lasso it."

Avery laughed.

"And you fell in?"

"Short-girl problems. And then the lid closed and well . . . I think you get the picture."

He laughed harder. She could feel the vibrations in his chest and his arms tightened around her.

"It's not that funny."

"Yes, it is."

"Okay, it kinda is humorous now that I'm rescued from the deep bowels of the washing machine. I was worried that it might spontaneously start that crazy-fast spin cycle at some point just to prove who was boss."

"Oh God . . . Sophia." His laughter subsided into little chuckles. "Do things like this happen to you often?"

"Actually, getting lost or stuck like this is more Grace's style. But let's keep this little mishap between us, shall we?"

"Not on your life." He continued to laugh making her get a little bit pissed until he kissed the top of her head, which made her anger melt like butter on the griddle at Walking on Sunshine Bistro. "Has the dizziness passed?"

"Yes." Sophia nodded reluctantly since she knew the admission meant she could no longer lean against his very nice chest and feel those arms holding her close. "I mean, I think so."

"Good," he said with a hint of humor remaining in his voice. He relaxed his grip, and then gently turned

her around. "So . . ." he began but his smile faltered.
"Whoa, wait, Sophia. Were you crying?"

"I, uh . . ." She shrugged feeling foolish. "Why do
you ask?" Dear God, she hoped her emotions weren't
that transparent.

"Your mascara is smudged."

"Oh." Great. She went for a grin that didn't quite
make it to her face. "It was the Tide fumes getting in
my eyes."

"A likely story." Avery shook his head and then
reached over and gently wiped the smudge away with
his thumb. His expression turned serious. "How long
were you trapped in there, anyway? Are you sure you're
okay?"

"Seemed like a lifetime, but I think about ten minutes, tops. Had I kept my wits about me I'm sure I
could have gotten out, but for some reason I decided to
have a bit of a meltdown. I should have gotten the front
loader but this model was a bit cheaper."

"Sophia . . ." He pulled her into his arms and gave
her a hug. "I'm sorry that I laughed. I didn't realize
you were scared."

Oh wow, he felt so strong and so steady. Her mother
had taught her to be strong and independent but . . . oh
this felt so very nice. And he smelled delicious, like
sunshine and spice and she could feel the steady beat
of his heart against her cheek. Her own heartbeat
wasn't quite so steady. "Truthfully, I was actually more
pissed at myself than scared. Being short really sucks
sometimes. Earlier, I tried to get a bottle of cleaner
down from the top shelf and . . ." She winced, trying to
distract him from her silly tears.

"And?"

"Let's just say it wasn't a good idea to stand up on a
chair with wheels. I did a little half spin and went zing-
ing across the tile floor."

Avery chuckled. "I'm sorry, but you're so damned
cute."

Sophia smiled but she felt a touch of disappointment. She was used to being called cute and she knew that Avery meant it as a compliment, but for once she wanted to be sultry and gorgeous instead of perky and cute. Her mother and Grace floated through life on those long legs of theirs being sexy without even trying. Well, granted, Grace was a bit clumsy at times but she looked the part.

"You need a step stool. I'll get you one."

"Thank you," she said, wishing she could think of a step stool as something more romantic. "That's thoughtful of you, Avery."

He gave her shoulders a squeeze and then stepped back.

"If you don't mind I need a quick trip to the ladies' room."

"No, not at all."

Sophia gave him a bit of a shaky smile and ducked into the bathroom. After relieving her full bladder, she washed her hands, and then dared to look into the mirror. "Dear God." Her mascara was smudged and her hair was a tragedy. She used a paper towel to wipe away the dark smudges and tried to smooth her hair down as best she could.

"Get it together," she said and inhaled a deep breath. After blowing her nose she decided not to look in the mirror again and opened the door.

"There you are. I was getting worried. Are you okay now?"

Sophia nodded. "Just a little stress of getting the salon ready. I let things get to me sometimes." She gave him a smile. "So what brings you around?" She tried to sound casual but the sight of him in that snug, long-sleeved T-shirt and those work boots really made her heart thud.

"Other than rescuing you from an evil washing machine?"

"You're not going to let me live that down, are you?"

"Not for a while, at least." He flashed her that killer crooked grin of his, but then tucked a fingertip beneath her chin. "But why the tears, Sophia? Is there something you want to talk about?"

"No." She waved a dismissive hand but was hit with an unexpected wave of emotion. "I think it's just all of the preparation for the open house party. I mean, we were lucky that this shop was pretty much set up for a salon to begin with. But still, there's so much to do. My mood swings from being super excited to absolute panic without warning."

"So you're warning me . . ."

Closing her eyes, she nodded.

"It will all fall into place."

She inhaled another deep breath and let it out. "Oh, I know. I'm just a worrier by nature. And Grace is such a marketing genius. Too good, actually. No wonder she drove Mason crazy with the opening of the brewery. And as if she doesn't have enough to do she's thinking of a line of cosmetics targeting the brides. An excellent idea, but come on! That girl just doesn't stop."

"Well, speaking of stopping. The reason for my visit was to ask you if you wanted to take a break from all of this and grab some lunch? Maybe something from River Row Pizza? I'm craving a calzone."

"Oh, sounds good." Sophia thought of her bum that had been sticking up in the air and told herself to order a salad and skip the amazing bread and herbed oil. And not to cave in to the oh-so-tempting dessert tray, not even if they had Italian Cream Cake. She could do that, right?

"So, you'd like to join me?"

"Yes, thanks. Just let me grab my purse and sweater," she said, wondering if this visit was spontaneous or was this planned to make a show of them out together?

"Let me," Avery picked up her red sweater from

where she'd draped it over a chair. When her hair got caught beneath the wide collar he reached in and lifted it from her neck. His fingers brushed against her skin making her feel warm and tingly.

Sophia longed to lean against him once more but she stepped away and picked up her purse. "Ready?" she asked briskly.

Avery looked at her for a couple of seconds, as if he was about to say something, but then merely nodded. Something in the air suddenly felt . . . odd. She couldn't quite put her finger on it. Not odd in a bad way, really, but he seemed to be holding something back.

"Hungry?" Sophia asked as they walked out the door. "Silly question, I guess," she added while turning the key in the lock.

"Yeah, I'm really hungry. You?"

"Yes." Sophia nodded. "My appetite is always at war with my metabolism. It's actually not too bad of a walk from the high-rise where I live. This hill is a bit of a trek but I'm going to start hoofing it here once the weather warms up a bit more. Although, I was certainly used to walking in all kinds of weather while I lived in New York City."

"Do you miss it?"

"The walking?"

"Living in a big city."

"Sometimes." The cool breeze hit her warm cheeks and she smiled up at him. One of the many things she liked about Avery was that he didn't make mindless small talk. When he asked a question, he was sincerely interested. "But I really like Cricket Creek. And being in the same town as my family sure is wonderful. And little Lily is growing like a weed! I don't want to miss one minute of her childhood."

"Family is important." Avery smiled back and took her hand, making her wonder if the gesture was for show or if he wanted to hold her hand. "I know that you first arrived in the summer but spring is my favorite season. Cricket Creek is really pretty when the buds bloom on the crabapple trees."

"I can imagine."

"Well, you won't have to imagine now that you live here." He smiled again making Sophia feel warm in spite of the cool breeze.

When they reached the entrance of River Row Pizza, Avery stepped forward and opened the door for her. The aroma of all things delicious wafted her way, making Sophia doubt she had the willpower to order a salad. Probably not.

Although the restaurant was fairly full, the hostess walked them over to a booth across from the bar and handed them menus. "Your server will be with you shortly. Enjoy your meal."

Sophia stuck to her guns and ordered a chef salad with dressing on the side. She was feeling pretty good about her decision until Avery's calzone arrived. Shaped like a half moon with golden brown crust, the oven-baked calzone smelled as delicious as it looked.

Avery took a bite, and then moaned. "Tony Marino makes the best calzones I've ever eaten. Have you ever had one here?"

"No," she looked at her salad and stuck a fork in a cucumber without much enthusiasm.

"Would you like a bite?"

"Thanks, but I'll stick with my salad."

Avery arched one eyebrow and put a steaming bite of calzone near her mouth. "You sure?"

"Oh, okay, you've twisted my arm." Sophia could resist the calzone but she couldn't resist Avery feeding her. She closed her eyes as she chewed the bite of heaven in her mouth.

"Good, huh?"

Sophia nodded. "Oh yes," she admitted, and then scrunched her nose at her salad. "Want to trade?"

Avery laughed. "Why didn't you order something more?"

"I'm trying to eat healthy. I had a granola bar this morning that tasted like cardboard but I felt proud of myself."

"Well, how about we share? I'll eat some salad and you eat some of my calzone."

"I like the way you think," Sophia said.

"I like the way you think and the way you look," Avery said with a slow smile that did funny things to her tummy. "In fact, I like everything about you." He reached across the table and put his hand over hers and squeezed.

"Do you, now?" Sophia's pulse quickened and she looked at him, trying to decide whether he was serious or if this was part of the pretend thing they had going on.

"I do," he said, and it appeared as if he was about to say something more but his eyes suddenly widened and he put his fork down.

"Avery? Is something wrong?"

He swallowed hard. "Ashley just walked in."

"Oh." Sophia tried to read his expression. "Did she see you?"

"Yeah, I think so. She did one of those quick look-away things that people do." He shrugged but also appeared uncomfortable. His hand that had been covering hers slipped away, which made Sophia have an odd hollow pang replace her earlier joy.

Sophia leaned forward and whispered, "Is she coming this way?" It occurred to her that she didn't know what Ashley looked like and she wanted so very badly to turn around but didn't want to be that obvious.

"I don't think so," he said but seemed uncertain. He stared down at his food as if he no longer wanted it and Sophia understood. Ashley showing up was a total buzzkill. She would give anything to know what was going on in his head. "But if she does—"

"I know. Be all lovey-dovey," Sophia said and smiled.

It was a fake smile but she thought she pulled it off. "I will stay in girlfriend character."

"About that, Sophia, I—" Avery began, but he groaned. "I was wrong. I think she's coming our way."

"Oh . . ." Sophia had dealt with a lot of touchy situations as a hair stylist, so she wasn't timid when it came to dealing with people, especially women. But this particular situation was a first. She knew at some point their paths were bound to cross, but she'd hoped that she would have been forewarned and not have this sort of chance meeting, especially when she and Avery had been having such a lovely lunch. But perhaps this was her little reminder that this relationship was for show.

Sophia signed inwardly. Not being in love when everyone else seemed to be in a relationship *sucked*— but unrequited love was so much worse. She was beginning to wish that she'd never agreed to this farce. But Sophia put a big smile on her face and hoped she could pull this off because she suddenly felt the silly urge to cry. Or bolt. Or worse, bolt while crying.

First there was the washing machine fiasco and now this.

Could the day get any worse?

Sophia watched a tall dark-haired woman weave her way past tables and chairs, pausing a few times to greet people. Some of the diners started glancing their way and it occurred to Sophia that this was exactly the kind of fodder that fueled small-town gossip.

Ashley wore a basic dark blue business suit that should have looked dowdy but she pulled it off with a touch of long-legged elegance. Sophia tried to remember if Avery had divulged what Ashley did for a living but came up empty.

Tall, willowy, with long flowing hair the color of midnight, Ashley was gorgeous. She just looked so . . . womanly, making Sophia feel like a teenager dressed in her sweater and blue jeans. And after the washing machine fail she knew she didn't look her best. Isn't that the way life happens? Go to the grocery store without makeup and you see everyone you know.

"Well, hello there, Avery." Ashley greeted him with a slow Southern drawl that made her words sound as if they were double-dipped in honey. "It's nice to see you." She gave him a wide smile revealing a set of perfect white teeth.

"Hello, Ashley," Avery said, and Sophia was secretly glad he left out the it's-nice-to-see-you-too part. Ever the gentleman, he stood up and there was a pause before what appeared to be an awkward, barely touching each other hug. But still, it was a hug. Avery gestured toward Sophia.

"I'd like you to meet . . . Sophia Gordon," he said. Sophia wondered if his slight hesitation was because he couldn't quite refer to her as his girlfriend. Did he not want to upset Ashley? It bothered Sophia, even though it shouldn't, because she really wasn't his girlfriend. Still . . .

Ashley turned her toothpaste commercial smile on Sophia. "Well, hello, Sophia." She extended her hand and gave Sophia a limp noodle handshake that Sophia returned with a firm grip the way a handshake is supposed to be. "I heard that you're a hair stylist. Zoe said she's going to you about doing her hair for the wedding. I guess, you know, she wanted to help you out. We're all so excited about the wedding, aren't *we* Avery? So many plans and activities! Just makes my little ole head spin."

Like in *The Exorcist*? Sophia shook that thought but almost giggled.

"So much fun lies ahead. I'm plannin' an a-mazing bachelorette party. Aren't you excited?" She didn't even look at Sophia.

"I . . . yes, I suppose," Avery said with a slight shrug.

When Avery failed to say more Ashley finally turned her attention to Sophia. "I was surprised to learn that you've opened that little salon." She gave her hair a little Cher-like flip. "I mean, I thought you were a short-order cook at that little bistro down by the riverside."

"I have many talents," Sophia said. She glanced over at Avery and was surprised that his gaze remained on her instead of Ashley. He gave her a reassuring smile. When Ashley cleared her throat, Sophia looked up at her. "I'm sorry—what were you saying?"

Ashley opened her mouth and then shut it. "Well, I will tell you ahead of time that I'm very particular about my hair." She put her hand to her chest. "You know that, don't you, Avery?"

Avery looked decidedly uncomfortable and remained silent.

"I'll keep that in mind," Sophia said. "I'm looking forward to meeting with Zoe." Sophia suddenly wished she had her mother's British accent so she could sound a little snooty, and then realized she was being super petty. Sophia was never petty. A little snarky? Yes. Petty? No. In fact, she hated pettiness and drama and always tried to steer away from it in the salon. But what she detested most was feeling jealous. Being jealous meant she was feeling insecure, and although she could be a bit quiet and sometimes shy and moody, she wasn't insecure and she didn't like the feeling.

Sophia took a sip of her water and told herself to cool her jets. There, her jets were cool.

But when Ashley put her hand on Avery's shoulder Sophia seriously wanted to smack it right off. Her jets heated up again.

"Well, it was good to see you, Avery." She squeezed Avery's shoulder and gave him a lingering look. Avery didn't say *same here* or *nice to see you too*. He just gave her a polite nod. Did being glad about that put her right back into the petty category? Sophia hoped not. But she was pretty sure that it did.

"And so lovely to meet you, Sophie."

"Sophia," Avery corrected in a clipped tone.

"Right. Oh, so sorry," Ashley said but didn't look sorry at all.

"It's okay." Sophia smiled and nodded but something of what she was feeling must have shown on her face because Avery reached down and took her hand. Was he feeling sympathy? Or was he suddenly putting on a show for Ashley? Or could he see the green-eyed monster sitting on Sophia's shoulder whispering snarky remarks in her ear?

"Well, I have a luncheon meeting with an important client so I have to run," Ashley said, but her megawatt smile had dimmed just a bit. "Hope to see y'all around," she said, but kept her gaze on Avery. Sophia was sure that Southern-plural thing was singular. Would it be wrong of Sophia to give Ashley a spiky purple Mohawk for her updo?

After Ashley gave Avery a little finger wave and finally turned away, he exhaled an audible breath and slid back into the booth.

"Are you okay?" Sophia asked.

"Wishing this water were a beer."

"Hey, you know what they say. It's five o'clock somewhere."

"Don't tempt me."

Oh, Sophia wanted to tempt him. She glanced down at her phone. "Yep, it's beer thirty."

Avery laughed and seemed to relax a little bit.

"I am *such* an enabler." Whether or not Avery still had feelings for Ashley didn't change the way Sophia felt about him and she didn't like seeing him upset. "But really. Are you okay? I mean it's awkward when your ex shows up and you're with another woman. Even if you're just pretending to be," she amended.

"Yeah, it was," he said. "You know that you have the ability to make a bad situation better?"

"As I said, I have many talents," she joked.

"I have no doubt, but that's not a talent, Sophia. It's called being a nice, caring person. You care."

Sophia swallowed hard but nodded. "I do."

Avery looked at her for a lingering moment, and then brought her hand up to his mouth and kissed it. Sophia felt the warmth of his lips all the way to her toes. "To answer your question, though, I'm just fine. In fact, better than I've been in a long time."

"Good." Sophia smiled back, telling herself not to read too much into the gesture. Maybe Ashley was watching and Avery was trying to send her a message. Sophia wanted to look over to see if that was the case but she kept her eyes on Avery and to her delight he kept his eyes on her.

But instead of glancing at Ashley, she asked, "So, are you going to share that calzone or not?"

11

Love Me Tender

"*I* WILL SHARE ONLY IF YOU FORK OVER SOME OF THAT salad that I've been drooling over," Avery answered with a grin. He was waiting for his feelings on seeing Ashley to hit him like a sucker punch to the gut the way it always did but, strangely, the feeling didn't happen this time.

"You've got a deal." Sophia busied herself sliding salad onto a small bread plate and losing a cherry tomato, which she then had to go stabbing after with her fork. She lost the battle and the tomato rolled off the table and onto the floor, stopping beneath a nearby table.

"Oops . . ."

"You've got another runaway."

"Can't take me anywhere," she said with a half grin and a shrug.

"On the contrary, I can't think of anyplace I wouldn't want to take you." *I want to take you to bed,* popped into his brain and refused to budge.

"Thank you, Avery." She sucked in her bottom lip while she drizzled a little bit of salad dressing on her half and then passed the little plastic cup his way.

Avery wanted to tell Sophia that he thought her curves were sexy and that she shouldn't worry so much about calories. But he knew from growing up with a sister that women tended to feel some sort of misplaced shame in eating anything fattening. And commenting about calories or weight always somehow got him in trouble. He remembered telling Ashley he thought she'd lost weight and she took it to mean that he thought she'd been fat. And Zoe was on a no-gluten diet, whatever the hell that meant, in an effort to lose weight for her wedding. Even his mother was fussing over fitting into her mother-of-the-bride dress. He wanted to tell them all to just chill the hell out. They were all beautiful.

Avery slid Sophia's half of the calzone onto an extra plate that Chad had provided. She took a bite of the salad, ignoring the calzone. "Aren't you going to eat it?" He pointed his fork at her portion.

"Oh, I . . . Yes," Sophia said and took a bite. "Mmm . . . really good. You had to go and tempt me."

"And this little temptation"—he held up a slice of cucumber—"is delicious." He stabbed an olive and popped it into his mouth. "Mmmm, to die for."

"Right, who needs cheese and pizza dough, anyway?" When Sophia laughed, Avery realized how much he loved the soft, throaty sound. Ah, damn, he wanted to kiss her. He'd wanted to for a long time now. But although he'd made her laugh he could see something stormy lurking in her eyes. She was trying hard, but her mood had shifted since Ashley's sudden appearance.

Avery felt guilty that he'd put Sophia in such an awkward situation. While he knew the day would come when his and Ashley's paths would cross, he'd preferred not to think about it and wished he'd been more prepared. He'd really wanted to introduce Sophia as his girlfriend, but since it wasn't true, he couldn't bring himself to say it to Ashley. Letting her come to her own conclusion was one thing, but a straight-up fabrication just didn't sit well with Avery.

When Ashley had cheated, he'd still been in love with her and he didn't know how to turn the love off or how to deal with her betrayal. Her tears, her pleading to give her another chance at their relationship got to him every time she'd asked, and in truth he'd tried, reached deep for forgiveness. And he'd supposed he *had* forgiven her, at least on some level, but he just didn't see how he could ever trust her again, and without trust what did they really have? "Aren't you glad that we shared?" Avery asked, wanting to switch up his train of thought.

"Well, I do believe your half is bigger," she said with the arch of her eyebrow.

Avery laughed, and was glad to see some of Sophia's humor return. He switched plates. "There, how's that?"

"No, I was just kidding!" She tried to switch the plate back and they ended up in a tug of war that had them both laughing.

When the laughter died down Sophia leaned back against the booth and smiled. In that moment Avery realized that seeing Ashley hadn't bothered him in the way that it used to because he loved being with Sophia. When he was with her everyone else sort of faded into the background.

Avery let the realization sink in for a moment just to make sure. He swallowed hard as he watched her lean forward to take a bite of her calzone. Yeah . . . he had no doubt.

He could fall in love for real with Sophia Gordon.

Truthfully, she'd captured his heart over the past few months when she served him breakfast with a sweet, shy smile nearly every morning at Walking on Sunshine Bistro. Her kind, gentle demeanor coupled with her wicked sense of humor chased away the darkness that had settled in his soul. In fact, she'd charmed the entire breakfast crowd, both young and old. Avery had witnessed her listening with concerned interest to customers bending her ear with their problems. She laughed at the corny jokes told by the old-timers from Whisper's Edge, the retirement community down by the river. And she'd often been the peacemaker if discussions about politics or sports became heated. Avery knew that the regular patrons had not only come to the restaurant for the melt-in-your-mouth biscuits and strong coffee, but for the company as well.

Sophia's smile was a really good way to start the day.

Avery watched her take another bite of the calzone and then dab at the corners of her pretty mouth with a napkin. But there was a slight edge of sadness to her too. Avery saw it there when she didn't think anyone was looking. He wanted to chase it away and keep that smile of hers in place.

"You've gone quiet on me again, Avery." She poked a tomato and tilted her head in question, tomato forgotten, while she looked at him with concern in her brown eyes. "You can talk to me, you know. About anything," she added and he knew she was referring to Ashley. Other than knowing that he didn't want to get back together with Ashley, he hadn't really discussed his relationship or why it had ended. "I will listen and what you tell me will go nowhere."

"I know that." He really wanted Sophia to know the real reason he broke off his engagement but of course he couldn't tell her. Why had he made that stupid promise? "Thank you, Sophia," Avery said, but hated the look of uncertainty in her eyes when he failed to elaborate.

She nodded. "Just remember that."

"I will." Avery had been about to tell Sophia that he wanted to give their relationship a try for real before Ashley made her unexpected appearance. And Ashley's behavior had been . . . odd. Not rude exactly, but coming close, and in truth, that wasn't like her at all. He supposed her seeing him with another woman hadn't sat well with her. The realization should have given him some satisfaction but it made him only feel somehow sad for her. She'd given up something good and strong for something sordid and fleeting.

"I'm serious," Sophia said after he'd gone quiet again. "Well, not always but I am right now. So . . . a penny for your thoughts? Wait, your thoughts are worth more than a penny. Let's try again. A dollar for your thoughts?"

"I don't know that my thoughts are worth all that much." Avery chuckled softly.

"Let me be the judge of that."

"Okay."

"Promise?"

"Is this where we do a pinkie swear?" Avery asked.

"Yes, I do believe it is." Sophia crooked her pinkie into his and laughed. "Now you are stuck with confiding in me or else."

"Or else what?"

"Not sure, but I think we'd better not chance it. Kinda like not stepping on a crack so you don't break your mother's back."

"I think you're right." Avery laughed. He remembered when he'd first met Sophia. He'd been in a really rotten mood and in dire need of strong coffee after tossing and turning all night long. He'd entered Walking on Sunshine Bistro with a scowl on his face and a chip on his shoulder.

And then Sophia Gordon smiled at him and he was powerless not to smile back.

The biscuit she'd served him was as hard as a damned rock but she was so frazzled that he'd slathered it with gravy that had sausage bits, which were like gravel. He'd crunched on it anyway. Her smile had been worth risking his teeth.

"You're still really quiet," Sophia said. "Look, if—"

Avery stopped the direction of the conversation by putting his hand over hers. "I was thinking about the

day I met you and ate the worst biscuits known to man."
He chuckled and looked up at the ceiling, before turning
his gaze back to hers.

"Oh, good gravy." Some of the worry left those
expressive brown eyes.

"Good gravy? You're learning some Southern lingo.
Pretty soon you'll be sayin' 'y'all.'"

"No, I meant my sausage gravy was good, wasn't it?"
Avery winced. "Well . . ."

"No, don't answer." Sophia rolled her eyes and
chuckled. "Oh, that first batch of biscuits was simply
horrible! You could have played golf with those suck-
ers." She shook her head. "I overworked the dough,"
she explained with a sort of shy smile. "And you were
such a gentleman for eating it. Rusty wasn't even interested in stealing any of those biscuits. I'm surprised
you didn't end up in the emergency room or break off
a tooth."

"As my granddaddy would say, I have a very strong
constitution."

Sophia laughed and Avery thought there wasn't a
sound more pleasant in the whole world. "Well, it's a
good thing! Giving indigestion to the good people of
Cricket Creek wasn't something I wanted to do. I'm
just glad that people came back and gave me another
chance."

"You were so cute and determined. Everybody was
pulling for you."

"And praying for Mattie to return."

Avery laughed.

"When I was asked to help out I agreed because I
knew I was a pretty darned good cook. I used to do my
homework while watching the cooks prepare meals
while my mother worked. I asked a million questions
and finally ended up being allowed to help out. Who
knew that a simple biscuit and the consistency of sausage gravy would be so difficult to perfect? I should
have done a trial run. Overconfidence is never a good

thing. But then again I came to Cricket Creek rather quickly when Mattie was put on bed rest."

"Well, practice makes perfect. You've got it down pat now."

"Let's just say I was determined. I hate to disappoint a customer."

"Another good quality of yours. You were so good-hearted to take a break from your career."

"Thank you, but in truth I needed a sabbatical from the salon in New York. I adore doing hair and makeup, but I was getting a bit burned-out, especially dealing with difficult clients who didn't always appreciate how hard I tried to please them. It happens in my industry."

"Understandable. Sometimes I get tired of fixing things."

Sophia raised her palms upward. "To be able to fix things is just awesome. I have absolutely no mechanical skills whatsoever. And then, for some reason, from time to time, I attempt to fix something, on my own. Fail . . . always a fail. Oh, but if I were ever able to finally fix something that was broken I'd brag about it for days and take pictures and show everybody."

Avery laughed. "I think I'll give you some handyman lessons. You'd look really cute in a tool belt."

"I might just have to take you up on that."

Avery smiled and said, "I can't imagine being away from my family for very long." He thought about how often his father was gone but at least he knew he was coming home. Sophia's family had been scattered all over.

"Yeah, I sure missed my family." She looked down at her plate and pushed her fork through the flaky calzone. "And of course now we have Lily!" She looked up with a bright smile. "That little girl changed all of our lives. She's just precious." When her eyes misted over Avery thought that Sophia would make such a sweet mother. His heart did a weird little thump at the thought. "And seeing Garret holding her and being so happy . . . Oh, it's just the best feeling." She cleared her throat. "I'm sorry for getting so emotional."

"There's no need to be sorry."

She smiled. "Thanks. I've been a bit more emotional of late and I really think it has a lot to do with little Lily. Her birth brought our family back together and made us grounded in a way that I've never felt before. The moment she wrapped her little finger around mine, I was a goner."

"Lily is a little beauty."

"Prettiest baby in the history of all babies."

"Except perhaps for her Aunt Sophia," Avery said. He watched Sophia wrap her tongue around the stretchy provolone cheese and felt a strong pull of desire. He'd certainly felt the connection before now, but he'd fought it thinking she would be moving back to New York. And now, he wanted to embrace the feeling . . . that, and he wanted to embrace Sophia. Kiss her and so much more. "Why, thank you, Avery."

"Just stating the truth."

"That's not what I'm thanking you for." She licked marinara sauce from her bottom lip making him swallow hard.

"What then?"

"I'm thanking you for looking at me like that."

"Like what?" Avery asked, his voice husky.

"Like you . . ." she began but then faltered and blushed a pretty shade of pink. "You know . . ."

"Like I want to kiss you?"

Pressing her lips together, she nodded.

Avery's heart pounded. The rest of the restaurant faded into the background. Ashley vanished from his mind like sunshine burning off the morning mist.

"Do you?" Her voice was whisper soft and her eyes echoed what he was feeling. "Want to kiss me?"

"Yes." Avery wanted Sophia with a sudden intensity that he hadn't felt in such a long-ass time. And he knew why. When he looked into those big brown eyes, he saw sincerity. *Trust*. For a while, he had been on a slippery slope that had kept him from fully getting back up on his feet. But when he was with Sophia, with her shy demeanor, crazy sense of humor, and compassion, it felt as if he'd finally landed on solid ground.

"You're way too far over there on that side of the table." He leaned closer, bumping against her knee. "I need to get closer to you."

"Perhaps we should get a doggie bag."

"Doggie bag? Who says that?"

Sophia laughed. "To-go box. My nan used to say that when we'd had leftovers from a restaurant. It just popped into my head. What can I say? I'm nervous."

"Nan?"

"Grandma. An English term, I think."

"Ah . . . so you're nervous?"

"In a good way."

"I get what you're saying. Me too." Avery motioned for Chad. "Can we have a doggie bag?"

"A what?" Chad asked.

Sophia's shoulders started to shake a little and she gave his knee a bump beneath the table.

Avery pointed to the food. "Leftovers for my dog."

"You feed your dog salad and calzone?" Chad looked a bit horrified. "Dude, that's not cool," he said with a serious expression. "That kind of diet will cause, like, really bad stuff. My dog got into my pizza box last weekend and . . . dude, you seriously don't want to know. The cheese—"

"Chad, I was just kidding."

"Oh," Chad seemed a little ticked, but then shrugged. "Whatever, dude."

"Ha! I can't believe you did that," Sophia said and started laughing.

"I want to do crazy things when I'm with you."

"Is that a promise?" she asked and her blush deepened.

"It is," Avery replied. "I like being with you, Sophia. No drama. Silly fun."

"About to get even more fun?" she asked and laughed while fanning her face.

"Yeah," he said as he tucked his debit card into the folder. "You know, you're just this quiet little thing and then you come out with those one-liners that just slay me."

"It's from being around my British mother. She has a dry and sometimes wacky sense of humor. Not everyone gets me. I'm glad you do." She grinned. "I have a line for that but I'll keep it to myself."

Avery laughed. When they were outside on the sidewalk it occurred to Avery that he hadn't given a thought to if Ashley was still in the pizza parlor or if she'd noticed him holding Sophia's hand.

What had begun for show was becoming very real.

"Oh, we forgot the doggie bag," Sophia said. "I'll go get it."

"No, have a seat on that bench over there. I'll run back in."

"Okay, thanks." She smiled and sat down.

Avery hurried back inside and made a beeline for the booth that they had been sitting in. Thankfully, the white plastic bag with the leftovers was sitting there and he picked it up. But as he turned to go he looked across the room and caught Ashley staring at him. She appeared stricken and tilted her head as if trying to figure out if she should approach him or continue with her meeting. She pressed her lips together as if trying to suppress emotion and lifted her chin as if to tell him that she hadn't given up just yet.

Avery turned around. He felt a little bit of sadness wash over him. He'd loved Ashley Montgomery for a very long time and it has been so damned hard to let that feeling go. But she no longer had that power over him. Sophia had filled the empty void with kindness

and laughter. Being with Sophia felt real and so . . .
right. He'd been fighting his feelings for her, *hiding* his
feelings for her, and now it was high time that he put
his broken engagement to rest for good and to move on
with his life. Today felt like closure; the end of the end.
Avery liked that feeling. Yes! He did an internal fist
pump.

Avery walked outside into the cool breeze and warm,
cheerful sunshine. Sophia. She sat on the bench looking
at the view of the river as if deep in thought. Avery
paused and watched her for a moment. The breeze ruf-
fled her hair and she tilted her face upward as if enjoying the warmth of the sunshine. What was going
through her mind? Avery wanted to know what she was
thinking. He wanted to know everything about her.

When he approached, Sophia gazed up at him and
smiled. Avery lifted the bag up higher. "Got it."

"Nice." She stood up. "The doggie bag retrieval was
a success."

"Yep," he said. "So, can I take you for a ride?"

She raised her eyebrows.

"Wait, that didn't come out right."

Sophia fell into step with him. "Why? I was about to
say yes."

Avery laughed. "You never fail to surprise me."

"Just keeping you on your toes. I know what it's like
being on my toes. Short-girl problems again."

Avery laughed again. "I don't see any problem with
you being short."

"Fun-sized?"

"Perfect-sized," Avery said, thinking he wanted to
have all kinds of fun with her. When they reached his
truck, which was parked outside of her salon, he stopped
and asked, "I know you're busy but would you like to go
for a ride along the river and maybe stop and have a
picnic with our leftovers? Maybe pick up some dessert
somewhere afterward?"

She glanced over at her shop. "I think I can manage an afternoon of playing hooky."

"Don't look so guilty. You're the boss, remember?"

She raised a fist in the air. "Yeah! And I'm gonna play hooky *like a boss*."

"Sweet. I'm on call but, as of yet, I don't have any repairs this afternoon," he said, but no sooner did that come out of his mouth that his leg vibrated. He reached into his pocket and fished out his phone. "Well, I spoke too soon. My uncle needs help repairing a deck."

"Oh." Sophia pointed at her cheek.

"What?"

"This is my crestfallen face." She stuck out her bottom lip.

Avery laughed. "Can I come in for just a minute?" He might not be able to spend the day with her but he sure as hell was going to get the kiss he'd been dreaming about.

"Sure." Sophia unlocked the door and he followed her inside.

Avery put the bag down and tugged her into his arms. Dipping his head, he kissed her. The touch of his mouth to hers sent a jolt of heat through his veins. He pulled her even closer, kissed her deeper, tangling his tongue with hers. She came up on tiptoe and wrapped her arms around his neck and he found the gesture both sweet and sexy, a heady combination that was simply Sophia.

Avery wanted to touch her, taste her, and be buried deep inside her. God, he wanted her naked in his arms. But he also felt tenderness for Sophia that went way beyond desire. When he ended the kiss, he tilted her chin up and tucked a lock of hair behind her ear. "You do need a step stool," he said and cupped her cute ass and lifted her up. "Or I could just do this."

"Avery!" She gave him a little squeal and wrapped her legs around him.

He kissed her again thinking that maybe he would just put off doing the repair job, but when his phone pinged he pulled back and groaned. Resting his forehead against hers he said, "Please tell me you'll see me tonight."

"I'll see you tonight. Come by my place around seven and I'll cook dinner."

"You don't have to cook for me."

"I know." She put her palms on his cheeks. "I want to cook for you. Anything special you want?"

"You. You're special."

"No, to eat, silly," she said and giggled.

"Surprise me." He let her slowly slide down his body. "Ah wow, it's going to be a really long day."

"Tell me about it." She arched an eyebrow. "We'll have to make up for it with a really long night," she said, and then slapped her hands to her cheeks. "Did I . . ."

"Say that out loud?"

She gave him a fake wince and burst out laughing.

Avery hugged her close. "Don't worry. You were reading my mind this time," Avery said in Sophia's ear, and then gave her one last lingering kiss. "I'll call you later," he said and turned away before he was unable to leave.

But when the cool outdoor air hit him in the face, Avery felt a bit of doubt wiggle into his brain. He blew out a breath and hopped up into the driver's seat. Avery liked his life to be uncomplicated. And the very last thing he wanted to do was to put Sophia in the line of fire.

Dragging her into this wedding mess might have been unfair. No, it was definitely unfair.

Now he had to decide what he was going to do about it.

12

Rock the Boat

EASTON HAMMERED A NAIL INTO THE WOODEN DECK he and Avery were repairing. Pausing, he braced on one knee and looked over at his nephew. "I'm takin' Carrie Ann on a vacation."

"What?" Avery looked up and grinned at him. "Really? That's awesome, Uncle Easton."

"Yep. Pete Sully hooked me up with a travel agent."

"Where to?"

"I dunno yet. Bahamas, maybe? Somewhere in the Caribbean? We gotta get passports first so I'm thinking 'bout going sometime in the summer."

"So, did you ask her already?" Avery reached for a bottle of water and took a long guzzle. The late-afternoon sunshine warmed the day up nicely.

"Not yet. I hope she will agree to go. She works hard and deserves a little vacation." Easton pictured them sitting on the deck sipping on some umbrella drink and smiled.

"And you're just the guy for the job?" Avery leaned over and gave him a nudge with his elbow.

"Yeah, it's a tough job but somebody's gotta do it. Might as well be me."

"Somebody? From the way things have been shaping up, I think you want to be the only man in Carrie Ann's life."

"Yeah . . ." Easton picked up his nail gun and examined it before looking back at Avery. "You're right."

"I mean, the only trips you've been on involved hunting, fishing, golfing, or boating. A cruise? Pretty out of character, wouldn't ya say?"

"It's about time I got out of my rut."

"Uncle Easton, you're one of the most active people I know. I'd hardly say that you're in a rut."

"Well, now." Easton tilted his head to the side. "You're right in a way. I do a lot of stuff but it's the same old stuff week in and week out. It's time for me to change things up and get excited about goin' places and doin' new things. I suddenly want to go on cruises. I've looked into traveling to Hawaii." He shook his head. "Drive up the coast of California. Hell, maybe even Europe. Who knows?"

"I think that your growing feelings for Carrie Ann has a lot to do with your change of attitude, Uncle Easton. I'm really glad for both of you. Having someone to do stuff with makes all the difference in the world. And you're trying to do activities she would enjoy. That says a lot too. It's not just things you want to do but experiences you want to share with her. Walking hand in hand down the streets of Paris or taking a cruise becomes much more important and enjoyable if you're doing it with someone you love."

"I'm finally realizing that, Avery. I avoided a serious relationship based on my parents' rocky marriage. Dumbass reason."

"We're all a product of our past. Don't beat yourself up."

"Kinda hard not to sometimes. But you're right.

What good does it do to worry about the past? Can't change a damned thing."

"Well, you've dated. Maybe the right person just didn't come along until now."

"You're right again, well sort of, anyway. I've had my share of lady friends. I mean I'm only human. But although Carrie Ann and I have been friends for a very long time, we avoided any kind of romance. I think I knew all along that she could be, as they say, *the one* and that's what scared me out of gettin' closer to her. Now look at all of the years I've lost not having her in my arms. I was a damned fool."

"You're hardly ancient." Avery gave Easton's bent knee a shove. "You've got a lot of years left to live. You're in great shape."

"Excellent way of lookin' at it." Easton grinned. "You're a smart man, Avery." He felt a little bit of emotion well up in his throat. "And a good man. Level head on your shoulders," he said gruffly.

"You've been a good role model, Uncle Easton. And you made me view my relationship with my dad in a different light. I wish I'd known sooner that he wanted to be around. I should have guessed but I was too busy being a teenager, gettin' pissed when he wasn't there for a baseball game. In truth, you were right. He was out busting his ass to put food on the table. I should have been more grateful and less critical."

"A wise man just told me that there's a lot of life left to live. Tommy's semiretired now. Like I said, give him a holler and take your old man fishing or somethin'."

"You're right." Avery nodded. "I'll do that."

"Good."

"Should we get back to work?"

"Ya know what?" Easton surveyed the deck. "I think we can button it up and finish tomorrow. I'd estimated three days for the job so we're good. Went pretty fast after you got here. I was lucky you were free." He stood up and started packing up his tools. "So whatcha doin' tonight?"

"Hanging out with Sophia at her place."

"Hanging out, huh? Is that what they call it these days?"

"Uncle Easton . . ."

"Just bustin' your chops."

"She's fixing me dinner."

"Ya don't say." Easton nodded slowly. "Not going out on the town for show and tell? Well now."

Avery snapped his toolbox shut and leaned against the railing. "This thing between us is getting kinda real."

"Kinda?"

Avery looked down at his boots, and then rocked back on his heels. "No, it *is* real. At least for me, anyway."

"Has been for a while, I'd say. You're another one who was in denial."

"Yeah, but get this. When we were at River Row Pizza grabbin' some lunch earlier today Ashley walked in."

"Holy moly." Easton stopped gathering up nails and raised his eyebrows at Avery. "How'd that go?"

"Awkward."

"I can only imagine. When were you gonna drop this little bombshell on me?"

"I dunno. Over a beer, maybe? I've got a few things I want to tell you about it. Wanna grab a cold one at Sully's since we're cuttin' out early?"

"Are you kiddin'? I've got to hear all about this. I'll meet you there in a few minutes."

"Sounds good." Avery nodded and picked up his toolbox.

"I'm gonna give Carrie Ann a quick call and then meet you there. Order me whatever's on tap from Broomstick Brewery, the darker the better."

"Will do."

After Avery left, Easton packed up his truck, but then paused to call Carrie Ann. He wasn't much into texting unless he had to. He couldn't quite understand why people typed a bunch of stuff when it was so much easier to just dial a number and talk. He leaned against the side of his panel truck and scrolled down to her number. Just seeing Carrie Ann's name made him smile.

"Hey, you," Carrie Ann said, making Easton wonder how just hearing her voice could get him aroused. "What's up, cutie pie?"

Me, he thought with a shake of his head. "God, I love the sound of your voice."

"So you called just to hear me chatter in your ear?" She chuckled. "You know how to flatter a girl."

"That's not all I know how to do."

"Well, now, did you call to get me all hot and bothered?"

"Not exactly, but am I?"

"Uh . . . yeah," she said, drawing out the words.

Easton looked up at the clear blue sky dotted with puffy white clouds and smiled. "Well, good."

"So get your sweet cheeks on over here. Or do you want me at that amazing cabin of yours?"

"Babe, I want you anywhere I can get you."

"Translating to . . . anywhere not in public."

"You are getting me all fired up, girl."

Carrie Ann laughed and he could see her with her head tilted back and shoulders shaking. "So, what time and where? I just finished up with my last client."

"Well, I'm going to stop over at Sully's and have a beer with Avery. Apparently Ashley showed up at River Row Pizza while Avery was having lunch with Sophia."

"Oh boy . . ."

"Yeah, I know I'm bein' a busybody but I want to know what went down. Avery seemed . . . I don't know, not upset but needing to tell me something."

"You're not being a busybody. He's lucky to have you to talk to, Easton."

"Thank you." Easton smiled at how easy it was to

talk to Carrie Ann about personal things. In fact, she was the first person he wanted to call when he needed to talk or had some news. "That boy has been good for me too. Hard for me to believe sometimes that Avery and Zoe are all grown up. And now Zoe's gettin' married." He shook his head. "Where's the time gone?"

"Oh, I know. I remember when they were both knee-high to a grasshopper." She chuckled. "First time I cut Avery's hair you would have thought I was trying to cut his ears off or something. Cried his fool head off. His nose running like a faucet."

Easton laughed, picturing the sight.

"I sure hated to cut all of that beautiful curly hair of his but he was starting to look like a girl. When I told him that people were going to think he was Zoe's big sister he finally settled down."

"I can just see him doin' that. But anyway, sugar, there's a key to my cabin tucked beneath a fat rock to the left of the front porch. I've got a couple of thick rib-eye steaks to toss on the grill later. Why don't you head on up there and take a nice soak in the hot tub and I'll meet you there after I talk with Avery?"

"Sounds like a nice relaxing night."

"We'll eat dinner by the fireplace, listen to some music . . . and take it from there."

"Mmmm, this is getting better all the time. I'll toss a salad and bring some russet potatoes. Do you need a bottle of Merlot to go with the steaks?"

"Gotcha covered."

"Perfect." Easton's heart pounded a little bit at what he was about to say. He swallowed and said, "Oh, and, Carrie Ann?" he asked, hoping his voice sounded somewhat normal.

"Yes, sweet pea?"

"Keep the key. I want you to have it and bring any clothes you want to leave at my place too. You know, in case you want to spend weekends there . . . or nights, for that matter."

"Oh . . ." she said, making Easton wonder if that was a good reaction or not.

Feeling a bit nervous at her silence he continued. "I know a lot of folks around here don't bother to lock up but some teenagers had a party at my place while I was out of town. Didn't do much damage other than depleting my liquor supply but still . . . Ever since then I've locked up the cabin."

"Oh, makes perfect sense."

"Locking the cabin or you having a key?" Easton squeezed the phone tighter waiting for her answer. He knew that for a lot of people this was expected after dating for a few weeks and because they'd known each other for so long this should be a natural and quicker progression. But he'd never given a woman a key to his place. Ever. And he sure as hell didn't ever tell anyone he dated to bring clothes to his place to put in the closet with an open invitation to stay over. "You know if you want to. I just think it would be convenient for you," he added, and then shook his head knowing he was saying too much.

"Yes, it would be convenient."

Oh damn, well, he really sucked at this. "Stupid way to word it." He inhaled a deep breath and continued thinking he might as well go for broke. "Carrie Ann, what I'm trying to say is that I want you to have things at my place so you can stay there whenever you want to and for as long as you want to. It will make me smile to see your clothes there and have your makeup and all of that stuff you put in your hair in the bathroom. Have the lingering smell of your perfume in my home. I want you to have a key so you can come and go as you please. With the emphasis on *come* . . . and not the *go*."

"I . . ." she began, but then paused.

"Hey," Easton said gently. "No pressure. It's just a key, baby." Even though they both knew it was much more than that. It was no secret that Carrie Ann shied away from commitment, just as he did, but he wanted to put the offer out there. He knew he needed to take baby steps with her. Easton understood. This scared the daylights out of him too, but living without her scared him even more. "We'll talk about it later but be sure to let yourself in if you get there before I do."

"Okay, I'll see you soon," Carrie Ann said, but the lightness in her voice sounded a bit forced. And she'd left off an endearment or funny remark.

"All right, bye for now, sugar," Easton said and tapped the red END CALL button with a bit of a heavy heart. He stood there for a moment, and then pushed away from the truck.

"Should have left well enough alone," Easton muttered as he opened the door and hopped up into the driver's seat. Blowing out a frustrated sigh, he turned the key in the ignition. This is the damned reason he'd stayed the hell away from commitment, he thought as he put the truck in reverse.

In truth, like Avery mentioned, Easton had always been a social guy, but when it came to his cabin he remained fairly private, inviting only close friends and family into his home. Avery's buddies used to stay the weekend now and then but, for the most part, his home was off-limits. To offer Carrie Ann a key and closet space had been a big deal for him even though he'd told her there wasn't any pressure . . . and there wasn't.

And yet, all of the sudden, he felt a big blast of hurt hit him in the face like an arctic wind. Common sense said that he had no right to be angry with Carrie Ann. She'd done nothing wrong. They'd both been hesitant for their own reasons.

Having grown up around constant conflict, Easton tried his best to remain levelheaded and not to lose his cool even in the worst of situations. And now here he was feeling angry and hurt and for no good reason. Being in love and in a relationship did that to a person . . . Made them unreasonable in reasonable situations, which was precisely what he was doing.

So, if Carrie Ann didn't want a key or didn't want to stay over at his place more often, who gave a rat's tail?

He sure as hell did, was the immediate answer but he tried to ignore it.

Easton drove over to Sully's telling himself that he was going to pull back from being so damned serious. He and Carrie Ann enjoyed each other's company so why mess up a good thing by handing out keys and thinking about a future? And who needed to go on a cruise anyway? He'd probably get seasick. No, he needed to go on his regular golf trip with the guys this spring and go on his usual fishing excursion in the fall. He'd never felt this kind of misplaced anger with Carrie Ann when they'd just been friends. "Shoulda left it that way."

Easton pulled into Sully's and parked next to Avery's truck. He firmly told himself not to bring any of this up with his nephew who was having enough problems of his own to contend with and didn't need to hear about his uncle's silly drama.

Because it was early, Sully's was fairly empty with just a few of the early regulars sitting around the main bar nursing drinks and talking about random things. Knowing they needed some privacy, Avery was sitting at a high-top table far enough from the bar to keep their conversation to themselves. Easton sat down on the stool, gave Avery a nod, and then took a big drink of the stout that his nephew had waiting for him.

"Uncle Easton, what's wrong?"

"Nothin', just thirsty."

"Right. You look like you just hooked an eight-pound bass that got away. You wanna talk about it?"

"Naw." Easton shook his head. "We're here to talk about when Ashley showed up at your lunch with Sophia." He popped a peanut from the snack mix in his mouth without much interest.

"That can wait," Avery insisted. "Dinner with Sophia won't be until late, anyway. She just sent me a text a few minutes ago that said she has a meeting with a potential client in a little while."

"That salon of theirs is coming along," Easton said, trying to head in a positive direction.

"Sure is. Weddings are big business these days. Zoe and Mom are going crazy with all of the plans. Who the hell knew you had to have a big photo shoot so you can send out postcards to tell everyone to save the date? Like we're all gonna be so busy here in Cricket Creek on the day they get married that if we don't put it in our planner months in advance, we'll forget." Avery shook his head. "Most everybody we know already knows the date."

Easton took another swig of his strong ale, hoping to mellow out a bit more. "True enough."

"Of course, I had a taste of wedding drama with Ashley," he said, but instead of the pain Easton usually saw on Avery's face all he mustered was an indifferent shrug. "All I cared about was where we were going on our honeymoon."

"I think most guys still feel that way. But as you know I've never given gettin' married any thought," he said, but then out of nowhere an image of Carrie Ann in a wedding dress popped into his brain. He shook his head thinking his emotions were all over the damned map.

"So, anyway, I've got plenty of time. Shoot."

Easton rolled his shoulders, reminding himself that he didn't want to get into this discussion. He sure as hell liked talking about other people's problems more than his own. Getting serious caused problems. He should have known better.

"You know what you tell me goes nowhere," Avery urged, looking a little bit hurt that Easton wasn't opening up to him.

"Okay, well . . ." He inhaled a deep breath and said in a rush, "I offered a key to my cabin to Carrie Ann."

"Oh wow, that's huge for you. Was she happy about it?"

"Well, no, she didn't act too enthused about it at all."

"Oh man . . . Uncle Easton, I'm sorry. Maybe you just took her by surprise."

"Maybe." Easton shrugged. "I know it's not right, but now I'm kinda mad at her. And I know I'm not bein' fair with my reaction and that makes me pissed off at myself. Almost makes me want to just stay here and get my drink on. I don't like my boat to be rocked."

"But it's gonna be rocked now and then, Uncle Easton. That's part of bein' in a serious relationship. Part of bein' in love."

"Who said anything about bein' in love?"

"You know you're in love with her. You just haven't admitted how you feel to yourself."

Easton remained silent and searched around for a sesame stick in the snack bowl. "Think so?" He already knew so but admitting it to someone else was scary.

"Well, yeah, otherwise you wouldn't be so damned upset about the key thing. But I guess denial is easier to deal with."

"Sure doesn't seem that way." Easton scrubbed a hand down his face suddenly feeling tired. He took a swig of his ale. "Nope, I've decided that I'm gonna back way off. Stop seeing her so much and get back to things being easy instead of complicated."

"Is that what you really want?"

"Am I bein' charged for this session?" he asked, tapping his fingers on the table.

"This first one is free." Avery chuckled. "But you're dodging the question. Think about it while I go get another beer. You want one?"

"No, these are pretty strong. I'd better nurse this one. Gotta drive home. You should too."

"I can walk to Sophia's from here if need be or she can swing by and pick me up. You know me better than that."

"I know, I'm just testy as all get-out." Easton nodded. "All right, go getcha one. I'll be sittin' here brooding in my beer."

"Okay, I'll be right back."

Easton looked around at some of the guys coming in after work. Pool games and darts started up. The jukebox came to life. Pinball machines pinged and blinked. Easton used to stop in Sully's a couple of times a week and soon his softball league would start having practice. He played basketball in a men's league down at the local YMCA. When the weather warmed up, he'd golf or maybe bass fish on the weekends, depending upon his mood. He was a regular diner at most of the local restaurants and made it a point to go to Wine and Diner on nights when Carrie Ann ate there, usually shooting the breeze and then popping on over to Sully's to listen to music or have a beer or two. They shared breakfast at Walking on Sunshine Bistro, lingering over coffee. He loved her company, there was no doubt. She always had him laughing in no time flat. And the sex was, well, phenomenal.

But still, he was used to coming and going as he damned well pleased. And so was she. Maybe they were both too set in their ways to make this serious stuff work. The thought made him frown.

Avery returned to the table and sat down with a bowl of freshly popped popcorn. He swung his long legs over the stool and sat down. "Okay, now where were we?"

"We were about to talk about your lunch with Sophia when Ashley showed up."

"Uncle Easton . . ." Avery shook his head and scooped up a handful of popcorn. "Come on, now." He popped a few kernels into his mouth.

Easton blew out a sigh. "All right, I was thinking that maybe I'm moving too fast and don't want to give up my freedom."

"Right and that's why you're planning a vacation

and handing out keys. She hurt your feelings. Like I said, it's gonna happen now and then."

"I know I'm being unreasonable and that's why I shied away from serious relationships to begin with. Avery, what if we argue? Shout at each other? I'll be done. Can't take one minute of that crap."

Avery shoved his fingers through his hair and eyed him for a moment. "All I'm seein' is you arguing with yourself."

"What do you mean?"

"Maybe you should just be honest with Carrie Ann and tell her that you love her."

Easton felt the bottom drop out of his stomach. Right, then she'd really flip out.

"Have you ever told a woman you loved her, before?"

"Nope." Easton took a swing of his ale wishing he had another one under his belt. A shot of tequila was sounding pretty good. "Don't know that I've ever been in love," he said, but realized that wasn't true. He'd loved Carrie Ann for a long time. Even though they'd not so much as even held hands up until recently, he'd still loved her.

"Maybe she needed to hear those three little words before you offered a key to your cabin to her."

"Oh . . . shit." He hadn't thought of it that way.

"Exactly."

Easton leaned against the back of the stool. "I guess I messed up." But the thing with his mother and father is that they yelled and screamed at each other, and then would make up and say *I love you*, get all sweetie pie with each other until the next big fight or sometimes even at the end of a big blowout. Which is why Easton never put much stock in those three little words and never used them. How could you scream and yell and call it love?

Avery leaned forward. "Do you love Carrie Ann?"

"Yeah. I do." There was no use in denying it to Avery.

"Then maybe you should let her know that little bitty detail."

Easton's heart thudded at the thought. He knew they would eventually have disagreements, but hopefully not fights. He would never raise his voice to Carrie Ann. He was pretty sure she wouldn't yell at him. And dammit, she deserved to be told that he loved her. "You're right, kiddo."

"About what part of it?"

"Everything. All of it. Carrie Ann needs to know how I feel about her. No more putting the cart before the horse."

"Sweet. I think that's a really good plan of action."

Yeah, unless she doesn't say it back. "Now, let's hear about you. That's why we came here in the first place. So, did seeing Ashley get to you?"

Avery nodded slowly. "Yeah it did, but not in the way that you might think. She was sort of rude to Sophia."

"Jealous, I suspect."

"But Ashley was never like that before. Took me by surprise."

Easton shifted in his seat not knowing if he should speak his mind.

"What?"

"Well . . . I always found her to be a little self-centered, Avery. I couldn't say it then, but I can be honest now."

"Really? Why didn't I see it?"

"When you love somebody you can overlook their faults or try to explain them away. You're just so good-natured that you didn't always pick up on it. I guess like the old saying says, 'love is blind.'"

Avery raised his eyebrows. "Wow, I never really thought about that."

"I think Zoe is the same way. She's so easygoing that she lets Ashley run the show most of the time.

Why do you think Zoe is trying so hard to get you and Ashley back together?"

"Mostly because Ashley wants it?"

Easton pointed his index finger at Avery. "Bingo, my boy. So go on with your story."

"Well, for the longest time, seeing Ashley would make me feel, I don't know . . . anxious, sad, sometimes angry or hurt. But this afternoon I didn't really feel, well, *anything* other than upset that she was rude to Sophia. As a matter of fact, I kind of forgot that she was even in the restaurant after she left us."

"A breakthrough if I ever heard one. And I'm guessing it's because you only have eyes for sweet little Sophia."

Avery nodded. "I'm fallin' for her, for sure."

"Why do I hear a big *but* in that statement?"

"Well, because I loved Ashley, Uncle Easton. I mean I trusted . . ." he began but clamped his mouth shut.

Easton leaned forward and said in a low voice, "And that's why you couldn't believe that she could cheat on you."

"How did you know?"

"I didn't."

"Well, I walked right into that one. That wasn't really fair of you to do."

"No, what isn't fair is that you're taking the heat for something she did and now has the nerve to try to get you back. And if Zoe knew . . ."

"Aw man, it would just devastate Zoe and mess up her wedding plans. You see where I'm coming from? It's one of those no-win situations."

"I do." And it really pissed him off. He took a swig of his beer and thumped it down.

"Please don't say anything to anyone. I promised Ashley that I wouldn't tell."

"You know I won't. I pretty much had it figured out

anyway." He popped a peanut into his mouth, thinking how horrible that had to be for Avery. "Can I ask you somethin'?"

"Sure."

"Did you ever really feel about Ashley the way you feel about Sophia?"

Avery looked down at the table and frowned. After a few moments he looked over at Easton. "No, there's just a gentle sweetness about Sophia that touches me in a way I've never felt before. I'm at ease with her and the girl can make me laugh like no other. And seeing Sophia and Ashley together at River Row Pizza made it even clearer to me."

Easton thought about how Carrie Ann made him laugh. "It's the best medicine and that's for damn sure. So what are you gonna do?"

"Once this wedding is behind me I need to let her know how I really feel."

"I'm gonna toss your advice right back in your lap. Why wait?"

"As usual, you've got a good point," Avery replied, but Easton could see some lingering apprehension in his nephew's eyes. Ashley had done quite a number on him. He guessed the old "once bitten, twice shy" was coming into play. At last, Avery said, "I guess you're right."

"I was wrong once and then it turned out I was right."

Avery laughed. "So you *were* wrong once."

Easton laughed along with him. He was so glad that Sophia had decided to stay in Cricket Creek. She and Avery made the cutest couple. Yes, she just might be the girl who will mend Avery's broken heart.

13

We've Only Just Begun

CARRIE ANN LOOKED DOWN AT THE SILVER KEY IN THE palm of her hand and swallowed hard. She'd been standing there on the front porch of Easton's cabin for about five minutes but had felt odd about letting herself inside. Maybe she'd just stand there until Easton arrived and pretend she just got there? Then again, the breeze up on the ridge was getting stiffer and she sure could use a glass of wine. But did she help herself and open a bottle or wait for Easton? Did she start puttering around in his state-of-the-art kitchen and try to learn how to use some of his newfangled gadgets?

What if she broke something?

Carrie Ann stared at the key, wondering if accepting his gesture was such a good idea after all. Were they moving too fast? After squeezing her fingers over the cold metal, she closed her eyes. This was stupid. By all rights, she should be over the moon that Easton had offered her the key with an open invitation to come and go. And having a selection of clothing and toiletries at his cabin would be so much less stressful than lugging her things over here each time she came for a visit. Getting dressed in the same outfit the following morning had a slight walk-of-shame feel to it.

But then would Easton soon go a step further and ask her to move in with him? Okay, she adored the cabin and wanted them to spend more time together during the week. But her house up in town was the only home she'd ever lived in. She could walk to A Cut Above, Grammar's Bakery, Wine and Diner, the park, or anywhere else she wanted to go. She just couldn't see herself ever moving, or heaven forbid, selling her home to someone else. That house held memories of her father. She could never let it go.

Could she?

Carrie Ann's heart thumped around in her chest at the thought. But then again, what would it be like to wake up every morning in Easton's strong arms? Drink coffee out on the back deck? Sleep in on the weekends or stay up late making love? Hot damn, the man knew his way around a woman's body . . . her body. And who knew that she could be so uninhibited after so many years of being celibate? And at her age? In truth, she never knew a man's touch could feel so good.

The very thought of making love to Easton made Carrie Ann feel warm despite the cool breeze blowing her carefully arranged hair across her face. She really needed to go inside and put the potatoes in the oven and the salad in the fridge. And she needed to pee.

And yet she stood there wondering if she had the nerve to go to her car and get the extra clothes and makeup she'd brought to leave in the closet and bathroom.

What if Easton someday asked her to . . . *to marry him*?

Could she give up her home? Change her name? Could she give up her independence and not have a place of her own to go to if she wanted to escape? Carrie Ann knew that Easton wouldn't give up the cabin and his magnificent view to live in her little brick house in town.

Dear God, should she toss the key into the woods and run like a bat out of hell? Well, putting it back under the mat would be more sensible, but she was starting to have a bit of a panic attack. Maybe she should run into the woods too!

And run where? Back to her empty home? Was she clinging to something that could be healthier to give up? Carrie Ann closed her eyes and tried to slow her breathing down. Losing the father she'd love so dearly was the deepest pain she'd ever experienced and she never wanted to feel that kind of despair again. "But running away in fear isn't what Dad would want for me," she whispered. Opening her eyes, she stood up taller, felt inner strength stiffen her spine. "I will not cave in!"

With a little growl of frustration at her silly self, she hurried over to her car and took the tote out of the trunk and put it on the porch next to the food. Before she could start another series of worries and doubt, she slid the key into the lock and opened the front door.

Flipping on the recessed lights, Carrie Ann stopped and inhaled a deep breath. The cabin smelled of pine and wood with a hint of vanilla and cinnamon. She took determined steps into the kitchen and put the covered dish of salad into the fridge and began to preheat the oven for the giant potatoes. With equally determined steps, she went back out to the porch and hefted the tote bag over her shoulder with her extra stuff. With her heart pounding she lugged her things into the master bedroom and flicked on the light in the huge walk-in closet.

And there it was . . . a big space created on the left for her to hang her clothing. The sight was so touching that it brought a lump to her throat. With her hand to her chest, she stood there for a moment and looked at the metal rod ready for her things.

And when she hung her feminine attire next to his masculine clothing she took a step back and managed to smile. "There, that wasn't so hard, now was it?" She'd brought a few bras and panties along with a brand-new black lace teddy that she planned to wear sometime soon.

As promised, he'd cleared out a drawer in his dresser and she put her satin and lacy lingerie there. The massive bathroom had lots of extra space for her toiletries . . . and oh, it smelled of his soap and after-shave. Easton's spicy masculine scent caused a tingle of anticipation. She looked over at the big open shower stall and recalled when they'd soaped each other up and made passionate love against the wet wall while being pelted with warm water.

"My, my, my," Carrie Ann said with a long drawn-out sigh. If they lived together would they grow tired of each other or would the magic wane after a while? She glanced at her flushed face in the big mirror and decided that she would never say no to making sweet love to sexy as all get-out Easton Fisher. "Well, would you just look at my hair?" she mumbled, and then frowned. "Mercy . . ."

"I think your hair looks just-out-of-bed sexy."

Carrie Ann yelped and looked in the mirror at Easton. "You scared the living daylights out of me!"

Easton leaned one shoulder against the doorframe and laughed. "I know. It was damned funny."

"You didn't have to sneak up on me. I am in the bathroom, you know."

"The door was open. And I called your name but didn't get a response so I came lookin' for ya."

Carrie Ann tried to glare but ended up laughing instead. "My mind might have been elsewhere."

"Like where?" When Easton crossed his arms she had to admire the sexy bulge in his biceps.

With a sideways nod toward the shower stall she said, "Remembering what we did there."

"We can re-create that memory later if you like."

"I'm sure I would like to," she replied, and was glad that he didn't mention the key or her clothes just yet. She wanted to keep things light and playful and not think about the future right now. "I need to put those potatoes in the oven to bake."

"And you need a glass of wine. I bought your favorite and a bottle of white if you're in the mood."

"Oh, I'm in the mood all right."

Easton chuckled. "Good. So am I. All I have to do is take one look at you." He shook his head. "No, I take that back. All I have to do is think of you, Carrie Ann."

"You're such a charmer."

"I'm being completely honest."

Carrie Ann felt a warm glow of happiness that he was learning her favorite things and thought of her throughout the day. He popped in the salon with fresh flowers at least once a week or brought her lunch if he was working in town and she was too busy to leave the salon. "Thank you."

"My pleasure."

"And what do you need, Easton?" When she arched an eyebrow he gave her a slow smile.

"I think you know the answer to that question."

"Say it."

"You." A moment later he had her pressed up against the wall giving her a kiss so hot that she wouldn't be surprised if the mirror steamed up. Big strong hands, callused from hard work, slid beneath her blouse and stroked her back. She felt her nipples tighten in response to his kiss, his touch, and she pressed closer wanting to feel the hardness of his arousal pressing against her mound. She loved how he tasted and the stroke of his tongue against her sent a jolt of desire so potent that she moaned.

Easton pulled his mouth from hers and said in her ear, "I think dinner can wait."

"I think you're right," she said, and caressed the steely hardness straining against his jeans. She found the buckle of his belt and laughed when all she could do was fumble with it.

"Need some help?"

She chuckled low in her throat. "I need you naked."

"We both seem to be needy tonight."

"I've thought about you all day. Nearly nicked the ear of one of my customers when my mind wandered to doing this . . ."

"Oh wow." Easton laughed. "Are you telling the truth?"

"I am. You're going to have to stop by the salon from time to time so I can get a little nooner now and then."

"Or we can make love in the morning before you go to work," he said.

Carrie Ann nodded but felt a little jolt of alarm and she stiffened. He must have felt it because he pulled back and cupped her chin in his hand.

"Carrie Ann, I . . ." he began, and for a heart-pounding moment she thought he was going to tell her that he loved her. "I think we need to get dinner going and get open the wine. The steaks need to come to room temperature." He gave her a light kiss on the lips and took her hand, tugging her forward. "I'll turn on the fireplace and we can relax and listen to some music while the potatoes bake."

"Sounds like a plan," she said, and was surprised by the pang of disappointment that gripped her heart. Maybe he wasn't going to say it, she reasoned. And if he had . . . would she have said it back?

"Maybe a soak in the hot tub after dinner and then back here to finish what we started?" He tilted his head back toward the bedroom.

"I do believe that you just described the perfect night." Carrie Ann smiled at Easton. She suddenly wanted to tell him how she felt. Why wait for him to say it? "Easton, I . . ." Her heart hammered and she felt a little light-headed.

"Are you okay, darlin'?" He stopped walking and gave her a look of concern.

The words were there.

In her brain. On her tongue. From her heart.

"I love . . . being with you." Her smile trembled.

Easton dragged her against him. "Carrie Ann, I love being with you too. I was serious. When I'm not with you, I'm thinkin' about when I will see you again. You're a dear friend and an amazing lover. Being with you is my favorite part of the day." He kissed the tip of her nose. "And my nights too. When you're not with me I feel as if something is missing."

"Oh, Easton, I feel the same way." *I love you. Just say it!* She inhaled a breath but the words stuck in her throat.

"Good because there's something I've wanted to ask you."

Her heart hammered but she could only nod.

"Why don't you go have a seat on the couch? I'll go get the wine and we'll sit by the fire. Then we can talk."

"Okay," she managed to say and walked over to the butter-soft leather couch. She sat down and stared at the flames of the gorgeous gas fireplace. Absently, she thought that the logs looked so real that if Easton hadn't told her she would not have realized that the stack of wood was actually a fake. The embers glowed and the whole thing came to life with a remote. Easton also had a remote for the overhead fan, television, and music. Carrie Ann shook her head and looked up when Easton approached.

"What are you shaking your pretty head about?"

"Wondering how you keep all of your remotes straight. I have trouble enough with one and even now it takes me forever to find the MUTE button." She took a sip of the wine, knowing she was rambling, but she was so nervous wondering what he was going to ask her. To move in permanently? "I remember when we had three television channels and had to walk over the ugly orange shag rug to turn the dial on the TV."

"And everything went off the air at midnight." Easton chuckled as he sat down. "Funny thing is that when we had those three channels there always seemed to be something on that I wanted to watch. Now I've got hundreds of channels, most of which I don't find one bit interesting."

"I hear ya on that one." What was he going to ask her?

"But I've always loved tools and gadgets."

"Did you always have a knack for fixing stuff?"

"Yeah." Easton took a sip of his wine. "It came in helpful, because I also had a knack for breaking things."

Carrie Ann couldn't stand it any longer. With a thudding heart she put her wineglass on the coffee table and shifted to look at Easton. "Weren't you going to ask me something?"

"Yes." Easton cleared his throat. "Carrie Ann . . . I'd like to take you on a nice vacation this coming summer."

"Vacation?" His offer took her by surprise.

"You know, that thing where people pack a suitcase and go someplace fun for a week or two? Take a break from work?"

"I know what a vacation is."

"Really? When was the last time you took one?"

"I went to visit my mother in Naples a few months ago."

"That was a *visit*, Carrie Ann. I want to take you someplace exotic and . . . fun. We can do whatever you want to do. A cruise? An all-inclusive resort? Hawaii? Europe?"

"Out of the country?" Her eyes widened.

"We will need passports, but yes, if that's what you want. Anywhere your little ole heart desires. I've been doing some research with Pete Sully's travel agent."

"You have?"

"Yes. You work your tail off. I want to take you somewhere where all you have to do is relax. So, what do you say?"

Carrie Ann smiled. "I think that's pretty much an offer I can't refuse."

Easton picked up her wineglass and handed it to her. "I was hoping you'd say that." He tapped the rim of his glass to hers. "To our first vacation."

Carrie Ann nodded and took a sip of the Merlot. "Thank you, Easton," she said, and felt a warm rush of emotion wash over her. "No one has ever . . ."—she had to stop and gather herself together—"done something this sweet and thoughtful."

"Well, those days are over." He leaned over and gave her a tender kiss. "Get used to being pampered because it will never end. So where do you want to go?"

"Well, I don't have any idea. But we can have lots of fun figuring it out."

"Then it's a yes?"

"Yes."

Carrie Ann thought that Easton made it easy to say yes. Instead of holding back she should be embracing each and every moment with this wonderful man. "Well, we should get to fixing dinner soon." *Say it!*

"Okay."

"But there's something else I have to tell you." She felt a rush of emotion.

"What, sweet pea?" He ran his fingertip over her bottom lip.

"Easton . . . I—I love you," she said softly. Her heart knocked against her ribs and her breath caught, but she'd said it, and she was suddenly very glad that she had the courage because it was worth seeing the happiness shining in Easton's eyes.

His finger stopped moving and he pulled her into his embrace. "I love you too, Carrie Ann. I've wanted to say it to you for a long time. I mean, I know we both knew it. But saying it just makes the bond so much stronger. We're older. Set in our ways. And our past has a lot to do with both our strengths and fears. But I'll be honest with you. I can't imagine not having you in my life."

Carrie Ann felt a hot tear slide down her face.

"Aw, sweetie." He rubbed the moisture away with the pad of his thumb.

"I'm sorry," she said in a husky voice. "I've wanted to say it too but I was so afraid. I know this sounds crazy but I felt like if I said it that what we have would somehow change. I was having an 'if it ain't broke don't fix it' kind of thing rolling around in my head. But I have to say that saying those words has strength and power that we both needed to hear and to say."

Easton cupped her cheeks with his palms. "Say it again."

"I love you, Easton Fisher." She put her hand on his chest and felt the solid beat of his heart. He was a strong, healthy man and would live for a very long time. She needed to put her fear of him dying, of losing him, to rest for good and to simply enjoy being with him every minute they had together. There would always be some complications but this was a solid beginning to what could be a long future together. "Now, let's get dinner going and then on to the other fun activities we have planned for the rest of the evening."

"No arguments here."

"I will have to start thinking about where I want to go on vacation."

Easton reached over and took her hand. "Like I said, wherever your little heart desires. And this is only the beginning."

14

Just One Look

SOPHIA OPENED THE OVEN A FEW INCHES AND peeked at the lasagna. "Oh, it's getting there." She nodded with satisfaction when she noted that the marinara sauce was bubbling around the edges. "I'll start tossing a salad now," she said over her shoulder to Avery who sat on a stool at the small kitchen island.

"Dinner smells wonderful."

"Oh, I love the aroma of Italian food." She smiled at him thinking he looked too cute for words. "I would pay a cover charge over at River Row Pizza just to walk in the door and sniff." Avery smiled back and it occurred to Sophia that whenever she was around him, she did a ton of smiling. All she had to do was look at him. That was all it took.

"I could do this all night, you know."

"Watch me cook? I tend to overcheck things and putter around even after everything is actually ready. You would get bored."

"No way. I think your puttering around is so cute."

"You do? Maybe I need a few moves." She danced her way over to the refrigerator making him laugh.

"I think I'll buy you a sexy little apron. Would you wear it?"

"For you, of course. Make sure it says, kiss the cook." She swiped her finger across her chest.

"Then you'll definitely only wear it for me."

Sophia knew he was flirting but she loved the fact that he spoke as if their relationship was real. "I can be very entertaining. I know I should leave well enough alone because at some point I'll knock something over or not be able to reach something and have to climb up onto the countertop to get to the upper cabinets."

"You do that?"

She nodded. "I've been doing that sort of thing since I was a kid. It used to drive my mother crazy. And you should see how I get things down from the top shelf at the grocery store. I would be good at mountain climbing."

Avery appeared horrified. "You could fall, Sophia. And the washing-machine thing?" He shook his head. "You need to stop doing that stuff."

"Or break my neck as my mom used to say?" She laughed, but felt a warm pull of happiness that he was concerned for her safety.

"I need to get you a step stool for here, too. Have you been using the one at the salon?"

"Yes, that step stool has become my best friend." And she thought of him every time she used it.

"Well then, I'm jealous."

"Of a step stool?" She opened the refrigerator and handed him a bottle of Black Magic Ale from Broomstick Brewery. "Why is that?"

"I want to be your best friend," Avery said in a teasing tone, but there was a hint of seriousness in his eyes. He lifted the swing-top from the bottle and poured the ale into the pilsner glass she'd provided.

Not knowing quite how to respond, Sophia put the head of lettuce on the island. Would he ever want her to be more? They'd already established a real connection that went beyond being friends. The attraction was there and it was mutual. But she thought after sharing the hot kiss that they might take their fake relationship into real territory. She felt her heart do a little tap dance in her chest at the thought. "We're already close friends, Avery." She washed the head of lettuce beneath the tap and set it on the cutting board to make a wedge salad.

"I was joking," Avery said with a slight frown. "Surely you know how much I care about you." He hesitated as if to say more but took another swallow of his drink. "Of course we're friends," he finally added. "You know that, right?"

"Oh, I do." Sophia suddenly wanted to ask him what was really on his mind but she didn't want to scare him off by getting too serious and ruining the playful mood. That would put a damper on the rest of the evening. "I'm sorry. You already know I'm an over-thinker. Worry is my middle name. Sophia Worry Gordon. That's me. Worry swirls around in my brain and sometimes I come to a conclusion that isn't really there." She made a twirling motion above her head. "My mother thought my frequent frowns was depression and I suppose in a way it is because worry can turn me into a Debbie Downer."

"I find you to be upbeat and pleasant, Sophia. I don't think of you as a Debbie Downer at all. In fact, you light up the room when you enter. You have a quiet way about you but you sure do make me smile. You make everyone smile."

"I've tried hard to overcome the whole worry thing but it rears its ugly head now and again."

"Worry is another sign that you care, Sophia. One of the many good qualities that I love about you."

She lifted one shoulder and tried to ignore the words "love" and "you" in the same sentence. "Oh, I know. I sure would rather fret than not give a fig."

"Well, there you go."

"But I tend to think about what the worst-case scenario could possibly be. As a hair stylist that can be stressful," she admitted with a shake of her head. "When doing color I'm still a little bit afraid that the result would be something crazy, like green or orange, even though I check the formula several times. Like I keep checking the lasagna every few minutes."

"And did unexpected color ever happen?"

"Oh yes, it's bound to happen from time to time. There are too many variables. Clients tended to fudge about doing home hair color or if they colored their hair at all. And then other factors come into play, like if they are taking any medication, things like that."

"So what did you do if the color came out all wrong?"

"I fixed it."

Avery smiled. "Well, there you go. I can tell you from personal experience that most broken things can be fixed."

Sophia chuckled. "I would imagine that you can. There's got to be such satisfaction in what you do."

"There is." He nodded, but a bit of a shadow crossed his face and she wondered if he was thinking that there are some things that can't be patched up, like a relationship. But then he brightened. "So tell me a mess-up story."

"Well . . . I can tell you some of those." Sophia took a sip of her wine and then licked her bottom lip. "But once in a blue moon the mistake became something the client ends up loving." She chuckled. "And of course I'd act like it was intentional. It could happen with a cut too. 'Oops' isn't something you ever want a hair stylist to say."

"I would imagine not. You know, I never really thought about the fact that your job can be super stressful."

She nodded. "And physically demanding too. I've had rotator cuff issues from so much blow-drying." She put her glass down and demonstrated the rolling motion. "And even though I had an assistant for a few years, I get carpal tunnel syndrome that causes numbness and tingling in my fingers. And I'm still young."

"And being on your feet all day long doesn't help."

"Oh, for sure." Sophia nodded. "A lot of stylists are going with stools now, but I never could get used to one. And of course I worry that we're exposed to a lot of chemicals, which are a part of the business that can't be avoided. I've made extra sure that White Lace and Promises has ample ventilation."

"I didn't really think about that either. Well, and of course hair is such a big deal to people too. I never really liked having curly hair. When I was a kid I would get it all buzzed off."

"I love your curly hair!" Sophia walked over and ran her fingers through it. "It's so nice that you take an interest in what I do. Honestly, I think that people take their hair stylists somewhat for granted."

"You're right. I think we take a lot of people in the service industry for granted. It's a hard job—you have to be precise and creative at the same time."

"Oh boy, it can be really nerve-racking when someone comes in and asks for a particular cut, you give it to them, and then they hate it. It's usually going from very long to very short. I had a girl with waist-long hair insist that I cut it off into a supershort pixie. I begged her to do a gradual change but she seemed so sure. . . ."

"I'm feeling an unhappy ending."

"Oh, Avery, she burst into noisy tears. And then *I* started to cry." She shook her head at the memory and had to take a sip of her wine.

"Did she come back to you?"

"Yes." Raising her eyebrows, she nodded. "And guess what."

"She's kept it short ever since."

"You guessed correctly. I'm probably boring you with my stories."

"Sophia, I enjoy listening to you as much as I enjoy watching you. In fact, I enjoy being with you, period."

"Well, the feeling is totally mutual," Sophia said. "And of course, being a hair stylist requires being a good listener. For many clients getting their hair done is such a pleasure. And it should be a really good experience from start to finish."

"So go on. Tell me more."

"Well, some people aren't all that good at communicating what they want."

"Then a picture is helpful, right?"

Sophia sliced through the head of lettuce. "Not always. The problem is that the photo is usually of some gorgeous celebrity and the client often thinks that getting the same hairstyle will totally transform them into looking like the actress."

Avery laughed. "So they think you can work miracles."

"Sometimes, I do. A new haircut or color can make all the difference. And product. At first, I hated trying to sell styling products, because I felt as if the client thought I was trying to push things on them but you can't re-create what I do in the chair if you don't have quality products at home."

"True. It's called maintenance and it's one of the reasons I do so many repairs on appliances."

"Oh, I didn't ask—do you like a wedge salad with bleu cheese dressing, bacon, and avocado?" She was enjoying the conversation while she prepared the final stages of dinner. Going out with Avery was fun but this was just so relaxing and intimate.

"Sure do. It's one of my mom's favorites. She makes it now and then."

"Oh good," Sophia said, thinking she would love to meet his parents. "I know that healthier salads with dark greens, like kale, are all the rage but I just love this one. I had it at Wine and Diner a few days ago with Grace and had forgotten how much I enjoyed this classic. Cold iceberg lettuce, the tang of bleu cheese . . . and of course bacon makes everything better. But I should have asked if you liked it. Bleu cheese is one of those love it or hate it kind of dressings. Personally, I like a wide variety of foods but I tend to drift toward older recipes."

"I've noticed that you like older music as well."

Sophia nodded and once again felt a rush of pleasure that he paid attention to what she preferred. "Oh, I enjoy pop music but fifties and sixties music is by far my favorite. My mother says that I'm an old soul. Even the updos and makeup I do usually have an older, classic look." She waved her hand through the air. "This apartment came furnished and I can't wait to have a place where I can put my personal stamp on it. I'm doing that with White Lace and Promises. But I also like trying new things." She smiled. "Well, maybe I should say new . . . old things. Anything retro captures my attention."

"I know how you feel. I'm having fun restoring my house. Old wood and worn brick has much more character and warmth than something brand-new. I'd much rather restore or repurpose a piece of furniture than buy something in a furniture store."

"Oh, I love thrift shopping! I adore anything vintage, including jewelry."

"Something else we have to do together. Cricket Creek is full of antiques shops up on Main Street but there are also other small towns close by that would be a fun day trip."

Sophia nodded, feeling excited at the prospect.

"I don't love only old stuff, though. I do like to try new entrées in restaurants."

"Me too!" she agreed, but then chuckled. "My mother would get miffed at me sometimes when we'd go out to dinner and I'd order something that I ended up hating." She sliced through the lettuce and put the wedges on small plates. "And I'd nearly always tried something different, which of course ran the risk of not liking it."

"But how do you know if you don't try it, right?"

"Exactly! We think alike."

"So, would she make you eat it if you didn't like it?"

"No, she would nearly always trade with me. People think of my mother as being this glamorous fashion icon but she grew up in working-class London. She's actually very down-to-earth."

"Your mother sounds like a really cool lady. I'd like to spend some time with her, Sophia. And I think it's really great that she and Jimmy Topmiller run the fishing camp for underprivileged kids."

"I have to say that I've never seen my mom this happy. Do you want chopped tomato on your salad?"

"I do. Would you like for me to do anything? I'm feeling useless sitting over here watching you work."

"No, but thank you. And this isn't work, Avery. I've enjoyed putting the dinner together for you." She drizzled the dressing over the wedges and sprinkled on the diced tomatoes and bacon crumbles. After adding the croutons she said, "Would you like to eat the salads first or with your lasagna?" She started slicing a loaf of French bread and glanced over at the oven.

"First would be fine. Okay, I can't stand it. I've got to do something. I'll take the salads to the table and slice the bread while you get the lasagna out of the oven."

Sophia laughed. "Okay, I'll take you up on that. And if you don't mind, would you fill the goblets with water?" She nodded to the long-stemmed glasses on the counter.

"I don't mind at all." He took the salads to the small high-top table in the corner of the kitchen. "Oh, in here or in the dining room?"

"I think the kitchen is cozy, don't you?"

"I do." Avery nodded. When he passed her to fill the glasses with water he paused to kiss her lightly on the lips. While he performed his tasks Sophia took the

pan out of the oven and put the lasagna on the counter
to cool just a bit before serving it. She noticed that
Avery hummed while he sliced more of the bread and
she thought to herself that they really did get along so
well. She'd worried a little bit about having him for
dinner, wondering if he would be relaxed in this intimate of a setting. After all, this wasn't part of the
warding off Ashley plan. But he seemed right at ease
so she decided not to question the situation. Perhaps it
was about time that she did more feeling and less ana-
lyzing.

Sophia joined him at the table. "I'll let the lasagna
cool for a few more minutes before I slice it."

"It smells wonderful." Avery nodded, and she noticed that he must have poured her a little more wine
without her noticing it. "Oh, this dressing is really
good, Sophia."

"Thanks. Salad dressing is really a lot easier to
make than people think."

"You did all of this even though you had a late client. I'm amazed."

"Being a hair stylist taught me how to do tasks quickly
and go from one thing to the next. It's all about timing."
She took a bite of her salad. "Mmmm, and it's also all
about bacon."

He grinned. "It sure is. I didn't know if I'd like the
avocado, but I do."

"Oh good. I also didn't really think about the fact
that we had the calzone for lunch so we are likely to go
into an Italian food coma."

He reached over and squeezed her hand. "I can eat
Italian six days a week and not get tired of it."

"What about the seventh day?"

"Anything with barbecue sauce on it. Ribs, chicken..."
He shrugged. "And fresh produce. We're lucky to have so
many local farms still around. And a lot of younger people are buying them up these days with the farm-to-table
movement getting stronger."

"I love going to the farmers' market." She rolled her eyes. "But I do have a weakness for French fries."

Avery took a bite of his salad and said, "We'll have to go to the farmers' market when it's harvest time. But we can do some thrift shop bargain hunting before that. I need a coffee table for my living room, and I'd love for you to help me decorate."

"I'd love to." Sophia tried not to read anything into his innocent comment since he was talking about several months from now. But she couldn't help herself.

"Maybe you'd like to go fishing when the weather warms up?"

"I've never been fishing but my mother sure seems to enjoy it."

"I'll have to introduce you to the great outdoors."

"I'm more adventurous than I look," she said. "You can introduce me to the outdoors all you like, and then I'll take you to New York. The city is an adventure in and of itself."

"You have a deal."

"Have you ever been?"

"No, and to tell you the truth I'd love to go to London, too, since you know your way around there. Looks like we've got a lot of exploring to do."

"That we do." Sophia's brain started to fast-forward. They went on to talk about other things while they ate their dinner but her mind kept drifting back to some of the comments he'd made that indicated he wanted a future with her. She told herself not to read too much into one kiss, one intimate dinner. Previously, she'd felt like Avery was holding back.

But tonight felt different.

"Are you ready for the lasagna?" she asked.

"Yes, but sit still and let me get it. Would you like more wine while I'm up?" He scooted his chair back.

"Yes, thanks," she said, thinking with the stress of opening White Laces and Promises it had been a while since she'd felt this relaxed. She watched Avery make himself at home in her kitchen and smiled. She could really get used to this.

Avery topped off her wine, and then brought over plates of lasagna.

"Thank you," Sophia said, hoping he liked her recipe.

"Oh wow, this is amazing," he said after taking a big bite. "Don't tell my mother but this is better than hers."

Sophia laughed. "Your secret is safe with me. I have a veggie one that I like too. I'll make that one for you one evening."

"Only if you come over to my place and let me grill something for you. I'm not what you would call a great cook but I can barbecue with the best of them. I have a gas grill but I still prefer to use charcoal. Brings back memories of childhood when we'd roast marshmallows after dinner. My dad was on the road a lot and those nights were really special."

"It must have been difficult having your dad gone so much."

A shadow passed over his face. "It was, but I didn't really get how hard it was for him too. I need to make an effort to get closer to my father," he said but then smiled. "But now I realize how special those summer nights were to us. Zoe and I would run around the backyard seeing who could catch the most lightning bugs."

"That sounds like fun, Avery."

"Then we'll do it soon," he said. They talked about a variety of subjects while they ate but even the silence felt natural. There was also an undercurrent of sexual tension, an awareness that had her wondering how in the world she could find watching Avery eat so very sexy.

When Sophia got up to clear the table Avery joined her, taking dishes to the sink and putting away condiments. Each time they brushed by each other Sophia wanted to grab him and kiss him.

"Can I help you do the dishes?"

"I'll just rinse them and put them in the dishwasher,"

she said, but then slapped her hand to her forehead. "Oh no!"

He appeared alarmed. "What?"

"I forgot to make the dessert!"

"You had me worried there for a minute. No big deal."

"Yes, but I have all of the ingredients and I wanted to impress you with my dessert-making skills instead of picking up something ready-made."

"I'm already totally impressed with your culinary expertise, Sophia. What were you going to make?"

"Chocolate mousse." She opened the refrigerator and pulled out a tall can. "Look, I even have whipped cream. Ugh, how could I have forgotten?"

"Um, maybe because you worked all day and then prepared this big meal from scratch?" He took the can from her and tugged her into his arms. "Did I tell you how amazing you are?"

Sophia looked into his eyes and shook her head. "No," she answered softly. Her heart pounded and she smiled. "I would have remembered."

"You are incredibly amazing and I'm not going to let you forget it." Dipping his head, he kissed her.

The moment Avery's lips touched hers she melted against him. She came up on tiptoe and wrapped her arms around his neck, loving how he tasted and how it felt to have his strong body pressed against hers. When the delicious kiss finally ended, she wanted to tug his head back and start all over again.

"Who needs dessert when I've got you?"

Sophia felt a rush of heat followed by aching tenderness at his bold statement and the look in his eyes didn't have one little bit of pretense. They were all alone with nobody to impress. "Are you going to swirl a dollop of whipped cream on top of my head?" she joked, but then realized that the cold creamy topping on her warm body would feel quite nice . . . especially if he chose to lick it off her.

Avery kissed her neck sending a sizzle of heat south. "Mmmm, I could think of other places for the whipped cream."

"Oh, could you now?" Sophia laughed. She felt mellow from the wine and had energy from the pasta. But most of all she felt desire for a man she was falling in love with. "So could I."

"Well then, I think it's about time for dessert. What do you say?" He looked at her through half-lidded eyes while rubbing his thumb over her bottom lip. "If you're ready," he added.

"I am more than ready." When she reached for the can of whipped cream, he scooped her up in his arms. She gave a little yelp, and then laughed while he carried her into her bedroom. She wanted this . . . she wanted him. When the worry gene tried to wiggle its way into her brain she shoved it aside.

Tonight all she wanted was love and laughter . . . with a little whipped cream on top.

15

Simply Delicious

UNTIL MEETING SOPHIA, AVERY DOUBTED HE'D EVER be able to love or trust again. Who would have thought that a can of whipped cream would have broken through that final barrier?

He was suddenly really glad that she'd forgotten to make dessert. The meal had been incredible and he was impressed that she'd pulled it all together with apparent ease and seemed to really enjoy cooking. Unless you counted reluctantly making a sandwich, Ashley had never prepared dinner for him and she would have turned her nose up at something as messy as whipped cream.

Although he hadn't meant to do so, Avery found himself making comparisons between Ashley and Sophia. What had he even seen in Ashley in the first place went through his head and Avery knew now that his uncle had nailed it. He'd loved her. He loved her so much that he'd made excuses for her selfish behavior. But his devotion to her had been largely a one-way street and now he realized once and for all that he was better off without her in his life. Avery guessed that part of him had known all along, but oh how he wished he could get back the endless hours of pining for a woman who didn't deserve it!

Tonight, though, Sophia's shy but playful smile and infectious laughter pushed away the last of his doubts about falling in love again.

Avery had wanted to hold her in his arms and make love to her for a long time, and after the kiss they shared he wanted her even more. Little by little her friendship helped to put the broken pieces of his life back together. Now that he felt whole again, he realized that Sophia was the main reason. And although he longed for her physically, he wanted her emotionally too.

She admitted to being a worrier and tonight he wanted to chase her worries away.

"Where to, Sophia?"

"Down the hallway and to the right," she said in a breathless voice that he found sexy as hell. "This is fun. I want you to carry me around everywhere."

Avery laughed. "Really?"

"Well, maybe just around here." She pointed to the bedroom. "On the way to there."

"That's not a problem." Avery carried her into a spacious bedroom overlooking the Ohio River. "In fact, all my problems disappear when I'm with you."

"I like that, Avery. I want to be your soft place to land."

"You already are."

"Good."

"I want to be that for you too, Sophia. I want to be the one you turn to when you're troubled or in pain and I want to be the first person you think of to tell good news. Will you do that for me?"

"Yes," she answered softly.

"And if you're worried about anything big or small, promise that you'll call me."

"I promise."

He kissed her again. A gentle, tender kiss meant to convey the way he felt about her. "I'm in your bedroom, sweet Sophia."

"That you are." She reached up and cupped his cheek. "And I'm glad."

"I've wanted this for a long time and as hard as it's been I'm glad that we waited until the time felt right."

"Me too."

A small lamp on a nightstand illuminated the room with a soft glow. The sweet, delicate scent of her perfume hung in the air and he imagined her spraying it on just after a shower. And then he imagined Sophia *in the shower,* naked arms raised while washing her hair. Later, much later, he'd shower with her. Wash her hair, and then slowly work his way downward beneath the hot, steamy spray of water.

Avery walked over to the sliding glass doors that opened to a balcony. "Wow, I bet the view is amazing during the day up here on the tenth floor."

"It is. I like it in the summer when the baseball stadium is all lit up. Sometimes barges go by and once in a while an old-fashioned paddleboat."

The mention of the baseball stadium used to bother Avery because it brought up memories of Ashley's affair, but he didn't even feel a slight pang this time. "So you like baseball?"

"Not especially, but I will take an interest in anything you enjoy."

"And I'll do the same for you." Avery smiled and the thought occurred to him that Ashley only went to events and did things that she liked to do. He'd often told himself that he didn't care about her lack of interest in the activities he enjoyed, that it was just a girl-versus-guy thing, but in truth he did what she wanted to do most of the time because he liked to please her. When you loved someone, you wanted to please them, make them happy, but it should always be a two-way street. Avery suddenly realized that with Ashley it was always a my-way-or-the-highway kind of thing.

Wow, he'd been missing out on what a meaningful relationship should be like. Looking back, he realized that now. What was that saying? Hindsight is twenty-twenty.

"Avery, what are you thinking?" Sophia asked softly and with a measure of concern. "You can tell me."

"That my breakup with Ashley was actually a blessing in disguise."

"Why is that?"

"Because it brought you into my life."

"Oh, Avery . . ." Sophia swallowed hard and she gave him a trembling smile. "Well, I hope the next blessing isn't in disguise and fully announces itself: 'Here I am and I'm your blessing!'"

"I think you just did." Avery tossed his head back and laughed. "Yeah, the whole disguise thing can throw a person off for a while."

"Well, now your life is back on track."

"You're right and I have you to thank." He took the can of whipped cream from Sophia and tossed it onto the bed. He loved the way her arms were wrapped around his neck. She clung to him and he suddenly felt fiercely protective of her. "You know, Ashley wasn't very polite to you today. I should have stood up for you and put her in her place."

"Avery—"

"No, I should have. She was trying to needle you and I should have immediately put an end to it. And I should have introduced you as my girlfriend."

"To throw her off?" Sophia asked lightly but her eyes appeared serious.

"No. To set her straight. There's no pretending, Sophia." He shook his head. "No, that's not quite true. I was pretending to pretend in the first place, if that makes any sense."

"Perfect sense."

Avery walked over to the bed, put her down, and sat beside her. "Let me back up. I should never have asked you to get involved in such a stupid plan to begin with."

"Avery." Sophia scooted around to face him. "I could have said no. We'd become close friends. I wanted to help your situation. That's what friends do."

Avery shook his head again. "No, Sophia. It was all wrong from the beginning. Having you offer to pretend to be my girl meant that I got to spend time with you without the fear of commitment. I told myself that if what we had wasn't real, then I couldn't get hurt. That was my screwy way of thinking."

"No, I understand."

"Yeah, but that wasn't fair to you. None of it was and I'm sorry."

Sophia lowered her eyes and then looked back at him. "In truth, I had to wonder if maybe you were trying to make Ashley jealous. If you were really over her."

"No. Absolutely not. And I am one hundred percent over Ashley." Avery blew out a frustrated sigh. "I hate that I can't tell you the details of why we ended the engagement. That's not fair either, but I made a promise."

"I don't need to know details, Avery. She hurt you. I saw the pain in your eyes the first time you walked into the bistro." She gave him a small smile. "And it wasn't just from the rock-hard biscuits. You were hurting. I wanted to give you a hug right then and there."

"Really?"

"Yeah, plus I thought you were really cute in spite of your dark scowl."

"Sophia . . ." Avery closed his eyes, suddenly filled with emotion. He wasn't a guy who liked to show weakness and he was coming close to it right now. He flopped back and watched the paddle fan going around and around. After a moment Sophia joined him. He reached over and took her hand. "You helped me through a tough time in my life."

She squeezed his hand. "I'm glad. About the helping part."

"Yeah, but as I said, I shouldn't have gotten you involved this way."

"I'm a big girl, Avery."

"No, you're a tiny little thing."

She nudged him with her elbow. "You know what I mean. I knew what I was getting into and I realized that I was setting myself up for a potentially huge fail."

"How so?" he asked, even though he knew the answer. He wanted to give her the opportunity to say what was on her mind and he was glad that she'd decided to open up to him about this.

"Either, A, Ashley would become super jealous, which would fuel her desire to get you back even more, or, B, I'd fall hopelessly in love with you, and then we'd have our big pretend drink-in-your-face breakup after the wedding and I'd be forever heartbroken."

"Like I said, Sophia, it was wrong of me to agree to a scheme like this. I was being really selfish and I'm very sorry. I should have just asked you out on a real date from the beginning. But to be truthful I wanted to and when you insisted on pretending to be into me I was afraid that the attraction was more one-sided."

"You were so wrong. I was already falling for you while working at the bistro. When you flirted it was so hard not to encourage you but I didn't want to be your rebound girl."

"I'm sorry for that too."

"Don't be so hard on yourself and stop apologizing. And pretend dating was one of my seemed-like-a-good-idea-at-the-time things. Everybody has those. I sure have had a few."

He kissed her lightly and said, "Name another one."

"Going on the Hulk roller coaster at Universal Studios. Grace called me a chicken and so I did it. Instant regret. I screamed from start to finish, and then I threw up three times."

"Why did it seem like a good idea?"

"Because I wanted to prove Grace wrong."

"Aw, you poor thing."

"It was a lesson learned that I don't need to prove myself. I'm scared of roller coasters. Who cares? And Grace felt so horrible afterward."

"Because she loves you."

"Yes, and I love her too. I'm very glad that I made the decision to move to Cricket Creek. I didn't realize how much I truly missed my family until I moved here. There's just something about this town that brings people together." She turned her head toward Avery. "The common denominator is love."

Avery looked into her gorgeous eyes and nodded. "You're right." But then he looked back up at the ceiling, wondering how he could have fallen in love with someone as selfish and untrue as Ashley.

"Love is an emotion, Avery," she said as if reading his mind. "We don't pick and choose who we fall in love with. It just happens. You think there is a particular type or certain criteria." She shook her head. "There's not. My mother told me that she adored Rick Ruleman but his rock-and-roll lifestyle wasn't something she wanted for Garret. And she also recently confessed that she was jealous of his music because it took him away from her. She married my father because he represented the stability that Rick didn't. They weren't suited for each other. For love to last you have to give and take, you know?"

Avery raised her hand to his mouth and kissed it. "Sophia, you're beautiful in so many ways but you're smart too. Levelheaded."

"Thank you." She scooted closer to him.

"You're so forgiving. But I've realized that the people with the biggest hearts get hurt the most. It doesn't seem fair."

"I have to agree with you but I'd rather be on that side of the ledger, wouldn't you?"

"Yes," he said, and thought that in that moment he fell in love with her even more. "Selfish people are never satisfied. Always wanting more and giving so damned little. I'm lucky to have found a sweetie like you."

"Hey, I can get feisty. My mother taught Grace and me to be independent and to stand up for ourselves. I won't allow anyone to walk all over me."

Avery chuckled.

"What, you don't believe me?"

"Oh, I believe you. I was just thinking I'd like to see you all fired up and in action."

Sophia laughed and when she moved her hand she knocked against the can of whipped cream. "Speaking of action . . . I think it's time for a little less talk and a lot more action. What do you think?"

"That I'm ready for dessert." Avery rolled to his side and pushed up to rest his head on his elbow. "But Sophia, before we take this next step I want you to know that what I feel for you is real. I want you to officially be my girl."

"Oh, Avery, my feelings for you have been real from the beginning."

"Uncle Easton was right. I was in denial." Avery knew he was falling in love with her but he wasn't ready to tell her just yet. He really did want to get the drama of Zoe's wedding behind him, and if he was completely honest with himself, there was still a little bit of fear in saying those three little words. Yes, after the wedding reception would be the perfect time to let Sophia know how he felt. But for right now he'd settle for having her in his arms.

Avery pulled her closer and kissed her deeply. He wanted her but he was caught by surprise at the intensity of his desire. When he cupped her breast, she arched her back offering him more. Needing to feel skin, he slipped his hand beneath her sweater. Warm, soft . . . God, he needed to taste her.

"Avery . . ." she said in a breathless, sexy tone.

"This might sound corny but I love it when you say my name."

"Avery," she said again. "Avery, Avery . . ." she repeated, and then gasped when he unsnapped the front clasp of her bra. Touching her wasn't nearly enough. He wanted to see her. Put his mouth on her . . .

"Sophia, I want . . . No, I *need* you naked. Come up to your knees," he said, and when she did he tugged her sweater over her head and tossed her bra over his head not caring where it landed or if they ever found it. "God . . . you are just gorgeous." He feasted his eyes on her breasts that were full, lush, and seemed to be begging for his touch, his mouth. "I could look at you all day long."

"Oh, Avery . . ." She gasped and threaded her fingers through his hair. "Touch me . . . taste me."

"Gladly." Cupping the lush fullness in his hands, he licked, sucked to his heart's content. When he nibbled just slightly she moaned and tipped her head back, pressing her body closer, filling his mouth. He found the snap and zipper of her jeans and a moment later he tugged the denim down her thighs exposing pink silk panties. He toyed with the lace edges until he felt moist heat beneath his hand. Rubbing his thumb back and forth over her mound, he slipped a finger inside to explore where she was wet and ready for him.

Avery moved in tiny circles with his thumb until she clutched his shoulders. "Take . . ." she began, and then groaned. "Take your . . . Oh." Her breath caught before she could finish her thought and when Avery sucked her nipple into his mouth she cried out with her release. "Oh . . . my . . ." Clinging to him, she buried her face in the crook of his neck. When her legs trembled, he held her tightly and then slowly lowered her onto the bed against a pile of pillows. "You . . . you just made my body tingle from my head to my curled toes."

"Good, that's what I was going for. And I enjoyed every second of touching you." He leaned in and kissed her again. "Now, I want to see and taste all of you."

After tugging Sophia's jeans all the way off, Avery came up to his knees and looked down at her. With her hair fanned out against the pillows and her curvy body lounging on the bed, Avery thought she was the prettiest, sexiest sight he'd ever seen. She held his gaze but then sucked her full bottom lip into her mouth and that slightly shy gesture went straight to Avery's heart.

"You're way overdressed for the occasion," she protested, making him chuckle. Her unexpected sense of humor would forever slay him.

"I can fix that."

"I bet you say that a lot."

Avery laughed. "I do but I only get naked for you." He stood up beside the bed and pulled his shirt over his head and then made quick work of his jeans and boxer briefs.

"Wow."

"Is that a good wow?" He raised his eyebrows. He hadn't been nude in front of a woman for a long time and he liked the look of admiration on her flushed face.

"No."

"I need to hit the gym?"

"No, that's an amazing wow. Come here. I want to touch you, Avery." She scooted up farther to rest her back against the abundance of pillows piled on the bed.

"Good, because I want to touch you too." He located a condom from his jeans pocket and then joined her on the bed. When his skin brushed up against hers he felt another hot rush of desire that started at his toes and made him absolutely rock hard with needing to be buried deeply inside her. But he wanted to go slow and savor this feeling.

"Can I explore just a bit?" she asked timidly but then added a wicked grin.

"To your heart's content."

"Oh, you did it now . . ."

Avery laughed. "I think I can handle the sweet torture."

"We'll see about that." Sophia straddled him and rubbed her hands over his chest pausing here and there to lean in and kiss . . . God and to lick. "I want Avery on my dessert menu every night," she said and although he knew she was joking he thought it was an excellent idea. She leaned over and licked his nipple sending another shot of heat to his groin. "Hmm . . ." She leaned back and tapped her cheek. "Delicious but missing . . . something." Raising her eyebrows, she nodded slowly. "I know . . ." she said, licking her lips.

When Sophia reached over for the can of whipping cream Avery's heart thudded. She shook the can up making her breasts jiggle. He was amazed at how she could turn from innocent to wicked in nothing flat.

When she let her fingers trail downward his abs tightened with anticipation. "I remember seeing you shirtless when there was a party late last summer at Mayfield Marina. I thought you were so sexy. But up close and personal is even better." She leaned in and started kissing his heated skin. "I'm so glad that you don't shave your chest," she said and then moved suggestively against him. A moment later she squirted a little curl of whipping cream on both of his pecs. The cold cream felt so good on his heated skin and when Sophia leaned down and oh so slowly licked the topping off his body Avery all but levitated from the bed.

"Sophia . . . God . . . you're driving me crazy."

"Your turn," she said and squirted a dainty little dollop just above her nipples.

With a groan Avery leaned forward and lapped the sweet cream from her breasts. She gasped, giggled, and rocked against him. "Sophia, I need . . ." he said and, knowing, she came onto her knees and tossed the can aside. He put his hands around her waist and helped her upward, guiding her to the tip of his cock.

But she didn't lower her body. Instead, she teased the tip, hovering while moving back and forth ever so slightly. His cock twitched with need and he arched upward trying to get where he desperately needed to be. . . . "Sophia," he said, half pleading, half moaning. "Ride me so I can watch your beautiful face while we make love."

Sophia nodded and slowly sank her wet heat onto his shaft until he was buried to the hilt. "Oh, you feel so good . . . fill me so perfectly." She closed her eyes as if savoring having him inside her. She inhaled deeply, clutched his shoulders, and came onto her knees, keeping just the tip inside her. Opening her eyes, she slowly sank back down to take all of him once more.

Avery's heart thudded, and he had to take a moment to get control because he wanted this to last, and he was already close to climax. "Go slow. You've got me so worked up, Sophia."

"Okay," she said. While clinging to his shoulders she started a slow and easy rhythm. When her breasts grazed over his chest, she made sexy little gasps. He slid his hands lower, cupping her cute ass cheeks but when her legs started to tremble he held her firmly, helping her, guiding her. She caught her bottom lip between her teeth and moved faster. "Oh, Avery . . ." She arched her back and started riding him harder and then faster and when she cried his name, he took a nipple into his mouth, sucking hard. He could feel her body clenching, squeezing, and when her moan sent him over the edge he thrust upward, finding his own hot rush of relief.

Sophia fell against his chest with a little moan followed by a weak giggle. He rubbed his hands down the sexy arch of her back and cupped her ass, kneading, caressing. She kissed his chest with light little smooches and then pushed up just enough so she could capture his mouth with hers. The kiss was so sweet and so tender that it touched him on a deeper level than he knew existed. "Mmm, better than Italian cream cake with none of the calories," she said against his mouth making him chuckle. "In fact, I think I burned enough calories to have seconds," she added in a lazy satisfied tone. She swung her leg over and laid her head on his shoulder.

"So you have a sweet tooth, do you?"

"I have an Avery Dean tooth."

He chuckled and kissed the top of her head. "Give me a minute. I'll be right back," he said. He headed to the bathroom, noting that his own legs were slightly unsteady.

Making love to Sophia had been even better than he'd expected. Like her personality, she was sweet but sexy, playful and fun, but with such emotion that Avery was blown away.

After splashing water on his face he looked into the oval bathroom mirror and smiled slowly. He felt a warm rush of happiness. He was ass over teacups in love and it felt so damned good.

16

Why Wait?

EASTON OPENED THE DOOR AND REACHED INTO THE passenger side of his truck. He hefted the shopping bag full of take-out dinner from Wine and Diner from the seat hoping that the paper wouldn't bust beneath the bounty of food packed to the gills. "White Lace and Promises," he said, looking up at the newly painted sign above the plate glass window. "Now that sure is a pretty sight."

The sun was sinking low in the sky and soon the streetlights would turn on, illuminating Wedding Row. Carrie Ann was thrilled that the quaint collection of shops was becoming known outside of Cricket Creek, drawing brides-to-be from Kentucky and nearby Tennessee.

Sophia and Carrie Ann had been hard at work all day long getting the salon ready for the grand opening celebration and so he'd asked if he could bring them something to eat. They'd eagerly accepted his offer and he had to admit that the fried chicken, mashed potatoes, gravy, and green beans smelled mighty good. Yeast rolls, golden brown and hot from the oven, made his mouth water. His good friend Myra, former owner of the local favorite, had been behind the counter working for her niece, Jessica, who'd returned to Cricket Creek several years ago when the old diner was in danger of closing. Jessica, an accomplished chef, put a modern spin on the old-fashioned menu and turned the restaurant into a popular spot for regulars and also for tourists who came from miles around for the amazing food. Jessica had married Ty McKenna, former major-league baseball legend who'd moved to Cricket Creek to manage the Cricket Creek Cougars for his friend Noah Falcon. According to Myra, Jessica, Ty, and their son, Ben, were on vacation in Disney World before spring training began.

Easton shook his head, thinking that the years were just flying by. He opened the door of White Lace and Promises to find Sophia and Carrie Ann sitting in the middle of the black tile floor surrounded by lacy and pearly things of all shapes and sizes. Sophia had decided to give the salon a black-and-white retro look with pink accents here and there. Easton didn't know much about this kind of thing but he thought the salon looked really cool.

Elvis's sultry voice crooned through hidden speakers and both Carrie Ann and Sophia sang along to "He Ain't Nothin' but a Hound Dog" with gusto. Unfortunately, neither of them could carry a tune in a bucket but they were cute nonetheless. Sophia started playing the air guitar, bringing the song home and it was then that Easton spotted a wine bottle and two glasses. He grinned, thinking he was going to have to swing back around later and pick those two up.

When Carrie Ann and Sophia looked up and spotted him and his shopping bag they both applauded. "Yeah!"

"Hungry?" Easton asked as he walked closer.

"Starving," they answered simultaneously.

"Well, good." Easton hefted the heavy bag a little

higher and grinned. "I've come to the rescue with two orders of food and a bunch of extras that Myra threw in."

"Praise the Lord," Carrie Ann said. She looked around for her wineglass, nearly knocking it over. "This deserves a toast." She raised her glass but frowned when she noticed that it was empty. "Sophia, did you drink my wine again?"

"No!" Sophia said emphatically, but then pressed her lips together and shrugged.

"I do believe you did."

"Maybe by accident." Sophia pointed to the bottle. "Pour yourself more!"

"Oh, good idea," Carrie Ann said and smiled up at Easton. "Come here and give me some sugar."

"Gladly." Easton put the bag down and knelt next to Carrie Ann and gave her a light kiss on the lips.

"Oh, you two are soooo cute!" Sophia clasped her hands together beneath her chin.

"Aren't we?" Carrie Ann asked and batted her eyes.

Easton gave her another quick kiss. "Let me pour you some wine."

"Please. Oh, I do believe I smell fried chicken," Carrie Ann said, sniffing the air.

"You're right. Myra was at the diner and she loaded you girls up with extra goodies."

"Not dessert, I hope!" Sophia wailed. "Between Wine and Diner and River Row Pizza I've put on five pounds. Fried chicken? I'm going to have a Kim Kardashian butt."

"Just don't take any selfies of it," Carrie Ann said with a laugh.

"No worries about me doing that!" Sophia's eyes rounded and she gave a shudder.

"I think Myra put some fresh-baked apple pie in there," Easton said and looked inside the fragrant bag. "Yep. Oh, and looks like chocolate cake."

Sophia stuck her index fingers in her ears. "I can't hear you!"

Easton laughed. "Are you two planning on eating here on the floor?"

"I think a picnic would be lovely," Sophia said and looked over at Carrie Ann for approval.

"I have to agree," Carrie Ann said, "but that's only because we've been sitting here so long that I don't know if I can get up. These old bones snap, crackle, and pop more than Rice Krispies."

"Oh, now you have me thinking about Rice Krispies Treats," Sophia said with a long moan. "I'm going to have my sweet tooth pulled."

Easton laughed, loving her humor. "I can help set up your picnic if you like. Should I get the paper plates out and let you girls get started?"

"Aren't you staying to eat with us?" Carrie Ann asked.

"Sugar, I would love to but I've got some errands to run and then I'm meeting up with Avery later. We're trying to decide whether to add another truck to the fleet or if we are growing too big. I think we're going to head to Broomstick Brewery to talk it over since it's trivia night."

"Are you good at trivia?" Sophia asked.

"I am chock-full of useless knowledge," he replied with a grin. "And you sure can't cheat, not that I would, but Grace marches around the taproom and glares at anyone using their cell phone."

"Sounds like fun," Carrie Ann said.

"Plus, they're tapping a new ale that I want to try."

"Ah, the real reason emerges. Okay, well, if there's any chicken left over do you want me to bring it up to the cabin?" Carrie Ann asked.

"Yeah, that would be great. Let me know if you need a ride later, okay?"

"Oh, happy hour is just about over," Carrie Ann said. "We've got a few more hours of work to do before we're done. But I'll let you know later. We've only had a couple of glasses each. We're both kind of light-weights. I'm sure we'll be fine once we eat."

Easton gave her another kiss, and then pushed up to his feet. "What is all that stuff?" He pointed to all of the fluff and baubles.

"Hair jewelry," Sophia explained.

"Of course it is," Easton said with a grin. "Hair needs jewelry."

"It's for special occasions and the bridal party." Carrie Ann rolled her eyes. She picked up a tiara and put it on her head. "See?"

"I don't think you need a special occasion for a ti-ara, princess," Easton said with a chuckle.

Carrie Ann adjusted it on her head. "You know? I think you're right. I'm going to wear it all the time. Every girl deserves a tiara. Sophia, my princess in ap-prentice, choose one."

Sophia reached over and picked a bejeweled tiara out of the pile. "I do believe you're right." She slipped it onto her head and nodded. "I feel pretty!" she sang. "Oh, so pretty!"

"You are both adorable," Easton assured them. And they were.

"Nicolina Diamante designed it all," Sophia said with a sweep of her hand. "Isn't it all simply gorgeous? She's really super talented. The brides are going to love all of the choices we have to offer." Sophia nodded so hard that her tiara slipped sideways and she had to right it. "There are a lot of creative, talented people living in this little town." She put her hands together in a circle. "It's like this super concentration of talent in a small area."

"You got that right." Easton nodded. "Our first claim to fame was having Noah Falcon make it to the major leagues. And then he became a soap opera star."

Sophia raised her eyebrows. "I know. His name is on the WELCOME TO CRICKET CREEK sign."

196 *LuAnn McLane*

"And rightfully so." Carrie Ann reached inside the shopping bag and located a roll. She tossed one to Sophia. "Good catch."

"I never miss catching food. Toss me a ball and that's another story."

Carrie Ann laughed and it suddenly hit Easton that although those two were friends, they could also be mother and daughter. He was so glad that sweet little Sophia decided to stay in Cricket Creek. She was good for Carrie Ann.

"Oh my . . . this roll is so scrumptious," Carrie Ann said and looked at Easton. "You want something? Chicken leg?"

"No, thanks, sweetie. I should get going and let you two get back to work. I'll get a bite at the brewery. They have catering from Walking on Sunshine Bistro on trivia night."

"Okay, well, thanks for the dinner. I'm sure there will be leftovers," Carrie Ann said. "You might want a midnight snack."

Easton nodded but thought to himself that Carrie Ann could be his midnight snack. "Have fun, ladies, and don't work too hard."

"Oh, this is more fun than work," Sophia said. "And thanks from me too! I would tell you to give Avery a hug from me but that might be awkward."

"How about if I just tell him you said hello?"

"That will work. Tell the whole crew hi for me. And if Mom and Jimmy are there, they rock at trivia—get them on your team or beware."

"Will do and I'll make a note of it. Have fun, girls." Easton said and walked outside into the cool, breezy evening. He liked it up here on the hill overlooking the Ohio River. The trees were turning the early shade of tender green and soon the redbud trees would be in bloom. He welcomed the change of seasons, even the bitter cold of winter, but springtime was his favorite. He loved when the earth came back to life.

After taking a step toward his truck, he decided to see if Flower Power was still open. Carrie Ann's delight when he gave her flowers never failed to bring a smile to his face and he decided to pop in and get a bouquet for the kitchen counter as a cheerful greeting when she came home. . . .

Home.

He'd been protective and private with his home but it seemed empty and quiet when Carrie Ann wasn't there in his bed at night and at his breakfast nook in the morning. Giving her a key had been a good move on his part.

And then it hit him like a lightning bolt. He wanted *his* to become *theirs*.

Holy moly! Easton wanted Carrie Ann Spencer to become his wife.

Easton scrubbed a hand down his face and went over to sit on a bench a few shops down from the salon, away from Carrie Ann's view. The thought hit him hard; it was something he wanted soon . . . as in yesterday.

"Wow," he murmured. Looking up at the darkening sky, Easton nearly laughed. For a man who avoided the slightest hint of commitment, and heaven forbid, *marriage* for his whole life, the fact that he suddenly wanted Carrie Ann to be his wife hit him like a hurricane force of nature. He couldn't explain the urgency, but there it was making his heart pound.

Sucking in a deep breath, Easton waited for a cold blast of anxiety to overcome his longing, but it didn't happen. He tried to imagine the sharp words, to hear the spiteful bickering of his parents clanging around in his head, warning him that marriage was nothing but a steel trap, but all he heard was the rush of his breath as it came out of his nose.

Easton closed his eyes and swallowed hard. As a kid he'd be sitting in his room trying to do his homework, when he'd overhear the fights between his parents, usually low and heated at first, and then louder, ending with his father shouting and his mother's tears. Never physical, thank God, but the words still sliced like a knife right through the walls, razor sharp and cutting deep. He'd turn up his radio to muffle the shouts and would often go looking for Carla. But more often than not his baby sister would knock softly on his door and come in, clinging to her favorite teddy bear. He remembered taking her by the hand and going outside to play games, even during the cold months of winter. She'd ask to be pulled around in her red wagon or to bounce a ball, and Easton would do anything she wanted until she laughed and the troubled look faded from her face.

His parents made up as fiercely as they'd fought, all hugs and kisses, more focused on their own drama than the damage done to their children. The truce between them could last for hours, days, and sometimes weeks, lulling Easton into believing the battles were finally over. But then the peace would shatter like broken glass when another fight, worse than the last one, would happen seemingly out of the blue.

When Easton got older, he escaped with sports, excelling in baseball and basketball. Carla turned to music and books, and to this day, she's remained quiet and thoughtful. He was certain that Carla and Tommy, who had been high school sweethearts, loved each other but Easton wished that Carla would stand up for herself more often.

Easton gripped the cold metal handle of the park bench thinking it was a damned shame that he couldn't have shed the ghosts of his past sooner and Carla needed to do the same thing. But then he grinned remembering that Avery had told him that he had a lot of life left to live. Well, I'd best get on with it, Easton thought, and pushed up to his feet.

"Flowers," Easton whispered. "Carrie Ann needs flowers," he repeated as he stood up. He felt slightly dizzy, almost light-headed, and then realized that he was feeling giddy. At least this was how giddy must feel, he thought. He wondered if he was capable of jumping up and kicking his heels but decided he was probably better off not trying.

Whistling under his breath Easton was happy to see that Flower Power was still open. When he pulled the door open bells tinkled announcing his arrival. He was hit with a sweet, earthy scent and mystical music and as if standing guard, whimsical garden statues, mostly gnomes and angels, mingled with the wide variety of potted plants and freshly cut flowers. Circular racks filled with greeting cards were crammed into the center of the shop. Shelves displaying local arts and crafts hugged the wall to the left. Easton smiled, knowing most of the offerings were from senior citizens living in Whisper's Edge, the retirement community down by the river.

For a moment he simply stood there, overwhelmed by it all.

"Can I help you?" called a cheerful voice from the rear of the shop.

"Yes," Easton answered and weaved his way through the maze until he found the source of the voice. He smiled when he spotted Gabby Marino, the cute little florist who owned the place. She was seated at a long table behind the counter and was surrounded by what appeared to be a million flower clippings and ribbons.

Gabby gave him a bright smile. "Well, hello there, Easton. You're certainly becoming a regular here, which means either you're a really sweet boyfriend or you have a lot of making up to do."

Easton laughed. "I just love giving Carrie Ann flowers. And your arrangements are so pretty, Gabby."

"I already knew that. I was just teasing," she said, and then pushed up to her feet. She put her hand to the small of her back and waddled over to the counter.

"When is the baby due?" Easton asked. "I know I keep asking but I keep forgetting."

"That's okay." Gabby chuckled. "I know I look

ready to pop but I'm not due for another couple of months. When I enter a room I make people nervous like they need to start boiling water or something."

"Well, that's because you're so tiny."

"Seriously?" Gabby looked down at her tummy and laughed. "I'd hardly say I was tiny."

"Well, you're a little bitty thing so there's not much room for a baby," he said.

"It doesn't help that Reese brings me food from the pizza parlor and insists on including dessert." She shook her head. "He keeps telling me I'm eating for two when I protest. I'm getting huge!"

"You're cute as a button. I'm sure Reese just loves to pamper you."

"He takes pampering to the next level." Gabby shook her head. "Reese gets all wound up when he comes in here and I'm on my feet." She rolled her eyes but the love that glowed there told the true story. Reese and Gabby were a star-crossed love story that people still talked about. "Now how in the world can I run this flower shop without being on my feet?"

Easton shrugged. "Well, I don't know."

"I have promised not to get on any ladders. Reese gave me this." She held up a stick with a grabber thing on the end. When she squeezed the handle it opened and closed. "As seen on TV," she said with a giggle.

"Does it work?"

"Not very well but it's good for pinching his rear," Gabby replied and laughed again. Easton had gone to school with Gabby's mother, a sweet girl who'd had a knack for choosing the wrong guys. She'd raised Gabby on her own, working double shifts at Sully's and had tragically died of cancer at an early age. It did Easton's heart good to see Gabby so successful and happy. "So what will it be today? A spring mix? Roses?"

"A dozen long-stemmed red roses," Easton replied.

"Well, now." Gabby tilted her head to the side. "A special occasion?"

"Yes," Easton said, thinking proposing is as special as occasions come.

"Well then, I'll round up a pretty vase and add some sprigs of baby's breath."

Easton wasn't sure what baby's breath was, but he nodded. "Thank you, Gabby." While she arranged the roses Easton browsed around the shop picking up items here and there but his mind wandered to what Carrie Ann's reaction would be to his proposal. After purchasing the flowers, he intended to head over to Designs by Diamante and pick out an engagement ring. He wasn't going to make a big fuss or do something public. No, he wanted to ask Carrie Ann to marry him in the privacy of his home on the back deck beneath the light of the moon, which happened to be full tonight.

After putting the flowers in his truck, Easton headed to the jewelry store. He was a man on a mission and hoped that he found a ring that matched Carrie Ann's personality. He didn't want to wait one more day to ask her to be his wife. But when he reached for the door handle of Designs by Diamante, the door was locked. Disappointment flooded him and he sighed. Proposing without a ring wasn't going to happen. Just as he started to turn away, the door opened.

"Come on in," said a gorgeous woman with midnight black hair and a wide smile.

"Are you still open?" Easton asked hopefully.

"It's been my experience that when a man walks into a jewelry store he has something special on his mind so I will stay open for you." She stepped back for him to enter, and then extended her hand. "I'm Nicolina."

"Nice to meet you," he said, but recognized her from photographs of her and her husband, Chicago business tycoon Mitch Monroe, who'd developed Wedding and Restaurant Row after moving to Cricket Creek. "I'm Easton Fisher."

"What can I show you today, Easton?"

"I'd like to look at engagement rings."

"Oh . . ." She rubbed her hands together. "How exciting!" She waved her hand for him to follow her across the store. After heading behind a glass case she pointed to the display. "I've designed everything you see here. If you don't see something that you like we can do some sketches and come up with a ring she will love."

Easton nodded. His heart hammered with excitement.

"Do you know her size?"

"Oh . . . no." He felt a pang of disappointment.

"Well, if she is average she should be about a size eight and if you get it wrong we can resize the ring."

He blew out a sigh of relief.

"Now describe your lady to me and we'll pick something out that she will adore."

"You probably know her. She's Carrie Ann Spencer and is opening White Lace and Promises with Sophia Gordon."

Nicolina raised her hands upward. "Well, you don't say! I love those two. Carrie Ann does my hair at her salon up in town." She leaned forward and whispered conspiratorially, "Not that I color my hair . . ."

Easton laughed and took an immediate liking to Nicolina. With the kind of money that Mitch Monroe had, she could get her hair done at some fancy schmancy salon outside of Cricket Creek and here she was at her shop working overtime.

"Oh, this is such exciting news!"

"Well, she hasn't said yes, yet," Easton joked but felt a little flash of alarm. Maybe he was going way too fast, he thought—not for him, but for her.

"Oh, get that look off your face. She's going to say yes."

Easton nodded and started looked at the selection she presented. After carefully looking at each ring he put his three favorites to the side. Nicolina, bless her heart, remained patient while he pondered, choosing one and then the other. When he finally chose a white gold diamond ring with a rose in the center surrounded by petals, Nicolina nodded. "Excellent choice."

"I like the delicate leaf on either side. Carrie Ann loves roses."

"I think she will absolutely adore it." She held up one hand. "I handpick my diamonds for the color clarity, cut, and carat, and this one is a beauty. This ring is delicate but with enough pizzazz for someone with her big personality. Perfect, Easton."

Easton inhaled a shaky breath making Nicolina smile. She put her small hand over his. "Congratulations!"

"Thanks for your help and patience."

"Oh, no problem." She waved a dismissive hand. "This is an important purchase. And if it doesn't fit just right just stop by and I'll size it for you."

"Thank you," Easton said. After he was back outside the cool air helped to calm his sudden bout of nerves but only slightly. Should he wait or ask her tonight?

Knowing he'd never be able to concentrate at trivia he called Avery and begged off. He needed to go home, take a long soak in the hot tub, and do some stargazing while he rehearsed his proposal speech.

17

The Long and Winding Road

CARRIE ANN DROVE HER MUSTANG OVER THE WINDING road leading to Easton's cabin thinking that she was exhausted down to the bone. Her hair even felt tired. When she'd left White Lace and Promises, Sophia was still buzzing around the salon doing this and that.

"Ah, the energy of youth," she said and yawned so big that her jaw popped.

Easton's big king-size bed and strong arms wrapped around her would never feel so good. "Mmmm," she said with a little shiver of anticipation. The thought hit her that she hadn't slept in her own bed for the better part of a week. Now when she got in her car after work, she naturally turned left instead of right and headed to the cabin—it was almost as if her car was programmed to do so. A little unexpected jolt of anxiety chased away some of her fatigue and she gripped the steering wheel tighter.

Maybe she should have gone home tonight?

Carrie Ann mulled that over for a moment. Was she overstaying her welcome? Did Easton want a break from her once in a while? Well, he *did* ask for her to bring the leftovers from dinner, Carrie Ann reasoned to herself. She eased her grip on the steering wheel just a tad. But she decided to have a little chat with him and ask if he wanted her to spend some time at her own house and not stay at the cabin for days on end like she owned the place. Perhaps Easton would want to stay over at her house sometimes too. Yeah, they needed to talk.

Carrie Ann's tires crunched over the gravel lane leading up to the cabin and she had to smile at the lights glowing through the windows as if in warm welcome. She hoped Easton wanted a late snack because a cold piece of crunchy chicken suddenly sounded pretty doggone good.

Carrie Ann wondered how he'd done at trivia and hoped that Easton and Avery had come to a conclusion about adding another truck to the fleet. Like her, Easton worked his tail off, and she thought that maybe it was time that they slowed down a bit. It seemed like a funny thought since she'd just become a partner in another salon. But Sophia seemed to have everything under control. The girl was as organized as they come—almost too much so.

After parking in front of the big garage, Carrie Ann hefted the bag of leftovers from the passenger seat and headed up to the front door. She shouted a cheery "Hello!" as she entered, and when there wasn't an answer she headed to the kitchen and smiled at the gorgeous bouquet of red roses sitting on the granite island. After putting the food in the fridge, she paused to sniff the flowers and touch a soft petal. And then she spotted a note requesting her presence in the hot tub, no swimsuit needed.

Carrie Ann felt a pull of longing and she had to shake her head. Maybe it was because she was making up for lost time, but she sure didn't know that she had this oh-so-lusty side to her. Of course Easton was, in her opinion, quite a good lover so maybe that little detail had something to do with it. The man loved to kiss every inch of her body, making Carrie Ann feel incredibly beautiful in her fifty-six-year-old skin. Feeling confident in her body had her tossing any inhibitions out the window, making their love sessions something of a workout. Much more fun than a treadmill, she thought with a laugh.

Being head over heels in love with Easton had a lot to do with lovemaking that often lasted for hours. Not that early-morning quickies weren't fun as well. "It's all good," she said. Touching, tasting . . . exploring; God she was suddenly oh so hot and bothered.

Fatigue vanished, leaving lust in its wake. While hurrying to the bathroom to freshen up, she thought to herself that she and Easton were the poster couple for finding love late in life. While they'd discussed how they wished they'd taken their friendship to this level several years ago, there was something to be said for treasuring each day instead of taking each other for granted the way Carrie Ann witnessed her married friends do.

And of course Carrie Ann knew better than most that life could be snatched away without a hint of warning. The thought made Carrie Ann frown. Now that she knew how good it felt to be in a committed relationship, had she been a fool for letting so many years go by without allowing love in her life? What would it feel like to have a family like her sisters or to have a daughter like Sophia?

And why in the world was her line of thinking going down this unusual path?

"Just enjoy the moment, you silly woman," Carrie Ann said as she shed her clothes. After pulling her hair up into a bun she found a big fluffy towel in the linen closet and headed for the back deck where her very sexy boyfriend awaited.

The sliding glass door opened with a quiet whoosh

and she stepped out into cool night air. A gentle breeze lifted the tendrils of hair framing her face and she shivered, hugging the towel closer. The wooden deck felt cold and damp against her tired feet as she walked closer to Easton. His arms rested on the back of the hot tub and his head was tilted up to gaze at the stars.

Fat vanilla-scented candles flickered, illuminating the deck with a soft glow. Apparently the sound of the hot tub's jets kept Easton from hearing Carrie Ann approach, allowing her the opportunity to admire his profile. She caught her bottom lip between her teeth. He really was a handsome man, she thought with a measure of pride. Nearly silver hair, skin kissed by days spent outdoors, and arresting blue eyes made him one of those sexy mature men who would turn female heads forever. He remained fit and toned from physical work and playing sports but his biggest lady-killing weapon was his charming smile.

Carrie Ann crept closer with the intention of surprising him with a kiss on the back of his neck.

"I know you're there," Easton said with a hint of humor in his voice.

"Do you now?"

"Mmm, yes."

"You have good ears."

"No, I could smell your perfume," Easton said just as the jets turned off. The bubbles ceased and the sudden silence felt almost physical, like you could reach out and touch the night. "I do love that sweet, sexy smell, Carrie Ann."

"And I love that answer."

"Especially because it's true. Come on over here, sugar. I need a kiss."

Carrie Ann leaned over to kiss him on the cheek but he turned his head so she could get his mouth. Oh, his lips felt so warm and soft but firm, masculine. She rested her hand on his damp shoulder while holding the towel around her with her other hand. When his tongue touched hers she felt a jolt of desire that had her kissing him deeply. She pulled back and ran her fingers through his wet hair. "You sure know how to kiss a woman, Easton Fisher."

"No, not any woman . . . only you."

"Good to hear."

"The truth again. Are you going to join me?" he asked, and the heat in his voice made her melt.

"Of course." She walked around to the front of the tub where he could see her and let the towel slip from her shoulders to pool at her feet.

"Now that's a pretty picture."

"I would stand here longer but I'm cold."

"It's warm in here," he said, and stood up to help her over the edge and into the hot tub.

"Oh wow, this feels amazing," she said and scooted close to him. "Whoever invented the hot tub should get some kind of award. Like pizza for life or something."

Easton laughed and reached over and took her hand. He pulled her fingers up to his mouth and kissed each one.

"You missed the thumb."

"I can fix that." He kissed her thumb and then sucked the tip into his mouth and ended with a little nibble.

"Are you trying to get me naked?"

Easton laughed again. "Worked like a charm."

"So did you win at trivia?"

"Didn't go."

Carrie felt a flash of surprise. "Why not?"

Easton shrugged. "I got a little bit distracted."

When he failed to elaborate she nodded. "Happens."

"I felt the need to do a little bit of stargazing."

She scooted close to him thinking she'd like to straddle his lap. "Always relaxing, especially out here away from the city lights."

"Do you like it up here in the woods?"

"I love it," she said, but felt a little bit of . . . what? Apprehension? Excitement? Was he going to ask her to move in with him? Perhaps he wasn't so tired of her after all, not that she really ever thought so, she supposed. "But I also love being up in town where I can walk everywhere," she added carefully.

Easton nodded and fell silent for a moment. "I did too, but coming home to the beauty of this ridge was worth the extra drive."

"No doubt." Carrie Ann could feel that this was leading up to her moving in. It was to be expected. Made sense, really. But what about her home? Parting with her home felt as if she would lose something of herself. Lose the memories of her childhood before her father died. Lose the laughter held within the walls. No, she couldn't.

"Carrie Ann?"

She nodded. "Easton, I—"

"Will you marry me?"

Her heart thudded and the jets turned back on. No, wait, that was the blood rushing in her ears. Before she could begin to form—what were they called again?— oh yes, words, Easton reached over and picked up a blue velvet box from the edge of the hot tub.

"I had a speech prepared. It had things like . . . I love you. I need you in my life forever. I want you to be my wife, Carrie Ann."

Her mouth opened and then closed.

"Aw damn." He shook his head. "The rehearsal was so much better." He scooted up exposing more of his chest. "And this proposal was supposed to be in front of the fire, not in the hot tub, but I lost track of time and the ring is out here because I kept lookin' at it and so . . . ?" He opened the box to reveal an exquisite white gold rose with a big diamond nestled within the petals. If she'd picked out a ring, she knew it would be this one. Emotion welled up in her throat. She looked at the ring and swallowed hard.

And then the jets came on.

Panic, much like the water, bubbled and churned in her stomach, in her throat, preventing her from answering.

Easton frowned. "Carrie Ann?"

"Easton . . . I . . ." Her voice sounded apologetic and unsure.

"The ring? If you don't like it we can get another one because—"

"No, the ring is beautiful," she assured him in a husky voice. "Perfect, in fact."

"Then?" His frown made her heart constrict.

Carrie Ann looked into those blue eyes that were so sincere and full of love. Was she crazy? She should be over the moon. No, she wasn't crazy. She was scared. "Easton . . ."

"Sweetheart, you know we can keep your house if that's what you're worried about. I wasn't thinking clearly when I asked if you liked it up here, only that I want you with me every single night of my life. But I know it's your family home and, darlin', we can keep it. We can stay there too. I've not been fair . . ."

Carrie Ann put a fingertip to his lips. "Hush." Tears—and she almost never allowed tears since her daddy died—leaked out of the corners of her eyes.

"Oh, baby . . ." Easton brushed at the tears with his thumbs. "I've bungled this . . . Damn, I—"

Carrie Ann laughed . . . Well, it was more of a gurgle. "No." She shook her head hard. "No!"

"Wait—you're saying no?"

"No, I mean you're not bungling it."

"No, as in yes?"

Carrie Ann nodded her head. "Yes, I will marry you, Easton Fisher." She cupped his cheeks while tears streamed down her face. "I want to spend the rest of my days with you."

"And nights?"

"Yes, I love those the best. Oh, wait . . . this might mean all of eternity, like in . . . forever. Are you still game? I can get pretty annoying."

"You're never annoying." Easton laughed. And then he pulled her into his arms. "Yes. Hell . . . yes."

"Well, are you gonna put that gorgeous ring on my finger?" Looking into his eyes, she put her left hand forward.

"Yes."

Carrie Ann noted, with more tears, that Easton's fingers shook just a bit. And so did hers, making sliding on the ring a bit comical and oh so tenderly sweet. But once it was on her finger she looked down, and exclaimed, "Oh my God . . . I'm . . . just . . . Easton, I didn't know happiness existed like I'm feeling this very moment." She laughed and looked up at the stars. "After my daddy"—she sniffed and then whispered—"died. I just knew he was one of those stars up there. I mean I know they are . . . stars, but—"

"Oh God, baby." Easton pulled her closer and hugged her hard.

"I'm so afraid," she admitted against his wet, warm chest. "Don't you dare die on me." Her shoulders shook and she let the emotion, the fear, flow out from her. Easton gently rubbed his hand over her head, patient and understanding. He didn't utter a word, waiting for her to cry it out. Finally, she pulled back and kissed him. "Now would you just look at me? One hot tub mess with my mascara runnin' everywhere . . ."

"You are and always will be the most beautiful woman in the world, even with raccoon eyes." He reached over and rubbed the smudges away.

"I don't know what tomorrow will bring, Carrie Ann. We're gettin' up there and I don't have any guarantee except for one." He held up his index finger. "If I live one more day . . . or to be a hundred, I will spend it loving you. And that's a promise."

"Oh, I love you so." Carrie Ann became overwhelmed and leaned her forehead against his chest. Finally, she pulled back and grabbed his shoulders. "What more could a girl ask for?"

"A trip to Hawaii?"

"Really? Okay, then a trip to Hawaii!"

"Our honeymoon or vacation before we get married. I don't care as long as you're with me. That's all that matters to me."

Carrie Ann laughed and threw her arms around him making water slosh everywhere. "I love you, Easton." She pulled back and pointed to the sky. "To the moon and back."

"Aw, sweetie, me too."

18

The Spice of Life

"SOPHIA, YOU NEED TO STOP WORRYING." CARRIE ANN brushed some product onto the foil before folding the silver square over Sophia's hair. "Avery loves you. I see it on his handsome face every time he looks at you."

Sophia met Carrie Ann's eyes in the mirror. "I'm not worrying."

"Right, so that's not a frown but a unibrow above your eyes. Do I need to get the tweezers out?"

"Okay." Sophia sighed. "I'm worried."

"Tell me, sugar. What are you fretting over?"

Sophia licked her bottom lip and played with the edge of the cape.

"Come on, now. You know what you tell me goes nowhere."

"He still hasn't, you know, *said it.*" Sophia felt a little bit guilty talking about something so personal about her relationship with Avery.

"That he loves you?"

Sophia nodded.

"Sugar, perhaps you should tell him. I think some-one gave me that advice once."

"I know, but I don't want to force him to say it back. I just need to hear it. And it makes me feel super needy saying that."

"Oh, Sophia, no, I think you do, too. But Avery doesn't strike me as a man who could be forced to say something he doesn't believe or doesn't want to say." She put another foil in Sophia's bangs. "He's been hurt. I think he's just afraid to fully admit how he feels. And men can be just plain stupid sometimes. Or maybe he thinks it's too soon and that saying it will scare you off or something. You just never know with men."

"I know." Sophia nodded because she'd thought the same thing. "I should just be patient. It's just hard for me to keep my feelings inside but I need to just chill, I guess. I tend to think way ahead of myself."

"It's understandable, Sophia. You also tend to be way too hard on yourself."

"I guess I'm just nervous about going to dinner with Zoe and Max because Ashley's going to be there. I asked Avery if she was bringing a date and he said that he didn't think so. Maybe having me in the picture has made her double her efforts to get him back instead of giving up. Some people are like that."

"Well, I do think that Ashley is one of those kinds of people who want what they can't have even more."

"I know Avery doesn't want to go, but they're dis-cussing the bachelorette and bachelor party details and he has to be there."

"Not a fun evening for you. Why don't you tell him you'll sit this one out?"

"Avery said he wouldn't go without me."

"See, Sophia, he's at the point where going some-where without you just won't feel right to him."

"I'm just worried that I'll feel like odd man out."

"If anyone is going to be odd man out, it will be Ashley. You know, I don't know her all that well but whenever she would come in here to get her hair done she always had something to say about the way I cut or styled it. Liked to tell me how to do my job. She's a royal pain in the rear if you ask me. You'll be just fine. All you have to do is be yourself, Sophia."

"I guess." Sophia nodded, making the foils tinkle but she wasn't really convinced. The four of them shared a long history and friendship. "It's just going to be weird. I'll be so glad when the wedding is over."

"Well, just one more month. And you're going to be so busy with White Lace and Promises that the time will fly by. After the grand opening this weekend, you're going to be slammed. Have you hired another stylist from the list of candidates I sent to you? I know you were torn between a couple of them."

"Oh, who knew that hiring people could be so stressful? I hate to disappoint anyone. I don't know how I'd ever fire anybody," Sophia admitted. She knew that Carrie Ann was changing the subject and she was glad to move on.

Carrie Ann chuckled. "So who did you finally choose?"

"Haley Hunter. Her updos were amazing. She has a knack for doing more trendy and unique creations while I like doing retro and classic, so she was a good choice."

"Variety is the spice of life."

"And I hired Callie Porter as a nail tech and Millie Cooper for the front desk."

"You're all set, sugar. I've known Millie for years. She's just gone through a painful divorce and really needs the job so I'm glad that you chose her. She'll be perfect."

"I thought so. Such a sweet lady. I didn't know about her personal life but I'm sure glad that I chose her now that you mentioned it."

"So, what time is this dinner of yours?" Carrie Ann asked.

Sophia blew out a sigh that lifted the foils on her forehead. "Avery is picking me up at seven," she answered in a glum tone.

Carrie Ann squeezed her shoulders. "You'll be fine. Just have a couple of those potent ales."

"Oh, trust me—I plan on it."

"And I'm touching up your hair to make you even more beautiful than you already are, sweet pea."

"Thank you, Carrie Ann." Sophia smiled. "And so are you! You are going to make the prettiest bride in the world. Have you set a date yet?"

"Oh, heavens no. I have to get used to being engaged first, which still blows my mind. But my mother and sisters are already making enough plans for me." Carrie Ann chuckled. "And they're already arguing. If it wouldn't break my mama's heart, I'd head off to Vegas and get married by Elvis."

"No! Don't you dare!"

"Oh, I won't, but maybe we can have the bachelorette party there and get all kinds of crazy." She held up her hand, tilted her head, and looked at the ring. "I just can't get over it." She swallowed and Sophia saw just the barest hint of anxiety.

"You okay?"

Carrie Ann met Sophia's eyes in the mirror. "Yeah, sweetie, but at our age blending two lives takes a bit of an adjustment, you know?"

"I know what you're saying. Kind of like my mother and Jimmy. But listen, you don't have to worry about planning a family or any of the stresses that come with being a younger couple. You can just enjoy each other. That's all that's required of you at this stage, right?"

"True enough." Carrie Ann pressed her lips together and nodded. Sophia knew there was something else she wanted to say but was holding back. "So, what are you wearing tonight?" Carrie Ann asked, deftly changing the subject once more.

"Well, after trying on everything in my closet, I finally laid out a flowing paisley dress with a wide leather belt. I've got some cute ankle boots and a fringed retro purse. I bought all of it at Violet's Vintage Clothing up on Main Street. What do you think about my choice?"

"Very bohemian. It suits you. I think you will look adorable, but then you always do."

"Well, I thought it was a good combination of feminine but with my own sense of style. Being so short means I can't carry off certain dresses and I didn't want to appear as if I was trying too hard or showing off too much cleavage. I put way too much thought into it, I suppose."

"Are you kiddin' me? I'd be doing the same thing. You'll look adorable no matter what you wear so don't fret about that."

"Thank you, Carrie Ann." She didn't add that she was feeling just a tad intimated by Ashley's tall, willowy stature, which was pretty much the complete opposite of Sophia's. She felt a bit angry at herself for the sudden lack of confidence or feeling the need to compete with Ashley on any level. Having grown up in a world of tall, beautiful people she'd learned to embrace being petite and to prove her confidence she should go with flats tonight but she'd put out boots with a heel taller than she normally wore. And here she was, having her highlights done, and earlier she'd had Callie give her a manicure.

"You've gone quiet, sugar. Speak to me."

"I can't help it. I'm just so nervous about tonight. Isn't that just silly? My mother taught me to never be intimated by anyone or any situation. I'm stronger than this."

"We can control certain things, Sophia, but not our emotions. I happen to think it's perfectly normal to feel nervous going out to dinner with your beau's ex-fiancée. But remember that she is his *ex* and you are *his girl* and there's a reason for that. Avery belongs to you. And it's well within your rights to let her know it."

"I'll keep that in mind," Sophia promised. While she no longer felt in danger of being the rebound girl, she wanted to be Avery's first choice and not the runner-up.

"Good."

Sophia smiled thinking that she was lucky to have someone like Carrie Ann in her life. *She would have made such a great mom* came into her head. Sophia had a close and wonderful relationship with her own mother but Carrie Ann was much more frank about things; Sophia's English mother tended to be a bit more subtle and Carrie Ann's hard-hitting advice was something she could cling to this evening when she felt even a little bit flustered. Judging by the encounter at River Row Pizza, Sophia was pretty sure that Ashley was going to try to get under her skin and she needed to do everything in her power to keep that from happening. And she didn't want Avery to come to her rescue. No, she planned to hold her own if need be. "I'll be fine."

"Promise?"

"I promise."

"Glad we got that settled." Carrie Ann gave her a firm nod. "Good girl," she added and went back to doing the highlights. As the conversation drifted back to grand opening plans for White Lace and Promises, Sophia pushed her worries from her mind.

After leaving A Cut Above, Sophia walked across the street and got a large coffee at Grammar's Bakery. She steeled herself from caving in to the enticing aroma of doughnuts, cakes, and cookies. It worked.

Almost.

The cheerful yellow smiley-face cookies seemed to be winking at her so she ordered one, telling herself that she'd indulge in only one sweet, crunchy bite. Like, only one chocolate eyeball's worth. Or maybe the smiley part. She could do that, right? With the giant coffee and little white bag in her hand she headed to her car and drove the short distance to her apartment.

And so the intense preparation for the evening began. . . .

TWO HOURS AND THE ENTIRE COOKIE LATER, SHE was in Avery's truck heading over to Broomstick Brewery. She tapped her toes to the latest Florida Georgia Line song and tried to remain calm.

"You're being awfully quiet, Sophia." Avery gave her a sideways glance. "We can blow this off if you want to. I can get together with Max later in the week."

"No," Sophia said with a determined smile. She'd decided that she would not let Ashley get to her at any cost. "I'm sorry I'm so quiet. I've just got a lot on my mind."

"That's understandable." Avery nodded but didn't appear totally convinced. "Soon all of this will be over and life can get back to normal. Will Grace and Mason be at the brewery tonight?"

"Grace will be bartending but she said that Mason is super busy in the brewery doing whatever magic he does to make his amazing beer," she replied. "I think she said he's doing some sort of thing where he's aging ale in bourbon barrels."

"Magic it is. Mason knows what he's doing. And having a craft brewery in Cricket Creek is so sweet. This little town has grown so much over the past few years." He glanced her way, making Sophia wonder if he needed reassurance that she liked living here rather than New York City.

"Cricket Creek has a lot to offer, especially the people," Sophia said with a smile.

Avery reached over and took her hand. "You're right." He squeezed her fingers. "The people have always been the strength of this town, and they always will be."

A moment later they turned into the Mayfield Marina entrance and headed down the lane to the brewery. The setting was lovely, with the main building right next to the water. The parking lot indicated that the crowd was light but Sophia supposed fairly normal for a Monday.

Avery came around to open her door and assist her down from the big step. Still a bit on the nervous side, her heart kicked it up a notch as she got out, but when Avery took her hand and brought it to his mouth for a quick kiss, she smiled. *Tell me you love me,* she thought, and then looked away before he could see the emotion in her eyes.

As soon as they entered the taproom Grace came running from behind the gorgeous handcrafted bar built by Danny Mayfield, her husband's talented brother.

"Sophia! Avery! It's so good to see you," Grace said, nearly bouncing as she hurried. Her witch's hat nearly toppled off her head in her haste. She righted it, laughing. As usual, she had energy to spare. Sophia used to think she was like the Energizer Bunny, never ready to slow down.

"Good to see you too," Avery said. "Casting any spells?" He pointed to her hat.

"Not yet, but the night is young." Grace gave Avery a kiss on the cheek. "I've been waiting for you guys to arrive." She turned and gave Sophia a hug. Tugging her a bit to the side, she whispered in her ear, "If you need a break from the loudmouth over there catch my eye."

Sophia hugged her sister and nodded. "Thanks," she whispered back.

"Your sister and friends are over there." Grace pointed to a picnic table hugging the far wall. Like many taprooms connected to a brewery, the atmosphere was casual but Grace's witches theme gave Broomstick Brewery a fun, festive vibe that brought in a female demographic that many neglected to cater to. Mason had balked at the idea at first, but had since warmed up to the concept, and the result was a resounding success story . . . as well as a love story.

"Thanks," Avery said.

"I'll let Mason know that you're here. Maybe that will get him out of the brewery for a little while. He's been obsessed with the whole bourbon-barrel thing."

"Yeah, I'd like to see him if you can pry him out of there," Avery said.

"I'll do my best," Grace promised. "What do you two want to drink?"

"Bring me whatever is new on tap," Avery replied. "I've tried everything else, I think."

"Coming right up. Sophia?"

"Oh, I think Black Magic sounds good tonight. Mason's chocolate porter is one of my favorites."

"Me too. That's the one Mason gave to me on the dark and stormy night when we first met right here in this building. I told him it was a girly ale and he didn't take that too well."

Avery laughed. "Wish I'd been there for that one. It might be chocolate but the AVB will sneak up on you."

"Oh yeah." Grace nodded. "I found that out pretty quickly. Well, looks like your sister spotted you, Avery. I'll bring your ales over to your table," she said and gave Sophia a discreet look that promised she'd come to her rescue. But Sophia wasn't about to be rescued by her sister or Avery. With a little lift of her chin she took Avery's hand and walked with him to the table.

Greeting and hugs were exchanged, friendly but with an underlying tension radiating from Ashley who sat down next to Zoe. Sophia had a moment of indecision of where to sit but Avery tugged her hand, urging her to sit next to him on the bench seat with Max. A moment later Grace arrived with their ales and Sophia barely suppressed a sigh of relief.

"Anybody else need anything?" Grace asked.

"A glass of water would be nice," Ashley said. "This ale is a bit on the bitter side." She wrinkled up her nose.

"Oh, would you like something different?" Grace

asked, in a polite but cool voice. "Or perhaps a flight to see what you prefer?"

Ashley lifted one shoulder. "No, it's okay," she replied in a sweet but slightly suffering tone.

Grace nodded. "Okay, well, if you change your mind let me know."

"Thank you," Ashley said, drawing out the words.

Sophia took a grateful swig of her ale and sat quietly while the conversation turned to the upcoming bachelorette and bachelor weekend. The guys were going to rent a houseboat on Norris Lake while the girls were going to Gatlinburg, Tennessee, for a weekend in the Smoky Mountains.

"Have you made the reservation for the houseboat yet?" Max asked Avery.

"I was waiting for the total head count," Avery replied. "Colby just said he could go, but I'm still waiting on Danny's answer. He had a fishing tournament scheduled for that weekend, and he was going to see if Jimmy Topmiller would take the reins for him."

"Oh," Zoe said. "Didn't you read my text earlier?"

"No, what happened?" Avery asked.

"There's been a change of date." She flicked a glance at Ashley.

"What? Why?" Avery asked. Sophia could feel the muscles in his leg tighten.

"We have to move the date up to this coming weekend. Ashley has a commitment the following weekend and anything closer to the wedding would be too stressful, so . . ."

Avery shook his head. "But that's the grand opening of White Lace and Promises."

"I'm ever so sorry. Business," Ashley said with a slight wince. "All of the bridesmaids are okay with the change of plans. Max, you checked with the rest of guys, right?"

"Yeah, and then Danny won't have to ask Jimmy to take over the tournament," Max said.

"See, Avery, it's better for everyone," Ashley said with a little smile.

"Well, not for me," Avery said tightly. "I want to be here for the grand opening."

"Oh, don't worry about it, Avery," Sophia said, eternally glad that her voice didn't shake.

"Zoe, this is very last-minute," Avery argued and gave Ashley a hard look. Ashley answered with a slight lift of one eyebrow.

"I know and I'm sorry," Zoe said, directing her answer at Sophia.

"It's okay," Sophia said.

"It couldn't be helped." Ashley pressed her lips together. She gave Zoe a pleading look. "I mean I could try to reschedule but then I risk losing a client."

"I can't have you do that," Zoe said to Ashley. "Avery, surely you understand."

"Well, I can't go, then," Avery said.

"You're the best man," Zoe reminded him. "And Sophia said she didn't mind."

Sophia swished her hand through the air. "Don't worry. It's fine." She turned to Avery and smiled. "Really. It's just an open house."

"See? No big deal," Ashley said, and then took a swig of her beer. She smiled at Sophia. "Thanks ever so much for being so understanding. It's so very nice of you not to put up a fuss."

"Don't mention it." Sophia shook her head.

"Well, now, you're just as sweet as can be," Ashley gushed, laying on the Southern twang. "I just adore your little paisley dress. It suits you. You're just as cute as a little ole button." She gave her hair a flip. "I could never pull something like that off but you somehow manage."

"Thank you," Sophia said, barely keeping an edge from her voice. "I don't follow trends."

"Or set them," Ashley said, drawing a surprised look from Zoe and a glare from Avery. "Oh, would y'all just stop? I was just joking."

"I leave setting trends to my mother," Sophia said, appalled at herself for dropping her mother's name. What was it about Ashley that brought out the worst in her?

"Your mother?" Ashley tilted her head, letting her long black hair slip over her shoulder. She snapped her fingers. "Oh right, the swimsuit model."

Sophia ground her teeth together, but nodded, trying not to get sucked into this but failing. "Yes, that's right, the swimsuit model. If you'll excuse me I need to visit the ladies' room," she said, hoping that Grace would get the hint and join her. She needed to vent or explode. She gave Avery's thigh a squeeze. "I'll be right back."

"Okay, don't be too long," Avery said and leaned over to give her a quick kiss.

"Y'all are just so cute," Ashley cooed and scrunched up her nose.

Was it wrong that Sophia wished her face froze like that?

Yes, it was wrong, Sophia thought as she headed toward the bathroom door that had WITCHES on it. Think nice thoughts, she said to herself, trying to catch Grace's eye but failing. She wished she'd picked up her purse so she could text her sister but in her haste to get away from the snarky Southern belle from hell, she'd forgotten to snag her belongings. After she was in the stall she heard the door swish open. She smiled, thinking it was Grace to the rescue but the black heels that clicked across the tile didn't belong to Grace and when Sophia came out to wash her hands, Ashley emerged from the other stall and gave her a snappy smile. "Well, hello there."

"Fancy meeting you here," Sophia tried to joke.

"Oh, you're so funny."

Sophia searched for something else to say, but before she could think of anything Ashley filled the silence. "Don't take this the wrong way," Ashley said slowly as if talking to a child.

"Okay." Sophia's heart hammered as she resisted the urge to cross her arms over her chest. Instead, she tried to appear casual.

Ashley leaned one hip against the edge of sink and continued. "I cheated on Avery."

Sophia blinked at her, stunned that she would admit what Sophia had already suspected and had to wonder what else was coming. "That's unfortunate."

"Yes." Ashley nodded slowly. "It is. See, Avery still *loves* me. He just can't forgive me."

"Why are you telling me this?"

"I want to save you some heartache. I am the love of Avery's life, So-ph-ia. He told me so when he put a gorgeous diamond ring on my finger. He will never get over me and he'll never be able to love anyone else."

"And just how do you know this, Ashley?" Sophia said calmly but her heart felt as if it might jump out of her chest at any moment and go running out the door.

"I know him much better than you do or ever will. You're not from around here and you don't know the ways of small-town folk. We're all family; you'll always be an outsider. Zoe is my best friend. The four of us are inseparable and we always will be. You'll never fit in."

"I'm not trying to fit in."

"Whatever." She gave her a little head bop.

"I'm guessing that Zoe doesn't know you cheated on her brother."

"No, she doesn't." Ashley shook her head slowly. "Avery promised me he wouldn't tell and he keeps his promises."

"Unlike you."

Her eyes narrowed. "It was a moment of weakness." She shrugged. "A hot baseball player I was working with. I'd had one too many martinis, and well, one thing led to another." She waved a dismissive hand. "Meaningless."

"Not to Avery. How did he find out?"

"That's none of your business."

"You're making it my business."

"Look, his ego was hurt but he'll get over it."

"You were engaged," Sophia said hotly. "How could you do such a thing to him?" she asked, angry that this woman had hurt him. She wanted to give her a hard shove.

Something flickered in her eyes. "It was a silly mistake. I regret it. Look, I thought it was only fair for me to tell you that Avery will always love me and that if you stay with him, you should know that you are his second choice. Do you really want that?" she asked in a fake tone.

No, screamed in her head.

"Don't you see?" she asked gently. "Avery is using you to make me jealous."

"Avery doesn't use anyone."

"He may not even know he's doing it," she said. "But I know it." She put a hand to her chest. "And deep down Avery does, too. Do yourself a huge favor and walk away before your heart is broken into tiny little pieces." She pushed up from the sink and gave Sophia a tight little smile. "Oh and if you decide to leak the little secret that I divulged to you, Avery will know where it came from. Other than him, you're the only other person privy to this information. So, if you blow your mouth and it ruins the wedding? Well, Avery will never forgive you. So this needs to be our little secret." She raised both eyebrows. "Okay?"

"I don't owe you any promises."

"True. But you owe Avery since he's taken you under his wing, wouldn't you say? Helped you to fit in where you don't belong?"

Sophia refused to dignify her question with an answer.

"Oh and I'm so *very* sorry about the change of date for the bachelor party." She raised her palms upward and shrugged. "It just couldn't be helped."

"I'm sure." Sophia gave her a level look and thought that the purple Mohawk might just happen after all.

"We'd best get back to the table. It's about time to discuss what you're planning to do with our hair for the wedding. I am very particular I'll have you know. But I'm sure you'll do a nice little job in your cute little salon." Ashley walked past Sophia leaving a cloud of her cloying perfume in her wake.

Sophia stood there for a moment, stunned. And then white-hot fury washed over her like a tidal wave making her feel odd and shaky. Anger this strong was a foreign feeling for Sophia and she didn't like it one bit. She shouldn't give Ashley the power to make her feel this way.

"What a nasty piece of work," she whispered, wondering how Avery could have ever loved someone so despicable.

But a nasty thought wiggled around in her head. Did he still love Ashley?

And is that why he hasn't said *I love you* to Sophia? Was she truly his second choice?

"Oh . . . *stop it.*" Sophia closed her eyes and had to grip the cool sink. If it wouldn't have ruined her makeup, she would have splashed water on her face. "Don't let her get to you," she said low and fiercely. Oh boy, but going back out there was the last thing she wanted to do. *Fake it till you make it.*

With that thought firmly in mind she inhaled a sharp breath, stiffened her spine, pushed the door open.

And came face-to-face with Avery.

19

Stuck in the Middle with You

AVERY TOOK ONE LOOK AT SOPHIA'S PALE FACE AND knew that something was terribly wrong. And he knew who had caused the problem.

"Sophia, sweetheart, what did she say to you?" Avery asked, trying to keep his anger at Ashley from exploding in his brain.

"Nothing you should be concerned about," Sophia replied in a calm tone that didn't reassure him one bit.

"Sophia, anything that bothers you is something I need to be concerned about."

"Worrying is my job, remember?" Sophia asked with a bright smile that didn't quite reach her stormy eyes.

Avery took her hand and led her down the hallway until they stood in the shadows. "Please tell me what happened in there."

"There's no need." Sophia gave him a jerky shake of her head. "Let's get back in the taproom and enjoy the rest of the evening."

"There isn't anything I can enjoy with *her* around. And I especially can't enjoy myself if I know you're troubled about something she said to you."

"Avery, tonight is your sister's wedding planning night. She deserves for this to be a fun evening. I won't allow Ashley to spoil it for Zoe."

"Well, I can tell you right now, I'm not going to the bachelor party or missing your grand opening. What Ashley did was bullshit and I see right through it. I can't believe that Zoe doesn't."

"Maybe she does and is still clinging to the hope that this thing with me is temporary and you'll come to your senses and get back with Ashley."

"I've come to my senses and that's why I'm with you," he said, expecting a smile or laugh but her expression remained serious. "I won't miss your special day that you've been working so hard toward."

"No, I really want you to go to the bachelor party. After all, you're the best man. I'm just having an open-house kind of thing. It's no big deal."

"It's a big deal to me."

"Actually, it would upset me more to have you miss the bachelor party on account of me. I would feel terrible. And Max would be so disappointed if you didn't go. It's fine, really."

"Are you sure?" In his experience, when a woman said something was fine, it really meant the opposite. Of course, his experience was with Ashley and not someone as kind and understanding as Sophia. Sophia nodded, and he let out an exasperated sigh. "What does Ashley think she's accomplishing by pulling this stunt?"

"Avery, she wants to cause problems. Come between us. Don't play into her hands."

Avery shoved his fingers through his hair, but then nodded. "You're right," he said and leaned over to kiss her. "We won't let that happen."

"No, we won't." Sophia finally smiled but something in the depths of her eyes told him that Ashley had already accomplished her goal. He wanted to press Sophia for answers as to what was said but she had a

fight-or-flight look about her and he didn't want to upset her further.

"Why don't we just get out of here?"

"Because we just arrived. There are plans to be
made and you're a part of them. Like I said, this is your
sister's wedding. She doesn't deserve tonight to be ruined because of something Ashley said to me." Sophia
reached up and cupped his cheek. "I'm okay, really,"
she insisted, but he knew otherwise.

Avery thought for the millionth time that he should
tell Zoe the truth, his promise to Ashley be damned.
And he sure as hell wanted to know what crap she just
shoveled at Sophia. He looked at her sweet face, sincere
eyes, and realized how very lucky he was to be here
tonight with Sophia instead of being married to Ashley.
"I don't know what I ever saw in her," he muttered.

"Love isn't something we choose, but something
that just happens. We can't control who we love," she
said gently, but something flickered in her eyes and
she glanced away. "And we can't control the actions of
others. I've never understood meanness, but in my experience, I've found that it usually stems from insecu-
rity," Sophia said and it seemed to be more to herself
than to him.

"Sophia, please tell me what happened in there.
What garbage did Ashley say to you?" He searched her
sweet face for clues. "It's driving me crazy. I need to
know."

Sophia tilted her head up to look at him. Her eyes
were shining with unshed tears and it clawed at his
heart. "You know, Avery, I think that forgiveness is the
hardest thing that we have to face in our lives. But it's
also the most freeing feeling. I finally forgave my father for loving money more than spending time with
his family. It was his loss and I feel sorry for him now
instead of anger and resentment. And he knows his
mistake but it's just the way he is. I love him in spite of
his faults."

When she stopped talking, Avery wondered where in the world she was going with this conversation. Confused, he prompted, "Sophia, I don't know—"

"Sometimes forgiveness is all it takes to make our world right again. We all make mistakes."

His heart thudded. "Sophia, if—"

"Let's just get back in there, shall we?" she asked lightly, but instead of waiting for an answer she started walking. Having no choice, Avery walked with her, turning over what she'd just said in his mind, trying to make sense of it all. But he could tell by her firm steps and the stiff set of her spine that Ashley wasn't going to get the best of Sophia . . .

Unless she already had.

Avery went through the motions. He ordered another round of ales, laughed at Max's jokes, and helped put the finishing touches on the bachelorette and bachelor party weekend.

When Ashley kept steering the conversation to old times, Avery quickly changed the subject, not wanting Sophia to feel left out. Besides, he didn't want to relive the past with Ashley; he wanted to start a future with Sophia. He was going to let Sophia know that important detail as soon as they could politely make their exit.

"So, are we all set?" Zoe asked. She looked down at the notes she'd taken. "The girls will drop the guys off at Norris Lake for a houseboat weekend, while the girls stay in Gatlinburg in a chalet."

"I've got a gorgeous one rented," Ashley said. "And if the boys make an impromptu visit, I'm sure we won't mind," she added with a wink in Avery's direction. "Just like they used to do when we had weekend sleepovers. Remember that, guys?"

"That's not going to happen," Max said with a frown at Ashley. Avery wanted to give him a high five.

"Oh, I'm just teasin'," Ashley said with a pout.

"Yeah, we already discussed that, Ashley," Zoe said

with a surprising edge to her voice. "We won't interrupt each other's weekend. We're only riding with each
other for the convenience and to save gas since the lake
is on the way."

"Oh, come on, Zoe, y'all just need to lighten up,"
Ashley said with a bit of a bite to her tone as well.
Could it be that Ashley was finally wearing thin on his
sister? It was about damned time. "I do believe that
you're getting a bit of wedding jitters." She rolled her
eyes and then looked at Sophia. "I don't envy you and
your little bridal salon. Brides can be such a pain." She
made a face at Zoe as if expecting her to laugh but Zoe
shook her head and took a drink of her ale.

"White Lace and Promises is a dream come true for
me," Sophia said. "I've always loved getting a bride
ready for the most important day of her life. Jitters are
normal. I'm very good at calming the bridal party down
and making the day extraordinary, as it should be."

"Better you than me," Ashley said and made a duck
face. Avery wondered if she realized how goofy she
looked. He wanted to take his phone out and take a
picture of her so he could show her.

"I'm okay with that," Sophia said airily. Avery
wasn't sure but by the sudden look of pain on Ashley's
face he had to wonder if Zoe had just given her a hard
nudge beneath the table. Good, Ashley deserved to be
squashed.

"We'll pick you guys back up Sunday afternoon,"
Zoe said, and then looked across the table at Sophia.
"And thanks for being so understanding about the
date change. I know it's sudden and I'm truly sorry."

"No problem. I'll be busy," Sophia assured her. "I
hope you guys have a really fun time."

"Thanks," Zoe and Max both said, but Ashley remained silent.

Avery took Sophia's hand and squeezed it. He was
a little bit ticked at Zoe for not being on his side when
it came to the date change, but then again, she catered

toward Ashley just like he used to do. He supposed old habits die hard. Lucky for him those days were over. "You ready, Sophia?"

"Yes." Sophia nodded. "I have a long day tomorrow. It was nice to get to spend time with you," she said to Zoe and Max, and then flicked a brief glance at Ashley. "I'm really looking forward to when you and your bridesmaids come in for the trial run for your updos. Start getting pictures together. I've got some lovely hair jewelry from Nicolina Diamante or you can go with a weave of fresh flowers from Flower Power to complement the color of your dresses. There are lots of fun choices and we'll explore them all. If you have any pictures to send me ahead of time that will be really helpful."

"I'm looking forward to it too," Zoe said, and Avery thought he caught a little look of guilt in Zoe's eyes. Well, good. Perhaps after having her seeing him with Sophia she would finally get the message that he was done with Ashley and had found someone really wonderful. "My mother wants you to do her hair for the wedding too. Have you met my parents yet?"

"Not yet," Sophia said. "I'm sure they're lovely folks."

"I adore Carla and Tommy," Ashley said with a smug smile. "My mama and Carla were best friends just like Zoe and me. Isn't that just the coolest thing?" she asked Sophia.

Sophia nodded.

Avery shifted in his seat, not liking the direction the evening was suddenly going. They seriously needed to get the hell out of there—and fast. "We'll see you around," he said and couldn't quite keep the impatience out of his voice.

"See you this weekend, Avery. It's going to be a blast," Ashley said. Avery pointedly ignored her comment.

"We promise not to get too wild," Max said to Sophia who smiled back at him. "I'll be the voice of reason."

"Since when?" Avery asked with a grin at his friend. Damn, he missed Max.

"Since I'm getting married."

"Speak for yourself," Ashley said. She put her hand to her chest. "I, for one, fully intend to get a little bit crazy. Isn't that what these weekends are for? One last hurrah?" Ashley cooed with a nudge to Zoe who shot her a frown. "What? Why on earth are you so uptight tonight?" She flicked Sophia a glance as if she was somehow the culprit. "Oh . . . I get it."

"Okay, we're heading out," Avery said and extended his hand toward Sophia. He grasped her fingers firmly as they made their way toward the entrance.

"I'm going to say good-bye to Grace, if you don't mind."

Avery leaned in and gave her a quick kiss. "No, take as long as you like, I'll meet you at the front door. I'm going to make a stop in the men's room."

"Okay, I'll meet you there in a few minutes." She smiled but he could tell that she was upset and rightfully so. He felt like going back in there and giving Ashley a piece of his mind but didn't want to give her the satisfaction of letting her see how riled up she'd gotten him. And since he didn't know what went on in the ladies' room he felt at a disadvantage. Damn, he wanted to know!

Avery tried not to dwell on what Ashley might have said to Sophia and put a smile on his face when he met her at the front door. After they were seated in his truck he finally said, "Well, I'm glad that's behind us. Thanks for coming with me, Sophia."

"Oh, Avery, your sister is really nice. She and Max make a great couple. I can tell that they are completely in love. She's going to make such a beautiful bride."

"Thanks, I miss hanging out with them," Avery said, and then could have bitten his tongue. "Max and I have been friends for a long time and you already know I'm close to Zoe."

"Oh, I know. This can't be easy for you."

"Yeah, it hasn't been, but now that Zoe's seen how good we are together we can start doing more things with the two of them. Why don't we plan a barbecue at my house soon?"

"Sure." Sophia nodded but her smile still seemed distant.

Avery felt a flash of anxiety grip him hard in the gut. After a moment of silence, he asked, "Do you want to come back to my house or head to your place?"

"Actually, Avery, I'm really tired so if you don't mind I'd like to go home."

When she didn't mention inviting him up, his anxiety kicked it up a notch. "Okay," he said with pointed reluctance and started up the truck. "But thank you again for coming with me tonight."

"You're welcome, Avery, but you don't have to keep thanking me."

Sophia remained silent on the short drive back but Avery was uncertain whether or not to approach the subject of what went on in the bathroom again. Unfortunately, whatever happened with Ashley felt like a time bomb ready to explode and he didn't have any idea how to defuse it since he was clueless as to what was said.

Avery reached over and took Sophia's hand and although she didn't pull away, she didn't slide a smile his way or make her usual cute remarks. She failed to sing along with the music on the radio and seemed deep in thought. When they pulled into her parking lot he found a vacant spot and killed the engine. "Mind if I come up for a little while?" he asked and when she hesitated, dread mixed with the anxiety he was feeling. "Sophia, are we going to talk about it?" he asked gently. "We need to."

Sophia looked at him with uncertainty in her eyes. After swallowing hard she lifted one shoulder. "I don't know."

"Can I please come up for a minute so we can figure this out? I don't want to do this in the truck."

"Okay," she finally softly agreed.

Dread made his footsteps feel heavy against the pavement. He opened the passenger door and assisted her down but instead of playfully falling against him like she usually did, she held herself away. He wanted to pull her into his arms and kiss away whatever was bothering her. She did take his offered hand and he felt a slight tremble as his heart pounded with slow dread. Whatever she was going to say wasn't going to be good. He could feel it hanging heavy in the air between them.

Instead of kissing in the elevator like they were prone to do, Sophia kept her eyes on the numbers. Avery's mind raced and he braced himself for whatever she was going to tell him. The abnormal silence felt thick and unnatural. He wanted to hear her laughter, see her sweet smile.

Once they were inside her apartment she walked over to the fridge and pulled out two bottles of water. "Want one?"

"Yeah, thanks." Avery nodded, thinking he could use something stronger but went over to sit down on the sofa. Sophia sat in a chair and unscrewed the cap on her water bottle. After taking a sip she inhaled a deep breath. She played with the cap, screwing and unscrewing as if the action helped her gather her thoughts.

"Sophia, please just tell me what's on your mind."

She went still for a long, agonizing moment. "Ashley confessed to me that she cheated on you with a Cougar baseball player."

Avery's pulse quickened and he sat there stunned, not knowing what to say. "She . . . she did?" What the hell!

Sophia nodded. "She also told me that you said that she was the love of your life." She looked at his face as if searching for answers.

"Of course, I did, Sophia. I proposed to her—remember?"

"Yes, I remember." She took another swallow of her water. "She said that you still love her but that you simply can't forgive her. And that I would forever be your second choice."

Avery felt a scorching flash of anger at Ashley and bit back an oath. "That's complete nonsense."

"Is it?" Sophia frowned and started playing with the cap again.

"Yes! Sophia, I enjoy being with you more than I ever did with Ashley. You're everything she isn't." With his heart pounding he shoved his fingers through his hair. "And that's a good thing."

"But don't you see?"

"See what?"

"You might *like me* more than you do Ashley. She might drive you crazy with her selfish ways but that doesn't mean that you don't still love her. Let's face it, if she hadn't cheated you'd be married by now, right?"

"But she did cheat!" Avery said hotly, and then it hit him hard what Sophia was getting at.

"Maybe you should just dig deep and find a way to forgive her. Then you could go back to the four of you hanging out like old times. She made a mistake, Avery. People do. She said it was meaningless."

"Well, it sure meant something to me. She slept with another man while she had my ring on her finger. That's not a mistake," he answered, while trying to tamp down his anger. It wasn't fair to Sophia for him to lose it. "Sophia, why in the world are you defending her? I don't get it."

Sophia was silent for a moment. She looked at him with troubled eyes and finally said, "I'm not defending her. What she did to you was horrible. But unforgivable? I don't know."

"Yes, it is unforgivable. How could I ever trust her again? Trust is the foundation of any relationship."

"And so is love."

Avery wondered where she was going with this but

it felt like a runaway train and he didn't know how to stop the momentum. "Of course. But you can't have one without the other."

Sophia played with the cap again so Avery knew there was more to come. "But Avery . . ." She swallowed hard, licked her bottom lip, and then finally said, "You've never told me that you love me."

For a second, her statement actually took him by surprise. "I . . . I haven't?" he asked, but he knew he hadn't and that was such a stupid reaction. He'd meant to, *wanted to*, but he supposed there'd been that lingering fear of saying those three little words that gave the other person so much power to inflict pain.

"No," she answered softly. "I think I would have remembered that little fact."

"Sophia, I—"

"Please don't say it now," she pleaded, her words trembling on her tongue.

"But—"

"I think we should"—she inhaled a breath—"stop seeing each other."

The runaway train picked up speed. "Sophia, no!"

"You need to take a step back and figure out where your heart is. Maybe search for forgiveness."

"I know where my heart is!" He held her gaze for a moment but she looked down at the floor as if studying the design of the carpet. "Sophia, my heart belongs to you and only you."

"I know that you want it to be so, but you have to take a step back, examine your feelings, and make sure."

"I don't want to take any steps back. Sophia, please don't do this."

"We have to." He could hear the anguish in her voice. "You know, I think that if we had simply started dating and not begun with the whole pretend thing, I would feel better about . . . us. But this started out being about Ashley. Tonight was about Ashley. I need to feel like . . . like this is about . . . me."

Avery squeezed his bottle of water so hard that the plastic crackled. "Sophia, I should have never made that damned promise to her! If I hadn't—"

"No," she interrupted. "You made the promise to protect her reputation and to save your sister the hurtful truth, but maybe there's more to it than you realize."

"What do you mean?" He shook his head, unable to believe this was happening.

"If nobody knew what she did to you then you could go back to her without risking your pride."

"No, I won't give you that. Sophia, you're reading more into this than what's there. You're overthinking this. It's your worry gene, remember?" he asked hopefully.

"Oh, Avery, it's more than just being worried."

He shoved his fingers through his hair feeling a wave of panic wash over him. "You're not really being fair to me. You said earlier not to play into her hands so why are you letting her win?"

"This isn't about winning or losing. And it's not fair to either of us. Maybe after the wedding . . . when all of this is behind you . . . maybe then we can . . . start fresh? When you have this all figured out."

"Sophia, no! There's nothing to figure out. I want you at the wedding with me." Avery patted his chest so hard that it hurt. "This is crazy. Look, I should have never asked you to come tonight. I knew she would pull something. But I couldn't have predicted . . . *this*."

Sophia closed her eyes for a moment, pressed her lips together, and then looked at him. Tears were shining in her eyes and he wanted to gather her into his arms. "Don't you see? It's still all about Ashley. Even right now."

"Then let's not allow tonight or any other night be

about her ever again." Avery wanted to stand up, pull Sophia to her feet and into his arms but he was suddenly afraid that she'd push him away and he wouldn't be able to handle her rejection. "Sophia, she pulled out all of the stops tonight. I should have put her in her place from the very beginning. And I should have refused to change the date for the bachelor party."

"You tried, Avery. She seems to always get her way and I suppose old habits die hard."

"I'm so sorry. I feel as if I've let you down. No, I did let you down." He leaned forward and rested his hands on his knees. "Sophia . . . can't we try to talk this out? If we break up this will be exactly what she wanted."

"I don't care what Ashley wants. This is about what I want."

"So then what do you want from me?"

"To be sure."

"I am sure." And he was sure but he didn't know how to convince Sophia. "God, I don't want to go . . . to leave things like this. I should have told you how I feel about you sooner."

"Avery, there had to be a reason for you to hold back," she said quietly, sadly. "Let's just give this some time."

Avery nodded because he didn't know what else to do. He was losing his composure. His heart raced. His chest felt heavy and bruised. He wondered if this was what a panic attack felt like. But he didn't want to lose it in front of Sophia. After all he'd put her through tonight, he didn't want her to see him break down. "Okay," he finally said. "I don't want to leave but if you want me to, I guess I will." He looked at her, hoping she would let him stay. He just wanted to go to bed and hold her. Surely if he held her in his arms she would feel his love for her seep into her body.

Sophia's lips trembled. She inhaled a shaky breath. "I don't *want* you to go, Avery, but I need you to. I have to sort all of this out and so do you."

Avery held her gaze for a moment longer, giving her time to change her mind but she remained silent. She looked ready to crumble as well so how could this be the right thing to do? "Okay," he finally managed. "But if you want me . . . *need me* to come back I'm just a phone call away. I will come over no matter what time it is. Please promise me."

"I promise." She gave him a slow, sad nod When she swallowed hard he knew she was on the verge of tears. How could he leave her? He saw a flash of indecision but she quickly hid it by taking a sip of water.

"Sophia . . ."

"I'll be fine."

"Call Grace, your mom, or Carrie Ann." Or let me stay.

"Avery, really. I'll be okay. I'm a big girl, remember?" she asked and the tremble in her voice clawed at his heart.

Avery shoved his fingers through his hair but reluctantly nodded. He wanted so much to tell her that he loved her and almost did but felt like it would be another mistake.

And so he pushed up to his feet and walked out the door.

20

Hope Floats

"SOPHIA, SWEET PEA, IF YOUR FACE GETS ANY LONGER your chin is gonna drag along the floor." Carrie Ann shot a concerned look Sophia's way while hanging bridal veils on a vintage hat rack.

White Lace and Promises looked absolutely stunning and she wished that Sophia could enjoy the fruits of her labor. With open house only two days away, her young friend should be over the moon instead of walking around with a glum face and a heavy heart.

Sophia glanced up from her laptop. "I'm okay, Carrie Ann."

"Then you don't know the definition of okay."

"I'm as okay as I can be."

"Which isn't okay at all, I'm afraid. Why don't you do yourself a favor and answer one of Avery's calls or at least send the boy a text message. Just give him a little crumb of hope. And don't you dare tell me there isn't hope for you two."

Sophia shook her head. "Avery needs to address his feelings for Ashley."

"Oh, sweetheart, the boy adores you. Easton said that Avery's been a hot mess ever since you two split up."

"We haven't exactly split up. We just need some time apart." She looked back down at whatever she'd been working on for the past hour.

"And just what will time away from each other accomplish except for both of you two being miserable?"

Sophia looked up from her laptop once more. "Please don't make me feel guilty."

Carrie Ann fluffed up the veil, and then fisted her hands on her hips. "I'm not laying a guilt trip on you, girlie. I just want you to face the truth." Carrie Ann walked over and squeezed Sophia's shoulder. "I know that love is as scary as walking into a spiderweb. You feel all trapped and try to escape and fly into a complete panic when there's really not any danger. Sophia, I have to say that you're overreacting."

"I can't help it."

"Oh, honey, you're speaking to the poster child for being scared of being in love. But you're so much better for Avery than Ashley ever could be. You've met her so you must know that he's so much better off with you."

"But it isn't just about that, don't you see? In a lot of ways my grounded, business-minded father was better for my mom than rocker Rick Ruleman, but they lacked . . . passion. I think she loved both of them in different ways but it wasn't until Jimmy that she found the right combination of love, commitment, and that certain special something. You have to have the whole package. Like you found with Easton."

"And you don't think that you and Avery have chemistry? I sure see it with you two. You were friends first just like Easton and me. Love that blossoms from friendship is something special. I just think you let that piece of work get under your skin just like she wanted to do."

"I know what you're saying." Sophia shrugged. "But Avery obviously fell for her. I mean he asked her to marry him for pity's sake. Some guys go for prissy women."

"I agree and I just don't get it. Just like some women continually fall for bad boys."

"Maybe it's the challenge or something but I've seen it before. My mother says I can be too nice, sometimes. Maybe nice is just simply boring."

"Oh, would you just stop that! You are anything but boring. Being nice is a good thing. You know some women think they're all that and a bag of chips and are somehow able to convince others the same thing. But friendship is a solid basis for a lasting relationship, not being uppity and prissy and just plain vain."

Sophia nodded but didn't appear convinced.

"You know, Ashley was Avery's high school sweetheart and boys at that age don't go beneath the surface. Physical attraction can be mistaken for love."

"They've been together that long? I didn't realize . . ."

"Yeah well, I bet if he'd met Ashley Montgomery now he wouldn't have gone past one date."

Sophia tilted her head. "Really? That's an interesting thought, but I don't know. She still can get to him. It makes me wonder if he will ever completely get over her."

"What makes you think Avery's not over her? Sophia, they broke up for a reason. A solid reason."

"Yeah . . ."

Carrie Ann peered at her closely. "Wait, do you know why? Because the rest of us sure as heck don't. Avery's always been closemouthed about it and I respected his privacy but I've always felt that there had to be something serious happen for them to suddenly break up so close to the wedding."

Sophia went very still, and then nodded. "I know why."

"Well, hell's bells, are you going to enlighten me?"

Carrie Ann could tell that Sophia wanted to confide in her and so she pressed the issue. "You know without a doubt that whatever you say to me will go nowhere. I won't even tell Easton."

"Oh, I don't know . . . It was Ashley who told me and—"

"What? Are you kiddin' me?"

"I wish."

"Did you promise not to say anything?"

"No, but she said that if anyone finds out her little secret that Avery will know it came from me and he will be really pissed."

"Oh, issuing threats, is she?" Carrie Ann felt a hot flash of anger.

"Yeah, and she's really good at it."

"Sophia, you trust me, right?"

"Absolutely," Sophia replied, but just as she started to say something Carrie Ann's phone pinged. "Go ahead and get that."

"Saved by the bell?" Carrie Ann was about to ignore the text message but when she looked down her blood ran cold. "Oh . . . oh my God!" She put a hand to her chest and thought she might pass out.

"Carrie Ann, what is it?"

"It's Easton. He's in the ER with chest pains! Oh, Sophia, what if he's having a heart attack?" Her own heart danced around in her chest and she felt as if she was hyperventilating. "Oh, God, I can't breathe!"

"Try to stay calm." Sophia jumped up from her desk and grabbed her purse. "Let's get over there right now."

"Can . . . can you drive? My hands are shaking like a leaf."

"Sure, come on!"

Less than fifteen minutes later they were standing in the brightly lit emergency room. They quickly learned that Easton had been taken back for tests and it was driving Carrie Ann crazy not knowing what was going on.

"Why aren't they telling us anything?" she asked. "Do you think that's a bad sign?" She was seriously considering busting through the double doors and going looking for him, hospital rules be damned.

"They must not know anything yet. Go and sit down. I'll get you something cold to drink. Preference?"

"A Coke, I guess." And a double shot of bourbon would be nice right about now.

"Coming right up."

"Thank you, sweetie." A couple of minutes later Carrie Ann accepted the cold Coke that Sophia pressed into her hand. She popped the tab and absently took a small swig. Icy fingers of fear slid down her spine and made her insides tremble. She should have probably opted for coffee but the machine was one of those where the paper cup filled with steaming coffee that tasted like pine tar.

"I'm sure it won't be long now. I'm going to make a quick run to the bathroom. I'll be right back."

"Okay, sweetie." Carrie Ann nodded and tried to calm down but fear felt like a living, breathing thing inside her body. The antiseptic smell of the hospital made her stomach churn. She pictured Easton in a small white bed with tubes everywhere and machines blinking and beeping just like when she had to go in and see her father for the very last time. Her sisters had been too young to go and her mother had said that she didn't have to go but Carrie Ann had done it in spite of her fear, thinking that if she could just talk to him that she could give her father the strength to wake up. She felt certain that she could will him back to life.

But fifteen-year-old Carrie Ann hadn't been prepared for the sight of her father in the hospital bed. He'd been deathly pale and bloated and didn't resemble anything like her robust, smiling dad who never failed to crack a joke. God, he'd been so small, so frail, and so utterly helpless.

Oh, how she wished she'd had the chance to hear his voice just one last time and above all else to tell him that she loved him. "I love you, Daddy. Please don't leave us." She'd whispered it to him, but was too afraid to touch him. Her mama had leaned over and had given him a kiss and brushed his hair back from his forehead but Carrie Ann had been too scared and had later felt guilty that she hadn't kissed her father good-bye.

What if Easton died too? The thought paralyzed her with mind-numbing fear.

Waiting was driving her insane with worry but if the doctor came out and said she could go back and see Easton, she wondered if her feet would obey. What if Easton looked small and helpless? Carrie Ann suddenly had the almost uncontrollable urge to flee right out the revolving door. She didn't know where she'd even run to . . . She just would keep running and running until her legs gave out.

Feeling nauseous, Carrie Ann swallowed hard. She looked at the red EXIT sign and gripped the metal arms of the stiff orange vinyl chair. Why in the world were hospitals always decorated dull orange and muddy brown? And what was with the speckled floor?

A moment later Sophia walked her way and after taking a look at what had to be her stricken face said, "Carrie Ann, are you okay?" She rushed over and sat in the chair next to her. "Stupid question. Is there something I can get you? Crackers?"

Carrie Ann patted Sophia's hand. "No, honey, I don't think I could choke them down. But thanks." In an effort to curb her panic she picked up a magazine from a scattered, ratty pile. "This *People* magazine is from last summer. Can you believe that?" She tossed it down. "Oh, Sophia, this is driving me out of my mind."

"I know," Sophia said in a small voice. She reached over and took Carrie Ann's hand. "Easton is a big, strong man. He'll be fine."

Carrie Ann tried to smile but couldn't muster one up. Instead, she grimaced and nearly broke down. "That's what I thought about my father," she said gruffly. Now she remembered why she steered away from puppies and relationships. Getting attached meant getting hurt. She wondered who just groaned and realized that it was her.

"Oh, Carrie Ann, I'm so sorry you're going through this. But there is so much they can do these days. I'm sure Easton is in good hands. And I know everything I'm saying sounds so trite and lame so I'll shut up now."

"Oh, sweetie, no, I'm so glad you're here with me. You've become so special to me." She patted Sophia's hand that felt warm beneath her ice-cold fingers.

"I feel the same way," Sophia said with a smile that trembled slightly.

Carrie Ann took another sip of the Coke hoping it might settle her stomach. Fizz tickled her nose and she coughed when the swallow she took went down wrong way.

"Are you okay?"

Carrie Ann held up her hand and nodded. "Went down the wrong pipe." She cleared her throat and then waved a hand through the air. "Although I could never understand that saying since there really is only one pipe." She reached up and touched her neck. "When I was a kid I thought there were two." And when she was a kid she thought her dad would live to be old and gray.

"And I believed in unicorns," Sophia said.

"What, you mean there really aren't unicorns?" Carrie Ann asked with widened eyes making Sophia chuckle. She inhaled a deep breath trying to get a grip and to not let her imagination conjure up the worst but she failed miserably. She handed Sophia a copy of *Good Housekeeping.* "Only four months old."

"What, no *Cosmopolitan*?"

"If there was it would probably go back to the Burt

Reynolds centerfold. And you probably have no idea what I'm talking about."

"Burt Reynolds naked?" Sophia shuddered. "Ew."

"Oh, forty years ago he was what we used to call a hunk. Three pages of chest hair on a bear rug. If I remember, and I do, he was smoking."

"The full monty?"

"His arm was strategically placed over his package, but for the time, it caused quite a stir."

"Yeah, my mother's one-piece swimsuit pose was considered super sexy."

"My, how times have changed."

"Yeah, now we have *Magic Mike* on the big screen." Sophia chuckled but accepted the old magazine and started to thumb through it.

Carrie Ann leaned back in the chair and looked up at the clock. They'd been there for only about an hour but it felt like a damned lifetime. Oh boy . . . how much longer?

Carrie Ann closed her eyes and tried to slow down her racing pulse. She hated this feeling of helplessness. A cold ball of fear settled in her stomach and refused to budge.

What in the hell was she doing getting married? She'd avoided this kind of mind-numbing fear all of her life and now here she was sitting in a hospital waiting room feeling like she needed to pass out or throw up or maybe both. In that moment, she made the decision that she was going to call the engagement off. She reached over and squeezed Sophia's hand suddenly knowing now why her young friend was afraid to continue her relationship with Avery. "Love is just so damn scary," she whispered.

"Tell me about it," Sophia answered and squeezed back.

"So now what are we gonna do?"

"I dunno." Sophia shrugged. "Run off somewhere where no one will ever find us?"

"Sounds like a good plan to me," Carrie Ann said with a mirthless chuckle. "Think we can find a deserted island somewhere?"

"We can look on Craigslist. Find one cheap."

Carrie Ann managed a halfhearted chuckle. "And hang out with Captain Jack Sparrow and drink lots of rum?"

"The plan keeps getting better."

"It does," Carrie Ann agreed but couldn't imagine life without Easton. In that moment she realized that running wasn't an option no matter what happened.

"Have you called Carla or Avery?" Sophia asked softly.

"No, but I suppose I should. Easton must not have or they would have been here by now. I was hoping to get some information first, but—" She stopped in midsentence when a nurse came through the door pushing Easton in a wheelchair. He appeared pale and somewhat irritated.

Carrie Ann jumped up and rushed over ignoring the rubbery feeling in her noodlelike legs. "Easton, are you okay?" she asked, relieved that there weren't any tubes or a beeping machine in sight.

"Yes, I'm gonna be fine." Easton nodded and gave her and Sophia a sheepish look. "I wanted to walk but I was told this is hospital policy or somethin'." He sent the nurse an annoyed glance over his shoulder but she didn't seem to care. "Foolish if you ask me."

"Oh, Mr. Fisher, I have to follow the rules," the young nurse responded in a cheerful voice. "Just sit back and enjoy the ride."

Carrie Ann looked at the nurse. "What was wrong with him?" Her heart refused to stop beating as fast as a hummingbird's wings. "His heart? Is he being admitted?"

"No, I'm sending him home. He's all yours."

"Easton?" Carrie Ann asked. "Is anyone going to tell me what in the world happened to you?"

"I . . . I was having chest pains and broke out into a cold sweat. Sorry to cause you such worry, sweetheart. I feel like such a fool. I simply panicked."

"No, Mr. Fisher, don't be so hard on yourself. Chest pains aren't anything to mess around with. Believe me—you did the right thing by coming here," the nurse said firmly. "It's much better to be safe than sorry."

"Well, now I'm safe *and* sorry," he said with a half-hearted chuckle.

Carrie Ann returned her attention to the perky nurse. "What was the cause of the pains?"

"Acute indigestion. Apparently those superhot wings for lunch didn't agree with Mr. Fisher."

Carrie Ann looked at Easton for answers and he said, "I feel like a complete ass. I'm so sorry to have caused you so much worry."

"Hot wings?" Relief made Carrie Ann feel weak in the knees but she also felt an acute flash of annoyance. "Is it wrong for me to want to box your ears?"

"No, feel free," Easton answered.

"How hot were those wings?" Sophia asked.

"Way too hot and I ate them on a dare over at Sully's." He shook his head. "Damned stupid of me."

"Did Avery dare you?" Carrie Ann asked. "If he did I'll—"

"No . . . it was *Sam Hanson*. I do believe he added a couple of shakes of extra hot sauce when I wasn't lookin'."

Carrie Ann felt another flash of irritation. "Okay, I *am* going to box your ears."

"Stupid . . ." Easton said, shaking his head as they reached the entrance to the hospital.

"Okay, you're all set, Mr. Fisher. Stay away from superhot foods from now on."

"Oh, don't worry about that," Easton answered.

When they were outside in the bright sunshine and fresh air Carrie Ann's stomach felt nearly normal.

"Why don't you go on home with Easton," Sophia

said. "I'm going to wrap things up at the salon as soon as I get back anyway. I'm more than ready for the open house and if I go back there I'll just start rearranging things for the millionth time."

"Sophia, White Lace and Promises is perfect. You don't need to change one little bitty thing." Carrie Ann looked at Easton. "That okay with you?"

"Are you sure? I don't want for you to cut your day short on account of my stupid drama," Easton said. "Sophia, I'm really sorry for all of the bother."

"No worries." Sophia shook her head and went up on tiptoe to give him a quick kiss on the cheek. "I'm just glad that you're okay. That's all that's important." She gave Carrie Ann a hug. "I'll see you tomorrow."

"Sure thing, sweetie. I blocked myself off at A Cut Above tomorrow and Saturday. White Lace and Promises is going to be a huge success. I'm so proud of you!"

Sophia smiled but Carrie Ann could see the sadness lurking in her eyes and it caused a hot lump to form in her throat. She watched Sophia walk away and had to sigh.

Easton took her hand. "She and Avery belong together. I hope they figure it out."

"Me too."

"Yeah, they shouldn't wait as long as we did to finally get together."

Carrie Ann smiled up at him as they walked to his truck. Once she was settled in the passenger seat, she inhaled a deep breath. Her emotions were all over the map, making her feel unsettled, and she wished she'd thought to have brought her Coke with her but she'd left it forgotten on the end table with the ancient magazines.

On the drive to the cabin, she remained fairly quiet, not knowing how she was going to react once they were home. She knew that Easton felt horrible and she didn't want him to feel worse after the scare he'd been through. The cold ball of fear finally thawed out, but some of the anxiety remained.

When they pulled into the driveway and stopped by the big garage, she felt a bit surprised and realized she'd been staring unseeing out of the window most of the way home.

Had Easton spoken to her and she hadn't heard him? Or was he just as unsettled as she was and needed to sort through his feelings too?

Well . . . she was about to find out.

21

Hot Sauce

EASTON OPENED CARRIE ANN'S DOOR AND OFFERED his hand just as he usually did. She gave him a brief smile but she seemed somewhere else. Of course he knew why. His heart attack scare had probably brought about memories of the death of her father. Although he wanted to kick his own ass for his damned stupid hot wings stunt, he wasn't about to let this come between them. In fact, he was going to address the situation with her as soon as he had a glass of wine in her hand. After entering the cabin he didn't even ask but went straight for the fridge and uncorked a fresh bottle of her favorite Chardonnay.

"It's only four o'clock."

"I think you deserve an early happy hour."

"I'm inclined to agree with you." Carrie Ann accepted the proffered long-stemmed glass and took a deep sip. "Mmmm, that hit the spot." She raised her glass in salute. "They should have wine in a machine at the hospital instead of that horrid stuff they try to call coffee." She grinned but failed to give him her usual throaty laugh.

"I think I need a generous pour of Woodford Reserve," Easton said, not caring if his stomach decided to rebel. To hell with babying his stomach today like the perky nurse suggested. A glass of milk just wouldn't do the trick. And yogurt? Was she kidding? He needed to take the edge off his nerves. "Let's go sit in front of the fireplace." He hoped that the flickering flames and cozy soft sofa would also have the usual calming affect they did at the end of a long day.

"Okay, that sounds nice," Carrie Ann replied and followed him into the great room.

After they were settled against the cushions, Easton scooted around to face her. "I can't tell you how sorry I am for scaring you today."

"You don't need to apologize again." She played with the stem of her glass and pressed her lips together as if holding in emotion.

"Yes, I do," Easton insisted and he was surprised at the wave of emotion that suddenly gripped him. "When I started having the chest pains I immediately headed for the hospital. Anyone who knows me will tell you that I'm usually very reluctant to go to the doctor but . . ." He had to stop to regain his composure. "Carrie Ann, all I could think about is how you would feel if something happened to me, so I didn't even hesitate. I hated sending that text message knowing that it would frighten you." He closed his eyes and swallowed the hot moisture clogging his throat. When she took his hand, he opened his eyes.

"I can only imagine."

"I'm not really afraid of dying. Not that I want to," he added with a wry grin. "I never have been. I know I'm on good terms with my maker and I've lived a good life. What scared the ever-lovin' daylights out of me is the kind of pain you might have to endure if something happened to me."

"Oh, Easton . . ."

"But what scares me more than anything in the

world is losing you." When she squeezed his hand he
felt a damned tear slide down his cheek. "And I don't
mean . . . dying. We don't have control over when we go.
But we do have control over how we spend these days
here on Earth. And I want to spend each and every one
of them with you by my side. We've waited way too long
and I don't want to miss another minute. Today only
reiterated my feelings for you."

"Oh, my sweet baby . . ." Carrie Ann reached up
and cupped his chin rubbing her thumb over the stubble. "I'll be honest. I looked over at the EXIT sign in
that ugly waiting room and wanted to run for the hills.
I thought to myself . . . What in the hell am I doing getting married?" She shook her head. "I wanted to avoid
this kind of heart-pounding fear at all costs. Easton, I
pictured myself going into your room and seeing you
in a hospital bed looking weak and helpless like my
daddy did." Inhaling a deep breath, she dropped her
hand and leaned over to set her wineglass on the coffee
table. "I know all too well how quickly life can be
snatched away."

"I know." He scrubbed a hand down his face. "Damn,
I know." He took a sip of his drink and looked down at
the cubes of ice.

"But I didn't run away, now did I?"

Easton looked up in surprise.

She met his gaze and lifted her chin. "Today I had
to face my worst fear full-on."

Easton managed a slight smile. "And you did it."

"Well, not exactly with what you'd call flying colors,
but yes, I did. Now don't get me wrong, it's still my worst
fear, no doubt," she said, but shook her head. "No, I've
got that wrong. My worst fear is letting my fear get the
best of me like I allowed it to for far too long."

"So you have nothing to fear but fear itself?"

She finally chuckled. "Well, and I don't like spiders
and snakes."

Easton sat up straighter and he smiled, relieved to

hear her sense of humor return. "Well, I can dispel that fear right now. Like I said, we might not have any control on how long we're gonna be on this earth, but we can do our very best to make the most out of the time we have while we're here."

"Exactly. So as much as I still want to box your ears for taking a dare from Sam, today taught me a lesson. I need to stop worrying about what tomorrow will bring and to appreciate today." She put both hands on his cheeks and leaned in to kiss him tenderly. Leaning back she wiped the tracks of his tears with her thumbs. "I love you, Easton Fisher. And I'm not going to let a day go by without telling you so." She started to cry as well, and then her tears turned to laughter. He joined her, laughing and crying at the same time.

"I love you too, Carrie Ann. And as stupid as it was to eat those damned hot wings, I'd do it again just to hear you say what you just did to me."

"Okay, but since we've got this out of the way, don't do it again, okay?"

Easton laughed. "I promise." He leaned in and kissed her. "Mmm, you taste so good."

"So do you. Like fine bourbon and sexy man."

"Really?" He nuzzled her neck, loving the scent of her perfume, the taste of her skin. He kissed the rapid beat of her pulse and shoved his fingers in her hair, shaking it loose around her shoulders. "So you think I'm sexy, do you?"

"You know it." She moaned when he cupped her breast. Needing to feel her warm, supple skin he put his drink down and slid his hand beneath her sweater. "Oh, your hand is cold!" She gasped, and then laughed low in her throat when he deftly unclasped her bra with one little flick of his fingers. "You're pretty good at that. Have you had a lot of practice?"

"I just have magic fingers."

"Oh really now? Care to show me?"

"Well, I think it stays with the theme of making the

best of the time we have together." He took her glass
from her and tugged her sweater over her head. She
shimmied out of her loose bra. Her breasts, full, lush,
tumbled forward begging for his touch, his mouth.

"Oh, Easton . . ." She tipped her head back, giving
him better access and he took it. When he sucked her
nipple into his mouth she moaned and started tugging
at his shirt.

"I want to make love to you on the rug in front of
the fire." He helped her to her feet and she landed
against him, laughing while they tried to kiss all the
way over to the soft, fluffy rug that she'd bought just
last week. He loved her feminine touches to the cabin
and encouraged her to make it her home as well.

Easton fumbled with his jeans, nearly falling over in
his haste to shed his boots. When he finally managed
to undress, Carrie Ann came up to her knees, cupped
his ass, and took him into her sweet, warm mouth.
He watched, thinking she was the sexiest woman alive.
She used the very tip of her tongue to tease him
lightly, licking and swirling until he was on the brink
of exploding. "Carrie Ann," he said gruffly, "I want to
be inside of you."

"Just where I want you to be." Nodding, she gave
him one last lick and eased down onto the rug. "Making sweet love to me. Or crazy love to me. Just love me."

"I do love you. All of you, inside and out." Easton
feasted his gaze on her naked body, caressing her with
his eyes. Her deep red hair fanned out in sharp contrast to the soft white fur of the oval rug. The glow
from the fire turned her skin a golden hue and for a
moment he could only stare. "Come to me," she said in
a breathless voice. She lifted her arms, beckoning him.

"Wild horses couldn't keep me away." Easton knelt
down next to her, rubbing his hands up her silky legs
and grazed over her mound. He leaned over and took
one breast in his mouth and then gave his attention to
the other until he heard her groan. He let his fingers

trail lightly over her body pausing here and there, and then dipping his finger between her thighs loving it when he found her wet and supple. He caressed her, knowing just how she wanted to be touched. He loved exploring her body, learning new pleasure points, and filing them into his memory.

"Easton . . . please . . ."

"Anything you want. Just tell me."

"I want you inside me."

He answered her plea by scooting his hands beneath her ass. Not just . . . *yet*." Tilting her up, he kissed her . . . *there*. She arched her back and threaded her fingers into his hair, looking wanton and lusty. He loved how uninhibited she was with him, giving and taking and offering herself to him fully.

"God . . ."

Easton took her to the brink, enjoying her scent, her taste, and the sexy, breathless way she asked for more. But unable to take another minute, he pulled back and entered her with one sure stroke. She felt so warm, so ready for him. Maybe it was because of the earlier scare or the way she'd promised to let go of her fear . . . Whatever the reason, making love to her took him to an emotional level he'd not experienced before now. Easton became keenly aware of every little nuance, making each stroke incredibly erotic. The sound of skin against skin, the scent of woman, taste of wine on her lips, all seemed intensely sharp, so very vivid. He kissed her deeply, drinking her into his body and when she arched her back he could feel her orgasm clutching and squeezing. It pushed Easton over the edge. His pleasure seemed to start at his toes and pulsated with a hot rush that made him see stars. His heart pounded and he buried himself deep within her warm flesh, riding the orgasm out with a hot shiver.

Easton pulled her close, kissing her, holding her, while he felt a love so strong that it took his breath away. "I love you so much," he said, gently tucking her hair behind her ear. "More than I thought was even possible." When his voice shook slightly, he wasn't embarrassed but hugged her closer, kissing the top of her head.

"I feel the same way, Easton."

"I can't wait to call you my wife."

She smiled. "I promise to become a better cook and to learn how to use all of those fancy gadgets in the kitchen."

"If you want to but I'm content to do the cooking or better yet cook together. We'll travel and just enjoy each other's company."

"I'm looking forward to all of it." She nestled her head in the crook of his shoulder and splayed her hand on his chest. "Now all we have to do is get Avery and Sophia back together and all will be right with our world."

"Yeah, this has me perplexed. It's obvious that they are crazy in love. I just don't get it."

"Sophia's fear is that Avery still carries a torch for Ashley."

"He doesn't," Easton said firmly.

"You know, Sophia was going to tell me what Ashley said to her in the bathroom at Broomstick Brewery but I got the hot sauce message from you and didn't get the chance to find out what happened. She said that Ashley divulged to her why she and Avery broke off the engagement."

Easton felt a flash of surprise and had to wonder what her motive could be in pulling such a stunt. "That's interesting."

"Yes, and she had the nerve to tell Sophia that if she spilled the beans to anyone that Avery would know she was the culprit so she was bullied into keeping her mouth shut. Can you believe the audacity of that girl?"

"I can." Easton felt a muscle jump in his jaw. "And I know the reason." He couldn't keep the anger from his tone.

"You do? Avery told you?"

"Actually, I'd had an idea. I figured that Avery was somehow protecting her and I was right. She stepped out on him with a Cougar baseball player."

Carrie Ann gasped. "Ruined her engagement for a roll in the hay. Stupid girl. Oh, I feel so sorry for Avery. But I guess it was better to find out her true colors before getting married to her."

"I never did buy the growing apart excuse. He'd promised not to tell her dirty little secret so as not to ruin Zoe's wedding. I also know he was trying to keep the knowledge from Ashley's parents. Avery's heart was in the right place but it sure did end up causing him a world of hurt that he sure didn't deserve. When I guessed the truth he unintentionally let it slip."

"Wow." Carrie Ann kissed his shoulder. "We should have put two and two together a long time ago. Poor Avery. Ashley was the culprit and he shouldered the blame this whole time. How can the girl look at herself in the mirror. Why would she tell Sophia?"

"I guess to take that weapon away from Sophia if Avery decided to tell her? Who knows what goes on in the mind of someone as heartless as Ashley? She's just a spoiled little princess who thinks rules don't apply to her. I wonder what else she said to get to Sophia the way she did?"

Carrie Ann sighed. "Most likely that Avery still loves her or some such nonsense. And Ashley changed the date of the bachelor and bachelorette party on purpose. You can take that to the bank."

"Oh, no doubt."

"Of course, Sophia told Avery that he needed to go since he's the best man. I personally think that he should have refused and made the rest of them take a stand instead of giving in to Ashley. The girl needs to be told no for once."

"Avery's problem is that he wants to please everyone. He didn't want to disappoint Max or Zoe and he told me that Sophia said she would be more upset if he stayed home and missed the bachelor weekend. The boy was caught between a rock and a hard place once again." Easton shook his head. "Think we should try to stop him from going?"

"I think you should at least call him and lead him in that direction. I understand that Sophia did the right thing by telling him to go but that was before Ashley pulled this little stunt."

"I do believe you're right." He reached for his pants and pulled out his cell phone. "Oh wow, I've got a text message from Avery." He slid his finger across the screen and groaned. "Damn, he said that he got finished early and so they're already headed for the lake."

"Now what do we do?"

Easton blew out a long sigh. "Damned if I know," he said, but then shook his head. "I take that back. I know exactly what I'm going to do."

"And what might that be?"

"I'm calling Tommy. As much as I want to, it should be his father coming to his son's aid, not me. Avery's been wanting to connect to his father, and this is a perfect opportunity to make what they both want happen."

"You're a good man, Easton Fisher."

"I've always aimed to be and that will never change." He came up to his elbow and leaned in to give Carrie Ann a lingering kiss. "Now let's set this plan in motion."

22

Got to Get You into My Life

AVERY SAT AT THE END OF THE DOCK SIPPING ON A cold beer without much interest. The rest of the guys were playing corn hole while getting their drink on even though it was early afternoon. The bridesmaids had stayed over last night since they couldn't get into their chalet until today but they'd left early and would return on Sunday. Avery had gone to bed before the rest of them, eager to get away from Ashley. Not that he'd slept. Between the noise and thinking about Sophia, Avery had remained awake until the wee hours of the morning. Even though he hadn't consumed that much beer last night, he still felt as if he'd been hit by a truck.

Avery looked out over the lake, absently watching ski boats whiz by thinking that he loved Max like a brother but he really wanted to be at the grand opening of White Lace and Promises. He'd bought into Sophia's insistence that she would feel worse if he failed to come to the bachelor party but now he realized he'd made a mistake. He also knew he should be up there chugging beer at least pretending to be having fun, for the sake of Max, but he just couldn't muster up the energy to fake it.

Avery watched a WaveRunner speed by and took another swig of his beer. Sunshine glinted off the lake making the water sparkle like diamonds and for some reason made him think of Sophia. He shook his head thinking that everything made him think about Sophia.

The weather had warmed up to the mid-seventies giving everyone a case of spring fever—well, everyone but *him*. Avery could smell the grill getting fired up, but burgers and hot dogs didn't hold any appeal either. Laughter and music drifted his way. He knew he should get back up there with the guys but his feet refused to cooperate. With a drawn-out sigh he leaned back so he could reach inside his jeans pocket for his cell phone.

Should he call Sophia and wish her luck?

At this point Sophia would be putting the finishing touches on the salon. Avery scrubbed a hand down his face. He'd already ordered a huge bouquet of roses to be delivered tomorrow morning from Flower Power. Maybe he should also send her one of those edible fruit things he'd seen commercials for or a box of her favorite Godiva chocolates? Or should he call Reese and order an entire Italian cream cake delivered from River Row Pizza? He wanted to do all of it but more than anything else he wanted to be there with her.

He should be bringing Sophia lunch about now or doing any last-minute thing that she might need. Of course, doing any of those things would require her to let him back into her life instead of this stupid separation that she thought he needed to search his heart. He didn't need to search for what was already there. If he had the power, he'd make his apologies to Max and hightail it back to Cricket Creek but he didn't have transportation so he was stuck until Sunday.

And it was killing him.

Avery took another swig of his beer thinking that he'd just get drunk and do some of the goofy stunts that they'd talk about for years. Wasn't it his job as the best man to get something crazy going? They'd talked about this weekend for so damned long and Avery felt as if he was letting Max down by sitting on the dock brooding in his beer.

Okay, he needed to quit sulking and get up there and get the party started.

Avery looked down at the can and willed himself to take a long swig. Surely once he had a buzz going he could muster up the energy to have some fun or at least do some serious pretending. Maybe he should have a shot of something, but his stomach churned at the thought. Damn, this wasn't good. He sighed deeply and was just about to try to chug the rest of the beer when he heard footsteps behind him. He looked over his shoulder, spotted Max, and tried for a grin.

"Dude, if that was a smile it was a total fail." Max sat down beside Avery and gave his shoulder a shove.

"I just have to get a few beers in me and I'll come around."

"Right," Max said with a shake of his head. "You trying to convince me or yourself?"

"Both, I guess. Max, I'm sorry. I promise to get my shit together and join in the fun."

Max took a swig of his beer and looked out over the lake for a moment. "No, I'm sorry. We shouldn't have caved in to Ashley's demands to change the date."

"Why do we always do that?"

Max shrugged. "I don't know. Habit? I should have stood up to her or at the very least insisted that you stayed home."

"I'm the best man."

"You are," Max said and Avery was a little surprised to hear deep emotion in Max's voice. "And you're also my best friend."

"Same here, Max. Man, I've missed you."

"For sure, me too. But listen, I've been thinking about this and of course Zoe and I have been talking about you and Ashley endlessly."

"There is no me and Ashley. Zoe needs to wrap her brain around that little detail."

"I know. Zoe just can't give it up." He took a swig of his beer. "You love Sophia, don't you?"

"Yeah." He hesitated, and then said, "But that night at the brewery, Ashley put it in Sophia's head that I'll always love her more and that Sophia is my second choice."

"Damn, that's cold."

"Yeah, don't tell Zoe, though."

"Maybe Zoe needs to know the truth. The *whole* truth, Avery. I know there's something you're not telling us."

"I don't want to mess up the wedding by getting drama started."

Max remained silent, but nodded. "I guess."

"Sounds like you have something more to say."

"Well, the four of us started hanging out together when we were just kids. When I fell in love with Zoe I think that maybe you and Ashley might have forced your relationship, you know?"

Avery nodded slowly. "Ashley pushed for it."

"It's what she thought she wanted. To be fair, I wanted for the two of you to be together, too. I know that Zoe and Ashley fantasized about having a double wedding when they were younger. They talked about how cool that would be." Max shrugged. "We were kids."

"Yeah, I get that. I mean, we had such good times together and she's a pretty girl. I was attracted to her. The two of us dating other people seemed odd, at the time, but looking back, we should have. Don't get me wrong—I did love her once." Avery glanced at Max. "But apparently she thinks I still do, which is not the case."

"Yeah, well, I think it's partly because she's just

used to getting her way. And it's human nature to want what you can't have. Especially her nature."

"Why did we always cater to her?"

Max shrugged. "We were kids and we all had our role, I guess. Ashley was the boss. I was the goof-off. Zoe was the perky one, always thinking of things for us to do."

"And me?"

"You tried to please everyone. You still do. So I have a question. What do you want?"

"To be with Sophia tomorrow. To have her back in my life where she belongs."

"Then do it, Avery. Look, I know you're trying to do the right thing by being here but you need to go back to Cricket Creek."

"But I'm your best man."

"And I'm the groom and I'm telling you to go home."

"How? I don't have a car."

"Call someone to come and get you."

"It's a three-hour drive. I don't want to—"

"Stop! Would you just listen to yourself? Avery, you would do it for a friend who needed a ride. Why don't you think that you deserve the same treatment from people who love you? Call your Uncle Easton. He'd be on his way in a heartbeat."

Avery nodded. "Yeah, he would. But even before we split up Sophia insisted that she wanted me to come here."

"Oh boy." Max chuckled. "You need to learn that women don't always say what they mean, but when we do what they ask we get in trouble for it. Trust me—she wants you at the grand opening."

"That's crazy. She insisted that I come here. How are you supposed to know what to do, then?"

"Look for clue words. *That's fine* means the opposite. *Maybe later* means never. And *it's up to you* really means you are supposed to guess at what they want to do. *I don't mind* is tricky but it mostly means that they kinda do mind but are trying to be nice."

"So you're supposed to be a mind reader?"

"Pretty much." Max laughed. "After a while you get pretty good at it. Well, sometimes." He lifted one shoulder. "I try, and you know how much I love Zoe. There's not a thing I wouldn't do for her."

"Yeah, I do. I couldn't have picked a better man to marry my sister," Avery said and meant every word. "And she loves you too, Max." He felt another wave of emotion hit him hard.

"Zoe means well but she's wrong trying to get you and Ashley back together. I see the way you look at Sophia. You've got to find a way back to Cricket Creek by tomorrow. I'd take you back myself but I'm already over the limit to drive." He put his hand on Avery's shoulder and squeezed. "I think you knew you two weren't really right for each other—even before she did whatever it was that broke you two up."

"Max—"

"Don't even try to deny it. She did something. I don't need to know what. Actually, I probably don't want to know."

"Yeah . . ." Avery looked out over the lake. "But you know, looking back maybe we both felt a little bit trapped and didn't really know it. Something was missing and I guess neither of us really understood what that something was. Maybe she was trying to end things in the only way she knew how."

"There you go defending her."

"Not really. Just trying to understand, that's all."

"Like I said, women aren't easy to understand."

Avery nodded his agreement but some things were becoming clear.

"Well, I'm telling you that I'm cool with you leaving if you can find a way."

"Thanks, Max. I mean, I guess I should have come to you sooner."

"Just promise me you'll start thinking about what's best for you, okay? Because ultimately it's what's best for those of us who care about you. You deserve happiness. So start thinking about your own life, for once."

"Thanks, Max." Avery nodded. "Will do. Now get on back up there and enjoy your last weekend of being single. It's about time for a 'watch this' moment."

"I'll leave that one up to Danny. He's been shooting some bourbon so it shouldn't be too long." Max pushed up to his feet. "Shit is about to get real."

Avery laughed, already feeling a sense of relief. Now, who should he call to come to pick him up? Uncle Easton? "Yeah." He picked up his phone but noticed that he'd gotten a text message that he'd missed. Avery read the message and felt a jolt of surprise. "Really?"

His father was on his way to pick him up and should be arriving within the hour. Now how in the world did his father of all people know that he needed a ride home? Avery shook his head and looked back at his phone wondering if there was something wrong with his mother, but no other messages were to be found. He thought about calling his father but he didn't want his father fishing for his phone while driving on the interstate.

Avery headed up to the cabin for his suitcase, and then said his good-byes to Max and the rest of the guys. They insisted that he do a shot so Avery decided to do one . . . or two. Avery grabbed a burger and by the time he'd finished eating his father called to say he was in the driveway. Avery hurried to the front of the cabin and spotted the red Ford pickup that had more miles than a truck should pile up, but his father refused to get a new one until this one quit running.

"Hop in, son."

Avery nodded and hurried around to the passenger side. Whatever was going on had a sense of urgency to it. After tossing his suitcase in the back of the cab he settled into the cracked leather seat. His father immediately threw the gear into reverse. "Dad, what's going on? Is Mom okay?"

"Yes, unless you count her constant indecision as to what her mother-of-the-bride dress should be. She's changed her mind a dozen times and the dress she favors is too small so she's been feeding both of us nothing but rabbit food and plain old boring chicken breasts night after night. I swear I'm gonna start clucking soon." He pointed to the fast-food bag he'd tossed onto the floor. "Best damned cheeseburger and fries I've ever had. Don't tell on me. Apparently, I should lose a few pounds as well. Ha."

"Did Mom really say that to you?" It wasn't like her to be so bold.

"Not in so many words," he said a little indignantly, and if Avery wasn't so confused as to why his father showed up in Tennessee to take him home he might have found the comment funny. "She's getting a little sassy these days, your mama is."

"Really?"

"Yeah, and I have to say that I like it."

Avery looked at his father in surprise. He waited for him to continue the conversation, namely why he was there but he started whistling as he pulled into the main road.

"Dad, are you gonna tell me why you're here?"

He slid a glance at Avery. "Isn't it obvious?"

"Uh . . . no."

"Son, you need to be at the grand opening of Sophia's salon," he said in a matter-of-fact tone.

"How did you know?"

"Easton called me."

"Oh."

"Yeah, and I know that you and your uncle are close but in the future I'd appreciate if you'd confide in me too," he said, and the even tone took on an unexpected edge of emotion.

"Dad, I'm sorry."

"No need," he said. Silence stretched out for a couple of heartbeats. "Son . . . I love you." Before Avery could reply he continued. "I haven't said that nearly enough to your mother, you, and Zoe. It was damned hard for me to be on the road so much. Hard on your mama but harder on me than I let on. See, being a hardass made it easier to deal with missing my family."

"Dad . . ." Avery felt moisture gather in his throat.

"I was jealous of your relationship with Easton and when you two went into business together it was . . . well"—he paused to clear this throat—"tough on me. See, I wanted to spend the time with you. All those weekends you and your buddies spent up at the cabin with Easton . . ." He shook his head.

"You should have joined us."

"I was invited but I stubbornly refused and Easton finally stopped asking. My damned pride turned into depression and I sat in my La-Z-Boy watching sports when I wanted to be hanging out with you. I was grumpy and hard to live with. Your mama should have set my sorry ass straight but she never said a cross word, mostly because your grandma and grandpa fought all the time as you already know."

"Yeah." Avery nodded but let his father continue.

"We married young and had you kids right off the bat, not really having any real time for us, and then I started driving a truck and, well, we weren't as close as we should have been. Your mama pretty much did the parenting on her own."

"Dad, you provided a nice life for us. I didn't appreciate your sacrifice, but I sure do now. Dad . . . I thought you didn't want to be around."

"Hell no. Killed me every time I missed a ball game or birthday party," he said gruffly. "I shoulda let you know that but being distant helped me cope, or at least I thought so at the time."

"I'm sorry. I should have picked up on that."

"Ah, Avery, you were just a kid. This wasn't your

fault. Look, I can't go back in time but I want to make up for what we lost. I don't want your relationship with Easton to change. In fact, he insisted that I should be the one to come get you." He gave Avery a wry smile. "Were you thinking of calling him to come and get you?"

"Yeah," Avery admitted.

"Well, like I said, I'm glad now that Easton filled in for me as a father figure. He's a good man. I wish that I had pushed my pride to the side because Easton and I could have been close, like brothers."

"There's still time."

"Damn straight. I love your mama. I'm gonna take her places and do things she likes instead of sitting in that damned chair watching nothing but sports. And I want to spend more time with Zoe, but especially you, Avery."

"I'd like that, Dad. And I'm glad it was you who came to get me. I shouldn't have gone to begin with but I was caught in the middle."

"You're like your mama and want to please everyone." He chuckled. "Zoe's more like me in that she is a little bit stubborn."

"Ya think?"

"It's good to want what you want and go after it but you have to give in sometimes, too."

"Well, in Zoe's defense, she was trying to get what Ashley wanted."

"See, you're like your mama that way too. Defending everyone. So tell me, are you in love with Sophia?"

"Yes, but she thinks I still have a thing for Ashley."

"Well, just ignore that silliness."

Avery chuckled. "Never thought of it that way."

"Yeah, sometimes women come up with the damnedest, craziest stuff . . . so out there that you just have to turn a deaf ear to it until they forget all about it."

"So it's that easy?"

"Sometimes. Just shut that nonsense about Ashley

down. Concentrate on telling Sophia how much you love her."

"How'd you get so smart?"

"Years of bein' stupid. I got all those years of doin' things wrong out of the way so much so that I plan on gettin' it right from now on."

Avery laughed. "Interesting way of thinking but makes a crazy kind of sense. And by the way, you're going really fast."

"Gotta get you home in record time. Gonna use that big rig up there as my front door." He looked at Avery and laughed.

"I like that."

"Me speeding?"

"Not so much. But I like hearing you laugh with me."

"Well, get ready for a whole lot more. We've got some making up to do. But first you have to make things right with that sweet girl of yours."

"Hope it's not too late."

"Hey, my new motto is that it's never too late to make things right."

"You're right. Hey, Dad?"

"Yes, son."

"I love you too."

23

Don't Worry, Be Happy

SOPHIA SMILED UNTIL HER CHEEKS HURT AT THE steady stream of people walking through the door of the salon. The weather had cooperated, warm but cheerfully breezy. Abundant sunshine spilling through the windows added sparkle to the silver and white decorations placed throughout the salon.

The turnout for the grand opening exceeded her expectations and within the first two hours they'd gone through their entire stash of goodie bags filled with products and wedding-related favors. At first Sophia had panicked but Carrie Ann pressed a cold flute of champagne into her hand and whispered for her to chill out and enjoy the success. Now that the open house was almost over she could breathe a sigh of relief.

"Cheers," Carrie Ann said with a big smile.

Sophia clicked her glass to Carrie Ann's. "To White Lace and Promises," she said but her smile faltered just enough for Carrie Ann to notice.

"Avery wants to be here," Carrie Ann said, reading Sophia's mind.

"I know." Sophia nodded. She'd regretted her request to separate but couldn't muster up the courage to call him. Plus, she didn't want to ruin his weekend by sounding needy, especially since she'd insisted that he should go. But damn, she missed Avery more than she thought possible.

"And my goodness, the boy sent that giant bouquet of roses, that edible fruit arrangement, and an entire cake that has already come in handy since we ran out of cookies and cupcakes in a blink of an eye. Even though I hated to give away that Italian cream cake that Reese Marino made. Everyone was raving about it. I'm thinking I'll have Easton take me to River Row Pizza afterward so I can get a slice."

"It's my favorite."

"Ah, that's why Avery sent it. He's a thoughtful boy, always looking out for others. And so sweet of your father to send the big bouquet of flowers too, Sophia."

"He said that he wanted to be here but he had to fly to Paris for a business meeting."

"Well, he's thinking of you so that's something."

"He cares in his own way." Sophia nodded but felt an unexpected urge to cry. She hid her wave of emotion by taking a healthy gulp of champagne and nearly coughed.

Carrie Ann looked at her with concern. "You need to take a break, sweetie? I can hold down the fort for a spell plus we're nearly finished. I think I'll actually start cleaning up a bit."

"I should help."

"No, Millie is doing a bang-up job greeting people and Haley and Callie are charming everyone who walks in. They can pitch in. Why don't you get off your feet for a little while?"

Sophia was about to refuse but her feet ached as much as her cheeks and so she nodded. "Thanks. I'll be in the laundry room if you need me."

Carrie Ann reached for a bottle of champagne and handed it to her. "Take this with you and drink as needed."

Sophia gave her a small grin. "Does it say that on the bottle?"

"No, it's my personal suggestion. This is my third glass and it's just what the doctor ordered."

"Okay, Dr. Spencer, I'll be in the back if you need me." Sophia chuckled as she walked away thinking that she was so lucky to have met Carrie Ann and she was abundantly glad she'd made the decision to move to Cricket Creek. Living in the same town as her family was such a blessing and, if today was any indication, White Lace and Promises was going to thrive even beyond her expectations. Her mother and Grace had come in early to help with the last-minute setup and had gushed over how lovely the salon looked, filling Sophia with pride. The fact that they'd all ended up in this quaint Kentucky town still blew her mind but she loved it here.

And she loved Avery.

Sophia sat down in a chair near the washer and dryer, toed off her heels, and propped her aching feet up on the seat of another chair. While sipping the champagne, she wondered if she'd messed things up by asking for the separation, and then chastised herself for allowing the worry gene to kick in. She raised the flute to her lips and realized that it was empty. "Hmmm . . ." She eyed the bottle of champagne thinking she shouldn't have another glass, but then again the open house was nearly over. "Oh one more won't hurt," she said.

"That's always been my motto."

Sophia looked up to find Avery standing in the doorway. He held up a flute of champagne in salute. His curly hair was tousled and dark stubble shaded his jaws. He wore a Kentucky Wildcats T-shirt, cargo shorts, and flip-flops making it seem as though he'd somehow morphed his way from the lake to her salon.

"You're here," she said and blushed at her silly statement. "Unless you're a figment of my active imagination."

"No, I'm real."

"Makes sense because I wouldn't have imagined you in shorts and flip-flops."

Avery chuckled. "Well, I would have been here late last night but my dad's old truck broke down in Tennessee." He shook his head. "We had to spend the night at a creepy hotel that looked haunted and get the truck fixed this morning." He pointed to his flip-flops. "I didn't have time to go home and change."

"Oh, Avery, you didn't have to come back from the party!"

"Yes, I did." He walked over, picked up the bottle of champagne, and filled her glass. "I wanted to be here all along and should never have gone away. Flowers and edible arrangements are no substitutes for being here. A bachelor party isn't a reason not to be here for your grand opening."

"But you're the best man."

He gave her a slight grin and shook his head. "I wasn't the best man. I was the miserable man."

"Oh, Avery . . ." She felt emotion well up in her throat.

"All I could think about was you. I should never have left."

"You needed the break to sort everything out." Her heart thumped hard while she waited for his response.

"Everything is sorted out." Avery took a step closer. "You come first in my life, Sophia. Not because you demand it, but because you deserve it. You're a beautiful person inside and out, and I'll be a lucky man if you'll have me back in your life."

Sophia smiled and her heart filled with joy. "Of course I will."

Avery sat down and tapped his glass to hers. "To no more *breaks* and no more *should nevers*."

"I'll drink to that," Sophia said and couldn't quite keep a tremor of emotion from her voice. After taking a sip she asked, "So you called your father to come and get you?"

Avery shook his head. "No, this is where the story gets kinda crazy. I was trying to put on a party face but Max finally took pity upon me and told me I should find a way to get back here to you." He leaned over and gave her a lingering kiss. "And then out of nowhere my dad shows up and tells me to get my tail into the truck."

"Wow . . ."

"Yeah, we had a great talk. When his eyes misted over, she took his hand. "But then the serpentine belt snapped and the truck broke down." Avery shook his head. "Dad felt terrible. I felt so bad for him."

"Aw . . ."

"Yeah well, now maybe he'll buy a new truck."

"Think so?"

Avery chuckled. "No. Oh, Sophia, I'm sorry I missed the grand opening."

"You're here now." She smiled. "And I'm so glad."

"I love you, Sophia. I wish I had told you sooner. I should never—"

Sophia leaned over and put a fingertip to his lips. "No more 'should nevers', remember?"

He nodded.

"I love you too, Avery. With all my heart." She put her glass on the table. "Now are you going to kiss me again or what?"

"Yes." Avery put his glass down, stood up, and pulled her into his arms. "I want to kiss you today, tomorrow, and for the rest of my life."

EPILOGUE
A Wish Come True

*A*VERY STOOD WITH THE WEDDING PARTY AT THE steps of the gazebo and watched Zoe and Max exchange their vows. Zoe looked so radiant, happy, and absolutely beautiful. Avery was already having trouble keeping his emotions in check, hanging on by a thread, and then he made the mistake of seeking out his parents. They held hands, smiling, and then his father reached up and swiped at tears. Ah, damn . . . Avery swallowed hard and nearly lost it. He inhaled a deep breath and then glanced over and saw that Ashley was also crying. She caught his eye, and then mouthed, "I'm sorry."

Avery's heart thudded. He swallowed the hot moisture in his throat, held her gaze briefly, and then nodded. He'd wished for so long that she hadn't broken his heart but, in truth, he'd wished for something that hadn't really existed between them. He knew that now because he'd found it with Sophia. Unconditional love. Avery had thought that love meant giving in when it simply meant giving.

Avery gazed over at Sophia who looked so pretty in

a soft pink off-the-shoulder dress. He thought back to when he'd first met her at Walking on Sunshine Bistro and she'd served him the rock-hard biscuit covered with the gravel gravy. He'd crunched through it just to keep the sweet smile on her face.

As if feeling his gaze upon her, Sophia looked at him and his heart filled with joy. She shyly mouthed *I love you* and he knew that his days of wishing and hoping were over. When he mouthed back, *Me too*, Sophia smiled and dabbed at the corners of her eyes. Avery felt a warm rush of happiness. While this may be his sister's wedding, in that moment Avery knew this was also the beginning of his future with Sophia and he would continue to do anything at all just to see her smile.

Sophia Gordon was the love of his life and he was one lucky man. She was and always would be his wish come true.

Don't miss the next charming
Cricket Creek Novel
by LuAnn McLane,

MARRY ME ON MAIN STREET

*Available from Berkley Sensation
in December 2016.*

*I*NSTANT REGRET WASHED OVER SUSAN WHEN SHE RE-
alized she'd underestimated the weight of the box of
mason jars clutched in her arms. The thick glass clanked
together as she stepped over the curb and onto the sidewalk. She eyed the front door of her shop, praying she'd
make it before dropping her precious cargo to the
ground. Setting the box down wasn't an option because
she feared she'd tip forward too fast, break the jars, and
face-plant onto the concrete.

"Oh, boy . . ." Panting, she continued what was supposed to be forward motion, but when she took another
careful step, her hefty purse slipped down her puffy
coat sleeve, sending her off-balance, causing a stagger-
ing dance sideways. A brisk breeze whipped her long
dark hair across her face, making her progress even
more difficult. Slightly disoriented, she tried to right herself, but the box started to slip down her arms. Panic
welled up in her throat, halting just behind her gritted
teeth. Blinded by her curtain of hair, she backpedaled
and came up against a big wall of something solid.

"Whoa there!" said a deep voice next to her ear. Long

arms wrapped around her from behind, keeping her from falling and the box from sliding to the sidewalk.

"Oh my goodness! Sorry!"

"It's okay. I've got you," he assured her.

"No . . . really . . . I'm okay now." Well she hoped so, anyway. Blowing at her hair, she tried to look over her shoulder, but she was trapped between him and the box. "You can let go."

"Can you hold the box? Sounds like something breakable."

"Yes," she said, although she had serious doubts. "Maybe . . ." She squirmed a little bit and the mason jars clanged together. "The weight of my purse threw me off-balance."

"Susan, please stand still and let me help. I'm guessing you're heading into the shop?" he asked, and his voice seemed to vibrate through her body.

She nodded. "That's the plan."

"Let's get you in there." The smooth Southern drawl sounded familiar but, then again, most of the men in Cricket Creek had a bit of an accent, so he could be anyone, most likely someone she knew. Oh wait—he knew her name. So many people knew her from her shop, and she hated when she couldn't place a name to a face.

She tried to look over her shoulder again. "Who . . ." she began but the box dipped sideways and she decided right that moment she really needed to make it to the front door without breaking the mason jars needed for her Christmas cookie mix. Casual conversation could wait. "I need to scoot my purse back up on my shoulder."

"Do you think you can hold the box long enough for me to scoot around in front of you to grab the bottom?"

"Oh . . . I don't know." She winced. "My arms are already protesting." Note to self: Join a gym.

"Well then, just move forward, and I'll keep holding on from behind."

"It's kind of hard because the wind blew my hair in

my face and I can't exactly see where I'm going," she explained.

"You have a lot of hair," her hero said with a low chuckle. "I'd brush it from your face, but I'm afraid to let go of the box."

Susan nodded, thinking she should get the unruly curls cut short. "I should head next door to the salon and get my problem fixed," she grumbled.

"Your boyfriend might not like that," he said, carefully moving her forward.

"I don't have one," she muttered, wondering why she'd just divulged that embarrassing information, but she wasn't exactly thinking straight at the moment. Just then, the wind kicked up again and she could smell his spicy aftershave with a hint of outdoorsy pine.

"We're almost there," he said near her ear. "Okay, Susan, I'm going to take a lightning-quick step to the right and grab the box."

"I'm afraid it will fall!"

"Don't you trust me, Susan Quinn?" he asked, but before she could react he suddenly had the big box in his arms. "See?" he asked.

"Not yet," she said, getting another chuckle from him. It took another moment to realize that her arms were suddenly free.

"You can brush your hair back now, Suzy Q."

Oh no. . . . With a thumping heart, Susan suddenly had a pretty good idea whom the sexy voice belonged to, and she wanted the sidewalk to open up and suck her beneath the concrete like quicksand. Inhaling a deep breath, she brushed the curls from her face and looked into the startling sky blue eyes of Danny Mayfield, the last person in Cricket Creek whom she would want to come to her rescue. "Hello, D-Danny." *Oh great, now I'm going to going to stutter,* she thought and nearly groaned. *Ain't life grand?*

"Hi, Susan," Danny said cheerfully and bestowed

upon her his killer smile. He nodded down at the box that he easily held in his strong arms. "What's in here?"

"M-mason. J-jars." Feeling heat in her cheeks, she lowered her gaze and dug inside her purse for her keys. She rarely stuttered anymore. *This is so embarrassing,* she thought with another inner groan. *Where in the hell are my keys?*

"If you open the door, I'll take them inside for you and anything else you have in your SUV that you want brought in the shop."

"Oh . . . you don't have to do . . . that." So happy to have kept the stutter at bay this time, she looked up from her key search and actually smiled.

"My mother would have my hide for not doing the gentlemanly thing," Danny said with an easy grin and lowered the box to the tiled floor of the alcove, between two big display windows. "And I value my hide."

Right. Just like back in high school, she thought and nearly cringed. "It's okay. I'm used to lugging th-things inside."

"Well, I'd love to see Rhyme and Reason, if you don't mind. My mom's birthday is coming up and she raves about the interesting stuff you have in your shop. You could help me pick something out for her."

"Oh, I'm sorry, D-Danny. I'm not really open right now. I stay closed on Mondays to restock after the weekend." Lowering her gaze to her purse, she frantically pushed past a pack of tissues, a tin of mints, a mini flashlight, and hand sanitizer. "My keys are playing hide-and-seek," she said. "I don't want to keep you. I can get it from here. Oh, but thank you so m-much." She glanced at him, not realizing how close they were. At just under six feet tall, Susan was used to towering over women and being eye to eye with men, but she had to look up at Danny. She'd forgotten how tall he was, and it made her feel feminine instead of gangly. "Okay, keys, this isn't funny anymore. Oh hey, there's my phone that I couldn't find."

Danny chuckled. "You're funny."

"I get that a lot. Problem is that I'm not trying to be funny," Susan said, and he laughed again. She lifted a corkscrew from her purse. "You know, just in case I need to uncork a bottle of wine on a moment's notice. S-sorry—you can get going. This could take a while."

Danny shrugged his wide shoulders. "I'm in no hurry. I was just going to grab lunch at the deli next door. I'm obsessed with Damn Good Sandwich," he said calmly while her heart raced.

"Ham Good Sandwich. City council made him change the *damn* part."

"I know, but I'm a rebel and John Clark does make a damn good sandwich, so I still call it that."

"Oh yes, the food there is amazing. Hard to resist the aroma of bread baking. I'll l-let you get back to your lunch," she said in a rush.

"Have you had lunch? I'll be happy to get something for you." Danny smiled. "Or you can join me. He has a few tables inside. My treat."

Lunch with Danny Mayfield? "Oh . . . n-no," Susan said, forgetting for a moment what she was looking for in her mess of a purse.

"You sure?"

Susan nodded firmly. "But thank you for the offer." She picked up another hint of his aftershave and had an insane urge to reach over and touch the dark stubble shadowing the bottom half of his handsome face. This was the closest she'd been to Danny since their prom date back in high school and her reaction to him had been just as instantaneous. He'd been a cute teenager, but he'd matured into a very sexy man, whom she'd done a very good job of avoiding for the past ten years, not an easy task in a small town.

"Did you find your keys?"

"Keys? Oh . . ." Susan scooped her hand around in her purse. "Here they are!" She lifted her Tinker Bell key chain and jangled it in triumph.

"How could you miss that big thing?" Danny chuckled and then gave her a high five, which she promptly missed. He laughed, thinking she'd missed on purpose, and she decided she'd let him think so.

"Gotcha," Susan said, hoping she didn't sound as nervous as she felt.

"You did," he said as he picked up the box.

Susan opened the heavy door and flicked the lights on, illuminating the main showroom. The calming scent of cinnamon and vanilla filled her lungs, and she glanced at Danny to see his reaction to her eclectic array of handmade gifts and repurposed items. She simply loved her store, and if she won the lottery tomorrow, she'd keep Rhyme and Reason open just for fun.

"Wow, Susan, this is really cool," Danny said, eyeing a display of old silverware made into wind chimes. He put the box down. "No wonder my mother loves to shop here." He walked over and touched one of the chimes, making the silverware tinkle. "Do you mind if I have a look around? I'm really impressed."

"Thanks." Susan felt a warm rush of pride. "Go ahead."

Danny picked up a colorful rug from a stack and looked at it. "Sweet. Mom would love something like this."

"Made from old T-shirts."

"Resourceful." He picked up another one. "Did you make them?"

"Most of them. My mom made a few too. They're easy to do."

Danny nodded and put the rug back in the stack. "I have plenty of old T-shirts I could donate to the cause. How about socks? I have a million of just one."

Susan grinned. "Socks are repurposing gold. Puppets, holiday snowmen, pincushions, pet toys . . . I have a display over against the wall called Sock It to Me."

Danny shook his head. "This is really amazing."

Susan felt another rush of pride. "I get such satisfaction out of finding new ways to use old things—especially if they are going to be thrown away." She pointed to a colorful display of candles in various shapes and sizes. "Those were all molded from pieces of broken crayons," she explained with a smile.

"Smart and useful." He seemed duly impressed.

"And see those bowls over there?"

Danny nodded. "Oh wow, I can see that they're made from vinyl record albums."

"Yes, but I only use ones that are too scratched to play. I collect vinyl. There's just something soothing about listening to music on a turntable," she said with a sigh.

"Yeah, I agree. My sister Mattie's husband got me interested in records. You should see Garret's collection. It will blow your mind, especially on his state-of-the-art sound system."

"I'd like that," she said without thinking, but her heart thumped when he nodded.

"Great, I'll be glad to take you, Susan. Oh hey, if you'd like to sit in on a recording session at My Way Records, I can arrange that too. Jeff Greenfield is working on a new country album, and Garret is one of the studio musicians. He said that Jeff's wife, Cat, is going to do a couple of duets with him and she wrote several of the songs."

"Oh, everyone in Cricket Creek is so proud of Jeff's success. I just love his old-school country voice. I was at the concert at Sully's when Jeff proposed to Cat."

"I was too. I think the entire town was there. Well then, that settles it. You have to come." Danny gave her another bone-melting smile and then pulled his cell phone out of his pocket. "Give me your number, and I'll let you know when we can sit in on a recording session."

"Oh . . . um . . ." At the mention of giving Danny Mayfield her number, reality smacked Susan in the face and she swallowed hard. "My schedule is rather full."

"There will be a lot of sessions to choose from." He looked at her and waited.

"Well . . ." What in the world was she doing getting cozy with the one person in Cricket Creek she'd wanted to avoid? How could she forget the embarrassing circumstances behind their one and only date? Feeling warm, she took off her puffy jacket, which had made her look like the Michelin Man. She seriously needed to shop for a cute winter jacket. And then she remembered she was wearing a green sweater embellished with Santa's sleigh and all nine reindeer, led by Rudolph with an actual blinking red nose. Susan's mother didn't get the whole ugly Christmas sweater concept and bought Susan a new addition to her growing collection at the beginning of each holiday season. Susan always accepted the new sweater with an "ooh" and "ah," along with an inward groan, but she wouldn't hurt her mother's feelings for the world. "I wouldn't want to be an imposition." She put her hand over Rudolph's nose.

"It wouldn't be an imposition," Danny insisted, and looked at her expectantly.

Susan would bet there weren't many girls in Cricket Creek who wouldn't readily give their number to Danny Mayfield. But just like in high school, he was way out of her league and she knew he was just being kind and she had sort of initiated the invitation even though it hadn't been her intention. "Well, I appreciate the nice offer, but I'm really b-busy with the Christmas season upon us," she said. "I have a lot of decorating to do before the parade and Christmas Walk."

"Okay. I understand." Danny slipped the slim phone back inside his jeans pocket, and his smile faltered. He pointed at the box of mason jars. "Where do you want the box?"

"Up in my . . ." she began and then stopped herself. "Oh, it's okay right there. You've helped enough."

Danny gave her a level look and then sighed. "Susan, I know you don't want that box sitting here in the middle of your shop. Instead of you having to struggle, I can take the box wherever you'd like it to go." He jabbed his thumb over his shoulder. "Or if you'd prefer, I can get out of your hair," he said with a slight frown. "I get the feeling I've overstayed my welcome."

Susan knew her cheeks must be as rosy as Rudolph's nose. "I'm sorry, Danny," she said slowly, struggling not to stutter. "I don't mean to sound ungrateful for your help. If you hadn't appeared out of nowhere I w-would have crashed to the ground."

"You don't need to be grateful. I was happy to help." Danny tilted his head to the side as if about to ask her a question, but then seemed to think better of it. He also appeared confused and maybe a little bit hurt, and if there was one thing Susan hated to do, it was to hurt someone's feelings. He was only being polite, and it was silly for her not to accept his assistance.

"If you wouldn't mind, I really need to have the jars taken up to my kitchen in my apartment above the shop," she said even though her pulse fluttered at the thought of having him in her home.

"I don't mind at all." Danny gave her a slight smile and nodded. He picked up the heavy box with ease. "Lead the way."

"Okay, follow me," Susan said, even though the knowledge that he was watching her walk ahead of him was quite unnerving. Was her sweater clinging to her butt? Was she wiggling her hips too much? She stood up straighter but then felt awkward and tried her best to walk normally down the narrow hallway that led to the staircase to her apartment.

Once she reached the landing, Susan opened the door and flicked on the overhead track lighting. The wide-open space and tall ceilings allowed her to decorate in the eclectic shabby-chic style she loved. As in her shop, Susan used old things for new purposes.

The clump of Danny's work boots sounded manly on the hardwood floor. She rather liked the deep sound.

Danny Mayfield is inside my apartment ran through Susan's head, and she wondered how this even happened. Oh yeah, she had fallen into his arms. And today had started out so normal. She shook her head. "Geez . . ."

"Something wrong?"

Oh damn, she had said that out loud. Talking to herself was a product of spending so much time alone. "Oh . . . no." Embarrassed where her train of thought was going, she shook her head harder.

"Where to?" Danny asked, following her inside.

"Over there in the kitchen." Susan pointed over to the far corner of the giant room that was sectioned off by a tall counter and really sweet bamboo stools she'd found at an estate sale.

"Okay." He followed her through the main living area, weaving past a wide variety of furniture that changed frequently. "On the counter?"

"On the floor is fine. I'm going to fill the jars with dry cookie mix, tie festive ribbons around the top, and sell them in the shop."

"A great Christmas gift idea. I'm sure they'll sell fast."

"All you have to do is add eggs and butter and you can make homemade cookies in a flash." She snapped her fingers and gave him a quick smile. "I've already done a few." She picked up a jar from the counter. "For you," she said, extending the jar rather awkwardly. When he accepted the gift his fingers brushed against hers and she sucked in a breath. "I appreciate your h-help."

"Thanks, Susan," he said, sounding not one bit breathless.

She bit her bottom lip between her teeth and nodded, wishing she wasn't wearing the silly blinking sweater.

"Your sweater is cute," Danny said, as if reading her mind.

"Oh!" Susan looked down at Rudolph, suddenly having a change of Christmas sweater heart. "A gift from my mom. She's crazy about Christmas. I have an endless supply of these, along with various earrings, necklaces, and hats."

"My family's big on Christmas too," Danny said but Susan noticed he hadn't specified himself. For some reason she wanted to know why.

"How about you?" The thought of anyone not loving Christmas made her sad. "Please don't tell me you're a Grinch."

Danny looked off into the distance. "I enjoy the family gatherings. Now that Mason and Mattie have kids, they're super into the holidays." He shrugged and turned his attention back to her.

"It's a fun time of the year, but can be stressful."

"Yeah, I try not to stress too much. Your place is awesome, by the way," he said, changing the subject. "I love the hardwood floors and exposed brick." He looked up. "The beamed ceiling is really sweet, and I like how the lighting is recessed between the wood." He turned toward the floor-to-ceiling windows. "And you have an awesome view of Main Street."

"Along with a very short commute to work."

"With no traffic." Danny chuckled and then continued to walk around, as if fascinated. He picked up a ceramic frog and examined it. "The poor guy is missing a foot."

"I tend to buy broken things that no one else wants. I drive my assistant, Betsy, absolutely nuts when I find something she knows won't sell."

"You feel sorry for it?"

Susan grinned. "My apartment is like living on the Island of Misfit Toys."

Danny laughed. "It's kind of like being in a museum. I wish everything had little cards so I could read the history."

"If you look closely you'll see that quite a few pieces on display are actually telephones," she said, wondering why her mouth kept moving when she should have been sending him on his way. It was like her voice had taken on a life of its own and her brain had taken a holiday. "Something else I can't resist."

"Really? Show me one."

Susan walked over to a shelf and picked up a red car. "See?" She lifted the top to expose the phone. "I collect odd things. Don't ask me why."

"You collect cool things," Danny corrected. "And it's what you do for a living."

"Some are items that didn't sell in the shop and I just couldn't toss away, and some things I buy to sell in the shop to begin with and then can't part with. Good thing I have a lot of space." She grinned. "Or then again maybe it's a bad thing." She put the car back on the shelf.

"Not at all. You just see beauty or value in things that other people miss."

"Thank you," Susan said, even though she suspected he was just being kind. "I suppose part of it comes from growing up on a farm. My mom used everything and wasted nothing." When Danny smiled she realized that she was starting to feel comfortable with him and her stutter, thank goodness, vanished. "We were green way before it became popular." She chuckled. "Or then again, maybe we were just poor but I somehow didn't know it."

"Hey, when hard times hit, everybody in Cricket Creek struggled. Our marina sure did. There was a time when we thought we would lose it," he said with a sigh. "Nearly put my father in the grave, trying to keep Mayfield Marina afloat."

"But you, Mattie, and Mason banded together and saved the marina not only for your family but for Cricket Creek. I can't imagine this town without it, Danny."

"Thanks." He gave her a warm smile. "Well, we have Noah Falcon to thank for coming home and building the baseball stadium. It was the shot in the arm we needed. His rookie baseball card is one of my prized possessions."

"Oh I know. For a while Main Street was becoming a ghost town, one store closing after another. It's so wonderful to see Cricket Creek thriving again. New shops are springing up all over Main Street. The deli next door is ham good," she said with a grin.

"Are you sure I can't treat you to lunch?"

A big part of Susan wanted to accept his offer, but she suspected he was only being nice. She wasn't about to repeat the mistake she made by going to the senior prom with Danny. She wanted to ask if his mother had put him up to this just like she did back in high school but she simply shook her head. "I really do have to get to work."

He hesitated for a fraction as if he might try to convince her, and she sure hoped he didn't because her resistance to Danny Mayfield was hanging on by a thread. "Okay. Well, I'll come back when you're open to shop for my mother."

"Great," Susan said even though the thought of seeing Danny again made her heart hammer. He was way too good at putting her at ease when she needed to keep her guard up. "I'll show you out."

Danny nodded and fell into step beside her, continuing to look here and there. Susan was used to people wandering around in her apartment, picking up items almost like they were in her shop.

They were nearly to the door when Danny stopped in his tracks. "Where did you get this rocking chair?"

"I bought it at an estate sale a few weeks ago, intending to sell it. She slid her hand over the smooth wood of the arm. "But I just couldn't bear to part with it."

Danny inclined his head. "Really? Why?"

"It's just so beautiful, obviously handmade. Rocking in it is so soothing after being on my feet all day long." She sat down in it and sighed. "It's like whoever crafted it made it just for me." She looked up at him.

"See, it's proportioned just right. I'm so tall that it's hard to find a chair that feels this comfortable. I change things around in here all the time but the rocking chair is a keeper," she said, but he had a strange look on his face, making Susan think she was going on way too long about a chair. "Anyway . . ." Feeling a bit silly, she stood up and headed toward the door. He followed her down the steps and through the shop.

"Anything else you need brought out of your SUV?"

"Nothing I can't manage, but thank you."

Nodding, he put his hand on the door to push it open but then hesitated and turned back to her. "It was good to see you, Susan. Funny that we don't run into each other more often."

"Literally," she said and he chuckled.

"I hope we do run into each other more often and don't mind if it's literally. If you change your mind about sitting in on a Jeff Greenfield session, let me know." He reached into his wallet and handed her a card. "That's the office at Mayfield Marina. Just leave me a message."

"Thanks." Susan nodded and wondered if he had any idea how hard she'd worked to avoid him. He stood there for another heartbeat and she suddenly felt shy again. Not knowing what else to say, she nibbled on the inside of her lip.

"Okay, well, I'll let you get back to work," Danny said and then walked out the door.

Susan stood there while fighting the oddest urge to run after him. Maybe she'd just head over to the deli and tell him that she was hungry after all. As if on cue, her stomach growled. "No!" Fisting her hands at her sides, she inhaled a deep breath. Danny was just being nice, and accepting another pity date, even if it was just lunch, would be stupid on her part.

"Just get a grip." After locking the door, Susan headed upstairs to start working on layering the cookie mix into the jars. But feeling a bit unsettled, she sat

down in the rocking chair and tried to sort out her con-
flicting feelings about her unexpected meeting with
Danny Mayfield. Closing her eyes, she leaned her head
against the smooth wood and rocked gently. After a
few minutes she didn't have all of the answers except
one thing was for sure: Her attraction to Danny was
stronger than ever, which meant she needed to avoid
him at all costs.